Praise for *New York Times* bestselling author Julia London

"Charming, witty and warm. This is perfect historical romance."
—Sarah Morgan, *USA TODAY* bestselling author, on *The Princess Plan*

"It completely charmed me... The chemistry is so delicious. I simply didn't want to put it down."
—Nicola Cornick, *USA TODAY* bestselling author, on *The Princess Plan*

"Warm, witty and decidedly wicked—great entertainment."
—Stephanie Laurens, #1 *New York Times* bestselling author, on *Hard-Hearted Highlander*

"Julia London writes vibrant, emotional stories and sexy, richly drawn characters."
—Madeline Hunter, *New York Times* bestselling author

"Charming...A fun, touching 'prince meets real girl' Victorian fairy-tale romance."
—*Kirkus Reviews* on *The Princess Plan*

"London is at the top of her game in this thrilling tale of political intrigue and second chances."
—*Booklist*, starred review, on *Wild Wicked Scot*

JULIA LONDON

A Princess by Christmas

HQN

ISBN-13: 978-1-335-08061-5

A Princess by Christmas

Copyright © 2020 by Dinah Dinwiddie

Recycling programs
for this product may
not exist in your area.

This is a work of fiction. Names, characters, places and incidents
are either the product of the author's imagination or are used
fictitiously. Any resemblance to actual persons, living or dead,
businesses, companies, events or locales is entirely coincidental.

This edition published by arrangement with Harlequin Books S.A.

For questions and comments about the quality of this book,
please contact us at CustomerService@Harlequin.com.

HQN
22 Adelaide St. West, 40th Floor
Toronto, Ontario M5H 4E3, Canada
www.Harlequin.com

Printed in U.S.A.

A
Princess by
CHRISTMAS

CHAPTER ONE

London, England
1847

Three ships flying the colorful green-and-blue flag of Alucia arrived at London Dock last week. On board was the official delegation that will participate in the Wesloria-Alucia peace summit, held in the name of Her Majesty, the Queen Victoria. Anticipation is high and hopes abound that some agreement can be struck between the two neighboring countries that will, at long last, foster peace between them.

Her Majesty will welcome the visiting foreign dignitaries at St. James Palace, and the summit officially begun.

Peace between the two rival nations is an admirable goal. But can peace be achieved between two countries that have been warring over the same land for generations? Is it possible that the family rift that divides the two nations runs so deep that it cannot be repaired? At the time of this writing, rumors abound that nefarious plots are underfoot. We will, of course, endeavor to keep our dear readers informed of developments.

Ladies, with the Christmas season upon us, now is the time to commission new suits of clothing for hus-

bands and sons to be ready by the New Year. Taylor
and Sons of Savile Row is accepting appointments.
ᕬ—Honeycutt's Gazette of Fashion and
Domesticity for Ladies

THE WIDOW HOLLIS HONEYCUTT was in a prickly mood as she waited admittance at the gates of St. James Palace. For one thing, she was standing in the middle of a throng of gentlemen, all of them chatting quite loudly in various languages, without any regard for other conversations occurring nearby. A warm-blooded woman of a certain age missing her late husband could have been intoxicated by the scents of citrus and tobacco that seemed to follow so many men about, but Hollis didn't care for all that privileged masculinity pressing up against all her femininity. It was as if they didn't sense how their bodies fit into crowded spaces—they kept bumping into her, tossing their casual *pardons* at her.

She was vexed that she had to wait in this line or anywhere else to take tea with her very own sister. It wasn't her fault that Eliza Tricklebank, formerly of the modest Bedford Square in London, was now the Duchess of Tannymeade and queen-in-waiting of Alucia, and the guest of Queen Victoria. She was still Hollis's sister, and being made to wait like a pauper at the gates of the palace to see her wasn't fair.

And Hollis was still vexed by an encounter earlier today with the odious, condescending Mr. Shoreham, who'd dismissed her out of hand. And not for the first time—she'd endured a weeks-long philosophical dispute with the gentleman from the London Library.

Donovan, her manservant, stood beside her in the queue, his hooded gaze following the movements of gentlemen as the group slowly advanced toward the guardhouse. He was the one man in her life who didn't care how long she nattered on…well, besides her father, of course. And Lord Beckett Hawke, her friend. Beck didn't care, but he didn't listen, either. Donovan always listened very patiently and then offered a fair opinion if asked. Sometimes, he offered one if not asked. Which he did at present. He said, "One of the problems here, if you don't mind me saying, is that you're quite stubborn. We've noted the inclination in you before, have we not?"

She clucked her tongue at him. "I grant you that at times I may suffer from pigheadedness, but in this, I am *right*."

Donovan laughed. The queue moved; he put his hand on her back and nudged her forward into the crush.

Hollis couldn't see over the heads of those before them, so she glanced around. Her gaze happened to land on a gentleman standing off to one side by himself. He was tall, and beneath the brim of his hat, she could see that his dark hair was longer than was fashionable. He wore a great coat that made his shoulders look impossibly broad, and she idly wondered if they were truly that broad beneath it. His head was cocked at an odd angle and he looked a bit confused, as if he'd found himself wandering a strange land. Little wonder—the line to enter the palace for the royal tea was ridiculously long and the guards didn't seem to know what they were doing. Why *were* so many people invited to tea? The purpose, as Hollis understood it, was to set a conciliatory tone for the peace negotiations between Alucia and Wesloria that would begin on Monday. Representatives of the two kingdoms had been invited to this make-nice tea, but were there really so many who needed the tone set for them?

The confused man moved behind some other gentlemen, and Hollis lost sight of him.

She turned back to Donovan and her vexation. "You ought to have seen how smug Mr. Shoreham was. Entirely too confident in his place in this world and in what he clearly believes are his superior thinking skills because he is a *man*. I tell you, he is one of the most supercilious and ridiculous men in all of London."

"Well, that's quite something, isn't it?" Donovan said. "There are an awful lot of men in London. A right proper feather in his cap." He stepped up to the guardhouse and handed Hollis's invitation to one of the guards. The guard disappeared inside with it. "What was it you called him, again?" Donovan asked, but before Hollis could answer, he leaned forward and said to the guard, "It won't do to keep Mrs. Honeycutt waiting, lad. She's the sister of the Duchess of Tannymeade."

"Hold your horses," the guard said gruffly.

Donovan looked at Hollis. "Ah, I remember. A bag of wind, wasn't it?"

Hollis felt only a twinge of remorse about that. "Well, I didn't *shout* it. I merely stated the obvious."

A group of three men jostled them as they pushed through the gate; Donovan pulled her to the side.

"Well," Hollis said, righting her bonnet. "Do you think they fear the tea will go cold?"

"Or that the queen will not have made enough cakes? Stay here. I'll see what keeps the guard."

He moved back toward the guardhouse, but another group of gentlemen who had just been given permission to enter very eagerly and loudly crowded through the gate. Hollis stepped back to avoid being trampled, but missed the curb and stumbled. She collided with what she might have thought was a wall had two hands not caught her by her elbows and effortlessly righted her. "Oh!" Hollis exclaimed, and turned to see who had saved her from taking a tumble.

It was the confused man. Except that he didn't look confused now—he looked slightly concerned. His gaze swept over her, as if checking to see if there was any injury to her person. Hollis noticed a thick tress of dark chestnut hair had escaped his hat and hung over his brow. His complexion was from a region of the world where skin tones were darker than the pale skin of the British. He had vivid golden-brown eyes, and Hollis was so startled that he was the one who had prevented her from falling that she couldn't speak. He clearly didn't need her to speak—he gave her a polite nod, stepped around her, and walked up to the guardhouse. She watched him hand his invitation to the guard, and when the guard handed it back, the man looked around, as if uncertain if he should actually enter the gates. Apparently, he thought not—he stuffed the invitation into his pocket, then walked in the opposite direction of the entrance, as if he'd meant to enter another palace and had just noticed he was at the wrong one.

Donovan suddenly appeared in front of her. "All sorted, then. This way," he said, and led her into the crowd of gentlemen going through the gate. "You're to meet Mr. Bellingham just inside the courtyard." He showed the invitation to another guard, who opened the gate. As Hollis stepped through, two more men elbowed past her.

"Why are all these gentlemen here for tea?" Hollis asked as she and Donovan headed for the courtyard. "I didn't think gentlemen really cared for it. I invited Beck once and he said that tea was for grandmothers and scandalmongers."

"I can't speak for his lordship," Donovan said, "but my guess is that these gentlemen are here to take tea." He reached up to rap on the door the guard had pointed him to. "It's not often one is invited to sit with the queen."

The door swung open. Donovan handed the invitation to the gentleman who stood there. "Ah, yes, of course, Mrs. Honeycutt. We've been expecting you. I am the underbutler, Bellingham, at your service. If you will come with me?"

"Thank you." Hollis looked up at Donovan.

"Shall I call for you in an hour or so?" he asked, looking at his pocket watch.

"No need. Eliza will see that I am sent home under proper escort."

He nodded and slipped the watch back into his pocket. He smiled. "How beautiful you look, madam. I should think today is an excellent day to look for a husband. There are bound to be many wealthy gents roaming about the staterooms."

Hollis rolled her eyes, but she could feel herself blushing. "Do you mean to go out this evening?"

Donovan's smile turned wry, and even though she understood that there could never be anything between them, his smile always caused her heart to flutter just a little. He was perhaps the most handsome man she'd ever known. "Better you don't ask," he said ebulliently. He put his hand on her elbow and turned her about so she was facing the door and the gentleman who was patiently waiting. "You're not to fret, remember?"

"I'm not fretting. I haven't the slightest bit of fret in me. I've already forgotten you."

Donovan laughed. "Go, enjoy your time with your sister and your niece. Bring home a story." With that and a wink, he turned to go.

Hollis watched him walk away with a definite spring in his step. Just as he turned to exit the gate, she saw the confused gentleman now striding purposefully across the courtyard at such a pace that the hem of his greatcoat kicked out with each step. He no longer appeared uncertain about anything at all—he looked perfectly at ease. He was following along where all the other gentlemen seemed to be going in groups of two or three, talking and laughing and carrying on as if they thought they were headed to a pub after a cricket match.

"Mrs. Honeycutt?"

"Oh! Yes," she said to the underbutler, remembering herself, and stepped in through the door.

CHAPTER TWO

All of London is eagerly awaiting a glimpse of the Duchess of Tannymeade, nee Miss Eliza Tricklebank, who is recently returned to London with her husband, the duke, and her newborn daughter, the heir to the Alucian throne. Princess Cecelia is said to be a little cherub with the green eyes of her mother and the dark hair of her father. Speculation as to who might be a suitable marriage match for the tiny princess has already begun in earnest, with the two-year-old son of a certain English minister receiving the most bets at a White's gentlemen's club.

It is inconceivable that a parlor game involving the young princess can entertain so readily when credible whispers of trouble persist in royal circles. It would behoove us all to remind ourselves of the true import of this summit.

Ladies, a reminder that stiff crinoline is a danger to your health. Do have a care when standing cliffside, as a good strong wind could send one racing out to sea like a balloon, which, unfortunately, the late Mrs. March of Scarborough discovered.

⁓—Honeycutt's Gazette of Fashion and
Domesticity for Ladies

THIS WAS THE second time Hollis had been escorted into St. James Palace like royalty, and the second time she felt as if she was perpetuating a terrible lie. She was much more at home in her drawing room, her feet before the fire.

Bellingham wore white gloves and a pristinely tied neckcloth as he led her up the main staircase and then down a long hall, past portraits and marble consoles and a spectacular view of St. James Park. He turned another corner and they carried on down another very long hall, past more portraits and enormous urns and velvet draperies, until they arrived at the door that led to the suite of rooms reserved for the Duke and Duchess of Tannymeade. He rapped twice. Someone inside opened promptly. The underbutler stepped through, bowed, and announced grandly, "Mrs. Hollis Honeycutt."

"Hollis!" Eliza cried happily from somewhere inside the room, and as Hollis stepped across the threshold, she spotted her sister darting through a veritable sea of people to reach her.

Hollis scarcely had a moment for a footman to take her bonnet and her cloak from her shoulders when Eliza burst through the maze and threw her arms around Hollis, bouncing them up and down like they used to do when they were girls. "You're *late*, darling. Where have you been? I feared you'd miss it altogether."

"I'm so sorry, Eliza. It couldn't be avoided."

It could have been completely avoided. Her pride and determination to prove Mr. Shoreham wrong was proving to be a bit of an obstacle.

Eliza stood back to examine Hollis's gown and nodded with approval. "It's beautiful. Caro said it was good, but not quite as good as the gown she's made you for the ball."

"But it's so *tight*," Hollis groaned, and glanced down at the ice-blue skirt. She pressed her hand to her middle in a pointless attempt to relieve the tight binding of her corset.

"It's supposed to be tight! Waistlines are all the thing. Not that I care a whit for mine." She laughed—of course she did—because it hardly mattered what Eliza wore. She looked regal, as if she'd been born to be a queen instead of the daughter of a justice. Eliza was fuller than when she'd left London, but then again, she'd married and given birth in the meantime. To Hollis's biased eye, her sister was gorgeous. Her *life* was gorgeous. She had a wonderful, handsome husband who adored her. She had a cherub of a daughter. She had a palace and servants and jewels and gowns, and would one day sit on a throne. Eliza had always been enviously pretty to her younger sister, but since bringing baby Cecelia into the world, she seemed practically to glow. Is that what love and companionship and motherhood did for a woman? If so, Hollis yearned for it terribly.

"I beg your pardon—will you not greet me?"

Hollis would recognize that male voice anywhere and turned around. She'd known Lord Beckett Hawke all her life. Beck, the older brother of Hollis and Eliza's dearest friend, Caroline, and the closest thing to a brother Hollis had ever had. He was insufferable and never tired of telling her what to do, but he also loved her and supported her when she needed him the most.

Just recently, an elderly uncle had passed away with no surviving heirs, and Beck had been made an earl. He was now Lord Iddesleigh. He had a new estate that was several hours from London and surrounded by nothing but a village that Beck had privately proclaimed only slightly larger than a horse turd.

He was the only one in the crowded sitting room who was actually sitting, enthroned on a red velvet chair, one leg crossed over the other like an old grandfather calmly surveying his brood. He tilted his head and examined Hollis.

"How lovely you look. Come here and tell me what you've been about. You never call anymore, Hollis. There was a time I couldn't rid my house of you, and now I can hardly entice you to come round at all."

"What on earth are you talking about?" she asked, laughing. "I dined at your house not three days past. Why are you sitting there as if you're ready to receive your tenants' rents?"

Beck glanced around him. "Is there a rule that says guests of the palace are not allowed to sit?"

"I never understood the point of having so many fine furnishings if they're not to be used," Eliza said.

"*Hollis,* darling!"

Beck's sister, Caroline, now Lady Chartier, as she had married Prince Sebastian's brother, Leopold, was sailing through the many men to greet Hollis, her arms outstretched. Prince Leopold strolled along behind her.

Caroline caught Hollis's hands and leaned in to kiss her on the cheek.

"Hollis," Prince Leopold said, and took her hand from Caroline. "I thought you'd gone missing." He brought her hand to his lips. "You look very well, as always." He smiled fondly.

Hollis curtsied. "Thank you, Your Highness. You are very kind to say so. And may I say that country living certainly agrees with the two of *you.*" She'd spent a lot of time with the prince and Caroline in Sussex. The Hawke family seat stood just outside the village of Bibury, and that is where Caroline, and eventually Leopold, had retreated after what everyone said was London's greatest scandal... until some four months later when a new scandal came along to claim the title.

Hollis and Eliza called the scandal Caroline's "courtship." But really, no one had believed that Caroline and Leopold would survive as much as a fortnight in the country, so far from society. The two of them separately had been the biggest prizes on guest lists for the longest time. Until they weren't.

It was impossible to believe, but the two most unlikely people in all of Britain had settled in the country and discovered, after years of being seen at every social event, that rural life, buckskins, and animals suited them. Caroline said it was peaceful and bucolic, unlike their lives in London. Beck said that was an invented excuse, and the truth was that they still weren't allowed in most Mayfair salons. "Scandals are slow to die," he'd said to Hollis. "Best you not put yourself in the middle of one, darling."

Caroline stood back to admire Hollis's gown. "Oh, it's lovely, isn't it? I knew it would be. I have a very keen eye for color, you know."

Caroline had discovered a natural talent for making gowns in the last year or so, and now, her creations were in high demand across London. She'd fashioned this one in a style that cut closer to the body, as the Alucians preferred, and with a lot of lace, as the English preferred.

"It's awfully tight," Hollis whispered.

"That's not *my* fault," Caroline said.

"Hollis, here she is! My little angel," Eliza cooed. Hollis turned back to her sister. In the sea of men behind her, one emerged, a head taller than the others. He was making his way toward them. It was Eliza's husband, Prince Sebastian, the Duke of Tannymeade and the future king of Alucia, carrying their firstborn child and heir. He had the baby high in his arms, his smile broad and proud.

"Should he carry her like that?" Caroline asked. "Shouldn't a nursemaid be on hand?"

"He prefers to hold her," Eliza said. "He's utterly besotted."

"Aren't we all," Hollis said dreamily. Princess Cecelia was seven months old and looked as if she'd just awakened from a nap—her dark hair was mussed, and one of her cheeks was pinker than the other, as if she'd been lying on it. She blinked at the adults gathered in the room, staring at them all sternly as if they were a new sort of animal she was seeing for the first time. But she quickly tired of the view and lay her head on her father's shoulder.

"Hollis!" Prince Sebastian beamed as he leaned down to kiss her cheek. "Would you like to hold your niece?"

"Please!" Hollis said, reaching for the baby. The little princess came willingly, but stared very suspiciously at Hollis. She had wispy dark curls, pale green eyes, and pursed, plump lips. She was all cheek and thigh, too—the sort that demanded to be squeezed with affection. "Oh, dear," Hollis said wistfully. "I can't possibly love her more."

"She's beautiful, Eliza," Caroline agreed.

"I don't mean to boast, but I do believe she is the most beautiful child I've ever seen," Eliza said, stroking her daughter's back.

Beck, having managed to hoist himself from his chair, wandered over to have a look at the baby. "Do you want to hold her, Uncle Beck?" Caroline asked.

"I do not. Firstly, I am not her uncle. Secondly, I held her earlier and she drooled on my shoulder. Even if I were so inclined to hold her after that unforgivable incident, her parents are so smitten they can't bear to let her out of their grasp for more than a moment."

Cecelia began to fuss. "Give her to me, Caro," Eliza said.

"My case is made," Beck drawled.

"Eliza, we are due to appear for tea," the duke reminded her, and lifted his hand, signaling someone.

Eliza pressed her baby's cheek to hers. "I don't want to

leave her," she said as a woman dressed in the gray of a nursemaid came forward and curtsied.

"She'll be well tended," the duke assured her.

"Yes, but I don't like being away from her, not with all this talk of rebellions and coups."

Sebastian—Bas, as he was known to his sister-in-law—didn't look at Eliza. He looked directly at Hollis and frowned darkly.

Hollis guiltily avoided his gaze. What was she supposed to have done? Pretend she hadn't heard what the two gentlemen at the London Library had said? Was she to be blamed when men of all ilk would speak of frank matters when she was within earshot, as if they assumed she was either an imbecile or invisible? As if she couldn't possibly make sense of words like *coup d'état* or *rebellion*? Well, she'd heard the gentlemen very plainly, and she'd made perfect sense of those words. She'd gone to the library, determined to speak to Mr. Shoreham. But the word *Wesloria* had caught her attention, and she'd looked back at the two gentlemen who'd been standing on the walk. One of them said he'd heard rumors of rebellion brewing in Wesloria.

"A coup?" his companion had asked.

"Perhaps," the other one had said. "The Weslorian economy is in shambles—it's hardly a surprise. It's been speculated for years."

"Does the queen or the prime minister know?"

"The PM said himself that a rebellion could happen here, as King Maksim is unable to defend himself as robustly as he might in St. Edys."

St. Edys, Hollis knew, was the capital of Wesloria.

"It's all conjecture, but we've assigned more guards to the Weslorian... Excuse me, madam, are you lost?"

One of them had finally noticed Hollis, standing not two

feet from them. "Pardon?" she'd said, and then had turned and walked into the library.

Of *course* she'd told Eliza what she'd heard. Sebastian and Leopold, having heard the tale from Eliza, assumed Hollis had misunderstood.

"You mustn't worry, Eliza," Leopold said. "Whatever talk there is concerns the Weslorians, and frankly, none of it can be believed." And then he, too, cast an accusing look at Hollis.

"But it's happened before," Eliza insisted, again repeating something Hollis had told her. She leaned forward and whispered loudly, "King Maksim's firstborn was kidnapped and murdered in the course of a failed rebellion."

Caroline gasped. Sebastian and Leopold again turned twin looks of exasperation on Hollis. Beck sighed wearily, as if Hollis had been taxing him all day. "Well, now you've done it," he muttered.

All right, all *right*, perhaps it hadn't been entirely necessary to tell her sister *that* part. But Hollis had read the whole, terrible account at the London Library. She'd studied the long and bloody histories of Wesloria and Alucia, because there was no lighter reading material to be had at the library, and because her sister would one day be queen of Alucia. God save Eliza, poor thing. It was one thing to enjoy the spoils of royalty, but quite another to have to shoulder *all* the trappings of a monarchy. Like this conflict between Alucia and Wesloria. It was true—the firstborn child and heir to King Maksim of Wesloria had been kidnapped at the age of eight months. Taken from his cradle, for God's sake, by rebels who meant to use him to force the king to abdicate. But the rebels were killed and the child was never seen again. Hollis read that the queen died of grief.

No one was ever certain who was behind the rebellion.

One theory suggested Alucia might have had something to do with the kidnapping and murder, which only added to the tensions between the two countries. Another theory posited it had to be someone inside the palace, someone close to the king.

The most plausible theory, at least to Hollis, was the one that laid the blame at the feet of Felix Oberon, the exiled half brother of King Karl of Alucia. Prince Sebastian and Prince Leopold's uncle had been cast out of Alucia many years ago for plotting an overthrow of their father, King Karl. Oberon had constructed the plot to kidnap Sebastian two years ago, as well. It seemed perfectly reasonable to Hollis to suspect him of kidnapping the poor royal baby.

Whoever had done it, Hollis had not told Eliza that story to alarm her. The reason she'd told her at all was that when the Weslorian king remarried a few years after the death of his wife, and Queen Agnes bore their first child, the Princess Justine, the Weslorian parliament had changed the rules of succession so that King Maksim's oldest daughter could inherit the throne in the event a son was born after her. Her *point* had been that Cecelia could one day be queen if Eliza pressed Sebastian now to see that the same law of succession was passed in Alucia. What if Eliza had a slew of sons after Cecelia? It was only fair that the little darling be allowed her rightful place on a throne.

"Eliza, my love, Cecelia is perfectly safe here," the duke said, slanting a look at Hollis that brooked no argument. "She is in a palace, surrounded by guards and nurses. It would take an army to penetrate these walls. And besides, it's time for her supper." He took his daughter from Eliza's arms, pausing to allow Eliza to kiss the baby's cheek over and over until Cecelia pushed her away. The duke kissed the top of Cecelia's head, then handed the baby to the nurse and signaled for the nurse to go.

Eliza looked helplessly at Hollis. Hollis winced apologetically as she looped her arm through Eliza's. "She'll be *fine*."

But Eliza didn't look convinced, and really, neither was Hollis.

"Shall we?" Sebastian said, and nodded to the head butler.

"I didn't mean to upset you, Eliza," Hollis said softly as everyone began to queue to enter the adjoining stateroom. "I only meant to help."

"How is that helpful?" Caroline asked.

"Caro," Prince Leopold said, and beckoned for her. Caroline frowned at Hollis, then moved to join her husband.

"Don't listen to them, Hollis," Eliza said. "You were right to warn me that Cecelia could be kidnapped."

"That wasn't... That was not what I..." Lord, look what she'd done. Hollis sighed. It hardly mattered what she'd meant—everyone was cross with her as it was.

"Well," Eliza said, and paused to check that her tiara was straight on her head. "Do you think we'll be treated to the queen's favorite lemon sponge cake? Lady Sutherland has said it's the best confection she's ever tasted."

"Eliza?" her husband said, reaching a hand for her.

"I hope so, but I think I would prefer a sandwich or two," Hollis said. "I'm famished," she added as Eliza moved to join her husband at the head of the procession.

Beck took his place next to Hollis. "What is the matter with you and all this talk of rebellion and kidnapping?"

"Not you, too," she muttered.

"Of course *me*. If I weren't here to steer you right, who would?"

She didn't have the chance to remind him that she didn't

need to be steered by him—the doors to the stateroom were thrown open, the duke and duchess were announced, and they began the promenade into the stateroom.

A very crowded stateroom. "I've never seen so many people at a tea," she said to Beck.

"It's for show, really," Beck said. "A show of unity. Of the British willingness to help the poor, misguided Alucians and Weslorians work out their differences."

"Eliza said Bas is rather nervous, as this is the first time he will meet the Weslorian king and his family. King Maksim must be nervous, too, do you suppose? *I* would be if I were him, as the Alucian economy is much stronger."

Beck looked down at her with a look of alarm. "What are you talking about?" he demanded. "What has happened to you, Hollis? You used to be amusing and now you're all dry and boring."

"I'm not… I've read…" Hollis sighed. No one, including her own sister, wanted to hear her thoughts about anything at all. "You used to be curious about things, Beck. What happened to *you*?"

Beck snorted. "The only thing I am curious about is how long I will be forced to endure this tea. Of course the Weslorian king is nervous, darling. He desperately wants peace and everyone says the duke's uncle Felix Oberon is just as desperate that they not have it."

"Why wouldn't Uncle Felix want peace?" Hollis asked curiously as the two of them inched forward.

"Because if there is peace and prosperity, no one will follow him into rebellion. And if no one follows him into rebellion, he loses power and his influence in the country will wane."

That made a lot of sense to Hollis. So did the potential for an overthrow.

When at last their full party had entered, people came forward to bow and scrape to the princes and their wives.

Hollis and Beck, being the least important of them all, stood to one side, among the Alucian gentlemen who were there, presumably, to lend their expertise to negotiations—ministers and lawyers and scholars who understood numbers. She and Beck were there as the family who would not be left out, no matter how little they contributed to the proceedings or to anything else.

Hollis was fairly certain she was the least important of them all. She was here for Eliza, obviously, but no one saw her as anyone other than the sister of Tannymeade. *Ah, the sister*, they said, and then she was forgotten. Really, for the time being, that suited her. She may be the sister of the Duchess of Tannymeade, but she was also the proprietor, author, and publisher of the *Honeycutt's Gazette of Fashion and Domesticity for Ladies*, a biweekly magazine she put together and published mostly on her own. Unbeknownst to her family, who would surely disapprove, she was currently working on a bit of news for it.

Recently, she'd turned the gazette toward the more important news of the day. Hollis reasoned that women were interested in more than the latest gossip and fashion news, and she intended to provide it. She was in the midst of penning an article on the true prospect of peace between Alucia and Wesloria and had all the information she needed from the Alucian side. She needed more information from the Weslorian side of things, and particularly, about this supposed rebellion. She figured a royal tea was as good a place to start as any.

She would like to make the acquaintance of one or two Weslorians. She thought that would be the easiest thing to do at this event, knowing that Eliza would be occupied and Caroline would be fluttering about the room. But as Hollis and Beck moved into the room, she discovered that introductions were made quickly and in passing, as everyone was jockeying for position to meet the rulers of the two monarchies. Most of the people she met looked right through her and directly at Eliza and Sebastian, or King Maksim and Queen Agnes.

And then Queen Victoria herself entered, and everyone stopped what they were doing and bowed before the diminutive woman. She went around the room to the various clusters of souls, welcoming them to St. James Palace, asking after their accommodations, wishing aloud that they would all work together for the good of all nations.

Hollis was not introduced to Her Majesty. She was pushed farther and farther back until she was standing in the company of others who were not deemed worthy enough to make Her Majesty's acquaintance.

Caroline was worthy, given her marriage to Prince Leopold, which somehow trumped her scandalous past. Even Beck was worthy, which surprised Hollis. "I didn't think *you'd* make the cut."

"I always make the cut, darling," he said, and straightened his neckcloth. "If you will excuse me, I mean to ask Her Majesty if she has any whiskey about."

"It's a tea, Beck," Hollis reminded him.

"We'll see about that." He sauntered away.

Hollis was left standing alone near a window. There was a time in her life she would have felt entirely conspicuous. But now, she felt a little…invisible.

She looked around the room for something to occupy her, and almost instantly spotted the gentleman who'd looked confused at the palace gates, but then had caught her before she fell. Like her, he was standing by himself.

His expression was serious, his gaze fixed on someone or something in the crowd. It was odd…he looked as if he'd somehow wandered into this tea quite by accident. Had he?

She rose up on her toes to have a better look. He'd removed his greatcoat and his shoulders, she noticed, really were that broad. He was thickly built, like a laborer. She imagined him cutting and hoisting stones, sweat trickling down his arms…

She shook her head—that made no sense. What would a stonecutter be doing here?

She studied his clothing as best she could from that distance. He was wearing the sort of formal suit popular in Wesloria and Alucia. The coat had thin lapels and hung to midcalf. His waistcoat was heavily embroidered. He wore his hair brushed back behind his ears, but one lock still stubbornly hung over his forehead.

He stood stiffly, with his hands clasped behind his back and his head slightly bowed. Was he Weslorian? Alucian? She couldn't see a patch of Weslorian green from here, that peculiar sartorial habit the Weslorians had of proclaiming their nationality. It was a bit like the Scottish tartan in that everyone knew that a man in plaid was most likely a Scot. A bit of green worn on a person signaled a Weslorian. It was generally quite small, such as a thin armband, or in a brooch, or cuffs or collars dipped in green. Unless one was a dignitary, in which case, they dressed more like Queen Agnes, who wore a forest-green gown.

There was something else about him that seemed a bit off. She suddenly realized what it was—in a crowded stateroom, where the goal was to make acquaintances, he was not attempting to make any. She pretended for a moment that, like her, he'd come with the intention of meeting someone, probably an Englishman. Here they were, the two of them, standing apart from all the rest, looking to meet someone new.

But it went without saying that the man had not sailed halfway around the world and found himself in a palace with nothing more important to do than meet someone from England.

So why was he standing alone?

The queen moved directly in Hollis's line of sight to speak to two gentlemen, blocking her view of the man. She leaned to her right, but the man had shifted, too—she couldn't see him.

"Look!"

Hollis gasped with a start and jerked toward the sound of Caroline's voice. "Caro! You scared me half to death." She pressed a hand to her heart.

"Do you remember what I said about—? There she is! Look now, Hollis. *Quickly.*"

"Look at who?" Hollis complained.

Caroline nodded in the direction of a woman with ginger hair. "The plump one. Do you see her? She's built for childbearing, that one."

"Caro! She's not a horse, and really, we're *all* built for childbearing when you think of it. The lady in pale yellow?"

"That's the one."

"And?"

"Why are you being so obtuse?" Caroline said. "I'm hardly in London at all and *I* know who she is—Lady Blythe Northcote, the daughter of the Earl of Kendal. I *told* you about her."

"I've never heard of Earl Kendal."

"You've never heard of him because he rarely comes to town. He's a bit of a recluse. But his daughter has come of age and gone very well past it, and honestly, Hollis, you spent an entire weekend in my company not a month ago, and I *told* you then I'd met the perfect woman for Beck."

There was a lot Caroline said that floated off into the clouds, particularly on the weekends Hollis spent with them in the country. But she heard her loud and clear now and gaped at her. "What do you mean, 'perfect for Beck'?"

"There is only one thing that can mean, Hollis. It's time he married."

Hollis gasped. "But you were so against it, Caro!"

"I was against it for *me*, darling, not Beck. He should have been married ages ago. Who is that vast fortune going to, I ask you?"

"Well, *you* if he doesn't have an heir."

"Hmm," Caroline said, as if she'd just considered the possibility. "That's tempting, I won't deny it. But why should Beck be allowed to remain a bachelor all his life? We all know he needs someone to look after him."

Hollis laughed. Beck had looked after them all these years, but to Caroline, it was the other way around.

"I am determined," Caroline insisted, and as she launched into all the reasons her brother ought to marry, Hollis glanced back to where the man had been standing. He wasn't there. She went up on her toes and looked around the room. He was nowhere to be seen.

"What are you doing? Oh, dear, Leopold is gesturing for me," she said. She grabbed Hollis's hand and squeezed it. "See that you don't interrogate the queen's guests. Eliza would be very cross with you." She went off to join her husband.

"I'm not going to *interrogate* anyone," Hollis muttered to herself. Why was it that she was constantly having to explain that the art of publishing had more to do with getting the details precisely right? That didn't mean she interrogated people, it meant she *clarified*. And, yes, she carried a pencil and a bit of paper with here wherever she went, another complaint from her family. But she didn't want to forget a blessed thing.

As Caroline glided away, Hollis tried to find the man in the crowd again, but he was nowhere to be seen. Where could he have gone? Why would he leave the room before the tea was served? Surely he wasn't allowed to wander about St. James unaccompanied.

She suddenly thought of baby Cecelia, away from her parents in this old palace, and a shiver of ice shot down her spine.

She was being ridiculous. He couldn't wander around the palace on his own—there were guards and servants and people everywhere. What was the matter with her? How could she find something sinister in a man for merely standing by himself? If that made people sinister, then she was sinister.

Cecelia was perfectly safe.

Hollis forced her attention to the tea.

The footmen began to move through the room, inviting people to take a seat at one of six tables set for tea. Hollis looked to the other end of the room, hoping to see Eliza.

There he was again! He was near the door now, but still quite alone, his gaze still fixed on someone in the crowd. If she wasn't mistaken, he was staring at King Maksim.

Hollis glanced to where Eliza and Caroline were sitting. They were very much engaged. And Beck was...well, she didn't know where Beck was.

She shifted her gaze to the gentleman again. She was curious about him. What was he doing here, all alone? Perhaps she ought to take the opportunity to thank him for being so gallant earlier. Hollis began to move casually around the perimeter of the room in the gentleman's direction.

CHAPTER THREE

At a royal tea welcoming guests from Alucia and Wesloria, Queen Victoria looked resplendent in a gown of gold silk and Chantilly lace, festooned with large silk flowers on the bodice and skirt, and a lace cap atop her curls.

There were many dignitaries in attendance, as the opportunity to take tea at St. James Palace is rarely realized. It was noted by more than one that a Hawkish English lord was very much enthralled with an auburn-haired beauty only recently come to London from the country. Might a courtship be on the horizon?

Overheard at the tea was a debate as to whether or not women are suitable teachers for the youth of our country. A rather antiquated notion abounds in the heads of many males that the fairer sex is inferior in matters of the mind. But if one considers the irrefutable truth that every gentleman has, in one form or another, been taught a thing or two by a woman, does that not disprove such ideas? Ladies, we are all teachers, are we not?

⌒—Honeycutt's Gazette of Fashion and Domesticity for Ladies

HE DIDN'T HEAR the woman approach him, didn't see her until she leaned into his line of sight, which gave him such a start that he must have jumped a good foot in the air. This happened to him quite often when someone approached him from the left. He was deaf in that ear.

He recognized her right away, of course. She smiled. She had a very pretty smile that matched her very pretty face, which he had noticed earlier today. She had deep blue eyes that shone with the light of a generous spirit. Her hair was very dark, almost black. He'd once heard that the Welsh had very dark hair. He wouldn't really know—he'd never met a Welshman in his life.

He realized, a beat too late, that she was speaking. Her voice was soft and he couldn't quite make out what she said in the din of so many voices. He leaned forward as was his habit, his gaze on her lips. *How do you do.* Aha. "Very well," he said. "Thank you."

"I really must thank you, sir!" she said. "I was so startled earlier that I couldn't utter a word after you saved me from all but tossing myself into the street."

He wasn't certain whether or not she meant she had deliberately tried to fall into the street, or if the expression was another English euphemism he didn't understand.

"Isn't this something?" she asked, shifting slightly closer. Now that he could see her lips, the words she spoke sounded clearer to him. "So many kings and queens and potential kings and queens in one room."

He looked around them. The people gathered here ought to have been kings and queens, given the purpose of this event.

When he looked at her again, she smiled prettily and asked, rather loudly, even to him, "Do you speak English?"

He blinked. "I—I just spoke English to you."

"Ah, so you did!" she said cheerfully. "You must be Weslorian. Are you Weslorian?"

Was *she* Weslorian? No, impossible—she had an English accent and wore no green. Why was she asking him this? Why was she asking anything at all? A dull throb of suspicion went through him.

"I spotted your patch of green," she said, as if she was proud of this, as if it was a special talent of hers. The green was on his cuff, clearly visible. He felt conspicuous. And a wee bit duped, as if someone should have warned him this would happen, that a beautiful woman would approach him from the left and startle him. But, then again, no one had expected him to be at this tea at all, and least of all, him. He'd received an engraved invitation, addressed to Marek Brendan, at the behest, he suspected, of Lord Dromio, the minister of trade.

The woman suddenly laughed, as if he'd said something amusing. "Do you at least have a *name*, sir?"

He'd failed to introduce himself, he realized, and now he was a bit reluctant. There was something about her that was causing him to feel a bit vulnerable.

In the space of his hesitation, she stepped closer. He caught a whiff of lilac or rosewater—something sweet and pleasurable. "I beg your pardon, I should have introduced myself—Mrs. Honeycutt." She held out her hand.

He hesitated, then took it, bowing over it. "A pleasure. Marek Brendan." The etiquette training he'd received all those years ago was slowly returning to his brain in something of a slow drip. It had been many years since he'd thought of those long, wintry nights spent on the shores of the Tophian Sea, playing a game with his aunt. *Enchanté, madam. Fork to the left of the plate, knife to right.* Funny, all that training was for naught, really—he lived a very solitary life in Wesloria, working in the capital city of St. Edys, going home to his little farm at the foot of the mountains in the evenings to water and feed his animals. This did not seem the time or place to renew his lessons, and really, he had more pressing issues to attend to. "Madam, if you—"

She seemed to sense that he was on the verge of excusing himself and blurted, "I have never been to a tea as crowded as this. How many teapots do you suppose the queen has in her kitchen?"

Was he supposed to guess?

She clasped her hands together. "Is it your first time here?"

Was she referring to the palace? Or to London? Either way, he had only one answer. "It is," he said. He glanced around for an escape. He wasn't good at this sort of thing, not with his hearing impairment. Not with his lack of practice. Not with his lack of patience. Not when his attention was sorely needed elsewhere. He didn't want to be distracted by a lady's smile or a guessing game of how many teapots. *If the queen had forty-eight people to tea, and each teapot held three and one half cups of tea, how many teapots...* "It is," he said.

The woman was smiling a little impertinently. It was indeed a lovely smile, and if he'd been a different man, in a different place, he would have basked a moment or two in that smile, no matter how uncomfortable. But he was not a different man. He was who he was, in London for reasons that had nothing to do with a woman like her.

He glanced across the room to King Maksim. The minister of trade, Lord Dromio, had his ear. The king looked concerned. Or was he confused? He tended to wear the same worried expression most of the time, as if he expected the roof to collapse on his head at any moment. Just behind him was the ever-present young man who watched the king's every move. He was his personal valet.

"I suppose you've come for the peace summit then, have you? The weather has been pleasant for this time of year, although one of my servants has informed me that it will snow soon. His hip is as good as a weathervane, he says. Rather like Wesloria, is it not?"

The man's hip was like Wesloria? "Pardon?"

"Snow. I should think it snows quite a lot in Wesloria."

Who *was* this woman? "*Je, yes,* indeed, it does."

Her smile brightened, as if she was pleased to have had that fact confirmed. "As I understand it, it has to do with the confluence of the sea and the mountains, or—or something like that," she said with a flutter of her fingers. "I've read quite a lot about Wesloria and filled my head with facts. Most of them not very useful."

"I see," he said, but he didn't see at all. Was she a scientist? Were there female scientists in England?

Marek glanced toward the king again, wondering how to kindly extract himself from this conversation. Fortunately, he was saved by the Alucian duchess and future queen of that country, as she came sailing toward them, her tiara slightly askew. She was clearly trying to gain Mrs. Honeycutt's attention. One of the advantages of Marek's poor hearing was that he was able to read lips in a variety of languages, including English, Weslorian, and Alucian. She was calling out to Mrs. Honeycutt. *Pardon,* she said. *Excuse me, Mrs. Honeycutt.*

"It seems you are wanted," he said simply.

"Am I?" Mrs. Honeycutt turned to look.

"It is a pleasure to make your acquaintance," he said, and took the opportunity to step away, disappearing behind a pair of footmen who were trying to corral guests to a table for tea.

Not everyone was invited to occupy a table—there were far more in the stateroom than there were places for tea. It appeared that none of the guests understood that at first, and so clumps of humans wandered from table to table, examining the place cards, then stood about, talking. Some of them seemed happy to peruse *all* the place names, as if they were shopping in a china shop. Others wanted to be seated and served. Others seemed entirely oblivious to the effort to seat the guests at all.

In the end, those who were not seated—the respective staffs and servants of the dignitaries, resident experts in a variety of subjects—were made to stand back and at attention in case they were needed to answer a question or remove an offending bit of food.

Marek stood by himself in the shadows.

Lord Dromio was seated next to Lord Van. Anton Dromio had been named the minister of trade in the way those things happened—as a favor to a favor for a favor, or some such. He was Marek's superior in the trade offices, and he was quite possibly the dumbest man Marek had ever known—excluding the lad who'd suffered a terrible fall from a horse and had then been suitable only as a helper to the stable masters.

But the difficult thing about Dromio was that he didn't know he was dumb. He pretended to know quite a lot, and when in doubt, which was often, he relied on Marek to explain things to him. He had a tendency to ask advice from any number of advisors, often changing his mind based on the last person he spoke to. He didn't particularly like the complicated topics of a country's trade and economic health, and waved off Marek when he thought his explanation was too taxing.

He was leaning close to Lord Van, speaking into his ear. Van sat immobile, his gaze fixed on the table in front of him, listening intently.

Van had recently been named the foreign minister after

it was discovered that the former foreign minister was involved in a deplorable scheme to sell poor Weslorian women to men of influence both at home and here in Britain. It was the worst sort of slave trade—young women for political favor—and none other than Prince Leopold of Alucia had exposed the plot. Prince Leopold had been the talk around St. Edys for weeks—he'd been engaged to the daughter of a Weslorian duke who was implicated in the scandal. It had caused quite an uproar. The prince had married an Englishwoman and settled here. As for the duke and the foreign minister, well...no one knew exactly what became of either of them. Banished to the hinterlands, Marek guessed. Or worse. King Maksim was not particularly ruthless, but it was known that people who acted in his name could be merciless.

On the other side of Dromio was Lord Osiander. The new minister of labor was young and stoic, and seemed to Marek to be fiercely determined. It was said around the halls of Weslorian government that he desired a new era for their nation, one that would foster good working conditions in the factories and in the ports. He hailed from the unforgiving terrain in the western part of Wesloria, where men worked for low wages in the coal mines. Osiander wanted to change that.

But from what Marek had observed, Dromio and Van were far more interested in clinging to the vestiges of their power and influence. It was obvious to him that the person who enabled them to hold onto that power was King Maksim himself. Unfortunately, the king was ineffectual.

Dromio said something to Van that prompted the two men to chuckle. Osiander glanced at them, then turned his attention away, almost as if he had no patience for their antics.

Marek looked to the right. King Maksim was seated next

to Queen Victoria. She had come alone to the tea, without her consort, Prince Albert. The table also included the king's wife, Queen Agnes, and their two daughters, Princess Justine and Princess Amelia, as well as the Alucian Duke and Duchess of Tannymeade, who would one day be king and queen of Alucia. That table looked like a picture of harmonious accord between the main parties, which, of course, had been the intent. And indeed, as servants dressed in turbans and red coats poured tea, the group did look rather at ease. As if they were all friends.

"Beg your pardon," someone said. "May I pass?"

The voice had come from Marek's right, and he turned slightly to allow whomever it was to pass. His gaze landed on Mrs. Honeycutt again. This time, she was on the arm of a gentleman who looked well fed and well privileged. She was giggling at something the gentleman was saying. But she was looking directly at Marek.

What the devil? He didn't like it, not at all. He stepped back, hopefully out of her line of sight, but Mrs. Honeycutt was not fooled. She leaned around her escort to see him. Was she...*good God*, was she trying to signal some sort of personal interest in him? Or was she an English spy?

Of the two possibilities, a spy seemed more plausible. Although he had never heard of a woman being a spy, he had to admit a woman would be excellent at teasing information out of powerful men. But neither was he generally the object of female attention and, in fact, could say with surety that it had happened to him only once or twice before. The most recent had been in St. Edys. The daughter of a colleague, a lovely young woman with golden hair and soft brown eyes, no more than twenty years or so in age and ten years his junior, had come to the offices every day carrying lunch for her father. Marek had always greeted her and exchanged pleasantries. One day, she'd come with sweetmeats for him. After a week or so of it, Marek began to realize she was not being friendly—she was signaling an interest in something more than a casual acquaintance.

He'd had to tell her that it was impossible. For reasons he could not explain to the young woman, or to anyone on this earth, it was *impossible*.

But it wasn't as if other women were asking their mothers or fathers or cousins to make an introduction. Quite the contrary. It certainly made no sense to him that this woman, as beautiful and privileged as she clearly was, would have any interest in him. It had to be something else.

Her escort, who hadn't seemed to notice Marek at all, said to Mrs. Honeycutt, "Will you take your seat?"

"Why don't you take your seat?" she countered.

"What, and be subjected to Caro's matchmaking attempts? I should rather perish," the gentleman drawled.

Mrs. Honeycutt laughed. It was a pleasing, silky sound, as pleasing as her smile.

The man sighed. "*Now* look what you've done, Hollis," the gentleman said. "A footman is coming to fetch me."

Hollis. Was that an English word? Marek's English was very good, but since being in London, he'd heard words and phrases he didn't know. Was Hollis a name?

"Oh, dear. I suppose you'll have to go, won't you? Don't fret for me, sir. I shall wander around here and make new friends."

"Wander around? Take a seat with Eliza. They'll make space for you. I never thought in all my life that you'd be reluctant to take tea with two queens and a king. You, of all people."

Why her, of all people?

"I'm not the least reluctant, sir, but I'm not invited to sit with the queens, and I will not be the one to break protocol and demand a chair be pulled up. You know very well how these things go, and so do I, and I'd much rather meet the people who have come so far than to listen to you complain about the cakes."

"You mean you want to interview them all. Take my advice and keep your pen in your reticule, darling. Now is neither the time nor the place. You will sit with me. Yes, yes, here you are, my good man," he said as the footman reached them. "Please make space for Mrs. Honeycutt."

The footman bowed and said he would, and the gentleman escorted Mrs. Honeycutt to a table. All the gentlemen at that table stood, and Marek watched as the footman placed a chair for her. She said something with a smile, probably offering an apology, and slipped into her seat.

Marek moved again, stepping up behind a pair of servants, their silver trays at the ready. King Maksim was speaking to Queen Victoria. He looked stiff and uncomfortable, and frankly, a little green around the gills. Maybe he disliked this setting as much as Marek. It was crowded, and too many people were milling about, up and down and out of their seats. Marek assumed that he'd heard the rumors about the threats to his throne. Who could blame him for looking ill at ease? How easy it would be for someone to step next to the king and slip a knife just under his ribs. It would only take a moment to spark a rebellion, here in London, right under Queen Victoria's nose.

Marek moved again, intending to return to his place in the back of the room. And just as he moved, he felt something shoot down his spine like the scrape of a ghostly finger. He glanced across the room…and right into the glittering eyes of Mrs. Honeycutt.

That woman was watching him.

CHAPTER FOUR

Peace talks between the Alucian and Weslorian lead-
ers have begun in earnest, and while it is speculated
that progress has been made, it is difficult to know
by what measure, as the talks are cloaked in secrecy.
Is it not true that peace flourishes in the light of day?

Ladies, Harcourt's Curl Cream has been deemed
superior to other curl creams, but should be applied
sparingly, lest it give the hair an oily sheen. One of
our most dedicated subscribers discovered how oily
at a fete last week when her headdress kept slipping
from her head. Her advice is to apply sparingly.

⌐—Honeycutt's Gazette of Fashion and
Domesticity for Ladies

MR. NORMAN KETTLE arrived at his desk in the United Kingdom's foreign-secretary offices promptly at eight o'clock
every morning, and every morning, he placed his hat and
cloak on the coatrack, carried his lunch pail to his desk,
and set it aside.

Mr. Kettle's desk was very orderly. On one corner, he
neatly stacked shipping and passenger manifests, as well as
correspondence from ship captains and trade companies.
On the opposite corner, he kept the reports submitted each
week by the gentleman in the customs office whose rose-
bud lips Mr. Kettle found uncomfortably attractive. These,

he collected on his noonday walks down to the docks and the Custom House.

Mr. Kettle's occupation was to keep up with matters of foreign shipments and travel that might be of interest to the foreign secretary. It was a duty he performed with verve. Today, he pored over the newest reports until a quarter past one, at which point he put away his papers and spread a linen on his desk for lunch.

He picked up his pail. It felt light.

Every day, his wife packed bread and cheese, an apple if they were in season, or, if he was lucky, some plums. On a good day, she added dried beef or a boiled egg. But last night, he and Mrs. Kettle had had a bit of a row. She said he needed new trousers, as it was impossible to let out even as much as a bit from the ones he had. Mr. Kettle reminded his wife that they couldn't afford new trousers on a clerk's salary and expressed his confidence that she could find a way to let them out.

Mrs. Kettle said she had let them out as far as they would go without the seams tearing completely apart, and that really, he ate too much bread, and he had no one to blame but himself for his tight trousers.

He did love bread. He ate two loaves a day. But Mr. Kettle pointed out that if Mrs. Kettle had been a better cook, he would not have to rely so heavily on bread.

Mr. Kettle removed the cheesecloth that covered the contents of his pail and carefully laid the items one by one on his desk: two carrots, and one boiled egg. He stared with confusion at the paltry meal. He leaned forward and peered into his pail on the slim chance he'd overlooked something. He had not—there was nothing but rusted tin at the bottom.

He was still staring at the items in disbelief when a

cheerful woman's voice sang out, "Good afternoon, Mr. Kettle!"

For the love of Christ, not again. He put aside the pail, braced his hands against the edge of his desk, and glanced up. "Mrs. Honeycutt. You've come round again," he said, hardly able to contain his irritation.

"I have indeed," she said, and removed her cloak, as if she meant to have lunch with him.

Mrs. Honeycutt was a woman whose ambitions frightened Mr. Kettle. The first time she'd come—at least a week ago, though, in fact, it felt like months ago—she'd handed him her calling card:

Mrs. Hollis Honeycutt, Publisher
*Honeycutt's Gazette of Fashion and
Domesticity for Ladies*

He'd instantly felt a sliver of dread run down his spine— he knew that gazette. His wife insisted he bring it home every Wednesday, when it was published. Mr. Kettle didn't like to spend five shillings on a gazette and argued there were better uses for their money. Mrs. Kettle said that she toiled every day for him with the housekeeping and laundry and meal preparation, and the least he could do was bring home a gazette that instructed her how to be a better wife. But Mr. Kettle knew that his wife was not concerned with being better. She wanted to read the gossip contained in those pages.

Mrs. Honeycutt had explained she was interested in writing a story for her gazette, one that would highlight the royal peace summit. She said it would be useful for her to have a look at the Weslorian ship manifests so she might "consult" some of the foreign visitors. Mr. Kettle had explained, and rather plainly, he believed, that he was not at liberty to provide those manifests to her, and really, was her gazette the sort of journal that should discuss such things as peace agreements?

Mrs. Honeycutt had not liked his answer. He knew this because she said it was nothing but sheer ignorance that led a man to believe ladies were not interested in peace between two rival nations. Mr. Kettle had refuted the idea he was ignorant and asked if there was not a gentleman in her life who might explain these things to her?

That was when the man who accompanied her had stepped in and suggested that perhaps Mrs. Honeycutt give Mr. Kettle a day or two to think about it. But Mr. Kettle didn't need to think about it. When she called a day or so after that, and again a day or so after *that*, the answer was still no.

Mr. Kettle had done a little investigating himself after her first visit and had learned that she was the widow of Sir Percival Honeycutt, who had published a superior gazette of politics and economic news. She was also the daughter of Lord Justice Tricklebank, a respected judge on the Queen's Bench. And she was, most notably, the sister of Eliza Tricklebank, who had somehow wooed a foreign prince to marry her and now, in the most unlikely of scenarios, would one day be a *queen*.

He fancied that Mrs. Honeycutt thought that her sister's notoriety gave her some entry into a world she knew nothing about and had wisely suggested she leave the topic of peace and relations between nations to learned men like her father. Once again, the gentleman who accompanied her had to intervene.

Today, her minder stepped just over the threshold and leaned against the doorframe, his arms folded. Mr. Kettle found the gentleman curious. He wasn't quite certain what his relationship was to Mrs. Honeycutt. He could be her carriage man. Or her blacksmith. Or perhaps her stable master or gardener. He didn't dress like a gentleman of quality, but he didn't dress like a regular bloke, either. And yet, it hardly mattered what he wore—he was so startlingly handsome that he caused quite a lot of chaos in the offices, what with clerks and visitors bumping into each other as they tried to get a look at him.

"Oh! I see you're at your lunch," Mrs. Honeycutt said brightly today, and leaned forward across his desk to have a look. She winced, then smiled sympathetically.

"Yes. I am," Mr. Kettle said gruffly. "So if you wouldn't mind."

"But is that all, Mr. Kettle? That hardly seems enough to keep a strong man such as yourself until tea."

Mrs. Honeycutt was a very handsome woman—he would give her that. She was softly rounded at the edges, just like Mrs. Kettle had been when they'd first married. "It is quite enough," he said pertly. Mr. Kettle had a sneaking suspicion that Mrs. Honeycutt was a fellow bread lover. Not that he could tell by the clothes she wore—they all seemed to fit her very well, indeed, and gave the appearance of a fine figure. Today she was wearing a gown of a deep sapphire color that made her ocean-blue eyes seem to leap from her face.

In the distance, someone dropped something that sounded like a wooden box. Mrs. Honeycutt's minder turned his head and looked out the door. No doubt the clerks were banging around like bowling pins out there, hoping to see that male beauty up close.

"I won't keep you from your, umm, carrots," she said, her gaze flicking to his meager lunch and back up again.

"I have come, as I am sure you realize, to inquire after the manifest of the two Weslorian ships that arrived ten days ago."

Lord. Of course he knew why she'd come. Did she think he would believe she'd found a new interest to bring her here again? "I do indeed realize, madam, and my answer is the same—no."

"Why not?"

He drew a long and tortured breath and tried not to look at her succulent lips. "As I have explained, those manifests are rather confidential and are not to be shared with regular people and certainly not women."

"Oh, yes, you did provide that absurd reasoning," she said, nodding. "But while it is true I am a woman, I'm not a regular person. So I will ask again—may I see the manifests of the Weslorian ships that came to port earlier this week?"

"I beg your pardon, madam, but you are indeed *regular.*" He hoped he didn't sound too officious.

"But I'm not, Mr. Kettle," she said gaily. "Because I am the sister of the Duchess of Tannymeade. Do you see? I should think that I, of *all* people, should be allowed to see your papers."

He didn't follow her logic, but he knew from his experiences with Mrs. Kettle that it was best not to point out when a woman was being nonsensical if one could help it. "Then please understand I am following established rules."

"Mmm," she said, and her lovely eyes narrowed a smidge.

Mr. Kettle didn't like it when a woman hummed an *mmm* at him. It never seemed to turn out well for him, and there Mrs. Honeycutt went, confounding him by daintily taking a seat across from him and smiling prettily. "As it happens, I am on my way to see the duchess now. She is residing in St. James Palace for the time being. It is entirely possible that while in her company, I might meet any number of Weslorians. It would be useful to know who they are. Surely you can see that."

"But—but can't you simply ask which ones they are when you meet them?" he asked, confused.

She sighed. "Let's think of it another way."

"Let's not."

"I won't know who is *not* in attendance if I haven't seen the manifest." She smiled again.

Mr. Kettle was hungry and growing cross about his meager portions. Plus, he didn't know what she was talking about. He sat up straighter, to his middling height, and said, "The answer, madam, is the same today as it has been on every previous occasion, and will be again tomorrow and the day after that—*no*. Frankly, it is no small wonder to me that your venerable father hasn't reined you in to proper behavior. Why he allows that silly gazette and for you to wade into matters that no lady should concern herself with is beyond me."

Her minder jerked his head toward Mr. Kettle, his expression one of alarm, as if he'd just seen the executioner and he was coming for Mr. Kettle.

Mrs. Honeycutt, on the other hand, smiled so silkily that he felt a little tingle in his groin. "Mr. Kettle, you *flatter* me! However did you find the time to peruse my gazette?"

That wasn't what he'd meant at all. "This is an unbearable assault on my time, Mrs. Honeycutt."

"*Unbearable* seems a bit of an exaggeration. I believe the information belongs to the public."

"I assure you, it does not."

She drummed her fingers on the edge of his desk. "All right, you force me to tip my hand." She leaned forward and said softly, "I'm gathering very important information for the duchess. You could play a heroic role, if you were so inclined."

He snorted and picked up a carrot. "Gather more dieting advice, Mrs. Honeycutt. You're better suited to it."

Her eyebrows sank low. "Why, thank you! I hope you will heed some of that advice soon. And yet, that is still beside the point."

"Madam. I have been very firm in this. You cannot look at the manifests. For any reason."

She tilted her head to one side. "When you say *firm*... precisely how firm do you mean?"

Mr. Kettle put down his carrot and stood from his chair. "Must I escort you from the premises?"

"Thank you, but if there's any escorting to be done, I'll do it," her Adonis said, coming forward.

"Fine. Then please, sir," Mr. Kettle said, and gestured impatiently at Mrs. Honeycutt.

She glared at him. She stood up. She leaned across the desk and said, "I will have the information one way or another, Mr. Kettle. You'll see." And with that, she swiped up one of his carrots and walked out of the room.

Mr. Kettle looked down at his meager lunch, suddenly reduced by half. That woman! Why did no one take her in hand?

CHAPTER FIVE

Quite a commotion was witnessed in the modest streets of Bedford Square when the Duchess of Tannymeade called at her father's home with the Princess Cecelia in her arms. Guards lined the street and kept onlookers at a respectable distance as the duchess and her party entered the residence. More than one witness reported gales of laughter coming from the open windows and, dear readers, one witness was this author.

The revered Justice Tricklebank, father of the elegant Duchess of Tannymeade, has said he means to accept a position on one of the new county court benches and remove himself from the London air. One hopes he will not remove himself as far as Kent, where neighbors to a very large and famous park mansion have complained that on nights the windows are kept open, the row between lord and lady can be heard for miles around.

♂—Honeycutt's Gazette of Fashion and
Domesticity for Ladies

It had required three large coaches to bring Eliza, little Cecelia, the nurse, and the number of guards the duke had undoubtedly insisted accompany her to the Tricklebank home. A crowd of onlookers and gawkers hoping for a glimpse of the little princess had gathered in the green, through which Hollis had to push to reach the door of her father's home.

She smiled up at one of the guards. "Mrs. Honeycutt," she said, and the guard allowed her to pass.

If her family didn't know she'd arrived, Jack and John, the family dogs, were on hand to alert one and all of the arrival of more foreign invaders.

"For heaven's sake!" Hollis cooed when Ben, the house steward, opened the door. She squatted down to greet the dogs properly, laughing as they tried to lick her face.

"Down, you bloody dogs, *down*!" Ben bellowed as Hollis stood to remove her cloak.

"It's quite all right, Ben," Hollis said cheerfully. "I am very happy to see them, too."

Ben shut the door and took Hollis's coat.

"Thank you, Ben. Has Caro arrived?"

"Aye, she has and is already at the telling of some long tale," he said with a fond grin.

"Mrs. Honeycutt!" Hollis's father bellowed from deeper in the house. "Is that you? Have you come at last?"

"I have indeed, Pappa!" she called back. She patted down her hair and entered the drawing room.

Poppy was the first person she saw, standing just inside the door, as if she'd just arrived herself. Poppy was the maid who had attended them all these years. Hollis's mother had discovered her, a proper orphan, and brought her home. She was so close in age to Hollis and Eliza that they had always viewed her as another sister. Poppy cried out with delight as Hollis walked into the room. Hollis grinned... but her grin fell when Poppy darted past her to the far end of the room. She saw then that Eliza and baby Cecelia were standing near the bookshelves, and Poppy's cry of delight had been for the baby. "May I hold her, please?" Poppy asked, reaching for the baby.

"Well," Hollis said, and toyed with a ringlet over her ear. "I will endeavor not to be offended."

"Both of us, darling," Caroline said from her place on the settee, where she was stretched out as if preparing for a nap. "Hardly anyone in this room has noticed me, and I am wearing a new dress."

"At least you're glad to see me, aren't you, Pappa?" Hollis crossed the room and stepped over a big basket of his yarn to kiss her father's cheek.

"Your arrival gives me a thrill like no other, except perhaps my granddaughter. Where is the cherub, Eliza?"

"I've got her, Your Honor," Poppy said, walking across the room to him.

Eliza followed closely behind, as if she thought Poppy might drop the baby. She pressed her hand to Hollis's cheek as she breezed by. "Happy you've come, darling."

Hollis rolled her eyes. She glanced around the drawing room, that familiar place where the four women in this room had grown up. Four motherless girls. Eliza and Hollis's mother was lost to cholera, and Caro's mother soon thereafter. She thought of how they'd puttered about this room as their father's sight had slowly left him.

She wondered what Eliza thought of this room now after living in palaces. It looked the very same as it had all those years. A bit more worn, of course. And the bookshelves were stuffed with even more books. Her father's knitting—a hobby he'd taken on after his sight had left him—took up more room than it once had. A basket of yarn—tangled, thanks to a very disobedient cat, Mr. Pris—was at her father's feet.

The mantel above the hearth was still cluttered with the clocks Eliza had stored there. She had a peculiar hobby of repairing clocks, and before Prince Sebastian had blundered into this house and demanded information from her—thereby starting a chain of events that had led to the darling little cherub—Eliza had taken in the clocks as extra work. When she had moved to Alucia, they remained precisely where she'd left them, still in disrepair, still clicking and turning and chiming at different times. It was as if Poppy was afraid to move them lest Eliza come bursting through the door one day, desperate to finish the repair of them.

In the front bay window, there was a pair of upholstered chairs, separated by a small table stacked with books. They were great readers, and even Ben and Margaret used to come round in the evenings to listen to Eliza or Hollis read to their father.

The hearth was lit and the room warm, but it needed a good airing, and the carpets a good sweeping.

As usual, Hollis's father was in his rocking chair, his feet on his own small footstool. A blanket covered his lap and his unseeing blue eyes strayed to one side of the room, where there was nothing but a wall.

"Here she is, Your Honor," Poppy said.

The justice put aside his knitting, and Poppy placed the baby in his lap. Hollis's father put his fingers to the baby's head, and a smile like she had not seen in many years illuminated his face as he slowly and carefully moved his fingers over her round head, then to her cheeks, nose and mouth. Cecelia was quite patient and looked on as he examined her with his hands.

"Oh, my," the justice said, his voice shaking a little. "She's beautiful, Eliza. Isn't she beautiful? I imagine she looks just like you did at this age. What an angel you were, as fat as a little pig. This one, she's a little angel."

The little angel had had enough of people petting her,

and she tried to turn. When she couldn't, she began to cry. Eliza picked her up and soothed her. She stepped over the inquisitive dogs and set Cecelia down on the carpet. All the residents of the house gathered around to watch—Ben and Margaret, Poppy, Hollis, Caroline, and Eliza. Even her father was smiling as if he could see the entire tableau.

A long braid of hair slid across Caroline's back and over her shoulder. There had been a time Caroline would not leave her house without her hair perfectly styled in the latest fashion, and her clothing impeccably outfitted. But today she wore a brown skirt and blouse, as if she planned to work in the garden when she left here. It reminded Hollis of how in just two short years, Eliza and Caroline's lives had changed quite dramatically. Eliza had assumed she'd be a spinster all her life, and now she was a duchess. Caroline had assumed she would be the toast of society for as long as she drew breath, and now wore buckskins and braided her hair and stomped around the gardens.

"What happened to Pappa's ribbons, if I may ask?" Eliza said suddenly as she sank down on the floor beside her daughter.

"What ribbons?" Caroline asked.

"You remember them, Caro—Poppy strung them all over the house so Pappa could feel his way around and move without assistance."

"I don't need them," Hollis's father said. "It's fourteen steps to the door, two shuffles to the right around the dogs. Twenty-eight steps to the stairs and one swift kick to the cat, who crosses my path without fail. And, besides, I mean to take one of those county court seats. Move the whole lot of us to the country."

This news surprised Hollis. "*Really*, Pappa? You'd leave London?"

"I need clean air," he said gruffly as he picked up his needles again. "And not two days ago, Ben and I were nearly flattened by a speeding carriage. It's too crowded in town."

"But what of Ben and Margaret and Poppy?"

"I'll go wherever His Honor goes," Poppy said.

"As would we," Ben said from his place near the door.

"But—but what about me?" Hollis asked.

"You?" Caroline laughed. "You have Donovan, darling."

Hollis did not miss the quick look Caroline gave Eliza. When Eliza realized Hollis had seen it, she blushed.

Well, then. Her sister thought she and Donovan were lovers, too.

"Hollis, love, you are welcome to accompany me," her father said.

"Am I?" Hollis asked dubiously.

Cecelia was fascinated by Jack, who was having a thorough sniff of her. Cecelia tried to grab his fur, but Jack darted out of her reach. Eliza dropped onto the settee next to Caroline. "It's good to be home," she said, and sighed with contentment.

"Where is your husband?" Caroline asked. "Mine's gone round to the club with my brother. I told Beck it was a terrible idea, but he shooed me away and told me to think about my saplings if that's what's kept me from London."

"Your what?" Eliza asked.

"My *saplings*. Leopold and I are both loath to leave them."

"What does that mean?" Eliza asked. "Is that a euphemism for dogs? Children?" She gasped. "Caro, have you brought a child into this world and not told us?"

"I have brought *trees* into this world and they require care."

John stood and stretched, then ambled over to join Jack

in his examination of Cecelia. The baby gurgled with delight then toppled over onto her side. Poppy righted her, and this time, Cecelia managed to grab a fistful of Jack's fur. Now, here came Pris, his tail swishing, signaling that he was miffed to have been left out of the fun. With his tail high, he rubbed up against Cecelia's chubby leg.

"Pappa, did you hear? Your oldest child has taken tea with the *queen*," Hollis said.

"I have indeed heard." His fingers were flying along with the yarn as he churned out another long panel of knitting. "Mr. Frink read the account to me as it was written in the most excellent *Honeycutt Gazette*."

The judge had been very vocal about not wanting Hollis to continue with the gazette after Percy passed away. But in the last few months, he'd admitted his admiration for her. "You've done what I never thought a woman in your position could do, Hollis. I'm very proud of my girl." It was true that the circulation of her gazette was quite good. Better than the legal gazette her father took once monthly, and far better than Percy ever managed to achieve with his gazette of politics and economics.

"I have also heard from Mr. Frink that the Weslorian king looks unwell. Is that true?"

"He looked well to me," Eliza said. "A bit worried, perhaps, but then again, everyone is. He's a slight man. Even his wife is taller. He has a thin moustache, long sideburns, and he keeps his hair combed neatly to one side, as is the fashion."

"How curious his hair, isn't it?" Caroline said.

"Why?" Hollis asked. She stepped up on the ladder that was always set up in the room near the bookshelves. It had occurred to her that there was a book about the Bow Street Runners, the lawmen who had preceded the Metropolitan

Police Force. She thought the book might be useful to her interests now, perhaps holding information about how one went about solving a crime. Not that she had a crime to solve, exactly. Not yet, anyway.

"And his daughters have the same affliction."

"Affliction?" Hollis repeated, glancing over her shoulder at Caroline.

"You didn't notice?" Caroline slid down on the floor to join Cecelia and Poppy.

"Oh, that," Eliza said. "I've heard it's not uncommon in certain families."

"What's not uncommon? What hair?" Hollis asked again.

"The streak of white," Caroline said, and gestured loosely at her temple.

"King Maksim's hair has a rather long streak of white, Pappa," Eliza said. "It's quite noticeable, really. It's as if an artist was painting a portrait and forgot to dash on a bit of color to fill in the hair. Very odd."

"His daughters have the same peculiarity," Caroline said. She lifted Cecelia up to her mother. "The oldest one, she has hair as dark as Hollis, and a thin strip of white, just at the front of her hair. The younger one has it, too, but her hair is fair and it's less noticeable."

Hollis was slightly alarmed that she could miss such an important detail. She'd read something about a streak of white in hair, but at the moment, couldn't recall where.

"I like Princess Justine," Caroline said. "She's an accomplished fencer."

"Really?" Eliza asked, looking up from her daughter. "How do you know?"

"She told me! I can't sit beside another woman in the retiring room and not at least speak to her. The princess and I had a lovely chat. She has the most beautiful eyes, have you noticed? More gold than brown, really, like her father, the king. He's a curious one. Have you ever seen another gentleman more full of nerves?" Caroline asked. She came to her feet. "I even said to Leopold, what could make a man so jittery? He said too much drink could make a man jittery."

"He's a bag of nerves because he's here, in London, gliding across a pond like a goose with hunters all around him," Hollis said.

"Pardon?" her father asked.

"Hollis, darling, not again," Eliza said sweetly.

"Well?" Hollis insisted. "I'm just pointing out that there are rumors that a coup or a rebellion might possibly be forming. And here he is, so far from home."

Eliza sighed. "They are *rumors*, Hollis. That's all."

"Speaking of rumors," Caroline said, "why on earth have you been going round to the foreign secretary's office every day?"

"The foreign secretary's office?" The judge put down his knitting.

"How did you hear that?" Hollis couldn't find the book she wanted and hopped down, dusting off her hands on her skirt.

"I didn't hear it—Beck did. Beck hears everything."

"Well, so do I, especially where my daughters are concerned," the judge said. "I had an earful from Mr. Gundy, Hollis, after you put those ideas into his daughter's head about teaching. The poor thing is making an application to Eton!"

"She's a cake," Caroline said.

"Why should she not?" Hollis asked. "Teaching seems an infinitely more agreeable occupation than cleaning chamber pots, is it not?"

"I assure you that Miss Gundy was never, not a single day in her life, destined for the chamber pot. And why would she be allowed to teach at a school that she cannot attend?"

"That, Pappa, is precisely the problem. As if that is somehow her fault! Perhaps if women began to *teach* at Eton, they might one day *attend* Eton."

"For heaven's sake, you and your fanciful ideas about the world," he said, as if she was a young girl with dreams of becoming a faerie. Hollis bit her tongue to keep from saying something she would probably regret.

"Beck said you were trying to obtain a ship's manifest," Caroline said. "Whatever for?"

Hollis huffed a breath of exasperation. "Did Mr. Kettle leave his carrot and skip off and report everything I said to Beck? How does he even *know* Beck?"

"I don't know what a carrot has to do with anything, but Beck is friends with the secretary. You know that. He heard it from Lord Palmerston, and later, Donovan confirmed it was true. Really, Hollis—why do you want a ship's manifest?"

"To know who has come, obviously," Hollis said, feeling a bit defensive. That sounded ridiculous, but she didn't think this was the time to explain all her goals and ideas.

"Why?" Eliza pressed.

"I should like to speak to some Weslorians, if you must know. One can't write a proper story without speaking to everyone involved."

"A proper story about what?" Eliza asked suspiciously, shifting around on the settee to stare at her younger sister.

Well, this was going poorly, and Hollis didn't like the way everyone was looking at her. Even Ben and Margaret, quiet as a pair of mice in the back of the room, appeared concerned. "About…some rumors," Hollis said vaguely.

"Hollis," Caroline said, her fair eyebrows sinking into a frown.

Hollis put up a hand before they could lecture her. "I know you think I'm out of place, but on my word, I've heard things that are unsettling." They didn't look convinced. "And then I saw a man at the tea who was clearly out of place." She probably shouldn't have said it precisely in that way, but when one was trying to make a point, well…there it was.

"What man?" Caroline looked concerned.

"A Weslorian gentleman. He looked like a sailor. Or a lumberman." What was she saying? She sounded mad to even herself. "I mean that he was broadly built. Muscular."

"What has that to do with anything?" Caroline asked.

Caroline and Eliza were looking at her quite closely. Hollis averted her gaze. It had to do with everything. He was unusual and a bit fascinating. She didn't mention Mr. Brendan's starkly amber eyes or his square jaw. She didn't say that his gaze seemed to land on her mouth more often than not, and that his hair was long and brushed back behind his ears, contrary to current fashion. She didn't say that, like her, he'd been a single person in a room where alliances seemed to be everything, and yet seemed determined not to make a single acquaintance. And she certainly didn't say that she found him attractive and was surprised that she did.

When she'd introduced herself and thanked him for helping her at the gates, he'd looked so serious, so intent. But in those golden-brown eyes, she'd noticed something else. A tentativeness, almost as if he didn't speak her language, when clearly, he did. She'd sensed his uncertainty for a second time that day and it contradicted the strength he exuded just by breathing.

"I didn't see anyone like that," Eliza said. "Hollis, I can't guess what you are involving yourself in, but you have no right to do it."

"But you don't know what I mean to do," Hollis said. "None of you do. Would you not agree that if there is trouble afoot, should it not be brought out into the open?"

"Not by you," her father said instantly. "Leave it to the men."

"Pappa!" Eliza cried at the same time Caroline said, "Your Honor!"

"Men don't know everything there is to know," Poppy snorted.

"You all know what I mean," the judge said, waving a hand at them before picking up his knitting again. "Hollis is perfectly capable of conjecture and speculation and, given a set of facts, will solve a puzzle faster than anyone. You're very clever, Hollis, my darling. But you should not *gather* the facts. That is dangerous and absurd, and I'll not have it."

"I don't like to hear those rumors," Eliza said. "Let's please talk about something else." She bounced Cecelia on her knee. "Let's talk about what everyone is wearing to the ball." She spoke in a singsong voice, and the baby laughed.

"*Another* ball?" Hollis's father complained.

"A costume ball!" Caroline said with delight. She was on the floor again, only this time on her back, so that Pris was compelled to jump on her chest and settle in, sinking his claws into Caroline and purring loudly. "Everyone is to dress as a figure from history, which means, of course, I'm going as Marie Antoinette. Eliza, I've made you a Grecian gown. And, Hollis, you'll be delighted when you see the medieval queen's dress for you."

"Is that all you do in Bibury? Make gowns and grow saplings?" Hollis asked. Poppy stood and picked up Cecelia, then walked to the window.

"Why not?" Caroline asked as she absently stroked the cat. "The queen loves a costume ball, you know."

"Oh, my," Poppy said. "The crowd has gotten much bigger, hasn't it?"

Hollis got up to have a look. So did Eliza. Cecelia put her palm against the panes of glass and babbled.

The crowd on the green was half again as large as it had been when Hollis had arrived.

"I wouldn't be the least surprised if Mrs. Spragg has made herself a town crier and let everyone know I am here with Cecelia. We should go," Eliza said. "Bas will not like that such a crowd has gathered." She turned. "Poppy, will you help me gather all our things?"

Poppy handed the baby to Hollis. Cecelia gurgled and reached for Hollis's curls.

"She loves you, Hollis," Caroline said. "What a pity you can't be closer to them."

"What a pity, indeed," Hollis murmured. She leaned forward to smell Cecelia's head, the sweetest scent in the world. It was curious to her that for so long now, since Percy's death, moments like this had been cloaked in grief. But today, Hollis was hardly thinking of him at all. She was thinking that she would like a cherub of her own. Maybe two or three of them.

She pressed her nose to the baby's neck, breathed deeply, and decided, very determinedly, not to let the sour thought that she would likely never have them ruin this moment.

CHAPTER SIX

The first week of the Alucia-Wesloria peace summit has been, by all accounts, rather subdued. One observer reports that the talks have begun with general agreement on the dependence of the respective economies. A most tedious subject to most, but a necessary one to all, as it is recognized that peace cannot be achieved if the parties do not establish a sense of fair play on both sides.

Ladies, as cold air settles over London, remember that Allman's plaster is considered the best to be applied to chests and backs as a cure for the cold. It will relieve the lungs as well as improve the function of kidneys in the most subtle of ways.

◦—Honeycutt's Gazette of Fashion and Domesticity for Ladies

LORD DROMIO SUMMONED Marek Brendan to his rooms early on the afternoon of the grand costume ball. He was in a state of half-dress, his legs bare and his shirttail flapping about and scarcely covering his bits. Marek felt a bit as if he was at the man's toilette with him, a very odd place to be.

But his lordship was not the most organized of persons, and he often called Marek to him while he was in the middle of something else. Once, he'd summoned him when he'd been naturally detained in the water closet and proceeded to ask questions about a trade imbalance with Norway.

This afternoon, Dromio was waving off his valet. The man fluttered like a moth around the minister as he desperately attempted to hand him trousers. Dromio avoided him and went instead to a table and, spotting what he was looking for, leaned across to fetch it.

Marek turned his head from the sight of the man's arse and pretended to examine a painting of someone's long-dead ancestor. But presently, the watery sound Marek knew to be someone speaking reached him and he turned back. The minister was waving a thick envelope in Marek's direction. "Your invitation to the ball," he said. "You'll need this to enter."

"Pardon?" The words *invitation to the ball* did not seem in any way applicable to him. He was not, generally speaking, invited to balls. He'd been to a grand total of two in his entire thirty-four years, even though his aunt had insisted on dance lessons in the event that he was, one day, invited to them all.

Marek was not invited to them, and didn't want to start now. He stared with some dismay at the envelope Dromio held out and didn't move to take it until Dromio began to wave it resolutely at him and he had no choice. He approached gingerly, his hand reaching well ahead of the rest of him.

"It's a costume ball, Mr. Brendan. That means you must attend in *costume*."

"Pardon?"

"A costume! Surely even a recluse such as yourself has some notion of what a costume is. As I said to Ratonkin here—" he gestured loosely to his valet "—we Weslorians view these things as something for children. Will we next be expected to dress as goblins and dance around a bonfire?"

Marek didn't see how a costume ball would lead to a pagan ritual, but Dromio was not exactly the most sensible man he'd ever known.

"Ratonkin informs me that is not the case, that one may dress in any costume one desires, and that the English queen and her consort intend to dress as an ancient king and queen, which I thought was highly ironic, given that they are a king and queen. Not terribly original, is it, would you not agree?"

He looked at Marek, as if expecting an answer. Marek responded with one half of a wry smile.

"Precisely my point," Dromio blithely continued. "You've some sort of costume, haven't you? Perhaps a military uniform? You've served in the military, haven't you, Mr. Brendan?"

"*Je.* Two years in the navy, my lord." Like all Weslorian men, he'd completed the compulsory requirement for every able-bodied man to serve in the military. He'd chosen the navy, of course—he'd been raised on the sea by his uncle, a captain.

"Wear that, then," Dromio said with a flick of his wrist.

Marek hadn't been a member of the navy for fifteen years and certainly hadn't thought to bring his old uniform to England. He'd come as the minister's assistant, not a naval officer. Sometimes he wondered if Dromio understood his role in the ministry.

"It's a costume ball, you see," Dromio said again, as if Marek couldn't grasp the idea. He took the trousers that the valet had been desperate to hand him and stuck one leg into them while his bits bounced around. Then he shoved in the other leg, and thereby proved once and for all that his lordship did indeed put his trousers on one leg at a time as did everyone else.

"I beg your pardon, my lord, but I had not anticipated—"

"Well, who had, Mr. Brendan? Who had?" the minister said gruffly. "Now, I need you to stay close by this evening. I've had a bit of a row with Montcrief from the Privy Council. He's a vile little prick."

Marek didn't know any Montcrief. He hadn't been to any of the peace talks—thus far, his assistance to the minister of trade had meant waiting in an adjoining room on the slim chance the minister or the king or some other Weslorian grandee needed information.

"I won't be caught wrong-footed again if he brings up the…" The minister turned away to stuff his shirttail into his trousers, and when he did, Marek couldn't hear what else he said.

"Pardon, my lord?"

The minister turned back and held out his arms so his valet could put a waistcoat on him. "The *engines*, Mr. Brendan. Our commission of four steam engines for the textile factories in Cormanda, for which we paid handsomely. They were routed to Helenamar."

Marek blinked. Engines for Weslorian textiles had been routed to the Alucian port city of Helenamar? Why?

"It wasn't *my* doing," Dromio said defensively, as if Marek had accused him. "It is the king's doing. He's convinced that the Aphidina is a bed of corruption and thinks it is better that the engines are transported by train from Helenamar."

Dromio was speaking of the Weslorian port town Aphidina, one of the major inroads into Wesloria. To reroute the shipment to Helenamar added so much uncertainty. There were border raiders, gangs of thugs who looked for transports between the two nations to rob. And since when did anyone believe that Aphidina was a den of thieves? Goods arrived through there every day.

He was suddenly reminded of another puzzling event. Wesloria was known for its superior grain. The climate in the north and vast amounts of arable land had produced the finest wheat and barley for centuries. Alucia was more mountainous and produced more coal than Wesloria, but had tried to produce grain at levels enough to trade.

Last autumn, a shipment of Weslorian grain, bound for Finland, had been held up at port. Marek couldn't find anyone who knew why, and while he tried to sort it out, the grain sat in storage and eventually began to rot. In the meantime, Finland took a shipment of grain from Alucia. How had Weslorian officials managed to make a hash of the one commodity they were adept at producing and selling?

Dromio said it had all been a misunderstanding. "A bad deal, I suspect."

Marek had frowned. "But…we have a solid agreement with the suppliers, my lord. We gave Finland a very good price."

"Je, it was a misunderstanding about the price," Dromio had added, as if that was an afterthought.

"Who's mis—"

"How should I know, Brendan? I can only report what has been said to me. I have much to do," he'd said, waving a hand at Marek and dismissing him.

It was one shipment, and sometimes these things happened. But it had bothered Marek nonetheless. It made no sense that the grain had not shipped as planned. It made even less sense that Finland had gone to Alucia for grain instead. Would they not have inquired after their expected trade? Asked for a remedy? Someone had intervened and sold Alucian grain to them.

It was much later that Marek had read a report from a neighboring state that Weslorian trade officials had set an export tariff on the grain. "Impossible," he'd muttered. There hadn't *been* a tariff. There had never been a tariff—who had introduced a tariff? Who would handcuff the landowners who produced the most reliable staple of Wesloria? Who would flood the Weslorian markets with grain they didn't need?

Once again, Dromio had no answer for Marek. "The king and his prime minister must have done it. You know that Lord Rubane tells him whatever he wants to hear."

But Marek knew the king hadn't done it—everything he'd said indicated he was desperate to expand trade deeper into Scandinavia.

Moreover, the economy of Wesloria was teetering on the brink of collapse. There wasn't enough work and people were struggling to make ends meet. Many laid responsibility for the poor state of the Weslorian economy at the king's feet. It didn't matter that his parliament had a hand in it—the king was an easier target, a lone man on top of a hill. They said that his plans to industrialize ignored the industries and occupations that had sustained Wesloria for centuries in favor of occupations that were foreign to them. They were not, the critics said, a textile nation, or a country of ironworks. They were shepherds and farmers and fishermen and glassmakers. They argued that the king was trying to turn them into Alucia, and powerful men were losing money on the delays of steam engines and the loss of grain shipments.

It was no help to the king to have a dullard as the minister of trade.

The tutor of Marek's youth, Mr. Ropas, was a wise man. He'd taught Marek that man didn't easily accept change, and like a new plant must push the mud and detritus aside to show its head, so, too, must change. Wesloria was the plant needing to grow, but there was so much old mud to push through.

"As for the ball, Mr. Brendan," Dromio said, gesturing loosely to the invitation, "stay close to me. I'll not have Montcrief insinuating that I don't know my nation's theories of commerce."

"*Je*, my lord," Marek said and glanced down at the invitation.

"That will be all."

But Marek wasn't ready to be dismissed and didn't move. Dromio looked at him curiously. "What?"

"If I may, my lord...how is the king?"

Dromio blinked, clearly surprised by the question, and gave Ratonkin an anxious look. "Why do you ask such an odd question, Brendan?"

Marek didn't think it odd. Seemed straightforward to him. "He's looked pale these last few days."

"Well, he's a pale man. When he stands next to his wife, he looks like a ghost."

Queen Agnes's skin was bronze in color.

"I mean that he looks paler than usual," Marek said.

Dromio's eyebrows dipped into a dark frown. He studied Marek. Marek remained still and impassive.

"He is perfectly fine, Mr. Brendan." And with that, he gave Marek a flick of his wrist to indicate he was dismissed, and then told Ratonkin he wanted a different neckcloth.

Marek walked out of his room, clutching the invitation to a costume ball, of all things, and wondering if Dromio knew the reason the king appeared so pale.

CHAPTER SEVEN

One thousand souls attended the queen's costume ball at Buckingham Palace, held in honor of the visiting dignitaries from the kingdoms of Alucia and Wesloria. Many of the costumes were carefully planned and created, while others seemed to have been pulled out of attic trunks and dusted off. Those in attendance called upon the near distant past and arrived in Georgian clothing. Others ventured deeper into their imaginations and appeared as important historical figures, including King Henry VIII with three of his eight wives, woodland faeries, and the goblins of youthful fairy tales. One enterprising guest chose to appear as a soothsayer and spent much of the evening divining fortunes for many people who sought her out.

Queen Victoria and Prince Albert were the most resplendent of all, choosing to appear as the effigies that grace the tomb of King Edward III and his wife, Queen Philippa. They arrived with an entourage of celestial page boys who attended them all night.

A twelve-piece orchestra provided the music for dancing, and a great feast was laid out, including marzipan cakes created to look like a map of the adjoining kingdoms of Alucia and Wesloria.

—Honeycutt's Gazette of Fashion and Domesticity for Ladies

BUCKINGHAM PALACE HAD been transformed for the costume ball. It was dressed in rich red velvet draperies. The chandeliers overhead were blazing with more beeswax candles than Hollis had ever seen in one place. Six-foot-tall floor-stand candelabras lined the room.

Above the queen's dais was a marble arch, topped with trumpeting angels. Behind those angels, an orchestra played for the dancers below. At least two dozen footmen were in attendance, all of them dressed in old-fashioned livery that had apparently come just out of storage, judging by the smell of mothballs emanating from them.

Hollis could never have imagined so many people in fanciful costumes. Ladies in the silk pastels and high waists and towering wigs of the Georgian period were numerous, as were a surprising number of ladies dressed as men in trousers and long tails and top hats. Gentlemen tended to be dressed in military uniforms, because, as she was certain women from all walks of life understood, the imaginations of most gentlemen did not venture into costumery. But there were exceptions—a few hearty gentlemen had dressed as women, and in the case of one enterprising sir, a wolf in sheep's clothing.

All around her, pirates and generals, princesses and courtiers, fortune-tellers and magicians and buccaneers and priests and angels danced.

Hollis was dressed in the garb of a medieval queen, a gown made for her, of course, by Caroline. It was pale blue and had long flowing sleeves that ended below her fingertips, a train as light as a feather, and a braided brocade belt that rode low on her hips. The crowning piece, which Caroline insisted be worn, was a tall conical hat. A tail of silk cascaded from its tip. It looked just like the hats in the old paintings Hollis had seen at the museum in Montagu

House. But it was not a good fit and kept sliding around her head, sometimes shifting so far back as to look more like a weapon jutting out the back of her head.

The gown was beautiful, of course, made of silk brocade and a dangerously low décolletage. Caroline was truly talented. Hollis envied her for finding this talent as she neared her thirtieth year. Hollis would love to find a talent to occupy her that did not include the gazette.

Hollis thought the gown was too revealing, but on the other hand, the simple design was quite comfortable to wear. It was lovely all but for that blasted cap! Hollis kept knocking into things with it, mostly gentlemen who were taller than she was. She managed to spear her brother-in-law with it twice.

"You'll hurt someone with that thing," Eliza complained. A flower from her floral crown had come undone and drooped over one eye. Her Grecian gown was exquisite, too, and her prince—who had dressed like a prince, thereby proving Hollis's suspicions about men and costumes—was as handsome as he ever was.

Caroline had made a spectacular Georgian court dress for her costume, including some very impressive paniers. She said she'd worked on it for a year.

"A *year*?" Eliza returned. "But we've only known about this ball for three months."

"What is your point, dearest?" Caroline asked breezily. "I didn't make it for this ball in particular. I made it because one never knows when a costume may be necessary."

"*I* know," Hollis said. "It is rarely, if ever necessary."

"Who is that?" Eliza asked, nodding at someone.

Hollis turned to look, and when she did, she whacked the duke in the shoulder again.

"I beg your pardon!" Hollis said, and helplessly put a

hand to her head. "I keep forgetting how tall it is. I should remove it—"

"Don't you dare," Caroline warned her. "It's perfect. Stop bobbing around so much."

"I'm not bobbing!"

"Where is Beck?" Eliza asked. "I would like to see *his* costume."

"He wouldn't come," Hollis said. "He said he refused to play the dress-up games of a child and said I looked less like a medieval queen and more like the Virgin Mary after she'd given birth to Jesus."

Eliza gasped. The duke laughed. "Ladies, if you will allow, I should like to dance with my wife."

A grin bloomed on Eliza's face. She returned his look with an adoring one of her own, and Hollis groaned. "Yes, please, we allow, we allow," she said, gesturing to the two of them to go on and dance.

"I should like to dance too, Leopold," Caroline said, turning one way, and then the other. "How else will all these people see my costume?"

"How could they possibly miss it, love? You take the space of three people. Hollis?"

"Of course! Go on, then. I am perfectly accustomed to wandering about on my own." In the last two years, whenever she was with Eliza and Caroline, she noticed how Alucians studied anyone who came near their duchess and countess. One could almost see the calculations being made—was she, Mrs. Honeycutt, English sister to the Alucian duchess, worth sidling up to? The answer was almost always no.

She righted her hat and looked around her, then made her way through a crowd that was still swelling, forgetting the monstrosity on her head and inadvertently assaulting a pirate by knocking his buccaneer hat from his head. He glared at her as she offered her apology and slipped by.

She happened on a small crowd gathered around the Weslorian king and queen. The couple had chosen to dress as a shepherd and shepherdess, which Hollis thought an odd choice—King Maksim was slight, and the shepherd's garb made him look emaciated. But Queen Agnes looked healthy and divine in her shepherdess costume, her long, thick black hair braided down her back, and a straw hat on her head.

Hollis pressed against the wall to move around the entourage, just squeaking by. Her cap was now sliding off to the right. She reached up to straighten it, and when she did, her gaze landed on a single gentleman who was not in costume, but formal clothing. A gentleman who was familiar to her. *Mr. Brendan, how do you do.*

He was standing quite alone again, his expression slightly pained. He reminded her of some country landowner on a windswept moor, staring off at the sea and contemplating his life.

Someone walked in front of her, and Hollis rose up on her toes, lest she lose sight of him. The person in front of her moved, and so did Hollis, falling backward to keep from colliding with him.

"Pardon, madam, have a care!"

She whipped around. A gentleman dressed like a priest was holding his eye. "I beg your pardon," she said as the silk tail from her conical hat settled down the front of her gown. She righted her bloody bothersome cap, then held out her arms and slowly turned a circle to make sure no one was within striking distance. By the time she'd come full circle, the king's group and Mr. Brendan had disappeared into the crowd.

For heaven's sake, he was just there! It was the tea all

over again—one minute he was there, the next minute he was gone. She guessed that all she had to do was find King Maksim and he'd be there, watching him. Why did he watch the king like a hawk? If she hadn't read and heard the things she had, she'd probably think nothing of it. But she had, and his behavior was odd.

She moved on and pushed through the throng, looking for a shepherd. And when she spotted the king, she spotted Mr. Brendan again, just as she'd suspected.

She darted around a man dressed as King Henry VIII. He had three women in period garb who, Hollis presumed, were some of his eight wives. They were standing too closely together to allow her to pass, so she squeezed between them and a woman dressed as Godiva, and nearly collided with a sideboard.

She quickened her step, holding one hand to her head to keep her cap from falling, and hurried to catch up to Mr. Brendan before she lost him. She didn't know what she meant to do when she caught him. Accuse him of the dastardly crime of staring at the king?

Fortunately, the king paused with his family, and so did Mr. Brendan. He stood at a distance, almost immobile. His neckcloth was Weslorian green, which Hollis took to be a silent declaration that he most certainly was *not* in costume. If he was plotting against King Maksim, why would he arrive at a costume ball in plain clothes? It had the effect of making him stand out in this festive crowd.

Hollis pushed forward. Souls swirled by in dizzying colors and in time to a waltz. It was almost as if he didn't see the dancers or hear the music, or any of the cacophony of sounds, while she could scarcely stand how loud the room was. He looked out of place, like an observer to this ball instead of a participant.

Hollis managed to slip between a lady and gentleman engaged in a tiff and could have reached out to touch him. She squeezed past the couple and landed as close to Mr. Brendan as she could.

He didn't turn. He didn't seem to sense her at all, so intent was he on King Maksim. How strange. She was so close she could see his coat was made of fine, soft wool. He was clean-shaven, but there was a tiny nick on his square jawline. His hair was brushed to a sheen and tucked behind his ears again, and she guessed that the gentleman did not have a valet to help him dress. Which meant he was not a lord.

He was clinging to a full glass of wine as if he feared he might drop it. She wondered if he'd even tasted it.

"Good evening!" she said.

He didn't turn his head or otherwise pay her the slightest heed at all. He kept his gaze on the king.

What was the matter with him? Surely he'd heard her. Was he ignoring her?

Hollis shifted closer to gain his attention, and her arm inadvertently bumped his. His head jerked toward her, and a bit of wine sloshed from his glass onto his shoes. He really hadn't heard her, then. No wonder he looked at her with the expression of someone who thought they'd been accosted by a stranger.

"It appears we meet again, Mr. Brendan."

"Oh," he said, as if confirming his worst suspicions to himself. "It's you."

Well, *that* seemed rather disagreeable. Hollis curtsied nonetheless, one hand on her hat. Let him see how polite society showed itself in England.

But while she was curtsying, he was shaking his fingers free of wine, and he gave her only a cursory bow of his head in return. He gestured to a footman, and put the glass of wine on the man's tray.

"Is the wine not to your liking?"

He looked at her, those unusual amber eyes piercing hers. "I beg your pardon?"

"The *wine*, sir. It seems you don't care for it." Or anything else, for that matter, she thought, and fluttered her fingers in the direction of the footman.

His gaze flicked over her, taking in the conical hat, the rope that rode on her hips, the long sleeves. "I'm not a connoisseur..." he said, his accent thick. "I thought it tasted a bit like dirt."

Hollis gasped with astonishment. She was *amazed* by this pronouncement. That anyone could stand in Buckingham Palace and have the gall to criticize the queen's fine wine was beyond the pale. That this man, this *foreigner*, could say such a wretched thing was remarkable in the annals of boorish behavior. *"Dirt?"* she very nearly shouted, her voice full of the indignation she felt on behalf of her queen.

He colored slightly; his gaze settled on something over her shoulder. "I didn't mean it as a criticism. I beg your pardon, I meant to convey that I have no taste for dark wine." He kept his gaze stubbornly over her shoulder, and when Hollis turned to see what had his attention, the tip of her hat knocked against his face. He grunted with surprise.

"Oh, dear... I beg your pardon, Mr. Brendan. This hat is bothersome. I don't... Did you hear me earlier?"

"What?" He rubbed the corner of his eye, and when he did, she noticed a bead of perspiration trickling down his temple. Granted, it was dreadfully hot in the ballroom with the candles blazing all around and the heat of so many bodies, in spite of the occasional bit of cool air that passed over them through open windows. But Hollis had the distinct impression that the tiny trickle of perspiration had more to do with her than the heat. Call it a woman's intuition, but this gentleman didn't care for her. That was entirely plausible, too—Hollis would admit he would not be the first gentleman who didn't care for a bored widow. Had he been any other man, at any other place, she might have been slightly wounded by this realization. But because she found him rather interesting, she was determined not to be upset. "It doesn't appear any harm was done," she said gaily, gesturing to his face.

"No."

"Why do you stand here all alone, Mr. Brendan?"

He seemed surprised by the question. "Pardon?"

Should she tell him it was suspicious? That a foreigner, with no obvious acquaintances, would welcome someone to talk to?

The orchestra suddenly struck up a reel; Hollis was jostled by a troubadour and a barmaid as they scurried toward the dance floor. She glanced back at Mr. Brendan—he had pressed two fingers to his temple, as though staving off a headache. He was quite possible the only person in London who could be made miserable at a royal ball. He'd greeted her like a leper, had made a disparaging remark about the queen's wine, and looked as if the entire affair was akin to being dragged through a crowded street by one leg.

A man dressed in a sailor's uniform suddenly appeared and clamped a hand on Mr. Brendan's shoulder. He leaned in close, swaying a little, and spoke in Weslorian. She didn't speak the language, obviously, but his words sounded slurred.

The sailor gestured at Hollis. Mr. Brendan's gaze flicked

over her again, lingering perhaps a moment too long on her décolletage. *"Je, mans isand,"* he said.

Whatever that meant. But the sailor seemed satisfied. He slapped Mr. Brendan on the back and carried on, bouncing off the backs of people as he went, too inebriated to walk a straight line.

"Well, sir, I should think that now your friend has remarked us, an acquaintance is certainly in order. Shall we start again? I am Mrs. Honeycutt and it is a pleasure to make your acquaintance."

He held her gaze as he reached up and brushed the shoulder the sailor had clamped, as if erasing the whole meeting. "I know very well who you are, Mrs. Honeycutt. I beg your pardon—it's quite loud in here and I haven't heard every word. How do you do?" he asked in his accented English. And then he gave her a hint of a smile that had the effect of making his eyes appear even more golden.

Progress! She smiled. "Very well, Mr. Brendan." She let out a breath she hadn't even realized she was holding in a whoosh. "I feel as if I've just climbed the highest mountain in my daintiest slippers," she added with a gay laugh. "Are you enjoying the ball, sir? Do you have costume balls in Wesloria?"

His eyebrows dipped and he leaned forward, his gaze on her mouth. "Pardon?"

"How do you find the ball?"

"Ah." He leaned back. "Agreeable."

Agreeable. She was beginning to see the problem here. In addition to having poor social skills, Mr. Brendan was woefully inadequate in making polite social conversation, which was exacerbated by the fact he couldn't hear well. What on earth did this poor man do for camaraderie and diversion in Wesloria? She pictured him in a field, dressed like the shepherds of biblical times, with nothing but a lot of bleating sheep to converse with him.

He squinted past her again.

Hollis followed his gaze and spotted the king.

It was so very peculiar. Hollis's interest in this man notched upward. He'd shown her kindness at the gates of St. James Palace. And he really was quite handsome. Not in a classical sense, certainly, but in a virile sense, and Hollis was utterly attracted to all that manliness. And she was dying to know why he kept such a close eye on King Maksim. She could forgive the inadequacies in his social manners in light of it.

She decided to try another tack and touched his arm to gain his attention. His arm felt like stone beneath her touch, not an ounce of give. "Did you see Queen Victoria and Prince Albert? They made quite the entrance, no? The young heralds dressed as angels were particularly effective. And the trumpets!" She teasingly covered both ears and glanced heavenward. The trumpets had been *very* loud.

Mr. Brendan looked as if he was trying to recall it. "Did you not hear the fanfare, Mr. Brendan?"

"I…no. It's quite loud in here."

"Yes, but the *trumpets*," she reiterated, because she couldn't imagine he hadn't heard *that*. "Really, Mr. Brendan, this is a royal ball! The queen's entrance was the most anticipated event of the evening."

"Was it?" He looked uncomfortable. "I didn't realize. I beg your pardon, Mrs. Honeycutt. I am not accustomed to being at events such as this."

"Interesting," she said. "Did you sneak in?"

"What? No!" he said, clearly appalled.

"I was teasing you."

He eyed her dubiously. "I don't think you were."

"You're right," she agreed, because she was a very honest person. "I truly wondered."

Mr. Brendan looked completely flummoxed. "I am here by invitation, Mrs. Honeycutt."

"Yes, of course you are." She smiled sweetly. "You seem so pleased to have accepted the invitation to this ball."

There it was again, that hint of a smile. "I am not pleased about it at all," he said. "But there are times when one's pleasure must be ignored."

Oh. She found the remark to be ridiculously titillating. Perhaps because she was imagining the different circumstances in which pleasure might need to be ignored. "I don't suppose you're the first to find yourself in extraordinary surroundings and not know what to do with yourself."

"What? That's not—"

"It hasn't been so long ago that I found myself in a similar situation," she blurted. "Do you know, I think I can help you, Mr. Brendan."

He looked entirely baffled. "Help me *what*?"

"The trick, as it were, is not to allow yourself to feel inferior. You must move about as if you are the king yourself. Oh, I know! We should dance!"

"No." He had the audacity to look appalled.

She sighed and pressed her fingertips to her brow a moment. "Mr. Brendan. You seem quite easily alarmed, and furthermore, I am well aware that some gentlemen like to be the driver in these things, and my very good friend tells me I am too forward by half. I truly don't mean to be, but candidly—and you will find me to be always candid—I really don't think much about the rules anymore. I'm a widow, and it hardly seems to matter who asks who to stand up, does it? Why should gentlemen have all the privileges of invitation? But never mind that," she said, noting that he seemed a bit stunned. "My intent was only to help you feel more comfortable here."

"That is not… I don't understand your—"

"My point is that if one attends a ball, even if one is not in costume," she said, her gaze flicking over his clothing, "one should expect to dance!" She suddenly leaned forward, catching her hat before it jabbed him in the eye. "If you are worried about the figures, Mr. Brendan, you are in luck. I happen to be a very good dancer and will help you along."

He stared at her as if she'd just slapped him across the cheek. "Madam… I know the figures," he said. "The figures are not the cause of my hesitation."

His eyes were so unusual in color that it was a little difficult not to be diverted by them in the middle of this conversation. "Then what is your objection, sir?"

He stared back at her.

Hollis gasped. And then she laughed with surprise. "*Me?* Your objection is to me? I am all astonishment! And here I thought we were well on our way to being friends. I will have you know that there are any number of gentlemen who would very much like to dance with me."

He glanced around them as if he expected hordes of them to present themselves.

"Perhaps not at this precise moment, but nonetheless," she insisted. "Never in my wildest dreams would I have imagined that *I* would be thought of as an objectionable dance partner." She laughed at the absurdity of it—she could dance circles around these people. "Oh, dear, I can't wait to tell Donovan."

"Did you say *friends*?"

This man was impossible. She abruptly curtsied and held out her hand. "Thank you, Mr. Brendan. I accept your offer to dance."

"I..." He looked at her hand. Hollis fluttered her fingers at him, impatient to get on with it.

"Very well," he said grudgingly, and in a moment of decisiveness, he took her hand in his large one and pulled her with enough strength that if she'd been a slender thing like Caroline, he might have launched her across the room.

Hollis grinned with delight. "It's a quadrille. The French invented it. Do you know the dance, Mr. Brendan? Do you know any Frenchmen?"

He pressed his fine mouth very firmly shut and led her onto the dance floor.

"I don't know any Frenchmen, but I've heard it said that they very much like their social gatherings and dancing."

He refused to comment on the French, but put her directly in front of him, facing him. Hollis debated telling him that she had never in her life met a more uncooperative gentleman. Well...he was not as uncooperative as Mr. Kettle or Mr. Shoreham, but they were *hardly* considered part of her social sphere. The *point being*, Mr. Brendan was as stiff as a board. But he kept looking at her mouth, and it had a surprisingly stirring effect on her.

She curtsied very low, and in doing so, knocked his chest with the tip of her cap. "Pardon," she said crisply. Why was she so reluctant to leave the man be? Should she not be seeking out Caroline and Eliza to tell them about this man, and the three of them could then laugh at the absurdity of it all? Part of her liked a good challenge, and he was certainly that. But it was more than that. In spite of his eccentricity, she was convinced that this man knew something about the Weslorian king, and she was determined to find out what it was.

She would just have to do it with something other than

feminine wiles, apparently, which, unfortunately, gave her very little to work with.

Another couple joined them and they had the required square for the quadrille. Hollis smiled as warmly as she could at her partner, and she thought she might have seen something flicker in those impenetrable eyes, but who could be certain? She leaned forward to say something, to put him at ease, but the music began and the first couple stepped forward. In the next moment, she and Mr. Brendan linked arms and went around in a circle, then joined together to step forward and meet the couple across from them. Mr. Brendan did indeed know the figures, but he moved as if his arms and legs were made of wood, and he scowled the whole time.

Hollis kept her steps light, and she made a point to laugh and smile as he handed her off to each partner, and in those moments they met again, she would speak, their gazes would lock, and she would say "Such a lively tune for a quadrille, don't you think?" Or "You're an excellent dancer, Mr. Brendan! What is your favorite dance? Mine is the waltz."

For his part, he said, "Yes," "Thank you," and nothing. But he kept his gaze locked on her, and when she spoke, his eyes slipped to her mouth, and by the time the dance ended, Hollis felt warmth curling around the core of her.

Mr. Brendan bowed, held out his arm for hers, and escorted her off the dance floor. When they reached the edge of it, he dropped his arm.

Hollis smiled. "Thank you, Mr. Brendan! May I say the experience was quite..." She sought an appropriate word—*daunting, tedious, excruciating...* So many to choose from.

"Thank you," he said, and bowed. "But now, I must ask you to excuse me." And he walked away.

Hollis's mouth fell open with shock. She watched him disappear into the crowd, and when she couldn't see him any longer, she folded her arms and closed her mouth. Of all the boorish, ill-bred, oafish men she'd ever had the displeasure of meeting!

She stood fuming for a moment or two, maybe three, until she felt someone's eyes on her. She turned abruptly, knocking her hat to one side, and righted it just as her gaze landed on Lady Katherine Maugham.

The peacock.

She was not dressed as a peacock, but that is what Eliza, Caroline, and Hollis had taken to calling her years ago, owing to the way she strutted around the same social circles as they. She'd been their nemesis for years, pursuing the same eligible gentlemen and social standing. The competition had been fierce. And now, Lady Katherine smiled so smugly that Hollis knew she'd seen every bit of what had just happened.

Well, that did it. Mr. Brendan was a guest in this country, and he did not have leave to treat her as if she was as bothersome as Katherine Maugham. Good God, she wasn't *that* bothersome, was she? Well, then. She had something to prove—if not to him, then to herself.

She whirled away from the peacock's prying eyes so quickly that her cone cap came off her head and tumbled to the ground. A gentleman stepped on it before she could stop him. He apologized profusely, but it was too late. Her medieval hat was ruined and, probably, so was her hair. Where was Caroline when she needed her? Where was Eliza for that matter? Where *was* everyone in her life now? Was she to suffer this indignity all by herself?

CHAPTER EIGHT

A peacock in Regency dress was spotted at the queen's costume ball dancing with a recently widowed gentleman. It has been whispered that he is on the prowl for a new wife who might attend to his brood of five, for which, it is said, he has no use.

There were several witnesses to the moment an Alucian minister shunned his Weslorian counterpart. The two gentlemen very nearly came to blows, and had it not been for the quick thinking of a Prime British person a crisis might have developed. Those close to negotiations say there is trouble brewing between the two countries, as there are many who stand to profit from war rather than peace.

Ladies, if an invitation to a costume ball should arrive at one's door, and one takes the charge to don a costume, remember that the heat of candles will melt paint on one's face and it will drip on one's clothing, putting it to ruin, as poor Lady Humbolt will attest.

↪—Honeycutt's Gazette of Fashion and Domesticity for Ladies

MUCH TO MAREK'S SURPRISE, the dance was not as bad as he'd feared. He truly hadn't meant to be so crusty with Mrs. Honeycutt, but his temples were throbbing, the effect of so much noise being forced into one ear. The music had only added to the strange mix, and when she spoke, her voice was lyrical and soft, and he had to strain to hear her, and there was the slight panic in him about stepping onto a dance floor after all these years and…well.

He hadn't been at his best. There was something about Mrs. Honeycutt that set him back on his heels. Her forthright manner, perhaps? He actually appreciated that about her. Her insistence on leading the way? He didn't mind it.

No, it was the feeling that she was watching him a bit too closely.

Well, he'd escaped her. He'd had to—had to leave that room before his good ear burst. He'd come to a halt near a pair of footmen who were manning the main doors. He put his back to the wall and breathed. The noise wasn't as dense here, wasn't as hard on his hearing.

He had enjoyed the dance, but he was not an efficient dancer. His lessons had come long ago, during some cold, dark nights at home on the shores of the Tophian Sea. The last time he'd attended a dance had been in the country near his farm. He'd danced a jig then, as he recalled. But a quadrille? He'd found it remarkable that he could remember the steps at all, much less remember what kind of quadrille it was—a variation that was Italian in its origins. It was amazing that after a few awkward steps, his feet had seemed to remember the rest all on their own. Even more remarkable given that every time he came round to Mrs. Honeycutt, her smile made him feel a little fluttery, and her lips, which he watched intently to know what she said, made his mouth water.

He still couldn't shake the notion that someone had put her up to befriending him. But why her? Who would use her in that way? The Alucians? Did they suspect something to do with King Maksim?

Speaking of the king... Marek couldn't afford to lose sight of him. With a sigh, he pushed away from the wall and began his trek around the ballroom again.

He'd gone halfway around when he spotted the king in his shepherd dress, dancing with the crown princess. She wore the costume of a French courtier and moved very gracefully. The king, however, danced as woodenly as Marek. His expression was pinched, too, as if he didn't feel well.

Marek shifted his gaze from the king to the edge of the dance floor. There he was, the young man with the dark hair, never more than a few feet away from the king. Like Marek, he wasn't wearing a costume, but a formal suit of clothing. He was holding a pair of wineglasses in one gloved hand, and from this distance, it looked as if both of them were nearly empty. Marek assumed they belonged to the king and Princess Justine. Who had access to their drinks besides that young man? Had they come from the trays of one of the many footmen? Had someone else poured the wine?

Marek glanced around the crowded room in search of Dromio. He hadn't seen the minister since he'd stopped to tell Marek that he looked peculiar, standing there as he was. "What's the matter with you?" Dromio had slurred into his good ear in Weslorian. "You look like a vile old man, ogling women as you are." He'd clapped his shoulder hard. "Have a care you don't look the menace, Brendan. Look at her. She looks alarmed by you."

He was referring, of course, to Mrs. Honeycutt. She hadn't looked anything but lovely and curious. And, really, if there was a menace between them, it was certainly her. She was very inquisitive. "Where is the man with the drink?" Dromio had asked, his concern over Marek's appearance apparently forgotten, and he'd stumbled away, his sailor trousers sagging in the rear to the point of distraction.

The dance ended, and the king escorted his daughter

from the dance floor. The young man handed them the glasses of wine, but the princess shook her head. She leaned in close to her father's ear, and then walked away.

The king stood alone with the young man. He glanced down at the glass of wine he held, almost as if he couldn't stomach—

"Mr. Brendan!"

Incredible. Marek turned around. It was inconceivable that Mrs. Honeycutt had sought him out again. This time, her conical hat was gone, and in its place, a flower was stuck into her very dark hair.

She was not alone. She was in the company of a woman he knew to be the wife of Prince Leopold of Alucia. That one was dressed in an elaborate eighteenth-century costume, complete with a towering wig in which three cloth bluebirds were perched.

"May I introduce you to Lady Chartier?" Mrs. Honeycutt asked. "Or, if you prefer, Marie Antoinette." The two women giggled. To Lady Chartier, she said, "This is my friend, Mr. Brendan."

There was that *friend* business again. Was it supposed to mean something? Was it some curious English custom to call a complete stranger one's friend?

She gestured quite unnecessarily to his neckcloth. "He's from Wesloria!"

"How delightful!" Lady Chartier said and curtsied grandly. "How do you do, Mr. Brendan? Welcome to London."

"Thank you." He clasped his hands behind his back and bowed. From the corner of his eye, he tried to keep track of the king. But Lady Chartier turned her head to say something to Mrs. Honeycutt. And to him, apparently, as both of them looked at him expectantly. When he didn't answer, Mrs. Honeycutt turned her head to her friend and said something more that Marek couldn't make out.

"I beg your pardon?" he said.

Mrs. Honeycutt and Lady Chartier exchanged a look. Mrs. Honeycutt spoke again, and this time, Marek watched her lips stretch and curve around the English words.

"She asked how you found the ball."

There seemed to be an awful lot of concern about how he found the damn ball. When he didn't respond right away, seeking the right words to convey how much he didn't care without appearing rude, Lady Chartier cocked her head to one side at such a sharp angle he worried her towering wig might fall off. "Oh, dear," she said plainly. "He really doesn't care for it, does he?"

"I don't think he does," Mrs. Honeycutt said as she studied him. "I'm not certain he cares much for our customs, really."

He looked between the two women. Was he supposed to deny it? Debate them? Rush to assure them that he'd never in all his life had a grander time?

Lady Chartier shrugged. "I suppose the ball is not for everyone, is it? I, for one, very much like a costume ball. And I adore the dancing. But then again, I'm quite good at it."

"You're a very fine dancer," Mrs. Honeycutt agreed.

"One of the best, I've heard it said," Lady Chartier said without the least bit of humility, obviously pleased with the compliment. "Which puts me in the mood to dance! If you will excuse me, I think I shall find my husband and insist he waltz with me again." She smiled prettily. "A pleasure to make your acquaintance, Mr. Brendan." She glanced at Mrs. Honeycutt, and a look passed between the two of them, some mutual understanding that Marek did not care for. He felt as if he had been whisked back to his thirteenth year. On a crisp, cool Sunday afternoon, he'd stood in the church-yard while Sarana and Felicia, two girls from his village, had whispered about him. He'd been just as inept at social chitchat then as he was now, and just as partially deaf. He guessed it was true that some things never changed.

Lady Chartier smiled and walked away, and in what was becoming rapidly predictable to him, Mrs. Honeycutt did not. Her smile was winsome and she asked, "Shall I leave you to sulk on your own, Mr. Brendan?"

"Sulk?" He didn't know that word.

Mrs. Honeycutt's smile deepened. "It means ill-tempered."

"I am not ill-tempered, Mrs. Honeycutt. Unfortunately, the ability to chatter idly is not in my nature."

One of her eyebrows arched above the other. "What makes you think my chatter is idle? I don't know you well enough to decide if you're truly morose, although I knew a gentleman like you once. Never saw even a corner of his mouth lift in a smile. When he died, it was discovered that there was an exceptionally large tumor in his stomach. Do you suppose you have a tumor in your stomach, Mr. Brendan?" A saucy little smile curved the corners of her mouth.

The last time a woman had smiled like that at him, he'd kissed her. The idea rumbled around in some remote reach of his brain. Marek didn't understand her, and in these circumstances, he didn't want to understand her, her comeliness notwithstanding. He didn't care how her eyes sparkled enticingly in the light of a thousand candles. She was becoming a nuisance and he had other much more important matters weighing on him. Which led him to the question once more—why was she bothering him? "Mrs. Honeycutt, if I may... Who *are* you?"

She laughed. "I've told you!"

"*Je*, but for the life of me I don't understand your—" he tried to think of the word in English, and gestured impatiently "—bother."

"My *bother*! How delightfully charming."

He'd insulted her again, which had not been his intent. His English was quite good, except when he was flustered. "Why are you following me?" he asked. Better to get to the heart of the matter than continue to misspeak.

She blinked as if the question caught her by surprise. She averted her gaze, and for a moment, he thought she would flee.

But, of course, she didn't flee. She tapped a finger against her lips, considering his question, and was he imagining it, or did she look a bit guilty?

"You *are* following me." Something in his chest tightened with the realization. Was she the only one? Were there others?

Her smile faded. She sighed. And then she nodded. "I am."

Marek was stunned. He'd expected her to deny it, to offer some excuse. When she didn't, it set him back even more. "You are *following* me?" he asked with disbelief.

"Yes!" She sounded remorseful. "I am, I *am*, Mr. Brendan, but I didn't mean for you to realize it."

He looked around them, half expecting guards or soldiers or someone to leap out and take him. But when none did, he frowned. "But why?"

She toyed with her earring. Bit her bottom lip. Sighed heavenward again. "This is very difficult to explain. The truth is that I have a gnawing suspicion about you."

His heart leaped. If she suspected him, who else did? "What sort of suspicion?"

Mrs. Honeycutt glanced down at her feet. "That you are—*may* be—plotting a…"

He didn't hear her clearly. "A clue?" he repeated uncertainly.

She looked up. "Not a clue, a *coup*. A coup d'état."

He stared at her. "Why in heaven would you suspect such a thing? What have you heard?"

She looked as if she meant to say one thing, but then her eyebrows rose. "What have *you* heard?"

He wasn't going to play games with her. He suddenly shifted forward, so much that she leaned back a little. "Tell me the truth, please, Mrs. Honeycutt. What do you know?"

She slowly straightened. "That's what I would like to ask you, Mr. Brendan. What do *you* know? Why are you keeping such a close eye on King Maksim? Why do you shadow him at every event?"

She had indeed been watching him. "He is my king," he said carefully.

"And Victoria is my queen, but I don't follow her every move. I don't seek her out and stare at her as if she's an unrequited love. You've been keeping a very close eye on your king, closer than anyone else." She lifted her chin. "For your information, I am conducting an investigation."

An investigation! Did the word mean what he thought it meant? How was it that this woman of privilege was in a position to conduct anything? Did she think this was some sort of parlor game? "You are speaking nonsense."

"Really?" She reached for the reticule dangling from her wrist. She pulled open the strings, then withdrew a calling card and handed it to him.

Marek eyed her warily before taking it. He glanced down at the card.

Mrs. Hollis Honeycutt, Publisher
*Honeycutt's Gazette of Fashion and
Domesticity for Ladies*

He might as well be reading Urdu, because he had no idea what that meant in reality. He slowly lifted his gaze from the card.

"It is unexpected, I know," she said. "One would not expect the publisher of a ladies' gazette to concern herself with political intrigue—"

"Darling! Where have you been all night?"

The Duchess of Tannymeade suddenly appeared, giving Mrs. Honeycutt a start. The duchess glanced at Marek, then at Mrs. Honeycutt. "We've been looking all around for you! You promised to stay close."

"Did I?" she asked, her gaze still on Marek.

He slipped the card into his pocket.

"I beg your pardon, sir, would you mind terribly if I steal Mrs. Honeycutt away?"

"Please," he said, probably a little more forcefully than he should have. He bowed curtly before Mrs. Honeycutt could make an introduction or try and extend this "investigation" any longer, and turned away, stepping into the crowd before she could think of a reason to keep him.

He went in search of the king once more—yes, he was keeping a close eye on the king!—*and* the young man who stayed so close to the king's side. But he was acutely aware of a calling card burning a hole in his pocket, begging to be examined and understood.

CHAPTER NINE

Dignitaries attending the queen's costume ball were seen leaving Buckingham well after sunrise. Not all danced until the morning hours. King Maksim of Wesloria, and the Duke and Duchess of Tannymeade, departed the ball at half-past midnight. Queen Agnes and the princesses danced well into the night and departed just before dawn.

Several have reported to us that the Marquess of Douglas, the heir to the Duke of Hamilton, has returned to London after an absence of more than a year, and that the very young and impressionable Princess Justine stood up with the notorious lord not once, but twice.

The Shoreditch Temperance Society has recently formed a new committee, styled the Coalition for Decency and Morality, with the express goal of ridding London of those they've deemed lacking in decency and morality. A noble endeavor, but one that perhaps should encourage the examination of one's own house before passing judgment on others.

Ladies, as colder temperatures dry our skin, brush iodine on the affected parts and cover with woolen mittens or stockings.

     ✑—Honeycutt's Gazette of Fashion and
            Domesticity for Ladies

COLD AIR SUNK DOWN and blanketed London the day after the ball and hung miserably over town for the next two days, culminating in a frigid, steady rain.

Hollis and Donovan pulled chairs and footstools to the hearth. Donovan had made them hot toddies, and they put their stocking feet before the fire and sipped on the drinks.

Hollis didn't know what she would do without Donovan. He was her manservant, her butler, and her driver, her houseman, her groom. In this large Mayfair mansion, Donovan worked alongside Ruth, a chambermaid, who functioned as a ladies' maid when the situation warranted. And Mrs. Plum, the housekeeper and cook, who went home to Mr. Plum every evening. And not to be forgotten, Old Man Brimble, an elderly gentleman whose position in her house Hollis had long ceased to question or understand. He didn't do much of anything other than feed the cats. But like Donovan, he'd been in the employ of the Honeycutt family for so long that it was inconceivable that he should go any other place in his dotage.

Donovan was also her best friend. He was the glue in her house and the glue of her spirit.

He'd been in the employ of her late husband long before Hollis had married him. And since her dear Percy's death a little more than four years ago, Donovan had become everything that her late husband had been to her.

Well…except her lover.

He would never be her lover.

Not that Hollis *wanted* him to be her lover—she didn't, she could *never*, because of Percy—but more importantly, because Donovan didn't want her to be his. In fact, in recent weeks, she'd begun to suspect he'd taken a lover. What else could explain his fine mood?

Hollis sipped the toddy he'd made. It was perfect. "I

remember my mother made my father toddies when the weather was bitterly cold. It's funny, the things I remember. I can't really recall her voice any longer, but I remember the toddies." She wondered what she would remember about Percy. He, too, was fading away. She glanced at Donovan. "Do you remember your mother?"

"I do." He smiled fondly. "She was a beauty, my mum."

"She must have been—look at you."

Donovan chuckled and shook his head.

"How long has she been gone?"

"I don't know that she is." He shrugged. "I left home and I've not seen her again." He turned his gaze to the fire and said no more.

Hollis really knew very little about Donovan's past and she'd learned early in her marriage not to ask. All she knew for certain was that Donovan and Percy had been childhood friends. The only thing Percy had ever said about Donovan was that he was the most loyal friend he'd ever had. Shortly after Percy's father had died, he'd hired Donovan, employing him first as a valet, and then as their "butler" of sorts. Donovan wasn't like any other butler Hollis had ever known. He was a man of many skills and talents and interests, and the least of all those was the proper way to set a supper table.

When Percy died, Hollis had dismissed half the staff. She didn't need so many people to care for just her, and honestly, at the time, she wasn't certain what her financial circumstances would be without Percy. "I'll go," Donovan had said to her one evening. "Say the word, madam, and I'll go. I'll do whatever you need."

Hollis had been surprised and alarmed by his offer. She couldn't imagine being without Percy *and* Donovan. She'd never contemplated dismissing him, knowing what his friendship had meant to her husband, and all that he took care of in her home. She'd refused his offer and their friendship had grown and deepened in the years since. She understood why Percy had cherished Donovan's friendship—the man would lay down his life for his friends, and he would for Hollis.

But it wasn't until two years after Percy's death that Hollis understood what Percy had meant to Donovan. Percy had been able to protect Donovan in ways he couldn't protect himself.

It was odd to feel such deep friendship and not know much about Donovan's past. She looked at him now, his head tilted back against the chair, his eyes closed. "When was the last time you saw your mother?"

Donovan opened his eyes. "I was fifteen years old." He sat up, scrubbed his face with one hand, then smiled at her. "Have you told me everything about the ball?"

"Did I tell you about the ballroom? You've never seen anything as grand," she said wistfully.

"I've no doubt of it."

She told him about the palace and its gilded finishes, the enormous chandeliers. She told him about the food and the many colorful costumes, of the sheer number of people who had attended.

She saved the best for last. She told him that she'd met the most curious man she'd ever encountered in her life.

"In what way?"

"He's curt."

"As curt as Mr. Shoreham?"

"Twice over."

"Remarkable. What else?"

"He's as unhelpful as Mr. Kettle."

"Impossible," Donovan said. "Tell me."

Hollis told him how she'd first encountered him at the gates of St. James. And then again at the tea, and then at the ball. She told him how she'd coerced Mr. Brendan into dancing, and how he'd raced away from her afterward, and worse, how the peacock had witnessed it all.

Donovan laughed roundly at that. "How does she manage to always be present?"

"It's astonishing, isn't it?" Hollis asked morosely. "There is something irregular about the gentleman, I fear. There can't be a good reason that he watches King Maksim so closely."

"Does he?" Donovan asked curiously. "Why do you suppose?"

"As I said to him, I think it's because he is involved some way in plotting a coup."

Donovan sputtered his sip of toddy. "You said what?"

"I said what I thought, Donovan. He accused me of following him, and I confessed that I was and I thought it only fair to tell him why."

"God save you, Hollis!" Donovan laughed. "My God, but you're incorrigible."

"I'm not! Well, perhaps a little. But I am also very honest, Donovan, you know that about me."

"I also know you're a bit mad." He turned in his seat to face her, his amusement apparent. "What made you think that he was planning a coup? Pray tell, what did the curt man say to your outrageous accusation? Did *he* say you were mad? Did he summon the guards to have you tossed out on your ear? Or did he admit that was indeed plotting a coup?"

"He asked me what I knew. And before I heard his full confession, Eliza chose that moment to pull me away."

"It's no small blessing that she did. You're dangling your

feet into some very dark waters, Hollis, and without a bit of proof other than a conversation you overheard."

"I'm only asking questions," she said defensively. "Why shouldn't I? I've nothing else to divert me."

He snorted at that. "You need diversion? You work yourself to the bone more days than not with the gazette."

"But that's just it, Donovan. The gazette is…" She groaned and looked at the hearth. It was difficult to explain, even to herself. The gazette was everything to her… or so the story went. And it was. But it was really Percy. Or rather, the gazette was all she had left of him. At least it had felt that way when she'd picked up the reins after he died. She'd felt connected to him. But lately, the gazette didn't feel anything like Percy. It had become something else entirely. "It's tiresome," she muttered.

Donovan stared at her a moment. He shifted around to face the fire. "Of course it is—you work too hard. If you published monthly—"

"It's not the frequency," she said, interrupting him. "It's *what* I'm publishing. There is more to life than the latest fashion! There are important matters in this world that women ought to think about—if not for themselves, then for the sake of their children. When Percy died I wanted to honor his name, I wanted to keep his memory alive and I thought the best way to do that was to keep the gazette going. But it doesn't resemble anything he published, and really, need *anyone* be told how to treat a chilblain?"

"Not me," Donovan said instantly. "I don't get them."

"I want to *do* something with my life. I want to have some purpose. I want…" Her voice trailed off. "I don't know what I want, not really. I only know that I have these feelings of restlessness that I can't explain. I feel as if something is missing."

"I understand," Donovan said softly. He reached across the space between them and took her hand, giving it a squeeze. "You work at a pace that exceeds that of any man I've ever known, and that would include the revered Percival Honeycutt. You're exhausting yourself, trying to do it all on you own. Why not hand the gazette over to someone who can take the burden from you? Then you'd have the time to explore those things that interest you."

Hollis clucked her tongue. "Now you sound like my father, advising me to give the gazette to someone else," she said, and slumped in her chair. "'You work too hard, Hollis. You ought to be about the business of marriage,'" she said, mimicking her father's deep voice.

"Mmm," Donovan said. "I don't know if you ought to be about marriage, but I do wish another love for you. And, frankly, I can't help but worry about this rumor you're pursuing. You've been privileged to know the best men society has to offer, love, but there are other sorts of men you're bound to run across. I know what those men are like—*all* men—and there are quite a lot of them that you shouldn't meet."

Hollis pressed her lips together. She didn't doubt that there was some truth to what he said. It wasn't as if she was unaware that the life she'd lived was a sheltered one. But how would she ever understand the world if she didn't experience it? How would she ever discover things that ought to be discovered? Like a coup. "It keeps me well occupied," she said, and glanced sidelong at him. "It keeps the nights from being so boring."

Donovan sighed. He had no solution to offer her. He stood up and went to the sideboard and poured whiskey into his glass. "By the by, I was down at the docks today."

Hollis loved Donovan too much to ask why he might have been down on the docks. "Were you?"

"I met a pair of sailors who'd only just docked on a return from the Continent. Oh, but they were chatty, those two. Nattered on at a pace. They'd been to France, they said, and Louis Napoleon has been elected president and favors imperialism. They mean to hire on to French ships because they think they'll be rich." He shook his head and came back to his seat. "One of them said something I thought you'd find interesting."

"Oh?"

"He said there were four Weslorians aboard their ship. Not just any four, mind you, but four soldiers."

Hollis didn't see the importance of it and waited for him to say more.

Donovan stacked his feet on the footstool. "That's what the bloke said. Said he recognized them because of the bit of green pinned to their lapels, aye? Said they were big men, strongly built." One of his dark eyebrows rose as he sipped his whiskey.

Hollis thought of Mr. Brendan, another man with a bit of green on his lapel who was strongly built. Unrefined, rugged good looks. Like a sailor, she mused. Hadn't she said exactly that? "What sort of ship?" she asked curiously.

Donovan shrugged. "Scottish merchant."

Hollis pondered that. She wondered if she ought to pay another visit to the insufferable Mr. Kettle. "What was the name of it?"

"The *Anna Marie*."

Hollis gasped. The *Anna Marie*! She knew that ship—everyone in Mayfair knew that ship. That was the name of the vessel that Lord Douglas had bought against his father's wishes—Hollis had reported the purchase of it. The gossip was that he'd won so much at a gaming table he hadn't known what to do with all that money, so he'd purchased the ship from a bankrupt merchant. Hollis knew Lord Douglas very well—they'd attended the same parish church as children. He could be quite charming when he was of a mind, but he had a notorious reputation and was abroad more often than not. He'd only recently come to London, some say to escape the very watchful eye of his father in Scotland.

"Why would four Weslorian soldiers arrive in London on a Scottish merchant ship?" she asked. "Do you suppose that—"

She did not finish her question because someone was suddenly knocking loudly on the front door. Donovan looked at the clock. "It's half past seven. Who would come calling on a night like this?"

Hollis's heart skipped. "You don't think something has happened to Pappa, do you?"

"No. If Poppy were sent for you, she'd come in without knocking."

"It wouldn't be Caro or Eliza, not at this hour. Beck?"

Donovan snorted. "I've no doubt he's completely at his leisure at this hour. I'll see who it is."

Hollis was suddenly filled with a sense of unease. "Let them knock," she said, even as the person knocked again, but more insistently.

"It's probably someone with something for the gazette," Donovan said. "You've handed those calling cards to everyone, haven't you? You've asked for news. You might at least hear what the person has to say."

Hollis groaned. "I'm not prepared to receive callers. And what could it be, really? I already know that Lord Farstowe is having an affair—*everyone* knows Lord Farstowe is having an affair. Except Lady Farstowe, of course."

The knock came again, only louder, as if the caller wasn't at all certain his first knocks had been heard.

"It might be Lady Farstowe herself," Donovan said. "I'll just have a look."

"Wait!" Hollis urged, but Donovan was already walking from the room.

With a groan, Hollis fell back in her chair. She pulled her wrap tightly around herself and hoped that Donovan dispatched whoever it was. The hot toddy had muddied her thoughts a little.

It seemed forever before Donovan returned to the room. "You've a caller, madam," he said, rather formally. "A gentleman."

"A *gentleman*!" Hollis stood up so quickly that she knocked over her footstool. "At this hour?"

"For you."

"I'm in my stocking feet! Who is it?" She put a hand to her hair—she'd tugged out the tight curls hours ago. "Wait. I don't care who it is, send him away. I can't receive anyone like this."

"He has your calling card," Donovan said.

"Yes, yes, I gave them around to everyone, as you said. I even gave one to Mr. Ket—" She suddenly gasped. "It's not *him*—"

"Not him. I would have tossed him out on his arse. This gentleman is drenched and said that you gave him the card at the costume ball."

"At the ball?" Hollis had to think about that. "I didn't give my card to anyone. Caro would have had my head if—" She suddenly gasped and her hand went to her throat.

"But I *did*, Donovan! How could I have forgotten it? I gave it to Mr. Brendan!"

"Well, the curt and impossible gentleman has come to call, Hollis. Best you hear what he has to say after accusing him of plotting a coup, aye? Better here in your stocking feet than in a dark alley when I'm not there to watch over you."

Hollis pressed her hands to the sides of her head. "Why did I not think to put calling hours on my card?" She sighed and dropped her hands. "Very well. Bring him."

"I will. But I'll not leave this room. Don't try and dismiss me, do you hear? This one looks a wee bit hard around the edges, he does."

Mr. Brendan did. And Hollis liked it.

As Donovan went out, Hollis grabbed her glass and drained the last of the toddy, wincing at the heat and the bitter taste. She put down the glass, whirled about, and ran to the window, frantically seeking even a shadowy reflection of herself. She tried to smooth her hair, but it was useless.

She was trying unsuccessfully to knot her hair at her nape when Mr. Brendan entered the room behind Donovan. Hollis dropped her hands. Half her hair fell and the other half stubbornly remained in some sort of loose bun. Donovan's eyebrows rose up his forehead at the sight of her before he announced like a proper butler, "Mr. Brendan calling, madam."

There was no point in trying to affect any dignity now. "Mr. Brendan. Good evening. What a pleasant surprise." She started forward to greet him, and the rest of her unruly hair tumbled down, one thick tress covering half her face. She brushed it aside and said, "I'm afraid you've caught me unawares, sir."

His amber gaze scraped down her body to her stocking

feet, then traveled up again, settling on her mouth for a slender moment. His expression was entirely unreadable, and yet the *way* he looked at her made a thousand tiny shivers run down her spine. She was, quite unnecessarily and ill-advisedly, titillated by this call.

But then Mr. Brendan took a small step backward and said, "It would seem that I have, indeed. I'll not keep you a moment longer than is absolutely necessary."

At that point, Hollis was only mortified.

CHAPTER TEN

One of our most trustworthy onlookers at events in London has reported that four Weslorian soldiers arrived Wednesday past on a Scottish vessel. Our observer thought it highly unusual, particularly as there were two Weslorian ships that came to port very recently. One cannot help but wonder at the reason for sailing in under a Scottish flag.

How strange it is to dine at a certain lord's home when all of his guests know of his affair, and his lovely wife seems blissfully unaware. Or is she merely indifferent?

Look for an abundance of large, colorful bows to grace the gowns worn this Christmas season.

༄—*Honeycutt's Gazette of Fashion and Domesticity for Ladies*

THE HOUSE SMELLED SWEET, like perfume. Like Mrs. Honeycutt. Marek pictured her gliding through these halls and leaving her scent behind.

Beyond the lovely scent, everything else in the house seemed a bit off-kilter. The manservant who had greeted him at the door seemed entirely too casual, as if he was master of this house instead of a servant. Moreover, Marek had the very uncomfortable impression that the bloke was eyeing him in a way that felt uncomfortably odd.

And then there was Mrs. Honeycutt. She was practically dishabille, what with her stocking feet and long, astonishingly thick dark hair hanging loose and uncombed down her front and back. Her dress was a deep ruby-red, cut low, and his eyes shamelessly strayed to the décolletage before he could rein them in. The color brought out the slight flush in her cheeks, and above them, her eyes shimmered like two deep pools.

She was frightfully appealing.

He glanced around at a richly appointed room with brocade draperies and fine carpets to remove his attention from her. It was sparsely furnished, but what furniture it did have was hand-carved and meticulously upholstered.

This space was a model of tidiness that he did not enjoy in his own home. His house looked more like a shop's odd storage, crammed full with books and trinkets he'd picked up at markets, old cookware and boxes of knickknackery that he guessed had meant something to him at some point, but what, he'd quite forgotten. He had toys he'd made for the dogs, and curiously—at least to his neighbors—a collection of cowbells. They were sentimental objects—they'd hung around the necks of some of his best cows. How he'd collected so many, he didn't know—they seemed to multiply on their own.

Two armchairs had been pulled in front of the hearth and placed side by side, separated only by a small table. On the table were two crystal glasses. One was empty, the other half-full. There were two matching footstools, arranged before the fire in the hearth. They'd been sitting there, these two. Were they lovers? What else would explain the easy manner of the manservant? And yet, something felt quite incongruent with that idea. Marek couldn't think of why, exactly, because they were both watching him expectantly.

He cleared his throat, looked down at the hat he held in his hand, and said, "Again, my apologies for calling so late, Mrs. Honeycutt. I've clearly come at a bad time."

One of her feet slid on top of the other. "It's quite all right, no need to apologize. Whatever brought you here must be very important." One eyebrow rose in silent question.

"It is…delicate," he said. Much like her foot.

"The intrigue grows! Would you like something to drink, Mr. Brendan? We've…" She turned her head and looked at the sideboard as she spoke, and what she said was lost to him. She gestured to bottles on the sideboard and then turned back to him.

"Pardon?"

She smiled with bemusement, as if she believed he had willfully not listened to what she'd said. In ordinary circumstances, that might have been the case. There were situations when he didn't know if he simply hadn't heard something or was so lost in his thoughts and questions that he missed what was said.

"I said we have wine and whiskey to offer you, or Donovan will fetch an ale if you prefer."

"No, thank you."

"A glass of water?"

He shook his head.

She seemed almost disappointed.

"I don't wish to impose," he added mildly.

"Oof," Mrs. Honeycutt said cheerfully, and propped her hands on her waist. "It's a bit late for that, isn't it?"

He opened his mouth to disagree. But then closed it. He couldn't disagree.

"It was a jest, Mr. Brendan!" she said cheerfully. "Do you see? Because you called so late, and then said…" Her voice trailed off, and she waved her hand. "Goodness, pay me no heed. I realize that my wit has an audience of one," she said, and pointed to herself. "And I'm not a terribly discerning audience. One should always remember that it is 'better a witty fool, than a foolish wit.'"

Marek cocked an eyebrow in mild surprise. "Shakespeare."

Her eyes widened. "*Yes!* How did you…?" She stopped. She smiled sheepishly and shook her head. "Never mind."

"I do apologize for the late hour. I've been occupied with the peace talks and they went well past the supper hour this evening."

"*You've* been at the peace talks?" she asked, clearly surprised.

"*Je,*" he said. "Contrary to your suspicions, I am here to aid our ministers."

"Oh. That's…wonderful." She looked mildly disappointed and sank onto one of the chairs before the hearth, eyeing him with renewed interest. "Is there progress?"

Very little, but there had been *some* progress, he supposed. Today they'd agreed to include the Astasian mountain region between their two countries in the array of issues to be discussed. One of the few paths of trade ran between the two countries through the Astasian Range, and there had been a long-held dispute about who had rights to it. Now that deep stores of coal had been discovered there, the dispute had gotten more vehement. The ability to extract and sell coal would be a boon to both countries. "Some," he said.

Mrs. Honeycutt inched forward on her seat. "Is *that* why you have come this evening, Mr. Brendan? I would be delighted to publish—"

"*No,*" he said quickly, horrified by the thought. He'd

done a little digging into *Honeycutt's Gazette*. He knew the history of it, how it had once been a paper focused primarily on financial news, and now was a gazette that recommended creams and unguents for ladies, offered marital advice, and kept track of the latest fashions. What that gazette had to do with any rumors of treason, he could not fathom.

Of course, he didn't want to convey that and make this rather uncomfortable situation even stickier.

He glanced at the manservant uncertainly.

"Oh! How terribly rude of me! Mr. Brendan, may I introduce you to Donovan, my butler and my confidant. He helps me with the gazette."

Her *butler*? If Marek hadn't been the fish out of water that he was in this drawing room, he might have laughed outright at that dubious title. This man may open a door here and there, but he was no butler.

"Donovan, this is Mr. Brendan. You know, the gentleman I told you about."

"So I gathered," Donovan said, looking at Marek.

Why had she mentioned him to this man? Or to anyone, for that matter? What could she possibly have said?

"You may trust Donovan completely, if that's what you're wondering. I vouch for him and his discretion with all my being."

Oh, he had no doubt of it. One had only to look at this quite handsome fellow to see he was the stuff of female dreams. There was even a dimple in his cheek, where one side of his mouth curved into a sly smile. "You misunderstand me, madam. It's not him. It's you I don't trust."

Mrs. Honeycutt drew a sharp intake of breath. And then she laughed, and loudly at that. "*Well*, then," she said cheerfully. "I'll prepare myself for the worst of news! Go on, then, Mr. Brendan—I'm on tenterhooks! Why *did* you come?"

"I came to inquire why you said what you did at the ball."

"Oh? What did I say?"

Her eyes were shimmering in a way that suggested she knew very well what she'd said. She wanted to hear him say it. In fencing, this would be the *appel,* her *en garde.*

And just as if she'd advanced while holding an epee, she said, "You look very serious, Mr. Brendan. Please do sit."

He didn't want to sit. He wanted proof that she knew nothing and was a woman dabbling in things better left to gentlemen, and then he could mark this off his list. But her manservant said, "Go on, then" in a low, cool voice. "Have a seat, Mr. Brendan."

He looked at Donovan. He looked at Mrs. Honeycutt. The only problem with taking a seat was that she would be on his deaf side. He reluctantly walked across the room and perched on the very edge of the empty seat, one leg stretched long to brace him on that edge, so that he could face her and see her lips when she talked.

She watched him like a cat, her dark lashes fanning across her cheeks when she coyly looked down and smoothed the lap of her skirt. "I will perish of anticipation, Mr. Brendan. Please do remind me what I said at the ball that would bring you all the way here on such a bitterly cold and wet night?"

He gave her a withering look. "I think you know very well. It was not something one would say lightly or forget easily."

"Ah." A smile slowly appeared. "You're right, I do remember. Did I distress you, Mr. Brendan? That was not my intent."

Distress him? She couldn't distress him. But she could

damn sure confound him and had been doing so since the moment he'd first laid eyes on her. "I suppose any man would be distressed when a woman unknown to him accused him of treason. But I'm not distressed, madam. I am curious. I would like to know who or what gave you that preposterous idea."

"Preposterous," she repeated, and smiled wryly at her butler. "He thinks I'm preposterous, Donovan."

Donovan shrugged. "A fool man thinks he is wise."

Mrs. Honeycutt giggled at yet another Shakespearean quote. What was the truth between these two people? Did they sit at the hearth each night and memorize Shakespeare? Astonishingly, that was what he did at times. The nights could be very long and cold in Wesloria, and reading Shakespeare helped him retain his English. "I didn't say *you* were preposterous, Mrs. Honeycutt. I said it is preposterous to believe I would have anything to do with overthrowing my own king. I would very much like to understand who led you to believe so?"

Her brow furrowed. "No one *led* me, Mr. Brendan. I freely came to believe it all on my own. Imagine that." She tilted her head to one side, and long waves of dark hair slid off her shoulder. "Why does it matter to you, if I may?"

"Is it not apparent? You accused me of something…" He struggled to think of the proper word in English.

"Vile," she said.

"Je. Vile. I'm a Weslorian—if there is something underfoot, I should like to know it so I can take appropriate steps to protect my king. Not displace him."

"Yes, but what if *you* are the thing underfoot?"

He stared at her. One of her dark eyebrows inched above the other, as if she thought she'd caught him somehow. She was terribly amused by him, he could see it, and that got his hackles up—this was deadly serious business to him. He leaned forward and looked her directly in her eye. "You can't be serious, madam. *Are* you serious? Do you accuse me again?"

"Oh, I'm quite serious, Mr. Brendan," she said confidently, then leaned forward, just like he had. "I'm also vigilant, and one cannot help but notice you."

"What have I done to give you cause for any suspicion whatsoever?"

"You must consider how you appear. You're a well-built gentleman, for one, and that draws attention. But when that attention has been drawn, it seems as if there is something a bit off about you. Something that doesn't fit with the exterior."

He leaned even closer. She matched him and upped the ante with a pert smile.

"How could you possibly pretend to know if there is anything *off* about me, or right about me, or anything at all? You don't know me, Mrs. Honeycutt—you've only seen me here and there."

"Only seen you here and there! We *danced*, sir! We've had entire conversations!"

Oh, but they'd had conversations, and he would never forget them. Conversations about the more absurd and ridiculous things he'd ever heard in his life. "Allow me to put it another way. Why would I come here if I were in any way involved? Would that not tip my hand in some way?"

Her pert smile faded slightly. She considered that, then nodded. "Fair point."

Yes, of course it was a fair point. He sat back, having dispatched the nonsense easily.

"And then again, you may have come here to intentionally mislead me. How am I to know?" She lifted her shoulders and the pert smile returned.

He could not fathom this woman. But what was she about? What game was she playing? Moreover, why?

"Oh, dear, you do look a bit piqued, Mr. Brendan. Are you sure you wouldn't like a bit of brandy? A finger of whiskey?"

He gritted his teeth and shook his head. "No, thank you. May I ask where you heard the word *coup*? Or did you very freely come to that word all on your own, as well?"

"Thank you for believing that I could! I heard it at the London Library."

"The library?" He did not understand. "Did you read it in a book or...?" Or had she invented this complete flight of fancy from some book?

"I *was* reading a book. As it happens I very much enjoy reading and have recently taken a dip into the history of Alucia and Wesloria. It's a very interesting part of the world. But I didn't *read* the word *coup*, Mr. Brendan, I overheard two gentlemen talking about it."

Now that gave Marek pause. He tried to think of the reason two men at a library would say or discuss a coup. "I don't understand. Gentlemen at a library were discussing a coup?"

"I should start at the beginning," she said.

"Oh, no," Donovan muttered.

"Mr. Shoreham is the persnickety and onerous chair of the London Philological Society." At his look of confusion—he didn't know what those words meant—she said, "It's a group devoted to the study of language."

He blinked.

"When I first heard of it, I was eager to join. I would adore the study of language! I do enjoy studying and reading. Most recently, I've been engrossed in the works of Shakespeare." She said this proudly.

"I don't understand—"

"She'll get to it…eventually," Donovan muttered, and leaned back against the sideboard, his arms crossed over his chest.

"But when I made my application to the society I was rejected tout de suite, with a reminder from Mr. Shoreham that a woman couldn't possibly be expected to comprehend the nuance of syntactic and semantic structures of English, much less any other language, without proper study."

Perhaps she hadn't understood his question.

"She fumed for days, she did," Donovan said.

"Well, it was *egregious*. And there is no recourse, no higher power to whom I could appeal. So I took my complaint to the head of the society, Mr. Shoreham, and he'd not give me as much as a glance. But I am not so easily deterred, Mr. Brendan, and I took to waiting outside their meeting room at the London Library every Tuesday and Thursday. I read about Wesloria and Alucia and, I should point out, that it appears I am indeed capable of understanding the subtle nuances of syntax and semantics, *and* grammatical structure."

Marek exchanged a look with Donovan. He returned his attention to Mrs. Honeycutt. "You were saying you overheard…"

"Oh! Yes, I did. One day on my way into the library, I heard two gentlemen speaking about rumors of a rebellion or coup." She twirled the end of a dark tress of hair idly around a finger. "If I knew who they were, I would have asked them directly who was plotting a coup. One said to the other that the rumors of a coup against the Weslorian king were so credible that the British had kindly assigned more guards to His Majesty and the royal family."

This news came as something of a shock to Marek. He had a dark feeling that it was true. He'd believed there was something more at work here in London, and these two anonymous men had confirmed it. "You've no idea who they were? Were they English? Weslorian?"

"All I can tell you is that they were finely dressed and clearly Englishmen. Londoners, I'd say."

"What did you hear, precisely, that led you to believe that I was somehow involved?"

"Nothing!" she said breezily. "I decided something was afoot with you all on my own when I noticed you rarely interacted with anyone and watched King Maksim like a hawk. Very suspicious behavior, Mr. Brendan."

"Did you consider that perhaps not all persons who attend a ball are inclined to chitchat?"

"I do know that to be true. In fact, you reminded me of it. What was it you said? You did not engage in idle chatter or something. Very chivalrous."

He was beginning to feel a little warm at the back of his neck. He didn't remember the exact words he'd used, but he very clearly remembered trying to move her along.

Mrs. Honeycutt settled back, her smile effervescent. "You watch King Maksim like a governess watches her charge."

Marek's neck warmed even more. "If it will disabuse you of your fantastic ideas, I will tell you that I was watching someone else very near to the king. I will also tell you that I am not involved in anything treacherous, and in fact, quite the opposite—I want to prevent any harm to the king. I am steadfastly loyal to him."

Mrs. Honeycutt glanced at her butler. Donovan lifted

his chin so slightly that Marek was surprised he noticed it. "What is the look between the two of you? Is there more? Is there something you've heard that might help me discover who is behind such talk?"

Donovan shrugged. "Aye, tell him, then."

Marek looked between the two of them. "Tell me what?"

"Should I?" Mrs. Honeycutt inquired, sounding uncertain.

"He seems harmless enough," Donovan said, and his gaze slid to Marek.

He didn't think he liked being called harmless, but that was neither here nor there. "Tell me what?" he asked impatiently.

"Very well." Mrs. Honeycutt folded her hands neatly in her lap, as if she was about to impart something very dire to him, something like his puppy had gone missing. "Earlier today, four Weslorian soldiers arrived in London on a Scottish merchant ship." She pressed her lips together, clearly anticipating a notable response from him.

But Marek didn't understand what this meant or why she would think it important. What was remarkable about four Weslorian soldiers arriving on a Scottish ship? "And?"

"*And?* Don't you think it's at least a little odd? Why would four Weslorian soldiers arrive today on a ship flying a Scottish flag when so many Weslorian ships have arrived in the last two weeks?"

"I can think of any number of reasons. Perhaps they've been sent to provide extra security for the king and it was the fastest way to get them to London."

"Yes, but," Mrs. Honeycutt said, and lifted one elegant finger. "It could also be that a Scottish ship is a way to arrive here in the middle of the peace talks without anyone noticing."

"You noticed."

"I didn't notice. Someone very close to me noticed."

"Really?" he drawled, and looked at Donovan.

"What does it matter? He heard it from two of the sailors and told me, and it seems very odd, knowing all that's been said."

She had a point, and it gave him a tiny bit of pause. He happened to notice the clock on the mantel. Dromio would be looking for him if he wasn't already. "Is there anything else you can tell me?"

"You want *more*?" She smiled. "No. Nothing."

He stood up. "If I may, Mrs. Honeycutt, it seems to me that you've made quite a leap to a conclusion that is not supported by any facts. But thank you for telling me what you've heard. I will leave you to your…evening."

She quickly stood, too. "Is that all?"

"Je." He bowed his head and started for the door.

Donovan walked out ahead of him, no doubt to open the door and kick him down the steps when he passed.

But Mrs. Honeycutt darted forward and stopped him with a hand to his arm. Marek glanced down at her hand. Her skin looked translucent next to the black of his coat. Her fingers were long and slender, and for some reason, made him think of a harp. They looked like the sort of fine fingers that could bring a harp to life.

"Perhaps I could be of service," she said. Her hand slid from his arm and she moved to stand before him, blocking his exit. "I have friends and acquaintances in positions of government."

She looked so earnest, and her skin so golden in the light of the hearth. What an odd woman she was. What a beautifully odd woman. He couldn't help himself—one corner of his mouth crooked up in a half smile. "You offer to be of service to a man you only moments ago suspected of plotting a coup against his king?"

Her skin pinkened. "I'm not so stubborn that I can't be persuaded to another point of view."

Marek actually chuckled. "I don't believe you." He didn't trust her in the least. And yet, his smile held, because she was pretty and she was unique and he was a man and he could feel a very stark longing for female companionship. Not just any female—*this* female. There were any number of questions he would ask her if she hadn't accused him of treason. What works of Shakespeare had she read? How often did she visit the palace? Was she having an affair with her butler? "Thank you, but I have what I need. Please don't feel it necessary to take any measures on my behalf." Advice that she ought to heed for many reasons, not the least of which was that she might come to harm if she poked around too deeply into business that did not concern her. But first and foremost, because he couldn't risk anyone knowing why he was really here. He couldn't have anyone—Weslorian, English, or Alucian—looking at him too closely.

She was looking at him very closely, as a matter of fact. Her eyes searched his and caused a bit of a quake in him. "Hmm," she said. "I suppose you're the sort that prefers to have a go at things quite on your own."

Yes, and he best remember that. "*Je*, I am." He tried to step around her to take his leave.

But Mrs. Honeycutt dipped to her right to keep him from it. "So am I, but sometimes, it helps to have an ally. Particularly if one is on foreign soil. How shall I contact you if I discover anything more about the soldiers?"

He would dearly love to understand what drove her. But once again, he looked at her lovely eyes, and the hair tumbling around her face. She reminded him of a painting, like the candid portraits of deceased Weslorian ancestors that lined the halls of the National Museum of Art in St. Edys. In that rare moment, he wished he was someone else. In this case, an Englishman. An unencumbered Englishman with nothing but time at his disposal.

"I don't mean to contact you at *all*, Mr. Brendan, if that's what you fear. But I should like to send a note if I learn anything more about the soldiers. Would you like to know? To, ah, protect your king?"

With her shining eyes, she was a dichotomy—speaking of matters that were deadly serious and all but laughing at it. It hardly mattered—she wouldn't learn anything about the soldiers because he didn't think there was anything to learn. He didn't believe they existed. "Yes, of course," he said charitably. "The Green Hotel."

"The Green Hotel," she repeated softly, and her gaze, ever so slowly, slid down to his mouth. Her lips parted slightly and while he was certain he hadn't heard it, he imagined the softest of sighs.

The heat that rose in him was startling in its immediacy and terrifying in its strength. Marek took one last look at the lovely, and slightly deranged Mrs. Honeycutt. He suspected it was the last he'd see of her.

"Good evening, Mr. Brendan," she said pleasantly, and moved out of his way.

"Good evening, Mrs. Honeycutt," he said, and walked out of the room, his mind still reeling a little from the rise of heat in him.

Donovan was at the door. "Thank you," Marek said, and donned his hat.

Donovan opened the door. But he didn't move aside, which meant Marek had to scoot past him to exit the house.

"Good evening, Mr. Brendan," Donovan said.

Marek touched the brim of his hat and jogged down the steps to the sidewalk. He stole a glimpse back at the door before carrying on.

Donovan was standing with one shoulder against the frame, his arms folded over his chest, watching Marek with a gimlet eye.

Marek strode down the sidewalk, moving as quickly as he could from that very strange house.

He didn't know what to make of Mrs. Honeycutt and was certain the task of understanding her was far greater than he had the patience for.

But she was a beautiful, intriguing woman.

CHAPTER ELEVEN

*New patterned silk fabrics from Brussels have arrived
at Debenham & Freebody for Christmas dresses.
Purchase by appointment, please.*

*The Alucian and Weslorian peace talks continue,
but it is commonly agreed that progress is still quite
slow. Does it not stand to reason that progress might
be improved if negotiations were open to public scru-
tiny? Alas, the secretive nature cannot help but suggest something is amiss.*

*Volunteers from the Coalition for Decency and
Morality have been seen around Piccadilly Circus on
some evenings, distributing leaflets warning against
the dangers of loose morals. Members of the metropolitan police were also on hand.*

*ᖚ—Honeycutt's Gazette of Fashion and
Domesticity for Ladies*

IF THERE WAS one thing Hollis Honeycutt did not shy away
from, it was a challenge. She'd learned that about herself
when Percy had died quite suddenly, the result of a terrible
carriage accident. At first, the shock of it and the inability
to comprehend that she would never see Percy again had
turned her into a wraith. When Hollis looked back on that
time, she realized she had come dangerously close to carrying on like that for the rest of her life. She could very well

have become one of those widows who never changed out of her mourning clothes, who aimlessly wandered the halls of her grand house, a mere shell without her husband. But even in the throes of grief and deep despair, in her paralysis at not knowing what to do without him, she'd heard the whispers. *What will we do with Hollis?*

As if she was a child. A mad child. A mad, mute child.

As she climbed the stairs to the master suite after Mr. Brendan left, she thought that she was indeed thankful she'd heard the whispers, because it had forced her to wake from her grief. It had cleared her muddied thoughts and made her see that decisions would be made for her if she didn't make them herself.

At first, she'd been frightened by the prospect. Like so many women of her social standing, she wasn't equipped to know what to do about anything much, other than her needlework. And menu planning, and how to set a table and make guest lists and attend church and participate in church bazaars with a few cakes her cook made and please her husband. She didn't know how to read her husband's financial ledgers or publish a gazette or ask complete strangers for help.

Hollis walked into the master suite of rooms she and Percy had shared in their marriage. They'd never had separate bedrooms, like so many couples in Mayfair. They had needed to be with each other. Through a door on the left was his dressing room. Through a door on the right was hers. They'd come together in here. This is where they'd reviewed their day, planned their future, read their books. This is where they loved.

The room looked exactly as it had at the time of Percy's death. Hollis hadn't thought much about it until a few months ago—she supposed it was one way of keeping him with her. In fact, his personal things were still on the bureau—a pocket watch he meant to give to Eliza to repair. A few coins, a handkerchief neatly folded. For the longest time, Hollis couldn't bear to even think of changing a thing. It felt as if removing a single item was removing him. But now it seemed…maudlin.

She walked to the bed and lay down, fully clothed, and stared up at the dark blue canopy above her head. It matched the dark blue draperies. The color, the heaviness of it all, had been Percy's choice. Hollis would have preferred something lighter and airier.

The chaise before the hearth, on which they'd made love on lazy rainy mornings, was collecting hats and gloves now. There was a desk and a wood-and-leather chair against a wall, and Percy's Bible was tucked neatly into a corner. Hollis got off the bed and, with her hands on her hips, she looked around the room. It was beginning to look a little drab. *She* was beginning to look and feel a little drab.

Her heart told her it was time to change. She'd loved Percy with all her heart, but what was the point of clinging to things? It didn't ease the loss. That had dulled all on its own, no matter how hard she'd tried to cling to his memory. Now, the idea that she'd clung to it for as long as she had made her sad. She was still a living, breathing thing. She was a person in her own right. She was not Percy's appendage.

It was time she changed this room to reflect her.

Just as she'd changed the gazette. That's what she'd done when she'd heard her family's whisper, *What to do with Hollis?* She'd understood that forging her own path before one could be forged for her was the challenge, but it was one she had to accept. She would be forever grateful to herself for it, too. The good Lord knew it would have been so easy to let her father and Eliza determine what was best for her. It would have been so easy to listen to Caroline and Beck tell her what she needed to do.

It hadn't been easy to refuse their offers of help, especially when she'd had to force herself to go through Percy's office and open his drawers and read his notes and see what he'd left behind of himself.

She'd found things that had brought her to her knees, like the ribbon he'd taken from her hair when he'd first begun to court her. She remembered that day—he'd stuffed it into his pocket and declared it a good-luck charm. She'd found a small jeweler's box, tied with another ribbon, and a diamond brooch inside. Was it for her birthday? Their anniversary? She read the ledgers into which he painstakingly entered the numbers of gazettes printed, the page lengths, the printing costs, the paper costs. His figures were so small and neat that when she rested her cheek on the ledger after one long night, she'd dreamed the tiny figures had danced their way into her skin.

And then there were the men upon whom Percy had relied to publish his gazette. The printers, the distributors. When Hollis had gone round to inquire about carrying on, they had looked at her with skepticism and disbelief. Or worse—some of them had laughed.

It was hard, it was aggravating, but Hollis had learned so much about herself in the process. She'd learned how to speak up for herself. She'd learned to ask for things she wanted and not to fold at the first *no*, because the first answer was always *no*. She'd learned that in the next life, she would like to come back to this earth as a man, with all the confidence and bravado that was granted to that sex by the mere virtue of being born.

She had changed the gazette, had seen it grow to tenfold

the circulation Percy had ever enjoyed. Would he be proud of her? Or would he be scandalized by the sorts of things she printed? Her memories of Percy, of knowing him like she knew herself, were fading from her marrow. She remembered specific things about him, and she remembered moments they'd shared. But she couldn't any longer remember how she felt when she was with him.

She walked to the chaise, pushed aside two hats, and sat heavily. Ruth had made a fire for her. The cold was seeping in through the windows. It would be Christmas soon, another one without Percy or Eliza.

Her challenge now was learning to live alone. Percy was gone. Eliza was gone. Caroline was gone. And from the sound of it, Pappa would be gone, too. Even Donovan was gone. Not *gone,* really—he hadn't said it, but she suspected something or someone held his interest. She supposed it was to be expected. He was a young man, a handsome man. But she wasn't ready to stop needing him.

Nevertheless, Hollis liked a good challenge. She very much enjoyed trying her hand at something new, to see how far she could go before she was pushed back. Mr. Shoreham was a challenge. Mr. Kettle was a challenge. But living without her loved ones in her daily life was the hardest of all challenges.

And then there was Mr. Brendan. He was a different, exciting sort of challenge. He was a nut she had to figure out how to crack.

The fact that he, and only he, had given any credence to the idea of a coup had thrilled her. She'd even suspected Donovan of humoring her when she spoke of it. But she was convinced something was happening—there were just too many odd little things that didn't make sense and couldn't be explained away. Why would those two gentlemen speak of it at all? What about those four soldiers? Oh, but she would dearly love to send word to Mr. Brendan that she was right about that.

A thought occurred to her—perhaps she ought to pay another call to Mr. Kettle to see what he knew.

She imagined Mr. Brendan's unusual amber eyes full of doubt when she told him that the four soldiers had come to harm the king. She imagined the furrow of his brow, the set of his square jaw, and how his eyes would change and fill with admiration when she laid out a logical case for her theory.

She was looking at his hands tonight when he spoke. His attention was so intense, as if he feared he might miss a single word. He gripped his knees as she spoke. They were broad, big hands. And the way he looked at her, as if trying to see into her, well… Hollis had had enough of the rum toddy to have a momentary lapse in judgment and imagine that piercing gaze and a hand on her breast.

The salacious thought fluttering through her brain had surprised her greatly—she hadn't thought of any gentleman like that. Donovan, perhaps, but that was only pretend. Mr. Brendan was the first man since Percy's death who had stimulated her in *that* way. And once the notion had escaped the box she'd locked all such notions into, it had spread. It was now taking over her thoughts.

Yes, she would very much like to look at Mr. Brendan again. Surprise him. Hand him information that was both useful and would cause him to look at her so intently again.

She felt warm just thinking about it.

THE NEXT MORNING, Ruth came into her room and drew open the drapes. Weak sunlight filtered across Hollis's face. With a groan, she sat up, pushing hair from her eyes. "Good morning, Mrs. Honeycutt," Ruth said cheerfully.

"Morning," Hollis muttered. She was not at her best upon waking, which was why Ruth always brought her hot coffee and toast to break her fast and to give her a moment to adjust to the idea of living. Percy used to say she was a bear in the mornings. Or had she said that about him? She couldn't rightly remember.

After Hollis had her coffee and toast, Ruth returned and asked, "All better now?"

"All better," Hollis agreed. She stretched her arms overhead and yawned. "I'm going to the foreign secretary's office today."

"Are you? Good day for walking, but there's a nip in the air." Ruth disappeared into her dressing room and returned, holding up a dark blue brocade gown with white piping. "What do you think?"

Hollis eyed the gown Caroline had made her. "It's tight, that's what I think. But then again, everything is." She suddenly recalled her supper two nights ago. Donovan had gone out for the evening, as he was doing increasingly, and it had been just her. She'd eaten a plate full of food and more. Come to think of it, she couldn't remember tasting any of the food. She'd sat there with her chin in her hand, mindlessly lifting the fork to her mouth and back again. *Good Lord.* She really had to find something better to occupy her than food.

She got out of bed and began her morning toilette, and when she was ready, Ruth helped her into the gown. Hollis had to suck in her belly just so Ruth could finish fastening it for her.

"This would be easier with a corset," Ruth said a little breathlessly behind Hollis.

"No," Hollis said. "Corsets are confining. They squeeze the air from me! Why must women be so confined?"

"Gentlemen wear them, too," Ruth said breathlessly.

"But not all of them. I think it very patriarchal, constraining us like that. We are people, too, Ruth! We need to be free! I begged Caro to let the gown out an inch or two, but she wouldn't hear of it," Hollis complained, and drew a deeper breath with the hope of assisting Ruth.

"Lady Caroline is very careful with her appearance," Ruth said. "There!" She triumphantly announced the last button fastened.

"Thank you." Hollis looked at herself in the mirror, her hands on her hips. It was not *very* apparent that she was stuffed into this gown like sausage into its casing, but it certainly felt that way. Was Caroline right? What she'd said that day was that she would not be part of Hollis's "downfall."

"My downfall? What are you talking about?" Hollis had demanded. "I'm only asking that if you insist on making a gown for me, that you make one that fits my body and not what society demands it be."

"I *mean*, darling, that you've given up," Caroline had complained.

Hollis had gasped. "I have not!"

"You have. You walk around this house in bare feet and with your hair down. You're completely unreasonable about wearing a corset and have equated it with some sort of liberation from society. You talk about politics to the point that I can hardly bear it. It's to be expected, I suppose. You lost a husband, your sister is in a foreign land, and your father is determined to move to the country. But really, Hollis, it's too much. Just wear a corset!"

"No," Hollis had said flatly.

Caroline had muttered under her breath.

Hollis had meant what she said about corsets and had become quite vocal among her acquaintances about her dislike of them. She had grown convinced of her argument that they were society's way of keeping women in check. But…this gown was *awfully* tight.

And Caroline was right—she had lost so many loved ones in the last few years. Even Caroline, who had been a staple in her house, had moved to the country and rarely came to town these days.

She placed the flat of her palm against her belly and took a deep breath. "I might faint dead away in this."

Ruth looked at her with some alarm.

"I won't…but I might." She turned to the side and eyed herself. Maybe she had given up a little. What was the point? It wasn't as if she saw anyone other than Donovan and Ruth and Mr. Brimble.

"There is nothing to be done for it. I am locked into the blasted thing and best be on my way." She wished Ruth a good day and went downstairs.

She stopped in what had once been her formal dining room, but was now the office of the gazette, in search of her favorite wrap. She startled poor Mr. Brimble. The old man was bent over, looking under the dining-room table that was now a very large desk, covered with gazettes in various stages of construction.

"What are you doing down there, Mr. Brimble?" Hollis asked as she picked up her wrap.

"Good morning, madam. I'm on the hunt for Buttercup. She didn't come round for her milk this morning."

"Have you looked in the sunroom? Yesterday, she spent the entire afternoon there watching the birds pecking about the mews."

"Aye, that I will. Thank you, Mrs. Honeycutt."

Hollis smiled, and with her wrap in hand, she went out. And when she did, she nearly stepped on Buttercup. "Here she is, Mr. Brimble!"

Donovan emerged from the drawing room. He had rolled up his shirtsleeves and was holding a feather duster. "Going out?"

"Yes. I mean to pay a call to Mr. Kettle and inquire about the *Anna Marie*."

Donovan's dark eyebrows rose. "Should I come along?"

"No, thank you. Poppy is coming with me. We've an appointment to look at the new silks that have come in from Brussels. It's right next to a chocolate shop."

Donovan walked to the foyer and retrieved her cloak from a coat stand. Hollis picked up a bonnet and fit it on her head.

"Mind you be gentle with Mr. Kettle. He's got tender feelings, that one," Donovan reminded her.

Hollis rolled her eyes as Donovan settled the cloak onto her. He rested his hands on her shoulders, leaned over close to her ear, and said, "Quite taken with the Weslorian gent, aren't you?"

She tried to twist about, but he held her in place. "What are you talking about?"

"Admit it. You esteem him."

It was amazing how quickly heat could rise in her neck, and she slapped his hand from her shoulder. "Don't be absurd. Why would you even think it?"

"Oh, I don't know. Running off to pay a call to Mr. Kettle after you said you'd never darken his door again. And you were a bit flirty with him last night."

"Flirty!"

"Aye, flirty. Leaning forward to speak to him. Smiling and twisting your hair around your finger."

"You're ridiculous," she huffed and fastened her cloak.

He grinned and opened the door. She stepped out. But she turned back. "What I—" Hollis lost her train of thought, as a gust of cold wind hit her and very nearly lifted her off her feet. "Oh!" she cried.

"Have a lovely day begging Mr. Kettle to give you even the slightest reason to send word to Mr. Brendan."

"Donovan, you—"

He laughed and shut the door before she could rail at him.

He was teasing her. She had not been *flirty.*

CHAPTER TWELVE

Observers say an earl of ill reputation has come to London from Leeds, daring to subject a town with his presence in the event a vote is needed in the Lords on the peace accord. The gentleman hasn't been seen since last summer, when a soiree in Belgravia resulted in a duel that left two men badly wounded and a woman disgraced. We look forward to his vote.

Ladies, if you or a loved one suffers from the disease of freckles, Dr. Herbert's Complexion Cream is guaranteed to remove all spots and leave your skin with a decided glow.

↷—*Honeycutt's Gazette of Fashion and*
Domesticity for Ladies

MR. KETTLE WAS mulling over the grim portions in his lunch pail. A slice of bread—one of his last—and two thin carrots. It was enough to nearly bring a tear to his eye.

Mrs. Kettle had gone to stay with her father in the country, marching out of the house and shouting from the street that he could do his own cooking. As if he could do that! It was all very embarrassing and noted by more than one neighbor.

It had been four days since she'd left, and Mr. Kettle felt as if he was withering away, turning into a ghost of his former self. He had learned, through the fiery trial of marriage, that when left to his own devices, he could hardly scrape a meal together.

He removed the bread and tore off a hunk. Tonight, he planned to enter the public house at the corner of the street on which he lived. He did not like to spend money on food in public houses, as the better value could be found at the markets. But he thought if he didn't do something soon, he might very well pass away. That would serve Mrs. Kettle right, to come home and find him dead as winter on the floor of the kitchen.

He had just stuffed the bread into his mouth when he happened to look up and see Mrs. Honeycutt. "Oh dear," he mumbled through a mouthful. She was walking into his office. He hadn't seen her in a week and thought he was done with her, but here she was, her fine looks and intense blue eyes fixed on him.

Lord. Now what? His mouth was full and his stomach was growling. He chewed frantically and looked around as she advanced on his desk. In a moment of panic, he spit the half-chewed wad of bread into his waste bin. He looked down at the glob and a queasiness filled him. It was as if a piece of his soul had just left his body. He had only one more bite of bread and two carrots. How would he manage?

"Good morning, Mr. Kettle!" Mrs. Honeycutt said brightly. She walked right up to his desk and leaned over it, peeking into his pail. "Oh. Very lean today, isn't it?"

He pressed both hands to the desk and rose. "Mrs. Honeycutt." He looked past her, his eyes seeking her personal Adonis. But instead of him, Mr. Kettle's gaze landed on an attractive young woman with brown hair and a delightful figure. Where was Adonis?

He scowled at Mrs. Honeycutt. "I am rather surprised to see you again. I thought I was very clear about the matter the last time you were here, wasn't I? If there is any doubt of it, I brought the matter up to Lord Palmerston, and he has said there is no reason anyone should see the manifests of the Weslorian ships."

"Oh." She smiled pleasantly. "Well, then, I suppose that settles it, doesn't it?"

That was not the answer he was expecting, and he found himself momentarily speechless.

"Out of curiosity, did his lordship mention Scottish ships?"

"I beg your pardon?" Mr. Kettle asked, confused.

"A ship flying a Scottish flag arrived yesterday or the day before that. You may know it—the *Anna Marie*?"

Of course, he knew the *Anna Marie*. It was a thirty-year-old clipper that ran between Le Havre and London at regular intervals. It had recently been outfitted with steam. He'd received the paperwork on her arrival just this morning. "And?"

"And…I have heard that four Weslorian soldiers were passengers aboard that ship."

Mr. Kettle's stomach growled. *"And?"* he said more insistently. "What business is it of yours?"

"Oh, Mr. Kettle. I should think the answer obvious, even to you. If there are four Weslorian soldiers listed on the manifest, a reasonable person might assume they arrived in London for unpleasantry."

That did not follow at all. "If there are *not* four on the manifest, one might assume they were not on the ship after all, and whoever has said they were has bats in the belfry. And what if they are on the manifest? What does that prove?"

"It proves that I am wrong and you are right, and I will be perfectly satisfied and will leave you to your potato."

"It is a *carrot*," he said tersely. "Once again, Mrs. Honeycutt, it appears you have no idea what you are talking about."

She laughed softly. "You're not the first to accuse me of that." She glanced over her shoulder at the other woman. That woman came forward and Mr. Kettle noticed for the first time that she was carrying a large shopping basket that bounced against her leg as she walked.

"I will concede that my thinking may not make sense to you, but I assure you, I know what I am doing and this is important information. Will you allow me to look, please?"

Mr. Kettle snorted a laugh. Why did she think a Scottish ship would be any different from a Weslorian ship? *"No,"* he said, his voice full of incredulity.

She folded her arms and fixed him with a stare, not unlike the cold stare Mrs. Kettle had given him the morning she left.

"Mr. Kettle, please allow me to introduce you to my dear friend, Miss Dumont."

"Good afternoon, Mr. Kettle," the woman said.

Mr. Kettle looked from one woman to the next, both of them looking at him in a manner that left him feeling unsettled. Was he supposed to greet this one? "How do you do," he said stiffly, and pulled himself up to his full height, which, disappointingly, was only eye level with Mrs. Honeycutt.

Miss Dumont noticed his pail. *"Oh,"* she said, sounding surprised and slightly disgusted. "Is that your luncheon, sir?"

"Very sad, isn't it?" Mrs. Honeycutt remarked. "Such a robust man with such a tiny bit of food."

"It's tragic," Miss Dumont agreed. "He must be very hungry."

Mr. Kettle's stomach growled again.

"Poor man," Miss Dumont said.

"What do you think?" Mrs. Honeycutt asked.

"The cakes?" Miss Dumont returned.

The cakes? *What cakes?* Just the mention of cake caused Mr. Kettle's stomach to growl again.

"Yes, the cakes," Mrs. Honeycutt confirmed.

Mr. Kettle looked from one woman to the other, then watched with great curiosity as Miss Dumont reached into the basket and removed a plain brown-paper package tied by a slender red ribbon. He saw the name printed neatly on the paper: *Charbonnel et Walker.* Mr. Kettle knew that shop. It was one of the best chocolate shops in all of London. He passed by their window several times a week to marvel at the chocolate delicacies and tiny cakes.

Miss Dumont untied the ribbon and folded back the paper. Four small chocolate cakes were nestled inside the paper.

He looked up at Mrs. Honeycutt. "Are you...are you *bribing* me, Mrs. Honeycutt?" he asked, his voice a whisper of disbelief.

"Bribing?" She laughed gaily. "We are concerned for your wretched lunch, Mr. Kettle! How can you possibly do the queen's work with no provisions? How uncharitable it would be to have these cakes on our person and not offer you one while you stand here before us with no food to speak of." She took one cake from the wrapping and put it on the desk. It sat on its own little island of paper, and with one finger she nudged it closer to him. "Perhaps you could enjoy this cake while I have a peek at the Scottish ship manifest."

Oh, but she was a devil of a woman. But he looked again at the cake and his belly rumbled. He shifted his gaze to the stack of correspondence from this morning, picked up the lot of it, and set it down before her. Then he drew the cake to him.

Miss Dumont perched on the edge of his desk. "Do you have any brandy, Mr. Kettle? I like a spot of brandy with my cake."

"Brandy, here?" he protested.

"Don't look so surprised. You'd be astounded by how many gentlemen like yourself will have a nip of brandy from time to time during the day. Particularly when it's as cold out as it is. Wouldn't you like a nip before heading home for the day?"

He would, actually.

Mrs. Honeycutt picked up the stack of correspondence and turned her back to him. She leaned up against the desk and quickly shuffled through it, pulling out one packet.

"Is it only chocolate? Anything else? Currant, perhaps?" Mr. Kettle asked, eyeing the cake.

"A very good guess, Mr. Kettle. You'll have to eat it to find out."

He picked up the cake and bit into it. The center of it oozed with jam. With a sigh of contentment, he closed his eyes and chewed.

By the time he'd finished his cake, Mrs. Honeycutt had returned the day's correspondence. She had what she wanted and he didn't even care. This was all Mrs. Kettle's fault—she should never have left him like she did. She should have stayed at home as a wife ought to and minded her husband. And these two ought to be at home minding husbands, as well, but that was the way of things these days. Women had minds of their own.

The ladies left him a second cake, even more delicious than the first, and he was so entranced with it that he scarcely noticed they had taken their leave. He kept his eyes closed as he savored the last bite of the last small cake.

What harm was there, really? What did it matter that she was looking for someone on a Scottish ship? It was of no consequence. His reward for defying the command of Lord Palmerston had been well worth it.

CHAPTER THIRTEEN

Quite a hubbub was witnessed at Piccadilly Circus recently when a throng of gentlemen stumbled upon a young soldier, an influential earl's youngest son, in flagrante delicto. The Coalition of Decency and Morality "volunteers" chased the young man down the street and flogged him. They have publicly proclaimed one small victory against sodomy.

Meanwhile, in Shoreditch, where many coalition members reside, as the vicar of St. Leonard's made his way to church one morning, he unexpectedly encountered a gentleman with whom he is acquainted. The gentleman, who is known to occupy the front pew of St. Leonard's with regularity, claimed to be calling on a sick friend at that early morning hour. However, that afternoon when the vicar called on the sick friend, he found everyone in the house very well indeed, and in particular, the young lady.

—Honeycutt's Gazette of Fashion and Domesticity for Ladies

TWO DAYS HAD passed since Marek had called on Mrs. Honeycutt—two days Marek had had to ponder those four soldiers. He had decided there was nothing to her claim. How could there possibly be? It was not unexpected that more guard relief might be needed in London and a few soldiers were sent on a merchant vessel. And he still thought it was quite probable that the men didn't exist or had been confused for someone else.

Marek had spent the last two days advising Dromio and, by extension, the king, of the national impact of their decisions during these negotiations. He had explained, in the simplest terms possible, that the tariffs on grain could be ruinous to the producers of the grain.

"*Je*, I understand," Dromio had said impatiently. "The king understands. Everyone understands, Brendan. We are not idiots."

That was open to debate.

They had just returned from the meeting room where the Weslorians, Alucians, and English met to hammer out the details of the agreement. Dromio had reported to all those assembled that King Maksim was keen to industrialize, yes…but that he would impose those tariffs. Marek had tried to make sense of it, to understand what the king hoped to achieve. He could come up with no plausible reason.

He fell in behind Lord Dromio as they made their way back to the Green Hotel. Dromio was walking along with Lord Van, the two of them quite animated in their conversation. Lord Osiander was behind Marek, looking entirely disgruntled. But then again, Osiander often looked as if he'd lost his glasses and couldn't find them.

Marek quickened his step, catching up to Dromio and Van, hoping to hear what they said. It was useless—with their backs to him, every word sounded as if it was spoken under mounds of wool.

When they reached the entrance to the hotel, Marek slipped in beside Dromio and asked for a word.

"Yes, what is it?" Dromio asked impatiently. His gaze was following Van, who disappeared into a common room where the ministers often met for brandy and port.

"The tariffs," Marek said. "I thought—"

"*Je*, that was very clever of me, I think."

Marek was taken aback. It was Dromio's idea? "But as we discussed, my lord, the tariffs will make the grain more costly for the Weslorian capitalists to produce, and those costs will be passed on to our people."

"Capitalists!" Dromio began to knead his side with his fingers, as if he had a sore muscle. "How do you propose, Mr. Brendan, that a government conduct its business? There must be some money to be had that doesn't come from the pockets of our poorest citizens." He smiled thinly and glanced over his shoulder at the men gathered in the common room. "Is there more?"

"No," Marek said quietly. Dromio walked on, his steps quick, as if he couldn't wait to be away from Marek.

Marek watched him go, thinking about what to do, when he heard something that sounded like someone singing underwater. He turned around to see a footman holding a silver tray. "Sir, a letter has come for you."

"Me?"

The footman simply held out the tray.

Marek took the letter. He didn't recognize the hand that had written *Mr. Brendan* neatly across the center of the folded paper. He unfolded it and read.

Dear Mr. Brendan,
I hope you are well and not disappointed with the dreadful cold. I have some exciting news and wish to invite you to join me for afternoon tea at half past five to hear it.

Sincerely,
Mrs. Honeycutt

What in bloody hell was this? What scheme was she playing at now? It was probably something ridiculous, a rumor she'd heard at the market that meant nothing to anyone. He pulled out his pocket watch and glanced at the time. It was nearly five o'clock.

"Is there a reply, sir?" the footman asked.

Marek glanced over his shoulder at the ministers gathered around a small table in the common room. Dromio stood up and waved at him, gesturing for him to come, then shouted across the room for him.

Which was the lesser of two evils? Lord Dromio? Or Mrs. Honeycutt? He closed his eyes and sighed again. Dromio was decidedly the worst option. He opened his eyes. "No need for a reply. I will deliver it myself."

The footman nodded and stepped away.

Marek waved at Dromio, but went in the opposite direction. He first went to his room to freshen up. He combed his hair and tried to buff his boots, but they were too worn to shine now. His hair had gotten too long, and while he would like to have it trimmed, there was never time to find a barber. He examined himself in the small mirror on the chest of drawers and frowned. He had the growth of a new beard on his face, and the knot on his neckcloth, no matter how often he untied it and tied it again, would not stay straight.

Why did he care? Maybe because it was the first time in a very long time anyone had paid any particular attention to him. Except for old Lady de Florent, who often brought him freshly baked bread, told him he needed a trim, inquired about his dogs, his horses, his sheep, asked whether or not he thought it would be a wet year, should she plant barley or oats, and various sundry other things.

Mrs. Honeycutt paid attention to him, and he realized,

as he brushed some lint from his shoulder, that for the first time in a long time, he cared how he appeared.

As a result of his fussing, he was a quarter of an hour late to her tea.

Someone had placed a wreath of holly on her red entrance door, reminding him that Christmas would be soon upon them, in a matter of a couple of weeks. He reached through the circle of the wreath and rapped with the door knock a few times. Moments later, the door was opened by an elderly gentleman holding a yellow cat.

"Well! Good afternoon, sir. Or is it evening?" the old man asked, poking his head out and glancing up at the sky.

"It is...evening," Marek said. His gaze flicked to the cat and back to the old man. "Ah... Mrs. Honeycutt sent an invitation."

"Did she?" He sounded pleased. "To what?"

Was he Mrs. Honeycutt's father? Grandfather? Marek gestured to the interior of the house. "To call."

"Ah. Shall I tell her who is calling?"

"Please. Mr. Brendan."

"You've an odd way of speaking, Mr. Brendan," the man said. "What accent is that? French?"

"Weslorian."

Mrs. Honeycutt suddenly popped up over the old man's shoulder. "Mr. Brendan! How good of you to come."

The old man turned around to see her, and she stepped forward, all smiles, dressed in a butter-yellow gown that had the effect of making her look somewhat ethereal.

Her smile sizzled in his veins. "I'm very happy to see you!" she said, and before he understood what was happening, she threw one arm around his neck and hugged him, patting him on the shoulder like someone's aunt. *Look how tall you've grown, lad.*

Marek did not return her effusive greeting. He stood stiffly, not knowing what to do. He'd never been greeted like that by an acquaintance. Certainly not a female one.

"Lord! I beg your pardon, Mr. Brendan," she said, and quickly let him go, stepping back. "I tend to forget myself. Come in, come in," she urged him, waving him forward.

He cautiously stepped into the foyer and removed his hat. He glanced at the old man, but Mrs. Honeycutt extended her hand for the hat, and put it on the console. The old man was too busy smiling at the cat.

"Mr. Brimble, you must be terribly tired, aren't you?" she said to the old man.

"Oh I am, a bit." Mr. Brimble was still stroking the cat. "Looked for Buttercup over an hour today, up and down those stairs."

"Poor dear. She looks as if she's a bit tired, too," Mrs. Honeycutt said, and stroked the cat's back. "Would you ask Mrs. Plum to bring tea?"

"I will indeed," the old man said. "She might have a spot of milk for Buttercup, mightn't she, kitty? Mightn't she?" he cooed as he wandered off, presumably in the direction of Mrs. Plum and milk for his kitty.

Mrs. Honeycutt watched him go, then smiled sheepishly at Marek. "He won't remember to ask for the tea."

"Your grandfather?"

"Who, Mr. Brimble?" Mrs. Honeycutt glanced over her shoulder. "He's no relation at all, really. At least, I don't think so. I'd really have to think…" She seemed to be pondering it over, and then smiled. "Never mind that. I won't bore you with my theories about him."

Did she not *know* the gentleman? Was there yet *another* person in her house who wasn't a servant or relative? And speaking of butlers who were not butlers, where was the very handsome bloke who was possibly, but possibly not, her lover?

"Come in," she said again, and scurried down the hall, her dress billowing out behind her. She paused at the door across from the drawing room and looked back.

Marek followed her.

The room he entered was completely different than the drawing room. *This* room was cluttered with papers and books and boxes piled up all around. He thought it might have been a dining room, judging by the twin chandeliers and the long dining table he supposed was beneath all that paper and books. On a wall opposite an enormous hearth, there were at least three paintings. He could make out the frames, but a linen sheet covered them, and pinned to that sheet were several pages of paper that he assumed was her gazette.

The smell of paper and ink mixed with smoke was a bit disconcerting—this room smelled like a factory, and the scent of her perfume was nowhere to be found. He took it all in, his gaze traveling over every surface, but there was so much clutter that it took him several seconds before he noticed a second cat, this one black and white, sitting on the table staring accusingly at him. It suddenly stood with its tail high in the air and daintily picked its way through the stack of papers and books before settling on a stack of broadsheets. It curled into itself with its back very firmly to the people in the room.

"Get down from there, Markie." She lifted the cat, dropped him on the floor, then glanced at Marek. "You're shocked, aren't you? I can see it in your face. You must excuse the state of the room, Mr. Brendan. This is where I do the work of the gazette. Donovan says I should have an office near the printing company, but I like being home. Here we are!"

She moved to the end of the table and gestured with a flourish to two armchairs in the bay of the window. Between them was a small table with a silver candelabra and three worn candles. The only other thing on the table was a small framed canvas of needlework that looked only partially complete. On the floor beside one of the chairs was a stack of newspapers. "It's not very pretty here, but interestingly, my thoughts seem clearer here than anywhere else in this house. Isn't that odd, to be in a room as chaotic as this and be able to think clearly?" She laughed and shook her head. "On my word, sometimes I hear the things I say and marvel at them. Will you sit? Please do—I'll just pop out and tell Mrs. Plum you've come."

She darted past him and out of the room before he could even answer.

Marek looked at the two armchairs. They reminded him of the two in the drawing room—as if two people often sat here to while away their hours. He chose the one the farthest from the needlepoint and sat on the edge of what he assumed was Donovan's chair. This house and this woman intrigued him. It was a puzzle to be unlocked, or a view into a life that looked fascinating in comparison to his boring routine.

A moment later, Mrs. Honeycutt fluttered into the room, smoothing the lap of her skirt as she came across the room to join him. "I'm so glad you've come, Mr. Brendan," she said again as he rose to his feet. She sat in a cloud of pale yellow in the chair beside him; he sat as well. She clasped her hands on her lap and leaned forward, her eyes sparkling with excitement. "I have the most extraordinary news," she said, as if confiding a secret.

"I thought you might."

"I should begin by...oh, wait!" she said suddenly. "How terribly ill-mannered of me, Mr. Brendan. Let me first inquire after your health."

"Pardon?"

"And your day, of course? How would you say the talks are progressing?"

Marek was once again reminded how inept he was in social situations, but he didn't understand why it was necessary to begin with social pleasantries as if they had met at some official function. She had said she had news, and he would like to know what the news was. "Mrs. Honeycutt, if I may—would you share with me your reason for inviting me here today?"

"I invited you to *tea*, Mr. Brendan, because I *do* have extraordinary news. But as we are friends, I should like to know that all is well with you."

This strange notion of friends again. "I appreciate your—" he searched his brain for the right word "—ardor for making new friends, but as I am here only a very short time, I don't think that possible."

"What?" She seemed surprised. "Of course it is possible!" she insisted. "One should not limit one's acquaintances, one should embrace them. What is the point of living if you don't?"

He could think of any number of answers to that. Procreation, for one, a thought that made his heart skip a beat or two. Study. Animals. There were many things that made a life worth living above and beyond simply making acquaintances.

"All right, I understand you're reluctant. But perhaps you will try for my sake? You happen to be the most interesting person to have entered my house in some time."

She asked with such a pleasant pair of dimples and arresting blue eyes that he couldn't rightly refuse her. "Very well," he said. "How do I try?"

Her dimples deepened into a beaming smile of victory. "You may start by telling me if you've at least had the pleasure of seeing some of the sights of London."

"I have not. What else might I tell you?"

"What? But we've some very fine museums, Mr. Brendan! I could make a list of attractions for you—"

"Thank you, but I've no time for it. Might you tell me your news now?"

She clucked her tongue at him. "Are you so entrenched in your occupation that you can't take the time to see a bit of London? And the parks—you *must* find time to walk, particularly through Hyde Park. It's very soothing, really."

He waited.

Mrs. Honeycutt groaned theatrically to the ceiling. "It is so desperately hard to entertain you, sir!"

"I apologize for it. Perhaps because the purpose of my visit is not to be entertained."

"Then why *did* you come?"

He stared at her incredulously. "You invited me. You sent a note round to my hotel. When last we spoke, you said you'd send for me if you had news. You said tonight you had extraordinary news. I have come, Mrs. Honeycutt, for your extraordinary news."

"Well, yes, but I thought you would be pleasant company now that we are acquainted...oh! There is the tea." Mrs. Honeycutt startled him by hopping to her feet and hurrying toward the door. He hadn't even heard the elderly woman come in. She was carrying a silver tray with a tea service. She and Mrs. Honeycutt seemed to have quite a discussion about the tea, but he couldn't understand what was said.

Mrs. Honeycutt took the tray from the older woman and carried it to a rolling tea cart near the wall on Marek's left. She was talking the whole time, not surprisingly. He was accustomed to very little chatter, also not surprisingly. She was talking about the tea, he thought, something about where it had been purchased. He wondered what it would be like to spend every night like this, admiring an attractive woman, listening to the lilt of her voice, the rise and fall, even if he couldn't make out all the words. He thought it might be lovely.

She busied herself with cutting two thick slices of a cake, each slice enough for two people. She handed him a plate and then a cup of tea.

Marek glanced down at the cake in one hand, the tea in the other.

"That won't do," she said, and leaned across him, the scent of bergamot and lemon wafting with her. She took the cake from his hand and placed it on the table between the two chairs. "There we are." She turned back to the cart and helped herself to cake and tea, too, and placed her cake on the table beside the needlework. And then she sat on the chair, kicked off her shoes, and drew her feet up under her skirts.

She was remarkable.

"You didn't say," she said as she forked her piece of cake. "What sort?"

"I beg your pardon?"

"On my word, I think you ignore half of what I say, Mr. Brendan. I was asking about the trees in Wesloria. For Christmas."

Christmas trees. Not tea, then.

She put down her fork. "Did you hear a word I said?"

He blushed hotly. He glanced down at the delicate china

teacup. There was no use pretending it wasn't so. "I, ah…as it happens, I am deaf in my left ear, and perhaps partially so in the right. When someone is standing to my left—"

"It's just as I thought!" She reached across the table and put her hand to his wrist in a move he was not expecting and almost saw him spill his tea. "I am so very sorry! It all makes sense to me now. My father is blind. Blind as a bat, can't see anything at all. He likes to knit." She removed her hand and picked up her fork.

He could not begin to guess what her father's blindness had to do with his deafness, but it hardly mattered because she was on to the next thing.

"I was saying that Prince Albert brought the tradition of a Christmas tree to London, and none of us have been the same since! I told Donovan we must bring a tree and trim it with all the proper things, and he asked me what the proper things are, and really, I don't know. Bows, I should think." She popped a forkful of cake into her mouth. "And then I asked if you have the tradition in Wesloria. Do you?"

"Ah…" He put aside the tea. "*Je*, we do. Small trees for the table." He held out his hand to indicate the height of the tree from the floor. More of a shrub, really, if one thought about it. He'd never had one in his house, and was fairly certain if he did, his dogs would think it an invitation to mark their territory. But last Christmas he'd been to dine with his neighbors, the Tarian family, and had spent the entire evening leaning to one side or the other to see around their Christmas tree.

"That sounds lovely," Mrs. Honeycutt said. "This is *delicious*."

"Mrs. Honeycutt," Marek said. He didn't know how long he was to pretend this was a social call, but he was getting a little antsy.

She waved a fork at him. "I knew you were going to ask." She set down her cake and shifted, propping herself against the arm of her chair. "I called on the foreign secretary today."

That was not the news he was expecting.

"Not Lord Palmerston, I don't mean him. But his office. There is a gentleman in his lordship's employ—his name is Mr. Kettle—and he has some responsibility toward the shipping industry, although I must confess it is hard to guess what or just how much responsibility, really."

Marek waited patiently, unable to fathom where this was going.

"Nevertheless, I asked Mr. Kettle if I might see the manifest for the *Anna Marie*. That's the ship, you know, the one we discussed the last time you called. Of course, Mr. Kettle refused, which, between us, I think it is simply his nature to be disagreeable. So I bribed him with cake." She paused and glanced at Marek's untouched piece of cake. Marek did, too. "Not *this* cake. A different cake. *This* cake is not a bribe, if that's what you're thinking. It happens that Mrs. Plum makes a delicious cake and I am forever looking for an excuse of have one." She laughed. "But he did allow me to look at that manifest."

Marek had to pause a moment so that his brain could catch up to her free-flowing stream of consciousness.

"Can you guess what I discovered, Mr. Brendan?"

Mr. Kettle's handwriting wasn't very neat? Mr. Kettle put a tree in his house at Christmas? He eyed the cake on his plate. "Not only can I not guess, I won't even attempt it."

"Just as well, because you'd never guess. Here it is— there were no Weslorians listed on the ship's manifest."

Marek waited for her to say something more, to explain why she found this news so remarkable that she'd summoned him here to eat her cake, which, he would admit, did indeed look delicious. When had he last had cake? Must have been the party to celebrate the birth of the Tarians' son. That had been several months ago.

Mrs. Honeycutt waited with visible impatience for him to say something. When he didn't, her eyebrows rose high. *"Well?"*

"You have me at a disadvantage, Mrs. Honeycutt," he said. "I don't understand the importance of this finding."

"Really?" She seemed shocked. "Surely you have some thoughts on the matter. You must make something of it."

"I do make something of it. I assume that whoever told you there were four Weslorian soldiers on that ship was incorrect."

She leaned back and considered him. "Well, that's one interpretation, I suppose. However, another one is to assume those four soldiers either stole onto that ship or were invited on, and they were not placed on the manifest for corrupt reasons."

Yes, well, when one had a vivid imagination, one might immediately leap to theories of corruption.

Marek picked up the plate of cake. "That is indeed one way to look at it. However, I choose to look at it from the most logical angle."

"Hmmm," she said, her eyebrows sinking into a fiendish little *V*. "Is it possible, Mr. Brendan, that you believe your theory is the most logical because you are male and I am female? Or would you, by chance, have another theory that I would be very keen to hear?" Her voice carried a pitch that he knew instinctively was the pitch of a woman who was displeased. That particular tone was the same the world over, in any language, at any hearing ability.

He took a bite of cake. It melted in his mouth and sent

a rush of pleasure through him that made his scalp tingle. He glanced at his hostess. As much as he hated to admit it, her hypothesis would make sense under the right circumstances. "I don't think your idea is inferior," he said carefully, although he did think it was a very long stretch. "But I think it's not as logical as mine."

"Naturally," she said crisply, and leaned forward, pinning him with a look. For a moment, he thought she meant to take away his cake.

He reluctantly set the plate aside and inched forward on his seat. Bracing his hands on his knees, he chose his words with care. "May I ask why you are so insistent in believing that there is a conspiracy against my king? You have presented scant evidence of it."

"But you believe it, too, Mr. Brendan," she pointed out. "Otherwise you would not have come again tonight. Why are you so insistent on believing I can't help you?"

He glanced longingly at his cake. "Please don't take offense when I say you cannot possibly help me. There are… circumstances that make it impossible."

"What circumstances?"

He couldn't possibly explain them to her. It would take a lifetime to explain his circumstances. It was complicated, convoluted, torturous, and tangled. Almost as tangled as the bit of silky dark hair that curled around her ear. "Nothing that I can share with you, unfortunately."

"Is that so," she said pertly. "I may be of more help than you can possibly imagine. I happen to know the owner of the Scottish ship, and he happens to be in London just now. We could simply ask him if there were four soldiers on his ship." She leaned over the arm of her chair again. "Aren't you just a *tiny* bit curious, Mr. Brendan?"

Yes, he was a tiny bit curious about many things in that

moment. His eyes traced a line from the curl of hair around her ear to her lips. He didn't know what to say to this lunacy. To think that she would go off on her own and perhaps stumble onto something villainous was unacceptable.

How in hell had he gotten himself into this predicament?

He was thinking how to respond carefully when something distant and thudding reached him.

Mrs. Honeycutt gasped. Her feet hit the floor. She sat up, wide-eyed, and looked at Marek.

"What is it?"

"Someone is pounding—"

She was suddenly on her feet, and Marek was aware of that distant thudding again. She was gone in a flash, disappearing out the door.

He took one last look at the cake and went after her.

He entered the hallway just in time to see her trying to catch a body coming through the front door. Or at least that's what it looked like—a body, falling through the door. He rushed forward to help her, reaching her just in time as Donovan was hoisted into the house by two men on the landing. Marek couldn't see their faces before they disappeared into the night, but he could see Donovan's—he'd been beaten and looked half-conscious.

"Oh my God!" Mrs. Honeycutt cried, and grabbed Donovan's arm. "What happened?"

Marek moved to catch the brunt of the man's weight. He hoisted Donovan onto his shoulders, one arm wrapped around a leg, the other holding his arm.

"This way," she said frantically and ran to the drawing room ahead of him, opening the door for Marek, and standing aside as he banged through with the butler on his shoulders.

"Have a care with me head, lad," Donovan muttered.

At Mrs. Honeycutt's frantic gesturing, Marek deposited Donovan on the settee. Mrs. Honeycutt crouched down beside him and soothed a lock of hair from his forehead. "What happened, Donovan? Who did this to you?"

"I didn't know the gents who did it," Donovan said. "Hired thugs, I'd wager." He lifted a hand and gingerly touched his busted lip. Both eyes were bruised, and there was a deep gash in his brow that Marek assumed would require some stitching. The front of his shirt was soaked with blood and his coat was torn at the shoulder.

Mrs. Honeycutt pressed her forehead against Donovan's arm for a moment. "It was them, wasn't it?"

"It was them," Donovan said, and shifted slightly. When he did, he gasped, breathless with pain.

"It was the sanctimonious Lady Hartsfield," Mrs. Honeycutt snapped. She stood up. "I'll get something to clean your wounds—"

"Don't," Donovan said, and tried to lift himself. "Let me to my room. I'll be all right."

"Don't move, Donovan!" she said sternly. "Stay where you are, I'll be back in a moment with help." She stood up and stared down at him, her lovely face full of concern and horror. "Why they can't leave one's decency and morality to be guided by one's own conscience defies all reason!" she said angrily as she rushed out of the room.

Marek looked down at Donovan. The man's brow was creased with pain and he was panting slightly. Marek frowned. "You've taken quite a beating."

Donovan actually chuckled through a grimace. "How did you work it out?"

"What is this about?" Marek asked.

"This, sir, is about people who fear their own instincts," he said tightly. He touched his lip again and pulled his hand away, looking at the blood. With a grunt, he managed to push himself up to sitting. Gasping from the pain, he looked Marek up and down. "Come round again, have you?"

"At the lady's invitation," Marek said. "What do you mean, 'people who fear their own instincts'?"

Donovan managed a sardonic grin. "You seem a clever man to me, sir. Have you not guessed by now?"

Marek didn't answer. He had some private suspicions about Donovan, but none that he would ever give voice to.

Donovan moved, and grimaced with pain again, his hand instantly going to his side. "I think they broke a rib or two."

"That should be bandaged. Be still—moving will make it worse."

"Said like a man who's had a broken rib."

"I have." As a boy, he'd fallen off a horse and broken a rib and his collarbone. To this day, he couldn't lift his left arm as high as his right.

"If nothing else, I suppose you might take this as proof that you can trust her," Donovan said.

"Trust her," Marek repeated. "What are you talking about?"

Donovan squinted at him. "You said you didn't trust her, aye? Is it not obvious to you now that she can keep a secret?"

Something clicked in Marek. All at once, everything made sense. His suspicions were born out—the strange relationship Donovan had with Mrs. Honeycutt. The way he looked at Marek. The talk of morality crusaders in the gazette and here again, tonight.

"Aye, you do understand," Donovan said, and averted his gaze.

What Marek understood was that there were men in the world who preferred the intimacy of other men. He'd had acquaintances through the years that he suspected of those sorts of relationships, but Donovan was the first gentleman he'd met who was admitting it to him.

Donovan shifted and sucked in a gasp of pain between his teeth. "You're shocked," he said.

"Not shocked," Marek said flatly. "Surprised."

"Revolted?" Donovan asked, his gaze on the hearth, and for the first time since meeting him, Marek thought the butler sounded a little less sure of himself.

"No," Marek said. To each his own. "Wary."

Donovan smiled lopsidedly and nodded. "Fair enough. Mrs. Honeycutt was wary at first, too. But you may take my word for it, sir—there is no better woman in London. She allows people to think what they will of us in this house, all for my sake."

Marek understood. And it seemed to him quite a sacrifice for a young widow on the fringes of high society to make.

"She can be trusted to keep your secrets and remain true to her word," Donovan said. He looked at Marek again. "But if you betray her, I will kill you."

Marek thought the threat unnecessary, as he didn't doubt for a moment that Donovan would. He might have offered that he didn't intend to betray anyone, and that Donovan was hardly in a position at the moment to make any threat at all, but Mrs. Honeycutt rushed into the room with a young woman behind her, and the two of them began chattering at once and fluttering around Donovan, and the threat was forgotten.

CHAPTER FOURTEEN

The Coalition for Decency and Morality has claimed victory in their uninvited war at Piccadilly Circus. Judging by the chatter around their latest round of violence, we may all look forward to the volunteers tidying up and down the Thames for us.

There are whispers that the peace talks between Alucia and Wesloria have stalled over disagreements to do with the Astasian region, a mountainous range between the two countries where rich coal deposits have been located.

Ladies, Mrs. Sutter of Lombard Street is making holly wreaths for purchase. Please do call Monday through Thursday.

♡—Honeycutt's Gazette of Fashion and Domesticity for Ladies

"WHAT HAVE YOU done, Donny?" Ruth cried. She came down to her knees before her friend and put her hand on his chest. "You've got up to some trouble, you did, and now look at you."

"I didn't beat myself, lass," Donovan said. "I didn't—*ach*," he said, wincing when she tried to take the neckcloth from his neck.

"We should get him to his room," Hollis said.

"Thank you, I can walk," Donovan said.

"You can't possibly walk!" Hollis insisted. She hurried

to the door to open it wider. "Will you help, Mr. Brendan?" Mr. Brendan did not respond. He was looking at Hollis curiously when she turned back to the room. His hearing! No wonder he'd seemed so aloof. He really couldn't hear very well at all. "Will you help us get Donovan to his room?"

"Je," he said, without a moment's hesitation, and moved to stand in front of Donovan.

"That won't be necessary, I can manage," Donovan protested.

"Don't be ridiculous," Hollis said. "You don't even know if you can stand."

She watched as Mr. Brendan leaned down, slipped his arms under Donovan's, and hauled him to his feet. Donovan stood uncertainly, testing his weight. When he tried to walk, his right leg buckled. Mr. Brendan draped Donovan's arm around his neck, then braced his arm around Donovan's waist. "Easy," he said, and together, the two men began to make their way out of the drawing room.

"Where?" Mr. Brendan asked Hollis as she darted ahead.

"Up the stairs, two flights, to the right," she said. "Ruth, bring something we can wrap around his rib cage. And tell Mrs. Plum we must clean his cuts."

Ruth hurried out, already calling for Mrs. Plum.

Hollis kept in front of Donovan and Mr. Brendan, pausing every few steps to see if they followed. On the first landing, Donovan looked as if he was wilting, so Mr. Brendan squatted down and lifted Donovan onto one shoulder. "It will hurt like Hades, but it's quicker," he said, and began to stride up the stairs with Donovan crying out every few steps.

In Donovan's room, Mr. Brendan said, "A hand, please, Mrs. Honeycutt. I'll need you to keep him from falling as I lower him down."

She quickly moved around to his right, and as he lowered

Donovan off his shoulder, Hollis braced Donovan to keep him from falling. But he was heavy, and he slid off awkwardly. When he did, his arm brushed against Mr. Brendan's hair, pulling it forward from having been combed back behind his ears. That's when Hollis very clearly saw the patch of white in Mr. Brendan's hair. She was so startled she forgot that she was helping, and Donovan bounced onto the bed.

"Bloody hell," he groaned.

Hollis straightened up and looked at Mr. Brendan. His attention was on Donovan—he was trying to swing his feet around to the end of the bed. He had brushed his hair back into place, but she could still see a tiny bit of white. *White*, Eliza had said. King Maksim and his daughters had those curious streaks of white in their hair. *As if the artist had forgotten to dash on a bit of color to fill in the hair.*

Her heart began to race. Her thoughts were divided between her concern over Donovan's well-being and the many puzzle pieces that were moving around, trying to fit into place in her thoughts. She stared wide-eyed at Donovan as she tried to absorb what she'd just seen and what it could possibly mean.

Donovan's face had gone gray, and perspiration was beading on his forehead. "Have you anything for the pain?" he implored her.

"Yes." She took his hand and squeezed lightly. This was the thing she'd feared for Donovan, the thing he always said she need not worry over.

Ruth banged into the room with a stack of linen sheets. "Here we are. Mrs. Plum is coming with the things to tend to his other wounds."

Ruth was still speaking when Mrs. Plum burst into the room. "Donovan!" she cried, breathless. She was a woman in her sixth decade of life, and while she had a great amount of stamina, which Hollis admired, the stairs left her breathless. "Oh, dear, lad, look at you!" she cooed. She leaned over him and touched the wound at his brow with her fingers. "We'll have to clean you up, won't we? I'll bandage him up, Mrs. Honeycutt. Ruth, bring the sewing basket, and fetch the laudanum from the cupboard in the larder."

Ruth dropped the linens onto the foot of the bed and raced out.

"What's all the commotion?" Mr. Brimble appeared, looking as if he'd been changing for bed—his waistcoat and neckcloth were gone, his shirttail pulled from his trousers and hanging to midthigh.

"Donovan ran into a bit of trouble this evening," Hollis said as everyone crowded around the bed.

"What's that?" the old man said, shuffling forward. "Oh! What a sight you are, lad. Hope you gave them what for."

"Tried," Donovan said. "But there were three of them to one of me."

Hollis gasped with outrage.

"You're going to have some lovely bruises, I'm afraid, love," Mrs. Plum said. "But they haven't ruined your handsome face, not one bit. In fact, nothing looks too terribly mangled. I suspect you'll live to charm again."

"Thank you, Mrs. Plum. I was worried," Donovan muttered.

"I should go," Mr. Brendan said. "Good luck to you, sir," he said to Donovan, then looked at Hollis across the top of Mrs. Plum's head. "Thank you, Mrs. Honeycutt. Good evening."

"No, wait," Hollis said, and looked frantically between Mr. Brendan and Donovan.

"Go on, Mrs. Honeycutt," Mrs. Plum said. "We'll take good care of him now."

"Yes, go," Donovan grumbled. "I won't have you all looking at me like this."

Mr. Brendan was already walking toward the door.

She didn't know how she could possibly think of leaving Donovan at this moment, but she couldn't let Mr. Brendan get away, either—not now, not with the new suspicions in her head. "Mr. Brendan?" When he didn't turn, she remembered he couldn't hear her. She darted after him and touched his arm. He looked at her. "Let me see you out—"

"Please. You've more than enough to do here."

Mrs. Plum had enlisted Mr. Brimble to help her remove Donovan's shirt. He was in good hands. "I insist," she said, and stepped out of the room with Mr. Brendan.

They walked down the hall in silence; Hollis's thoughts were racing ahead to what she would say, *how* she would say it. When they reached the stairs, she said, "Thank you so much for your help, Mr. Brendan."

"You mustn't mention it."

"I hope you weren't...scandalized." So much had happened tonight that she was only now thinking of what he must have thought when he surely realized what had happened to Donovan.

But he looked at her as if he didn't understand at all.

"Because of..." She gestured vaguely in the direction of Donovan's room. She had never spoken of his affinity to men to anyone, not even her sister. She had sworn to Percy she would never tell anyone and she had kept that promise.

Mr. Brendan started down the steps. "Rest assured, Mrs. Honeycutt, I don't make other men's business my own."

She followed him to the first-floor landing. He paused there and his gaze flicked down the length of her and up again, settling on her eyes. "Thank you for the tea." He said it softly, as if she'd done him a kindness. "Please, go back to your...butler." He started down the second flight of stairs.

"Wait," she said, following him down, catching up with him as they reached the ground floor. "Mr. Brendan?"

He paused once more and waited politely for her to speak.

Unfortunately, Hollis couldn't think how to say it.

His gaze flicked to the front door. She was pestering him now and had to speak up or lose him. "There is one more thing I have to tell you. Please," she said, and unthinkingly, impulsively, grabbed his wrist.

Mr. Brendan very slowly looked down at her hand on his wrist. Hollis did, too. Why did she keep doing things like this—hugging him, and putting her hand on him? She should have let go immediately. But she didn't. She stared at her hand on his wrist and imagined that her fingers couldn't close all the way around it. She stared at the bit of hair that peeked out from his cuff, at his knuckles, and noticed one of them was scarred. When she did at last look up from his wrist, she found Mr. Brendan looking at her. And his gaze was incendiary.

She let go.

"It's important," she insisted. "And...you left your cake." She tried to muster a laugh as she gestured lamely to the door of her dining room.

His gaze was still locked on her, and she wondered if her flesh was turning fiery red. "Lord Dromio will be expecting me shortly."

"Mr. Brendan, please—it won't take more than a minute. Or two. Possibly three." She was hoping that was a lie. She was hoping he would stay and tell her everything. She wanted to know it all. "Do you remember what I told you about the London Philological Society?"

"How could I possibly forget it?"

She took a step backward, toward the door of her office. "And do you remember I told you that they meet every Tuesday and Thursday afternoon at the London Library?" She stepped into the dining room.

Mr. Brendan glanced at the front door, then at her. He followed her. "I do."

She started toward the far end of the room, to the armchairs where she'd spent many afternoons with her needlework. She turned back to face him and spoke louder. "And do you remember that I said I wait for them every Tuesday and Thursday to press my case?"

He had taken a few more steps into the room, watching her. He nodded.

Hollis made it to the chairs and picked up his plate of cake. He'd taken only a bite of it. She held up the plate. He watched her set down the cake again near the chair he'd taken earlier. "I recall everything you said, Mrs. Honeycutt." He walked to the chairs, looked at her, then at the cake.

Hollis sat. So did he. She hid her smile by looking at her lap a moment. "The short of it is, Mr. Brendan, that while I have not been able to persuade Mr. Shoreham to give me entrance, I have had a lot of time to study the history of Alucia and Wesloria."

He picked up the plate. "I would hope that you would have used that time to engage in something far more pleasurable than reading dusty history books." He took a generous bite of the cake and made a sound of approval.

"They're not dusty books to me," she said. "I find them fascinating. My sister will one day be queen of Alucia and

I should like to know as much as I can about the country where she'll live."

"Yes, I suppose she will," he said, nodding. He took another bite of cake. "Frankly, I had forgotten your relation."

So had everyone around her, quite honestly. "The history of Alucia is terrible, what with all the betrayals and rebellions. It's very encouraging to see the country move in a more productive direction, isn't it? Or at least in the direction the duke will take it once he becomes king."

Mr. Brendan shrugged. "That could be many years yet."

"True." She drew a breath, seeking her courage. "But I must say, it is the Weslorian history that fascinates me."

His fork stilled on the plate. His gaze seemed to darken slightly. "How so?"

"It's dark and bloody, too, isn't it? So much fighting and many betrayals. At least until King Maksim took the throne."

He eyed her warily as he put aside the plate of cake. Hollis tried to keep from fidgeting, but she felt like she was sitting on a hive of bees.

"The king's father is the one who brought peace, such that it was, after years of rivalries between the lords," Mr. Brendan said.

"Ah," she said, because she couldn't quite think with him looking at her so intently. But here, on the very tip of her tongue, the thing she wanted to broach. She hesitated, because for a very long time, she had behaved precisely in the way society expected a woman of her standing to behave. It was her duty to do the responsible, polite things— she was a married woman, after all. Caroline was lawless, and Eliza had spent the last several years before meeting her prince walking about the markets looking for clocks to repair. Who else would hold up the decorum of the Tricklebank family in the face of the world?

And then Eliza moved to Alucia, and Caroline moved to the country, and Hollis was left behind. She'd always been the one who could be relied upon to do the right thing, say the right thing, *be* the right thing, and they'd gone off and left her to do all the right things on her own. She had nothing to occupy her. The gazette, as unusual as it was, was not the answer. The gazette was about a whole other life that really didn't exist any longer. She wanted something more for herself. She wanted a life that had meaning. She wanted to put the past behind her and find her way forward.

Mr. Brendan was looking at her. He was frowning dubiously. Perhaps he thought she was having a stroke, or the cat had got her tongue. What made her hesitate was that what she was about to say was so rude and improper that her former self would have been ashamed of her. But the new Mrs. Honeycutt—the bored, lonely, I-need-more Mrs. Honeycutt—was sick of what she'd become. She cleared her throat. She smiled with empathy for the man who she was certain had once been destined to be a king.

"What I found most tragic in Weslorian history was the loss of the baby crown prince. Stolen from his cradle in the middle of the night and never seen again."

The color drained from Mr. Brendan's face. He braced his hands on his knees as if he expected to be struck.

"I can't imagine the horror for his parents."

Mr. Brendan's face mottled. Something seemed to change in the air around them and Hollis knew in that instant she was right—Mr. Brendan was that missing prince.

It all made perfect sense. He was partially deaf, which was not an uncommon result of childhood fevers, and by all accounts, the prince had suffered from scarlet fever.

He had the white splotch of hair, just like the king and his daughters. And now that she really looked at him, she could see a resemblance to King Maksim in the amber eyes. How could she have missed that connection before?

Her heart was beating so fast that she felt almost dizzy. She leaned closer. "Mr. Brendan...are you the lost son of King Maksim?"

"What?" He looked as if she'd suggested he kicked babies and puppies up and down the green.

"Isn't it possible? After all, you look—"

He surged to his feet. "That is the most absurd thing you've said yet, Mrs. Honeycutt," he said crossly. "It is a *ridiculous*, dangerous assumption! What is the matter with you?" He stalked to the window, his hands on his hips. He said something more in Weslorian, and judging by the tenor of his voice, it was not kind.

But did it not stand to reason that if her idea was as absurd as he seemed to want her to think, that he would laugh? He was not laughing—he was furious. "It doesn't seem ridiculous to me," she pressed.

He didn't respond. He hadn't heard her. So she came to her feet and joined him at the window. "Mr. Brendan?"

He would not look at her, and she realized she was on his left side. She touched her fingers to his hand. That made him turn. "It makes perfect sense," she said calmly. "You have certain features—the bit of white in your hair like the king and his daughters. The color of your eyes, too, which are quite unusual, just like the king's."

He looked at the door, almost as if he was considering escape. She had the sense that he didn't know what to say, what to do, or where to go. She had the sense that he was reluctant to admit the truth. "Your secret is safe with me, sir."

He gave her a disdainful snort. "You could not be more

mistaken. Forgive me for saying so, Mrs. Honeycutt, but you are the worst sort of person, kicking up the dust of lies and rumors with absolutely no proof of anything. It's a dangerous and irresponsible way to behave. You could see yourself hurt for it."

She would ignore his opinion for the time being, although in truth, his stark words stung a bit. She liked to think she was helping. "Then tell me why you're so captivated with King Maksim," she persisted.

"I haven't been *captivated*," he said angrily. "I am a patriot."

"If you are a patriot, then help me find the soldiers."

"There *are* no soldiers," he exclaimed, casting his arms wide. "You interfere where you have no business being."

"Well, now you sound like Mr. Shoreham at the Philological Society. Who, exactly, has any business looking into the possibility of a coup? Is there someone special I should share my suspicions with? I don't think so. It seems to me that we are the *only* two who think it is a possibility, and the only two, therefore, who will try and uncover it."

He put his hands on his hips and stared down at her with incredulity. "You have taken complete leave of your senses," he said, his voice full of wonder. "Have you considered that there might be greater things at stake than something to print in your gazette?"

"Then educate me. I can help you back to the throne—"

He cried out with alarm. "*Never* say that!"

"Do you deny it, Mr. Brendan? Do you deny that you are King Maksim's rightful heir?"

He stared at her. He pushed a hand through his hair and looked wildly around them. "I don't believe this," he said, shaking his head. "I *can't* believe it." He looked at the ceiling, then down again. His eyes appeared to be shifting color, going from light to dark to light to dark with his changing emotions.

He was truly distressed, and Hollis pressed her hands to her belly. It was never her desire to be the cause of someone's pain, and yet, here she was. "Am I wrong?" she asked quietly. "Tell me I am wrong and I will never mention it again, on my word. I will never speak to you again if you like. But tell me I am wrong."

"No, *I* am wrong," he said. "All these years, I've been so wrong."

She didn't know what he meant but considered it a denial.

"All right," she said, holding up her hands. "I understand."

"You are incredible," he said. "Outrageous. In all my life, no one has ever asked me such a thing. Not a single person. So tell me, Mrs. Honeycutt, how is that *you*, of all people, would be the one to do it?"

Hollis's breath caught. Had he just admitted to being King Maksim's son? The crown prince? The missing baby? Good God, she might faint. "Do you mean…?"

"What, you don't believe me now?" he asked with exasperation, and stalked away from her, falling into the chair in a cloud of defeat.

Hollis's breath lodged in her throat. She was right. She was *right*! She had somehow stumbled onto this without even looking! She had sussed it out all on her own, had found the path to the truth, and—*and…*

And she'd promised to keep his secret. She returned to her chair.

"I would hope that you understand that no one can know of this. *No* one."

"No one," she agreed. "Why didn't you deny it, Mr. Brendan? If no one must know, would it not be simpler to deny it?"

He laughed darkly. "And have you print something in your gazette? Draw more attention to me? You left me no choice."

"No, I—I didn't intend—"

He held up a hand to keep her from speaking. "It doesn't matter what you intended. It's done." He sighed and dragged his fingers through his hair, revealing that bit of white to her again, before his hair fell back into place. He noticed her studying him. "Do I have your word?"

"Yes. Of course," she said.

He looked skeptical.

"I give you my word, Mr. Brendan."

He gave her a curt nod. "I hope your butler spoke true. He said you would not betray me, and by all appearances, you've not betrayed him."

"I would *never*," she said breathlessly, with conviction. She still couldn't quite grasp that she'd stumbled onto his secret. She had so many questions but had to proceed carefully. She stood up and went to the sideboard, poured two snifters of brandy, and returned, handing one to him.

He took the glass and looked at the bronze liquid. "I've long believed I'd be discovered. But I never imagined it like this."

"Will you tell me?" Hollis asked.

Mr. Brendan sighed twice. He swirled the brandy in the snifter as he gauged her. She wondered if she looked trustworthy to him, or if he thought her a villainess now.

Mr. Brendan suddenly put the glass to his lips and tossed back the brandy. He coughed, put aside the snifter, and began. "I didn't know the truth of who I was until I was seventeen years old." He rubbed his face with his hands.

And then he told her.

CHAPTER FIFTEEN

*What a dilemma it must be for a certain diminutive
lady from a good Lake District home to have married the heir to a great Northumberland fortune and
discover she is in love with the younger brother. We
suspect the heir will find his brother a clergy position somewhere far, far away.*

*Ladies, a Christmas tree will brighten the decor of
every home. Colorful ribbons and paper ornaments
should be added to the tree. Some recommend that
candied breads and fruits be placed in the boughs to
give the scent of the season.*

         *—Honeycutt's Gazette of Fashion and
         Domesticity for Ladies*

IT WAS AMAZING to Marek how the words streamed out of
him. As if they'd been locked in his chest for a very long
time, dreaming of being set free, then escaped in a rush
the moment he opened the door. Every word that slipped
from his mouth felt heavy with the emotion of having carried his burden for so long.

It was also amazing to him, once the words were freed,
how much lighter his soul felt for having shared his extraordinary story. He had never allowed himself to do it
before this. Why hadn't he? He'd become close with the pas-
tor of his parish. Paul came round Sunday evenings from

time to time to have a glass of port and look in on Marek's spirit. They talked about worldly things, about spiritual things, about why Marek did not attend services at the small church. Marek had not been tempted to reveal his secret to a man he considered a friend. It had seemed like an impossibly heavy burden to put on him. It had seemed dangerous, too, like setting free a lion that would ravage you.

Neither had he shared it with the one woman he supposed he'd loved in his own way. He still wasn't certain what love was to him in this body with this unique view of the world. But he'd been fond of Mariska—more than fond, he believed. He'd contemplated telling her the truth about himself. And yet, there was something about Mariska, a facet to her that made him wonder if she was entirely trustworthy. He had a feeling that a secret like his would be too great for her to keep to herself and she would be compelled to share it, for love or money.

He couldn't say why he chose Mrs. Honeycutt, either. She was the only one who'd ever guessed the truth. She was the only who had ever looked at him closely enough to notice the things that she had about him. Even Mariska had never commented on the patch of white in his hair.

It was entirely possible that it was because of Donovan, too—that Mrs. Honeycutt had kept the man's secret, had even harbored him.

Maybe he was a fool, but the moment Marek started to speak it was too late—he could no longer contain the truth.

He told her he was raised by two people he thought were his aunt and uncle on the Tophian Sea in a remote part of Wesloria. From the time he could remember, he was told that his parents had died of cholera. Marek accepted this explanation, just as he accepted that he was deaf because of an accident—a bad fall and blow to his head when he was only two years old. "My childhood was idyllic," he said.

He told her about his life growing up on the sea, of the days spent on a fishing boat with his uncle, bringing in the catch. Of the tutoring his aunt insisted upon, the wide range of subjects in which he was educated, her determination that he learn several languages. It was odd, he admitted, that a common lad in a common house was tutored in this way…but he didn't question it. His aunt and uncle wanted the best for him. If he'd known at the time a substantial portion of the income his uncle brought in went to his education, he'd have given it little thought.

He told her he never aspired to anything more than to captain a fishing vessel, like his uncle. "My dreams, my hopes were all rather ordinary. I was happy," he said. "I enjoyed my life. I never had reason to believe it should be anything other than what it was…until I was seventeen years old."

That was when his aunt had become gravely ill. She was dying of a cancer. Days before she succumbed to it, she called him to her deathbed and told him something that changed his life forever.

"That's when she told you who you were?" Mrs. Honeycutt asked, wide-eyed.

He nodded. "She was not my aunt. She'd been my nursemaid at the palace."

"Your *nursemaid* kidnapped you?" she asked, clearly stunned.

"She was part of it," he said.

The woman he had always believed to be the sister of his poor mother was no relation to his mother or to him. The mother his aunt had described never existed. "I should have realized this," Marek admitted. "Neither my aunt nor uncle had the same coloring as I do," he said. They were both very pale, whereas his skin color was tawnier. His aunt—nursemaid—confessed to him that he was the first-born son of the King of Wesloria, presumed kidnapped and dead. She confirmed the history that Marek knew through his studies—the king assumed the throne at a young age after the death of his father. He was green, untried, and there was a lot of strife in the country. Rumors abounded that members of the king's family—cousins, uncles, what have you—and other disruptive factions wanted to invade Alucia. But Maksim's father had been an advocate of peace, and the young king vowed to continue on that path.

"It was the half brother of the Alucian king who was the most troublesome. He was—and still is—hungry for power and wealth, and will stop at nothing to get it. If he can't depose the Alucian king and claim the throne, then he'll depose the Weslorian king and claim it."

"Felix Oberon," Mrs. Honeycutt said.

Marek paused. "You know of him?"

"Yes. He tried to kidnap my brother-in-law."

Of course. Marek had read about the attempt to kidnap the crown prince of Alucia when he was in London two years ago. The plot had gone wrong, resulting in the death of the prince's private secretary. "Felix Oberon has been a threat to King Maksim and his family since the king ascended the throne. I believe I am living proof of it," Marek said darkly. "His claim to the Weslorian throne is through a distant relation. There are many in Wesloria who would welcome his rule—he is ruthless and sides with the capitalists who seek wealth. Many have long suspected him of attempting to usurp my father's throne. If he were successful, he would undoubtedly wage his war against his half brother in Alucia and unite the two countries under his iron fist."

Mrs. Honeycutt released a breath when he said it. "That's my sister," she said softly. "She is an Alucian now. A Chartier. So is my dearest friend, Caroline."

Marek nodded. "He would stop at nothing to depose them, I think. All those years ago, everyone assumed he had something to do with my kidnapping. And I have read that many thought he had murdered me, because a king with no heirs is a very weak king."

"Was it him?" Mrs. Honeycutt asked. "Can you be sure?"

"No. All I have is the confession of a woman on her deathbed."

"Did she know him?" Mrs. Honeycutt asked.

"I don't think so," Marek said. "She had an illicit affair with one of the traitors. She was to make sure I was accessible to them. A window left open, a door unlocked. I suppose her conscience got the best of her—on the night the kidnapping was to happen, she couldn't bear it. She took me, and with the help of a friend, she fled with me. There was a fight in the fields outside of St. Edys, and she became separated from her friend. I gather it was a wild chase, and her friend did not survive. Somehow, she escaped to her brother's house. She made the trek across Wesloria with a child who was not her own, and there, on the rocky shores of the Tophian Sea, she hid for the rest of her life."

"Oh my," Mrs. Honeycutt said, her voice full of wonder.

Marek looked down at his hands. His aunt, his nursemaid...had been a good mother to him. He'd loved her unquestionably, up until the moment she told him the lie that he'd lived all his life. He still hadn't worked out his true feelings for the woman who had raised him as her own, all the while holding such a devastating secret from him.

He still hadn't worked out how he felt about himself. He was the son of a king. He should have grown up in palaces and been shown the world. But then again, he'd liked his life on the sea. Now, he supposed he didn't quite know where he belonged.

Mrs. Honeycutt spoke, but the words were watery, and he looked up.

"I said, I'm so sorry," she repeated. "How extraordinary it all is. I can't imagine how hard it must have been for you to learn the truth."

"Quite," he said darkly. "I didn't believe her at first. It was too outrageous to be believed. My uncle was very little help—he swore he only knew what she'd told him of the affair."

"And you're certain it's true?"

He smiled ruefully. "Aren't you? You have noticed the bit of white in my hair, and the color of my eyes, my partial deafness owing to a fever I had before I was abducted. The missing prince was made partially deaf by the fever—that's been well-documented."

"I suppose there are those who could argue those are coincidences."

It was an astute observation, and Marek had thought the same himself. "*Je*. But there is one more thing." He reached into his collar, and with some effort, pulled out a thin gold chain. Dangling from the chain was a small gold cross. It was encrusted with pearls and inscribed on the back was his given name, Villu Marek Ivanosen, and the date of his christening. He removed it from his neck and handed it to Mrs. Honeycutt.

She examined the cross. "It's beautiful." She turned it over and squinted at the inscription. "How did you get the name Brendan?" she asked.

"An old fishing village that had once flourished near

my home but had disappeared in years past. It was called Brendan."

Mrs. Honeycutt handed the cross back to Marek and watched him slip it over his head, then tuck it under his collar. "I believe it's true. I believe you are the missing prince."

As shocked as he'd been by Aunt Laurlena's confession, at the same time, things had almost immediately started to make sense. Like the tutoring, which he'd received well past the point other young men were being educated, and especially young men who were destined to become fishermen. Or his Uncle Dondan's obsession with keeping him safe when they were on the sea. Even their lack of society, in hindsight, seemed strange. They lived remotely, and no one ever came to call except the tutor.

And there was something else, too, something that had been with him since as far back as his earliest memories—a feeling as if he didn't belong to that sea or that land, at least not really. A feeling that he was, in some ways, a stranger in his own life, and had somehow stumbled into it.

"Why have you never told anyone? Claimed your place in your family? At least sought their help?" Mrs. Honeycutt asked.

That was a difficult question to answer. He'd certainly thought about it. When he'd reached his majority, he'd left his uncle and the sea and had gone to St. Edys in search of answers. Or at least some meaning. He didn't have a plan for anything other than catching a glimpse of his real family and the father he never knew, of the half sisters who had come after Marek's mother had died, it was said, with a broken heart. After a few years his father had remarried, a woman from the Mediterranean who was younger than the king and capable of giving him the heir he needed after his son had been lost.

Marek would see the royal family during formal parades or when his father gave the occasional speech. But it wasn't until he came here, to London, and had sat across the room from His Majesty as the ministers discussed the various planks of a peace plan, that Marek had actually seen him up close. It had been jarring to see the white forelock of hair and the amber eyes so eerily similar to his own.

"I didn't see a way to do it that wouldn't be terribly disruptive to the family," Marek said simply. And that was the truth of it. He'd come to St. Edys to see them, with fantasies of appearing before his father. *I am your lost son.* But the more he'd seen the royal family, the more he understood it would not be a joyous reconciliation. His claim would be suspected and challenged. He could even be jailed for pretending to be the long-lost heir to the throne. And then there was the question of Princess Justine and Princess Amelia, trained from the cradle to take their place in this world. The Weslorian parliament had amended the succession documents so that Princess Justine would become queen by virtue of being the oldest living child born to the monarch. Would Marek take that from her? Would he plunge the country into deeper turmoil when they were working hard to bring peace and stability to the region?

After a time in St. Edys, Marek had sought employment and found it in the Office of Trade and Commerce. His job was to take reports from various industries and compile written summaries for the minister of trade. It wasn't long before he began to offer recommendations for remediation of trade issues. He wrote reports on what the figures meant below the surface. After a few years, he'd become the right-hand man of the minister of trade.

Two years ago, Lord Dromio had been named the minister. He'd confessed to Marek that he'd never been entirely comfortable with the notion of economics, which he proved every day. He'd come to rely on Marek's opinion quite a lot and had insisted he come to London with him.

"All this time, you've been watching the king from afar?" Mrs. Honeycutt asked.

"I have. My work is in the study of economics. It is the closest I come to him."

"But what of you, Mr. Brendan? What sort of life do you have there?"

"A simple one." He told her a little about the work he did on his small farm, with his two milk cows, a few sheep, two dogs, and some chickens. He hired a lad from the closest village to tend things while he rode into St. Edys every day, without fail, no matter the weather. At the end of his day, Marek would stop by an inn that sat at the crossroads of two main arteries for a pint. The proprietor, Mr. Karetzo, was friendly with Marek. The man had heard everything there was to hear in and around St. Edys and liked to tell it. Once he had the news from Mr. Karetzo, he went home to tend his animals and sit before the hearth.

Marek's life was solitary, with one foot in the world he'd grown up in, and one foot in the knowledge that he belonged to a world that had been stolen from him. It was a simple existence. He remained a loner, fearing discovery, fearing accusations and reprisals. He had no real proof of what he thought to be true, and the only person who could vouch for what he said was his uncle. But Uncle Dondan had been nowhere near St. Edys the night he was abducted. Moreover, to mention his uncle's name would be to turn the jackals that surrounded the royal family on a poor lamb.

So Marek had kept his secret buried deep within him, and there he thought the secret would remain all his life.

Until tonight.

"But you haven't kept your distance entirely," Mrs. Honeycutt said. "Something has led you to suspect a coup or trouble afoot."

"Je," he said. Over the last several months, he'd begun to notice some anomalies in the work that came across his desk, disturbing patterns that went against the stated policy of the Weslorian trade. "In the course of my work, I've seen things that don't make sense. Exports that are never exported. Grain left to rot. Imports that never arrived or were waylaid en route. The Weslorian economy has always been weaker than our neighbors, but we've made some strides in recent years. We've begun coal production, and we are importing technologies that will help the effort to industrialize. So these…events," he said, trying to think of the right word, "have made some powerful capitalists unhappy. They say the king and his parliament are making poor trade decisions that are flittering away the gains we've made."

Mrs. Honeycutt smiled wryly. "Is not the same said of every government by every capitalist?"

He was mildly surprised that she would know of things like that. It didn't keep with what he thought he knew about privileged British women. "In this case, it feels true."

"Do you believe your father is ruining the economy of your country?"

"No," Marek said instantly. He'd read everything King Maksim had ever said about trade and prosperity. The king wanted change. He wanted a modern society. "But I think it is being made to look like he has. He's given speeches stating the goals he has for the country. But some of his ministers are doing the opposite and makes it appear as if the king and his prime minister are making bad decisions."

"Really?" she asked skeptically. "But how?"

Marek thought about how to frame this vague feeling he had. "Today," he said, finding his example, "Lord Dromio, our minister of trade, gave away a majority share of the coal mines in the Astasian region. He said the king had specifically told him to offer the coal mines for a bigger share in the grain trade. None of that makes sense. Weslorian grain is superior to Alucian grain and we've always had a bigger share of the export market. Furthermore, I was in the room in St. Edys when our country's trade postures were decided before coming here. Nothing of the sort was said. That coal is critical to our nation's wealth, as I expressed to his lordship today. I've made several recommendations grounded in fact, which he has ignored in the course of these negotiations. He says he follows the desires of the king, as if His Majesty has changed his mind since arriving in London. The Alucians take advantage of our weak position, and the British are caught in the middle and try to appease everyone." He glanced away, mulling it over again. This was more than he'd said to anyone in weeks. "And the king looks ill to me. His pallor is...unhealthy."

She frowned. "Is he ill?"

"I don't know. But I can't but help suspect the worst."

"What do you think is the cause of his illness? A cancer?"

"Poison."

Mrs. Honeycutt gasped. "No! *Here?* In London? But he's a guest at St. James Palace! How is it possible?"

It probably wasn't possible, and now that Marek had voiced his fears, it sounded quite wild. "You must think I'm mad. Only a madman would suspect such things. I hardly know the king and I've seen him only in crowded rooms. How could I possibly know?"

She didn't try and convince him that he did.

A silence stretched between them for several moments. "May I ask…what was it like?" Mrs. Honeycutt asked.

"What?"

"When you saw him up close. What was it like?"

It was an experience unlike any other. He'd desperately wanted his father to recognize him, but at the same time, he'd desperately hoped he would not. He was ashamed for the king to see the ordinary man he was. No longer a crown prince and king in waiting. A simple man with some sheep and goats and chickens and cows, and superior knowledge of trade mechanics.

He'd wanted to study his father's face, to see his features. He'd wanted to examine his hands, to hear the stories of his youth. He'd wanted his father to be robust and strong, like him, but instead, he'd found a slight man with a sickly pallor. "It was…*outré,*" he said, unable to think of an English word that described how bizarre and extraordinary it was to see him on a throne, surrounded by men that were bigger and more robust than him. "This sounds mad. *I* sound mad."

"Not to me," she said firmly. "Tell me, Mr. Brendan, given your suspicions, what do you really make of the four soldiers?"

Marek shook his head. "I don't believe it. I don't think there were any soldiers on that ship, or any ship. The king and his family arrived with sufficient guard."

"But what if it is true?" she pressed. "Why would they be here? There *is* sufficient guard around the king now, both British and Weslorian—I've seen them myself. What reason would there be to send four soldiers to London via a Scottish merchant ship?"

Marek considered the question. He got up and walked to the window, staring out at what had become a very dark night. What if it was true? What if she was right, and there was something odious afoot? If something were to happen to the king here, what would it mean? Queen Victoria would call in her best physicians to help to save the king. His family would be taken to safety. The ministers would gather around the king. Where did four soldiers fit into that scenario?

Mrs. Honeycutt came to her feet and joined him at the window, peering into the night. She touched his hand so he'd turn his head to her. "I think I know what we have to do."

"We?"

"Yes, we. We must find if there are indeed four soldiers, and if so, who has sent them, and for what purpose." She smiled.

Marek had a feeling that her smile would haunt him long after he'd departed London. "Ah, I see. It ought to be as easy as looking for the four horsemen of the apocalypse."

Her smile broadened, and she shrugged. "'When the hurly-burly's done,'" she said cheerfully.

"'When the battle's lost and won.'" Marek's gaze went to her mouth.

She made a sound of delight. "You beguile me with your knowledge of Shakespeare! None of my acquaintances have the patience for it."

She beguiled him, too, and not because of Shakespearean quotes tossed into conversation—he'd learned to speak English reading Shakespeare and other English works.

"I know what to do, Mr. Brendan, but you have to trust me."

Whom had he ever trusted since his seventeenth year? No one but himself. He'd relied on no one else, had learned to forge a single path, had kept his solitary place between two worlds. And now, this woman, this beautiful woman, who'd appeared from seemingly nowhere, was giving him the smallest hope that he *could* trust. He impulsively reached up and touched her cheek with his knuckles. "I have no choice but to trust you, Mrs. Honeycutt."

Her smile deepened and those lovely eyes shone at him. "My name is Hollis."

Hollis. A strong name for a daring woman. "All right, you have me. What do you suggest we do?"

"Find them."

He admired her spunk, but he was dubious of her sleuthing abilities. "And how, pray tell, do you suggest we do that?"

She didn't answer; she suddenly turned toward the door. Once again, Marek hadn't heard anyone enter, but the older woman was standing three feet in the room.

"How is he?" Mrs. Honeycutt asked.

"Sleeping, madam," she said. "I gave him a good dose of the laudanum. He's a bit battered, but nothing too serious by the look of it. He'll be right as rain, I suspect."

"I'll be up shortly to look in on him," Mrs. Honeycutt said.

The woman nodded and went out.

"I'll leave you to your patient." Marek was surprisingly reluctant to go, but he sensed she wanted to go to Donovan.

In the entry, he took his hat and put his hand on the door handle. He paused. "You never said how."

"How to find them? I have an excellent idea."

"I'm afraid to ask."

"I think we need a tree gathering."

"A what?"

She laughed. She put her hand on his arm, and he felt the heat of her touch through his coat. "To gather round a Christmas tree. That's the safest way to speak to Lord Douglas without drawing attention. He owns the Scottish ship, apparently. Unfortunately, we had a bit of a tiff the last time I saw him, and I suppose I'll need to apologize. Which is why I can't simply call on him. He's a bit notorious, too, and such a call would be noticed all over town." She gave his arm a light squeeze and let go. "Leave it all to me."

This was utter madness. "I can't leave it all to you."

"Then leave at least this to me."

He ought to say no before this went too far. He imagined that after a good night's sleep, he'd be kicking himself for having said anything at all. But at present, he couldn't bring himself to say anything that might deny him the opportunity to see her again. He took her hand in his, brought it to his lips, and kissed her knuckles, lingering a moment too long, letting the scents of soap and rosewater fill him. Her skin was smooth against his lips. He thought of all her skin, and what he imagined would be the softness of her inner thighs, and her abdomen… He lifted his head and opened his mouth to tell her that he couldn't leave this to her, but what came out of his mouth was, "My given name is Marek."

CHAPTER SIXTEEN

Lady Dammer of Belgravia was delivered a healthy baby girl last Saturday. The child has, at the time of her birth, a dowry estimated to rival that of the children of the queen. The long line for her tiny hand may commence.

At a private supper this week, it is reported that the King of Wesloria was taken ill and rushed from the room by his ministers. As he appeared the following afternoon at a tea, we may all be hopeful that his health has returned to him, although many noted the shadows under his eyes. Perhaps the stress of brokering a peace agreement that has resulted in a severe disadvantage to his country has taken its toll on the monarch.

౨—Honeycutt's Gazette of Fashion and
Domesticity for Ladies

HOLLIS FELT MORE alive than she had in a very long time. She bounded up the steps to Donovan's room, found him sleeping deeply, and pressed a kiss to his forehead. In his sleep, he frowned.

She retreated to her master suite and glanced around the room. She was holding herself, she realized, as her arms were wrapped around her body in a hug. Of course she was! She'd pulled Marek Brendan's extraordinary secret from him and was holding it in herself.

She wanted to help him. Poor man—what a burden he'd carried all these years! She guessed, giving what she knew about Weslorian history, that he was thirty-one or thirty-two years old now. Which meant he'd been keeping this secret for about half of his life, and with no one to talk to. She couldn't imagine how hard that must have been for him.

No wonder he was such a mysterious man—a darkly handsome, mysterious man who had suddenly appeared in her life from half a world away.

She was captivated by him.

THE NEXT MORNING, Hollis brought tea to Donovan's room. He was sitting up, dressed in trousers and a shirt. His face was red from the exertion and the pain it had caused him.

"You should stay in bed."

"I'm fine," he said, wincing.

She sat down on a chair beside his bed. "What happened?"

"Hollis…you know our agreement."

"Our agreement is that I won't ask, but I agreed before you were beaten."

He slowly gained his feet, testing his weight and taking a few wooden steps. "The authorities, or ruffians—I don't know who they were—were waiting outside of a particular establishment."

He meant a molly-house, where men of all feathers flocked together. Percy had told her about them once, and it didn't take much imagination to know that the reason Percy knew of them was because of Donovan. "Were they waiting for you?"

He laughed, and it caused him to suck in a sharp breath. "Not for me, love, but anyone. Lying in wait, looking for a fight. They might have left me for dead, too, but a gent who holds a seat in the Commons was unfortunate enough to exit the establishment after me. They went chasing after him. My friends helped me home." He smiled ruefully. "I'd not have brought it to your door if it were up to me. But I wasn't thinking properly."

"You must always come here, Donovan. But…is it necessary to go to such places?"

He sighed. "If it were possible to change my nature, I would have done so a long time ago. It's not easy to be what society abhors. But I can't change it and I won't fight it. You know that."

They'd had this conversation once before, shortly after Percy had died. He'd told her then that he'd not apologize for who he was or hide it from her. Hollis had been so grief-stricken that the thought of losing him had been more than she could bear. She'd never regretted it, but she did worry for him. And for herself, honestly. There were many in Mayfair who would make a pariah of her if they knew Donovan's true nature. It was odd to her—they would titter and laugh over the idea that she was sleeping with her butler without much regard for the morality of it. She was a young widow, after all. But that her butler desired other men was something she knew many would never forgive. She knew this crowd well—two years ago, a man was hanged for the crime of buggery. "Donovan, I—"

"Where are you off to?" he asked, cutting off what more she would say about last night. He was not going to tell her more than he had.

She suppressed a sigh of exasperation. "To call on Beck."

"At this time of the morning?" Donovan looped his neckcloth around his collar. "He won't have had his breakfast."

"Then I'll join him as he dines. He complained I haven't gone round to see him, so I thought I might."

Donovan looked dubious. "Hmm… Has it anything to do with Mr. Brendan's call last night?"

Hollis unthinkingly sat up straighter. "Of course not. Beck was very clear that he was displeased I never called. That's all." She'd learned this trick of diversion from Percy. He'd once complained that a man he often did business with never answered a question directly, but answered another one that hadn't been asked, and before he knew it, they were talking about something else entirely.

But Donovan was not easily put off the scent. He looked her in the eye. "Did you learn anything from Mr. Brendan?"

Hollis hesitated only briefly before shaking her head. Oh, but she hated to lie to Donovan, but she'd given her word to a man last night who had kept something to himself for half his life. He trusted her.

"You're certain?" Donovan asked skeptically.

"I don't think a team of horses could drag anything out of that man." *That* was not a lie, at least. But Hollis thought it best to be on her way before she found herself talked into a corner she could not talk herself out of. She stood up, walked to Donovan, and pressed her palm against his cheek. "Please be careful. I'd be utterly lost without you."

He gave her a wry smile and wrapped his hand around her wrist. "You would not be lost without me, Hollis. You would miss me, I would hope, but you'd be perfectly fine."

"That's what you think. I can't do without you."

"I think you do very well without me all the time." He pulled down her hand and laced his fingers with hers. "Should you not prepare for the possibility of it? One day you will want someone or something more than this."

"For heaven's sake." She yanked her hand free of his. "Why would you say such a thing?"

"Because it's true." Donovan turned back to the mirror to tie his neckcloth.

Hollis turned away from him before he could see the wild fear in her eyes. Do without Donovan? That was impossible. Whom would she talk to? Who would tell her the truth? Who would be there when the nights were the longest and coldest and loneliest? "I really must go. I don't want to miss Beck."

"Good day, madam," Donovan said.

She walked to his door and glanced back. "Take care," she said softly. She didn't wait for him to assure her he would when they both knew he wouldn't change a thing.

She was determined that her ebullient mood return to her on the brisk walk to Beck's house. She had a purpose, an important task, and it mattered to someone other than her. By the time she reached Beck's doorstep, she was smiling again.

Garrett, the longtime butler at the Hawke home, gave Hollis the barest ghost of a smile when he opened the door. "Mrs. Honeycutt, how do you do?"

"Very well, Garrett, thank you! Is Hawke in? His sister perhaps?"

"Both are in residence. Won't you come in," he said, and stepped aside.

"Mrs. Honeycutt!"

That was Beck's deep bellow from down the hall. He'd just come down the stairs in his dressing gown. Hollis handed her hat and cloak to Garrett, and hurried forward. "Beck!" she cried, and upon reaching him, threw her arms around him in a hug.

"What in blazes?" he demanded before kissing her cheek. "You can't just go about hugging people, Hollis. What are you doing here? I've become quite accustomed to having breakfast at my leisure now that you've all gone off and are not eating all the food before I have a bite."

Hollis linked her arm through his and pulled him toward the dining room. "You admonished me for not calling, so I have come to call." She let go of Beck once they entered the dining room and went straight to the sideboard. She was famished, she realized, and accepted a plate from the footman.

"Coffee, Brockman. And for the lady."

Hollis filled her plate with food and set it down on the table.

"Do make yourself at home," Beck drawled, watching her. Another footman entered and began to fill a plate for him.

"This looks divine," Hollis said appreciatively. She cut a piece of bacon and put it in her mouth, closing her eyes at the delicious taste of it.

"Save some for the prince and his bride," Beck said, and picked up a toast point.

"Where is Caro? Still abed?"

"I most certainly am not." Caroline sailed into the dining room, her golden hair down her back, her silk dressing gown flowing behind her. She took one look at Hollis and frowned. "What are you doing here so early? Has something happened? Is it the judge?"

"It's nearly eleven o'clock, Caro. Why are you still in bed?"

"Oh, but we were out quite late last night," she said, and with a loud yawn, fell into a chair beside her brother, curling up on it.

"Really? Where were you?" Hollis asked curiously as she buttered her toast.

"A supper party at the, ah..." Caroline abruptly sat up.

Hollis looked up from her toast.

"I forgot," Caroline said with a wince. "We weren't to tell you."

"Ah, so you were with Eliza," Hollis said with a shrug. "I've told her a thousand times if I've told her once that I don't expect to be invited to everything in the course of her visit. I understand, she's a duchess, and you are a... What are you again?"

Caroline clucked her tongue.

"The point is that I know how these royal things are played," Hollis said, gesturing with her knife. Indeed, she understood it all too well—she was no one of any import, no one but the poor sister of a royal duchess. All right, it did sting a little that she wasn't allowed to blithely follow her big sister as she'd done all their lives. But she did understand.

"You were missed terribly, Hollis," Caroline said.

"Mmm." Hollis smiled dubiously at her friend. "I am certain you scarcely had a moment to think about me."

"You're right," Caroline agreed. "But I've brought you the most amazing news to share with you. *Douglas* was there—"

"What?" Hollis exclaimed, surprised. "Where?"

"Montford's house," Beck said, reaching for the morning paper.

"Robert Ladley!" Hollis exclaimed. Now she was offended—Lord Montford had been Beck's friend for many, many years and Hollis knew him well. "I'm not to be included in *his* invitations?"

"Not my fault, darling," Beck said casually. "It's his father who wants to hobnob with all the foreign royals."

"Douglas isn't a foreign royal."

"But he will be a duke," Beck said with a shrug. "And a powerful one at that."

"There is more, Hollis," Caroline said eagerly. "The Weslorian king had to be helped from the supper table when he became ill."

Hollis's belly dipped at that news. She put down the knife. "Ill?"

Caroline nodded vigorously as she took a toast point from the caddy. "Just after the soup, he complained of feeling poorly, and he did indeed look terrible."

"Did he faint?"

"Very nearly. One of his ministers noticed him flagging and helped him from the room."

Good Lord, Mr. Brendan suspected something or someone was making him ill.

"The queen and her daughters, however, stayed behind and finished the meal. What do you think about *that*?" she asked, pointing the toast at Hollis.

"It all sounds very distressing," Hollis said. "His wife didn't tend him?"

"She did *not*. I daresay the crown princess scarcely noticed, either, because Douglas held her completely in thrall."

"No!" Hollis cried again as the footman returned with coffee.

"Please, the two of you, no shouting," Beck complained. "I've not had even a swig of coffee yet." The footman put coffee before Hollis, then quickly moved around the table to serve Beck.

"He must be seven, eight years her senior, isn't he?" Caroline mused. "How old is the princess?"

"She is seventeen, and he is two years younger than me, which makes him a twenty-six-year-old bounder," Hollis said darkly.

Beck laughed.

"You should have seen him, smiling and holding her gaze," Caroline said. "Do you suppose he finds himself a bit short on funds and intends to help himself to the dowry of a princess?"

"Well *you're* awfully cynical, darling," Beck said from behind his paper. "Douglas has got a behavior problem, not a funds problem. He'll make a bloody fortune with his merchant ship, and the family estate takes up half of Scotland."

"Perhaps we ought to invite him to the tree party," Hollis said. "It would be a considerate gesture, seeing as how he and I shouted at each other the last time we met."

Beck lowered his paper and looked at her.

"Why is this the first I'm hearing of it?" Caroline asked. "What tree party?"

"I know I will not like the answer, but I'll ask the question all the same. What *is* a tree party?" Beck added. "And what cause would you have to shout at Douglas?"

"We shouted at each other about his roving hands," Hollis said. "I told him firmly to keep them off my person, and he said I had a vivid imagination as everyone knew from the gazette, and that apparently I dreamed he had touched my person but that was impossible, as he was a gentleman. But he very plainly did." She turned her head to one of the footmen. "Is there someone about who might poach an egg or two, please?"

"Oh, me, too," Caroline said.

"Yes, go on, both of you, eat through my stores." Beck turned the page of his paper. "You haven't answered my question, Mrs. Honeycutt. What is a tree party?"

"A party to celebrate the arrival and trimming of a Christmas tree," Hollis said. "It's a very fashionable thing to do. Everyone is doing it. I mean to invite Douglas along with everyone else. I will apologize for calling him a beast."

"*You're* hosting a party?" Caroline asked. "What will you do with that dreadful dining room?"

"Oh, I can't do a thing with that," Hollis conceded. "That's why I thought we might do it here? We could invite family, of course, and acquaintances, including those we've not seen in a very long time. No more than three dozen souls."

Beck's paper came down onto the table with a slap and he fixed her with stare. "What the devil are you talking about?"

"Where is the tree?" Caroline asked, confused.

"We'll have to fetch one."

"A tree. In my house," Beck repeated.

"A *Christmas* tree," Hollis corrected him. "Decorated in the spirit of the season. They're all over Mayfair salons now that the queen's done it."

"The queen's done *what*?" Beck demanded, growing exasperated.

"But we are days and days from Christmas," Caroline pointed out. "The queen's tree doesn't make an appearance until a day or so before Christmas."

"We'll start a new tradition."

"No," Beck said, sounding very firm about it. "If you want to drag in a tree and dance like a pagan around it, you may do that in your own home, Hollis."

"But your house is much grander than mine, dearest. Everyone would be much more comfortable here."

"Don't try to *dear* me into it. My home *is* grander than yours with that blasted gazette everywhere, and grander it shall remain. I despise gatherings where all people do is stand around and speak of inane things and eat my food and drink my spirits. I will not mar my house or my spirit with a *tree*."

"I think it sounds delightful," Caroline said. "Eliza and Bas will come, and the baby, of course. Cecelia would love a tree! Your father and Poppy, naturally."

"Everyone!" Hollis said. "Even Beck."

"Most of all, Beck," Caroline said, smiling at her brother. "It wouldn't be a festive occasion without him."

"I said no," Beck said.

"Who else would we invite?" Caroline asked Hollis, ignoring him.

"The peacock?" Hollis asked.

"The peacock!" Caroline burst into laughter. "Katherine Maugham! You do recall that she desperately wanted an offer from my husband, do you not?"

"And Eliza's. In fairness, she has long wanted an offer from anyone with a purse, Caro—you know that. This would be the opportunity to do something entirely in vogue and show her you're still very much a part of this society."

"But Caro is *not* a part of this society, and frankly, I doubt any of our old friends would come if this bit of scandal does the inviting," Beck said, jerking his thumb in the direction of his sister. "Do you think anyone has forgotten what happened last year? If there is any inviting to be done, I will do it."

"Thank you!" Caroline cried, and leaned over the arm of her chair in an attempt to hug him, which Beck easily rebuffed. "Hollis and I will give you the guest list."

"I didn't say I would *do* this."

"I think you did," Hollis said lightly. She sipped her coffee then forked another piece of bacon.

"That was the last bite of bacon," Beck huffed.

"Still, Hollis, I'm a bit suspicious," Caroline said. "Why

do you want to have this party here? And *why* do you want to invite Douglas? Whatever you said to him, I'm certain he deserved. There is no need to make amends. Unless..." Caroline suddenly surged forward. "Unless you've come to *esteem* him?"

"No!" Hollis cried, horrified by the thought. That would be akin to esteeming someone's pesky little brother.

"Remember who you are speaking to, Caro," Beck said as he made a serious study of a new plate of bacon the footman slid onto the table before them. "I would wager her desire to have it here has to do with that blasted gazette. Doesn't everything? I sometimes imagine what my dear friend Percy would make of all his hard work being turned into a women's gazette."

"He'd be terribly proud," Hollis said. He would have been...after an acceptable period of being scandalized. But when he saw the figures of copies sold and the money brought in, he would be quite proud. He'd been a man who'd responded well to facts. "Shall we say Saturday?" she asked lightly as a footman placed a poached egg before her.

"Say Saturday for what?" Beck asked, examining the bacon.

"The tree party."

"Saturday?" Beck exclaimed, looking up from the plate. "Where am I supposed to get a tree, for God's sake? And I suppose I am to feed these friends and acquaintances, as well, is that it? Does no one have a care for my purse or my wishes in this?"

Caroline very gently laid her hand on her brother's arm. "No."

Beck yanked his arm away from her.

"Hollis will send Donovan to chop down a tree, won't

you, darling? It should be tall, shouldn't it? How tall was the queen's?"

"Donovan is a bit under the weather. I rather thought the Earl of Iddesleigh might have one sent from his estate."

"Mrs. Honeycutt, you simply cannot glide into my home and demand a party and a tree from my estate. I'll have to send a messenger and ask for the tree. What do you think? It will mysteriously appear?"

"Then we'll have one brought up from Bibury," Caroline said. "Leopold will be delighted! It is a custom in Alucia, you know, to decorate a tree for Christmas. Oh! I just thought of someone else we ought to invite."

"Who?" Hollis asked.

"Lady Blythe Northcote!"

Beck dropped his fork to his plate with such a clatter that everyone in the room jumped a foot. "I swear by all that is holy, if you mention her name one more time, I will stuff a napkin into your mouth."

"I've forgotten this name, Caro. Will you remind me? Is she Beck's beau?"

Beck pointed a finger at Hollis. "Don't you dare play at this game, Hollis. If you want your tree so badly, you will think twice."

"If I promise never to mention her again, will you concede?" Hollis asked.

"Done," he said.

Caroline and Hollis exchanged a look. Blythe Northcote would certainly be invited.

"Shall we set the invitation for eight o'clock?" Hollis asked.

"Yes," Caroline agreed. "And don't mind Beck. He's happy to be the host—it will give him something to complain about."

"Ha. As if I were lacking in topics for complaint with the likes of you two in my house again," he muttered.

"Beck will get a proper tree, and we'll do the rest," Caroline said brightly.

"What the devil is a *proper* tree?" Beck asked, annoyed.

Hollis saw her opportunity and stood. "I'll leave you to explain it Caro," she said. "Come pay a call to Pappa today, and we'll make the list. He'll be thrilled to see you."

"Naturally. Everyone is always thrilled to see me," Caroline said without the slightest hint of humility. But that's why Hollis loved Caroline—she was a confident woman who said what she was thinking.

Hollis came around the table and hugged Caroline, who kissed her cheek, then Beck, who complained again that she was "hugging willy-nilly with no thought to the comfort of it," but squeezed the arm she'd put around his chest.

For all his bluster, Beck loved her like a sister and he always—*always*—did what they desired.

CHAPTER SEVENTEEN

*Lord Iddesleigh of Mayfair, notorious for his pro-
claimed dislike of soirees whilst being one of the
most frequent guests to all, is planning a gathering
to install a decorative Christmas tree in his drawing room. It is reported that the tree comes from the
Thetford Forest in Norfolk, with a girth so large that
his lordship has been forced to move his beloved arm-
chair from directly before the hearth to make room.*

*While the size of the tree and the space it requires
precludes sending invitations to all of Iddesleigh's
friends, it has been whispered that one eligible lady
from the north will be in attendance, having received
permission to remain in London for the winter from
her formidable father.*

*Ladies, the most attractive of Christmas wreaths
is made of holly, yew and evergreen, decorated with
pine cones and, if you can spare it, apples.*

                *—Honeycutt's Gazette of Fashion and
                           Domesticity for Ladies*

THEY WERE HURTLING toward a peace agreement with terms
that were hardly favorable to Wesloria, terms that seemed so
lopsided, in fact, that one British official had urged Dromio
and Van to reconsider the allowances they'd granted in the
name of the king. The Alucian ministers and the Duke of

Tannymeade had stared in disbelief when Van agreed that Wesloria would reduce its grain exports by a very small percentage, designed to allow Alucia access to markets.

"Is that the king's wish?" Osiander demanded after the meeting. "It flies in the face of everything we agreed before leaving St. Edys."

"His perception of the negotiations has changed his opinion," Dromio said with a shrug.

"Then perhaps he ought to attend the negotiations himself," Osiander snapped.

"Calm yourself, sir," Lord Van said coolly. "The king has an ague. He can hardly negotiate from a position of strength if he is sniffling and sipping hot tea."

"What is happening is unacceptable," Osiander said.

Dromio smirked. "Then perhaps you'd like to question his thinking yourself?"

Osiander hesitated, no doubt wondering how, exactly, he would question the king. And in that brief hesitation, Dromio had slid into another conversation, complaining about the British arbiter.

It was baffling to Marek and, apparently, to Osiander, who continued to look as if he was quietly fuming.

When the day concluded, the Weslorian delegation returned to the Green Hotel, and there, in the entrance, Osiander confronted Dromio and Van again in their native tongue. "I want to attend the next meeting with the king. You have given away everything Wesloria holds dear and gained nothing in return."

Dromio's brow drifted upward with surprise. "You think peace with Alucia is nothing?"

Lord Van sighed and shifted his gaze to a window. "He is the king, Osiander. It's his decision to make, and this is his wish."

"How do we know his wishes other than to hear the two of you tell them?" Osiander asked. "Why doesn't he meet with all of us?"

"We told you," Dromio said curtly. "He is ill. As always."

Osiander's gaze narrowed. "All I have ever heard the king say is that he wants Wesloria to prosper. Wesloria will not prosper with no industry or trade."

Van sighed. "You exaggerate."

"Do I?"

Van's eyebrows sank and his expression turned dark. "It would be a mistake to overstate your feelings, my lord."

Osiander looked at the two ministers, and then his gaze flicked over Marek. Marek reflexively leaned back. He didn't want Osiander to think he had anything to do with what was happening at the negotiating table.

Osiander returned his gaze to Dromio and Van, but when he did, he put his back to Marek. He said something to the ministers in Weslorian that was lost to Marek. Whatever he said caused Dromio to look a little ill himself.

Osiander strode away, and Van and Dromio exchanged a look. "I'll speak to him," Van said, and went after him.

Marek and Dromio remained. "He's right," Marek said. "We are giving away too much. The coal, the concessions on grain."

Dromio slowly turned to look at Marek. "Who the hell are you to tell me where you think your king has erred?"

He was a trusted advisor, someone who understood the economy of Wesloria better than Dromio could ever hope to understand it. "I am your advisor, my lord, as I understand the economic forces better than most."

"That may be, but you don't understand the political landscape, Brendan. You don't understand how the king holds power. I do. Stay out of it."

He moved as if he meant to walk away. Marek spoke before he could. "What ails him?"

Dromio's brows dipped lower. He didn't like being questioned.

"You said he was ill," Marek said.

"How can I know? If you ask me, he drinks too much."

That was a lie. The king did not drink to excess—Marek would stake his reputation on it. He'd never heard it said, and he'd not observed it in these last few weeks. If anything, the king seemed very careful of drinking at all. Like father, like son, he thought idly.

"He ought to have a physician brought in to have a look, but he refuses," Dromio added.

"Refuses?" Why would the king refuse the advice of a physician? If he was ill in a foreign land, he'd want to be made better. He'd want a medical opinion...unless he didn't trust either the physician or the person bringing the physician to him.

"You don't understand that His Majesty is a—"

"Beg your pardon, sirs."

A footman stood off to the right of Marek, holding a silver tray with a calling card on it.

"What now?" Dromio said, annoyed. He gestured at Marek to take the card.

Mrs. Hollis Honeycutt, Publisher
*Honeycutt's Gazette of Fashion and
Domesticity for Ladies*

Marek felt the color drain from his face.

"Who is it?" Dromio asked impatiently.

"No one. Someone from one of the local papers," Marek said, and shoved the card into his pocket.

"Take care of it," Dromio said with a flick of his wrist. He glanced irritably at the footman, who was still standing there. "What do you want?"

"The lady is waiting," the footman said.

"The lady," Dromio repeated.

"Where?" Marek asked.

"Just outside, sir," the footman said.

"*Je*, thank you."

"The *lady*," Dromio drawled, and a salacious smile lit his face as the footman retreated. He waggled his eyebrows in Marek's direction. "You surprise me, Brendan," he said. "I'd begun to think you were a eunuch."

"I beg your pardon?"

"Go on, then. Far be it from me to stand in the way of a man's pleasure. But don't let anyone see you. You shouldn't bring your paramour here."

The color flooded back into Marek's face. Dromio was stupid and vulgar, two things he despised in a man. "She is not—"

It didn't matter what he said—Dromio was already walking away. Marek bit back a sigh of exasperation and turned toward the entrance of the hotel.

Mrs. Honeycutt was standing on the walk with a female companion, and the two of them looked terribly out of place among all the gentlemen coming and going from the hotel. She was bundled up in a heavy wool cloak, a scarf around her neck and a bonnet firmly on her head. But he could see that her cheeks and the tip of her nose were pink with cold. And as he walked toward them, he could see the happy smile that bloomed on her face. Remarkably, Marek could feel that light power through him.

"Mr. Brendan!"

"Good afternoon, Mrs. Honeycutt."

She beamed at him for a moment, then remembered her companion. "May I introduce my friend, Miss Poppy Dumont?"

Miss Poppy Dumont, a thin woman with auburn hair and a hat worn slightly askew, was smiling with great anticipation, almost as if she expected him to do something remarkable, like turn a cartwheel. She dipped a curtsy.

"Miss Dumont."

Miss Dumont unabashedly looked him up and down. "How do you *do*, Mr. Brendan?"

An enthusiastic greeting, he noted. "I am well, thank you. Mrs. Honeycutt, is something wrong?"

"Not at all!" she said cheerfully. "Things are positively right, isn't that so, Poppy?"

"Right as they can be, I'd wager!"

"I've come because I have something for you," Mrs. Honeycutt said. She withdrew her hand from a fur muff. She was clutching an envelope, and by the bend of it, she must have been clutching it for a time. He could see his name plainly written across the front of it.

"What is this?"

She laughed. "Read it!" She handed it to him.

Marek opened the envelope and withdrew a single card of heavy stock. It was an invitation to a gathering at the home of the Earl of Iddesleigh. The invitation proclaimed there would be a tree to be trimmed in the spirit of Christmas, and Christmas pudding would be served. Lord, she'd done it. He looked up; she beamed at him. "You can come, can't you?"

Could he? "What of Lord Dromio?"

"Ah. The problem, you see, is that the tree will take up some room, so we must limit the number of guests."

That presented a bit of a problem, as Marek didn't quite

know how to absent himself from Dromio's company for a Saturday evening without a proper explanation. He didn't know how to accept an invitation to a gathering like this if Dromio wasn't also invited.

"I'm sure you'll think of something," she said, as if reading his mind.

Marek looked at the invitation again.

"Lord Douglas has already sent word that he'd be delighted to attend."

"Did he!" Miss Dumont said, her eyebrows lifting with surprise. "I hadn't heard he'd come down to London."

"Do none of you read my gazette?" Mrs. Honeycutt asked her.

"I've read every one of them," Miss Dumont insisted. "*Most* of them," she amended. "And those I haven't read are stacked by my bed."

Mrs. Honeycutt shook her head and turned her attention to Marek. "*Anyway*, Mr. Brendan, will you come?"

"I—I fear it may prove difficult." He had to think of a way to dodge Lord Dromio.

"Splendid," Mrs. Honeycutt said, her bright smile returning. She refused to take no for an answer. "Shall I send a carriage for you? Donovan can fetch you, if you like."

"Thank you, but I'll make my own way."

"How very independent of you," she said cheerfully. "Well then, Mr. Brendan, our duty has been dispatched. Until we see you again, then."

He felt exposed on this sidewalk, as if he shouldn't be here. He'd spent so much of his life in the shadows that he imagined the whole of the Weslorian delegation behind him, sniggering. On the slim chance that they were, he slipped the invitation into his coat pocket. He bowed.

Miss Dumont pulled her cloak about her. "A pleasure to make your acquaintance, sir."

"The pleasure is mine."

The women started to walk away, but Mrs. Honeycutt glanced back once more. She said something to her friend, then skipped back to him. "Don't fret, Mr. Brendan. You look as if you are fretting."

"I'm not...fretting?" He wasn't certain what that meant. "No, Mrs. Honeycutt. I'm thinking."

"Think of it as the same sort of party you'd attend in Wesloria. Perhaps even the same tree."

Forget that he would never attend a party like this in Wesloria. He asked curiously, "How could it possibly be the same tree?"

"It will be a lively evening. Doesn't that sound enticing? And there will be some very important people attending." She glanced around them, as if she suddenly worried someone might see her or hear her. "Someone who will be very helpful to our cause."

"It's our cause now, is it?" he asked, smiling a little.

"Have you not realized it by now?" She laughed, and the sound of it whispered through him on butterfly wings. How could he resist her or her invitation? He was curious about the soldiers. If they indeed existed, and she had the person to verify that they did, he wanted to find them. But, mostly, he wanted to bask in her warmth a little more.

"Oh, I can see by your smile that you will come," she said. "And may I say, I couldn't be happier. Good day, Mr. Brendan!"

He said nothing as she hastened down the street, looping her arm into Miss Dumont's when she reached her.

At the corner, both of them paused and looked back at

him, then carried on with what looked like, from where he was standing, a burst of laughter.

A funny feeling came over him. A premonition that one day he'd watch her skip away from him forever…and that astonishingly, he would be very unhappy when she did.

CHAPTER EIGHTEEN

*The invitation to the Iddesleigh Christmas gathering
became the most coveted in all of London when it was
announced that the Duke and Duchess of Tannymeade
would be in attendance and would graciously escort
the Weslorian princesses. King Maksim and Queen
Agnes remained behind at St. James Palace, where
it is noted that the king's health has not improved.*

A gift of la fée verte *from the Marquess of Douglas and three sprigs of mistletoe from Lady Chartier made the evening much more festive than anyone
might have anticipated. Neighbors reported that carolers threw open the windows and the sound of their
voices could be heard blocks away. Three hackneys
were called the following morning to cart some of the
most ardent revelers away.*

*Ladies, one must take care not to mix an incalculable
amount of spirits into one's Christmas punch. Please do
follow the recipes provided in this publication.*

*ᧁ—Honeycutt's Gazette of Fashion and
Domesticity for Ladies*

ELIZA INSISTED THAT Hollis come to St. James Palace to prepare for the party. "It's like it used to be, isn't it?" Eliza
asked breathlessly as she moved around her suite of rooms.

"Yes!" Hollis said brightly. "Well, mostly." As in, not at

all, really, other than they were together. But everything else was different. They were in a palace, for one. Eliza had three women to dress her while Hollis had none. And Cecelia was on the floor at her mother's feet, gnawing on a little wooden horse.

Really, nothing was as it used to be for any of them.

Nevertheless, Hollis was happy to allow Eliza to think so, and she gratefully accepted the assistance of one of Eliza's attendants to help her fasten her gown after complaining how tight it was.

"Yes, well, you've bubbled up, haven't you?"

"I have not 'bubbled up,'" Hollis said missishly. When in fact, she had bubbled up. But she didn't need anyone to point it out to her, and least of all her beautiful, glowing sister.

"Your gown is beautiful," Eliza said, standing back to admire it.

"Thank you," Hollis said. She looked down at the gorgeous, cream-colored silk gown. The skirt was sewn with tiny crystal beads that caught the light when she moved. This was the dress Caroline had worn at her debut many years ago, but had been refashioned for modern times and Hollis's "bubbled up" body. It had a row of sprightly bows cascading down the front. The bodice was awfully low—Hollis had pointed this out to Caroline, and Caroline had sniffed indignantly and said that was the fashion of the day, which clearly it was not. If Hollis bent over, half of her would pop out of the gown altogether.

Hollis glanced up from her study of the gown and saw that one of the attendants was fitting a tiara on Eliza's head. "You mean to wear that to Beck's?" she asked with great amusement. Beck would groan and roll his eyes. Eliza was destined to be queen, but in Beck's eyes, they were all still pesky children.

"Of course," Eliza said, and leaned forward to look at herself in the mirror. "It will vex him terribly." She winked at Hollis in the mirror. "I'm still Eliza, darling, and he's still Beck, and I shall delight in tormenting him."

Hollis laughed. "Thank God for it. I've had to do it all on my own in the last year."

Eliza smiled, and Hollis thought she'd never looked lovelier. In fact, every time she saw her sister, she was astonished all over again how love could transform a person so completely. Eliza had always been lovely, but she'd never glowed with happiness. Hollis wondered if she'd looked so content with Percy? She could scarcely remember that version of herself any longer.

Cecelia babbled at her mother's feet, drawing all their attention. She was holding up the horse, slick with baby drool.

"Oh, my little rose, listen to you," Eliza cooed to her. "You'll be a great orator, like your grandfather." She looked at Hollis. "Speaking of Pappa, I went round to see him yesterday. He was packing for a trip to the country."

"Was he?"

"He didn't tell you?" Eliza asked. "The entire household is set to tour Sussex this weekend, and they are all very keen to go. I think even Jack and John will make the trip."

"Is it a holiday?" Hollis said, confused as to what that meant. She sat next to Eliza.

"A holiday—no, darling. Pappa means to move to the country, remember?"

"Yes, but *now*?" How had Hollis missed this? Why hadn't anyone told her? No one had ever said it would be soon.

"I don't know when, exactly, but Poppy said Ben's been having a look around when he's able."

So that was that? They were *all* going to leave her? Just desert her here in the middle of London? Surely Poppy would stay behind. Hollis couldn't imagine her in the country.

"I went round to see him earlier this week. Caro tried to convince Poppy she ought not to go, that her prospects for marriage were better in London than in the country."

"What? Caro was with you?"

Eliza looked curiously at Hollis. "Well… Leopold and Bas were meeting with the ministers, and she wanted a diversion."

Hollis wondered why they hadn't come to fetch her, or at least sent a messenger. This wasn't at all as it used to be.

Eliza suddenly laughed. "Caro even advised Poppy that she ought to marry Donovan and keep it in the family."

Hollis snorted. "Caro should keep to her own patch of country and leave well enough alone."

Eliza leaned down to pick up the baby. "You mustn't worry, darling. Poppy proclaimed Donovan much too handsome to marry…but he's not too handsome for you, is he?"

Hollis nearly choked. "Don't be absurd, Eliza."

"Why is it absurd? Everyone suspects what I think must be true. Isn't it true?" she asked with a sly look at her sister.

Hollis could feel the heat rising in her. "*No*, it's not true. That's not…" She paused to draw a breath to steady herself. These were the moments she hated keeping Donovan's secret. "Donovan esteems someone else."

"Oh." Eliza sounded very surprised. "I didn't… But that… I mean, he seems so devoted to you."

"He is devoted to me because he is a very loyal man. But he's not in love with me."

Eliza buried her face in Cecelia's neck, kissed her cheek, and put her on the floor again. "Then he's a fool."

That was the sort of remark any loyal sister would make. But she almost sounded disappointed. "Oh *dear*," Hollis murmured.

"What?" Eliza asked.

"I've become the relation everyone frets about, haven't I?"

Eliza laughed, but it sounded forced.

"I have! I say too much, I involve myself in things that everyone says I ought not to do, I've bubbled up—"

"Hollis!"

"But I never thought you'd fret about me, Eliza."

Eliza's face fell. "I didn't say any of those things—you did. All I want is for you to be happy. Is that so wrong?"

"No, of course not. But being married for the sake of marriage would not make me happy. Donovan would not make me happy."

"Then what would make you happy?" Eliza asked.

A very good question. She wanted a happy marriage. But she didn't think she wanted this. She wanted something simpler. Unfortunately, when one was sister to a future queen, *simple* wasn't a ready alternative, unless one was prepared to enter a convent. "Not Donovan," Hollis said.

Eliza pursed her lips. "Then I'll never say another word about it. But what *would* make you happy? You've been widowed more than four years now—you can't live with Percy's ghost forever."

Hollis laughed at that. "But I do live with it. He's everywhere in my house."

Eliza turned back to the mirror. "Then perhaps you ought to remove him or yourself from your house. I loved Percy like a brother, but I don't think even he would want you to spin like a top."

Hollis wasn't spinning like a top...or maybe she was.

Lately she'd felt as if she'd been spinning around and looking for anything to give her meaning.

But there was more to it. For the first time since his death, there *was* someone other than Percy to think about. Someone who was in many ways just as ill-suited to her as Donovan, and just as unattainable. But when she thought of his amber eyes, or the way he spoke English so perfectly with a deep accent, or how she tingled when he intently watched her lips when she spoke, or how she imagined his broad hands on her body... Well, maybe she was spinning a little.

When they'd finished dressing, Eliza studied Hollis. "I have just the thing." She went into an adjoining dressing room and returned with a necklace. An enormous ruby was attached to a larger, circular gold chain. Below the ruby, three smaller rubies, separated by diamonds, dangled.

"It's beautiful," Hollis said as Eliza put it on her.

"The biggest stone was a brooch originally," Eliza said. "King Tomsin presented it to Queen Verity two hundred years ago as an anniversary gift. He pinned it on her himself. The very next day she was found dead in her bed. Some say it was poisoned."

"Eliza!"

"Pay that no heed," Eliza said breezily "What else could they say about it? It's not poisoned now, I assure you—I wore it myself to a state supper."

Hollis admired the ruby in the mirror. "I've never in my life seen anything so beautiful."

"You must have it," Eliza said. "A gift from me. It suits you with your black hair and that dress. You look voluptuous."

"Ladies?"

The duke had entered, all smiles. Cecelia began to gurgle at the sight of him, and he scooped her up, holding her high overhead, and cooed to her.

"Look, darling, I gave this necklace to Hollis. Doesn't it suit her?"

"Gave it? I can't keep this," Hollis insisted.

"*Je*, it suits her very well. And, of course, you must keep it, Hollis. My wife has made it so." He winked at her. "You are both ravishing, if I may say," he added, although he was looking at Eliza, his gaze raking over her. "It's time we departed. Darling, you and Hollis will follow me in another coach so that I might escort the Weslorian princesses." He kissed his daughter and handed her to Eliza with a warning that she not be late.

They said their goodbyes to Cecelia, and after Eliza reviewed a very long list of instructions for the baby's nursemaid, the sisters made their way to the grand home on Upper Brook Street.

A LIGHT SNOW had begun to fall when Hollis and Eliza arrived at Beck's. Because of the crush of carriages, they were made to wait a full quarter of an hour before they could enter. Light blazed through the windows facing the street, and they could make out the flickering flames of dozens of candles on what looked like an enormous tree.

Beck's home was palatial, but Hollis guessed there had to be at least one hundred and fifty people present when they finally squeezed inside. There were far more souls than the two or three dozen people she'd suggested. The tree Beck had brought from the country was so large that it covered half the salon and was so tall that the tinsel star someone had set atop it scraped the ceiling.

"Where on earth did you get that tree?" Hollis asked as Beck came forward to greet them.

"How would I know?" Beck said with a shrug as he leaned down and kissed Hollis's cheek. "I put Garrett on the task."

Hollis hugged Beck tightly to her. "Thank you for this."

"Oof," Beck grunted when she squeezed him. "For heaven's sake, Mrs. Honeycutt, there you go again, hugging as you please." He pushed away from her grasp and tapped the tip of her nose with his knuckle.

"Your tree is too big, Beck! I had in mind something smaller. Something you could actually gather around. You can hardly see your guests around that thing."

"I don't need to see my guests as I've seen them all before. And if I may, I should like to point out that I was quite right about having a tree in one's home—it's ridiculous and fills the room and there are needles everywhere. By the by, you are a vision of loveliness this evening. The color suits you."

"Doesn't it?" Eliza said, as Hollis murmured a thank-you. Eliza leaned forward to accept Beck's kiss. "Where is my husband?"

"Taking the princesses around to introduce them to all the dastardly gentlemen in the room. They are the star attraction this evening, and after I've gone to all the trouble to bring in that monstrous tree."

"I'm so glad they've come. Can you imagine how dry and tedious the—" Hollis suddenly lost her train of thought because she happened to catch sight of Mr. Shoreham wandering by. She gasped. "Is that—" She jerked her gaze back to Beck.

He smiled like a cat.

"Did you— Beck, did you invite *Shoreham*?" she asked in a whispered shout. "That wretched excuse of a man?"

Beck's smile broadened. "Quite obviously. He's here, isn't he?"

"But *why*?"

"Why not?" Beck asked gaily. "I like the man. He's an interesting chap." He leaned down to whisper in Hollis's ear. "If you plan a party in a man's house without his consent, you best be prepared for the man to invite a few people of his own choosing." He patted her cheek. "Enjoy your evening, darling."

And with that, he wandered off to greet his guests.

"Oh dear, there is Lord Russell," Eliza muttered, nodding in the direction of the prime minister. "Sebastian doesn't care for him. He says he won't stop talking once he starts, and it's impossible to get a single word in. I'm going to intercept him before he reaches Bas," Eliza said, and before Hollis could respond, she was hurrying away, expertly dodging those who tried to stop her and speak to her.

And just like that, Hollis found herself standing alone in a crowded room. She found herself standing alone quite a lot these days. She looked around for the other person who stood so often alone, but Mr. Brendan was nowhere to be seen. Surely he was coming. *Surely* he would have sent word if he'd declined the invitation. Or would he have sent it to Beck, from whom the invitation had been issued? She should have sent Donovan to ask, but Donovan had been gone more than usual.

She rose up on her toes, trying to see over the heads of all the guests, scouring the corners of the room where Mr. Brendan was prone to lurk. She didn't see anyone resembling that brusque man, but it was difficult to see much, really, as the crush of bodies was thick. So she began to make her way through the crowd to have a better look.

He *would* come, wouldn't he? She would be crushed if he didn't.

Beck had done quite a lot of decorating, she quickly discovered. For a man who claimed to hate gatherings like this, he'd certainly outdone himself. He'd put boughs of evergreen and holly on the mantel, which was decorated with candied apples, and anchored with candelabra that had been wrapped in gold bows. The light from those candles flickered against the painting of Caroline and Beck's father, and the old man appeared to be laughing.

And the tree! It was lit with at least two dozen beeswax candles, the flames dancing perilously close to the needles of the tree, and wax dripping onto the boughs below. She would never say it aloud to anyone, and certainly not Beck, but that looked awfully dangerous. Some enterprising person had strung garlands made of raisins and nuts and berries around the tree, and she made a note to ask him who, exactly, had done that, as it bore the careful touch of a woman.

Interspersed throughout the tree were more gold ribbons tied in bows and candied oranges. She couldn't imagine where he'd found so many candied oranges! Had he gone to the markets? Some had been scooped out and fashioned into little baskets to hold sweetmeats.

As she neared the archway that led into the entry, she heard a commotion near the staircase and looked up just as Caroline and Leopold made their way down. Caroline's hand skimmed over the stair railing that had been roped with garlands of evergreen and holly. She was wearing a dark green gown made of silk and satin, and descended like a queen. And her husband, who insisted Hollis address him as Leo, looked very happy and regal beside her. He held Caroline's hand, with the other behind his back, and beamed as they descended into the madness of the tree party. At the entrance to the large salon, Caroline and Leo looked up. Hollis followed their gaze and saw the mistletoe hanging there. Leo kissed Caroline beneath it. Oh, Beck, that cheeky man. He'd made every possible accommodation for a Christmas party, and she couldn't wait to commend him for a job well done.

A footman appeared before her and bowed. "Merry Christmas, Mrs. Honeycutt."

"Merry Christmas, Donnelly!"

He held out his tray. "Christmas punch, compliments of Lord Douglas."

"Really?" She took a glass from the tray. "Did he ask you to bring it to me directly? Is it poisoned, do you suppose?"

"I suppose not, madam. Several guests have tried it and are upright."

"Thank you, Donnelly." She took a crystal glass from his tray, and as he moved away, she sipped…and coughed with the burn of it. "What in blazes?" She peered down into her glass at the pale green liquid, wondering what abominable and deadly spirit had been poured into the punch. She began to feel as if someone was staring at her. *Marek Brendan.* She turned around, all smiles…but no one was looking at her.

Quite the contrary.

People were talking and laughing, and no one noticed her at all.

Well, except Leopold, who startled her when she turned back around and his head was just there.

"Hollis, you look dazzling," he said, and took her hand and brought it to his lips.

"Thank you!"

"I made it for her!" Caroline appeared, too, and smiled

with delight as she examined Hollis's gown. "Is it not beautiful? Is *she* not beautiful?"

"She is," Leopold agreed.

"Well, now I'm blushing," Hollis said. "*Thank* you. I rather worried I'd not be able to wear it at all since you refused to let it out so much as a smidge."

"Wear a corset," Caroline said. She couldn't help herself—she reached up and straightened one of the bows, and then Hollis's necklace. "What do you think, Leopold? I think I've outdone myself this time," she said proudly. "I wish Percy were here to see you."

The mention of her late husband thudded into Hollis's gut, landing in a vat of guilt. She hadn't thought of Percy much at all in recent weeks, other than she was ready to let him slide into fond memories.

"What are you drinking?" Leopold asked, looking at the glass Hollis held.

"Beck's footman said it was Christmas punch, a gift from Lord Douglas. It's horrid, really."

"Horrid? Or Potent?" Leopold asked, and put his hand under her glass and lifted it to his nose. He sniffed. "Potent," he said. "This punch, darling, is generously mixed with *la fée verte*, a French spirit that will give you nightmares if you drink too much of it. It is also called absinthe."

Hollis and Caroline gaped at him. Leopold shrugged. "I spent a bit of time in Paris."

"Well, now I must try it," Caroline said. "I would never recommend drinking from any bowl that Douglas has brought, but then again, he was always very diverting, wasn't he?"

"*Too* diverting," Hollis reminded her. "He locked you in a closet."

"We were children," she said with a wave of her hand.

"You were seventeen."

"Nevertheless, I shall try his drink in the spirit of the season," Caroline said, and turned to her husband. "Shall we?"

"Please," he said, and nodded in the direction of the sideboard, where very large silver serving bowls held the absinthe punch, and two footmen worked furiously to fill cups.

"Perfect," Caroline said. "I had hoped for an opportunity to walk through this great throng so that everyone who still speaks ill of me can see my dress." She winked at Hollis.

Leopold held out his arm to Hollis, but she didn't move.

"What? Aren't you coming?"

"I mean to find Lord Douglas and extend my warm wishes." Which meant, more precisely, that she was going to look for Mr. Brendan.

"Ha!" Caroline countered. She paused and put a hand on Hollis's arm. "Don't start a war with Mr. Shoreham. I told Beck he was asking for trouble with that one."

"What do you mean? I would never!" Hollis said. Not without a bit of punch in her, she wouldn't.

She moved on, sipping the drink. She found the second sip wasn't as foul as the first, and the third even better. It traced a lovely warm path down the middle of her body.

She reached the end of the room in her search for Mr. Brendan and took a spot by a wall near the tree. She was leaning to her right, trying to see farther behind the thing, when someone tapped on her shoulder. She spun around, certain she'd find Mr. Brendan.

It was not Mr. Brendan.

Alas, it was William Douglas, the Marquess of Douglas, the future Duke of Hamilton. It never failed to amuse her that the boy she'd known would be a duke, as he seemed more suited for roughhousing in the stables. He still had that look about him in spite of his tailored clothing—he was tall, with dark hair carelessly tousled, and a sparkle in his gray eyes that made one think he was a scoundrel.

"Fortune smiles on me today, does it no', for here is the lovely Hollis Tricklebank, as I live and breathe."

"Honeycutt," she corrected him, the rotten bounder. He knew very well her last name.

"Ah, yes, you married the fellow, didn't you?"

"You attended my wedding, sir."

"Did I?" He feigned confusion. "I can't possibly remember all the weddings I've attended. There have been many in the last few years."

"And yet, never your own wedding. Your mother must be beside herself with grief."

He chuckled. "As I have explained to my dear, grieving mother, how can I possibly marry when the best ones have been taken? You appear to have mourned your husband very well indeed, madam," he said, his gaze deliberately skimming over her.

"Oh, William. You were a rake when you were a lad and still are." She laughed.

"*Och*, Mrs. Honeycutt—I am not a *rake,* but an ardent admirer of feminine beauty."

"That's what all rakes say." She lifted the glass with the pale green drink. She'd had a few more sips of it and she was beginning to feel a little fuzzy. "Did you really contribute this to the evening?"

"I did, indeed. I've just come from France with it."

"Did you bring it on your big new ship, Captain Douglas?"

"Aye, madam. I should like to invite you onboard. Allow me to spirit you away," he said with a flourish of his hand. "Would you like to see India?"

"I would. But I'd heard that you'd been ordered home after your purchase."

"Who, me?" He smiled again...but he was looking past her.

Hollis wanted to ask him about the soldiers. She wasn't quite certain how to bring it up and to tell him she knew they were aboard his ship. And she'd lost the moment—he had clearly lost interest in her, and she turned to see what had caught his eye. He was looking at Princess Justine. She was dressed in a beautiful blue gown with a long, embroidered train, a style popular in Alucia and Wesloria. "Look away, sir. She is only seventeen."

"And her sister?"

Hollis frowned. *"Fifteen."*

A lopsided grin turned up the corner of William's mouth.

"You're despicable!"

"You wound me, Hollis. I would never dream of defiling a princess...if she is unwilling. Let's go and make their acquaintance all the same."

"What's the matter? Have your coffers sprung a leak?"

"My coffers are fine, thank you, but it's not every evening one is presented with the opportunity to meet a princess. And before you say so, Eliza is hardly what I mean."

"Well, she *is* a princess. A duchess, even. And Caroline, too."

William laughed. "Caroline Hawke was destined to be a princess if she had to steal a crown and kick some poor miss off her toadstool. Come, Hollis Honeycutt. Let us meet a true princess." He put his hand on her elbow.

"You're so cynical."

"You're so right," he said jovially, and escorted her across the room, admonishing her not to spill her drink, as it was very expensive.

Hollis strained to see around him, looking for Mr. Brendan.

CHAPTER NINETEEN

Absinthe is a very pretty drink, but one should be cautious in serving it, as it may lead to some unbecoming behavior, particularly if there is a sprig of mistletoe nearby.

Ladies, if your husband refuses your counsel and takes to absinthe, this home remedy should ease his discomfort: Brew magnesia, peppermint water and sulfate of iron until it boils, then have him drink while hot. If you don't have the ingredients, it is also effective to have him drink a full glass of vinegar.

༈—Honeycutt's Gazette of Fashion and
Domesticity for Ladies

MAREK COULDN'T ESCAPE his duties as quickly as he would have liked, and by the time he arrived at the address on Upper Brook Street, everyone was well into their cups. Perhaps at the very bottom of their cups by the look of it, and the dreadfully loud sound that accompanied all that merrymaking. It was so overpowering he had to work to resist the urge to cover his good ear.

Damn Dromio. He was amused that Marek was going out for the evening and badgered him as to where. In order to escape him and his insidious questioning, Marek finally intimated, if only vaguely, that it had to do with a woman. "Damn me if I didn't guess it," Dromio had said with a slap to his knee. He didn't ask Marek more—men never questioned the idea of a woman, no matter who or where they were. But Dromio wanted to laugh about it. "You've dressed very well for a lightskirt," he said jovially, noting Marek's formal coat and embroidered waistcoat. In Wesloria, the more embroidered the waistcoat, the more formal the occasion. He'd brushed his hair, too, forcing it behind his ears. He didn't want to look unkempt. "You could do with a shave, lad. Ladies don't care for the stubble."

There was nothing Marek could do for his face—no matter how well he scraped a blade across his cheek, he could never get a shave as close as a barber.

"I won't keep you from your paramour," Dromio said, when he'd finished with his teasing. He was in front of a mirror himself, fixated with a curl near his temple. "We are dining with the king this evening, Van and I."

Not Osiander? Marek noted. "I thought the king was under the weather."

Dromio waved that off. "It's an excuse, Brendan. He's not one for public gatherings, you know. He'd rather spend every evening before his hearth with his wife. Unfortunately for the queen. She would prefer to dance, I think."

A week ago he'd been too ill to attend the negotiations. And now it was an act to keep from going into society?

"I mean to review some papers with him," Dromio added.

The explanation was entirely unnecessary and therefore, strange. It was a Saturday evening in London. They would not reconvene the peace negotiations again until Tuesday. If the king preferred a quiet evening, why not allow him to have it? And what could Dromio have to review with the king? "My lord?"

"You don't trust me, Brendan," he said, still studying

himself in the mirror. "But you should congratulate your-self, as I've learned quite a lot from you. I mean to speak to the king about the coal mines once more. The deal is not done yet, is it?"

He was referring to the last sticking point in the peace negotiations. Both Alucia and Wesloria wanted the rights to mine the coal in the Astasian region. Marek had pro-posed an equitable sharing, but as the week had gone along, Dromio and Van had agreed to a little more chipping away until there seemed hardly anything left for Wesloria.

Dromio clapped Marek on the shoulder. "Mind you don't do anything to embarrass the delegation," he said, and saun-tered away.

Embarrass the delegation? Marek shook his head and bit back the remark he would very much like to have made, which included the observation that he wasn't the ass in the room.

When he was certain Dromio had gone, he'd walked to Upper Brook Street. It was a greater distance than he'd thought, and he had a slight panic when he arrived—he'd forgotten his invitation. The panic, springing from nowhere, surprised him. He had come this evening to learn anything he could about the four soldiers. But the feeling of nerves he was experiencing had nothing to do with soldiers and everything to do with the idea of missing an opportunity to speak to Hollis Honeycutt again.

That's how he thought of her now—Hollis Honeycutt. The name of a mythical creature, as if she was too much woman for just one name and required both to convey the full measure of her.

When he presented himself at the door, the butler didn't ask for an invitation and merely pointed him in the direc-tion of the earl.

Marek went the other way. He'd never met Lord Id-desleigh and would require a proper introduction. He looked around the room for Hollis Honeycutt, his gaze moving over so many female faces that they all began to look alike to him. Pale-skinned and with ringlets framing their faces. None of them had the dark hair and piercing blue eyes he was searching for.

There was another impediment to his search, and that was the sheer size of the tree in the drawing room. It was enormous. Half the candles had already burned out—not that anyone seemed to notice or care. The room was crowded and hot, and he could hear what he thought was caroling coming from another part of the house, the watery undertones forming a familiar song in his head.

He spotted the Duke and Duchess of Tannymeade. They were smiling in a way Marek had never seen them smile, and it gave him a small jolt—that was joy, simply put. He envied the way they looked at each other and found their smiles for everyone else endearing and even a bit contagious.

The Alucians were here in force, he noticed, and very few Weslorians, with the notable exception of the two royal princesses. He was taken slightly aback at the sight of them—he'd never been this close to his half sisters. Justine was engaged in conversation with a British man. She was lively and pretty, and the man was clearly amused by her. The younger one, Amelia, seemed terribly ill at ease. She kept her gaze on the floor and fidgeted with the bracelet on her wrist. She only looked up when Lady Tannymeade stooped down to speak to her.

A footman suddenly blocked his view of his sisters and held up a tray with several crystal punch glasses. Marek took one from the tray and brought it to his nose. *Ah, absinthe punch.* Or, as they said in Wesloria, *Diablia en verte botillia*—the devil in the green bottle. He knew of no other drink that could make a man see things, but this drink certainly could.

No wonder the people packed into this house were having such a grand time.

He waited until the footman was gone, then put aside the drink and pressed on through the crowd, past boughs of holly, underneath sprigs of mistletoe, around embracing couples attempting to dance to the caroling in another room.

He couldn't see Hollis anywhere. He felt a bit conspicuous, as he didn't know a soul and sought a corner where he could stand a moment to get used to the throbbing in his head. He closed his eyes, took a few deep breaths, and tried not to let the deep, watery sound bother him. He didn't know how long he'd been standing there when he heard, in the constant, low-grade din that lived in his head, her voice.

He snapped himself straight and looked around him, but still couldn't see her. What he did see were the two sets of shoulders belonging to a pair of men on the other side of a thick cluster of garland portieres beside him.

He heard her voice again. Marek stepped toward the garlands. He could see her dark head over the shoulder of one of the men. His heart quickened like a besotted fool. He parted the portieres and stepped through so he could see her.

Good God, she was beautiful, a true vision in a glittering, cream-colored gown. Her hair looked even darker tonight, and the rubies at her throat drew his attention to the pale skin of her bosom. He could feel parts of him twitching like a cat's whiskers, waking up and taking notice.

She appeared to be making a point to the gentlemen. He guessed, knowing her—and he did know her a little, didn't he?—that the point she was making was either extremely important or extremely fantastical, given the way she used her arms to assist her. He cleared the last of the garlands and stepped through.

"This is precisely the sort of thing that's needed in the country," she said to one of the gentlemen. "But we are often overlooked because of antiquated thinking."

"Mrs. Honeycutt. You miss the point entirely," said the smaller of the two men. He was older, stately looking. "We don't discuss words, we discuss *language*. That you fail to understand the difference only solidifies my opinion that you are not equipped to be a member."

Hollis's lush mouth, painted scarlet red, formed a perfect *O* of surprise.

"Mrs. Honeycutt," Marek said before she could launch into a tirade, as she seemed poised to do.

She jerked toward the sound of his voice. She looked stunned, as if she was surprised to see him, and for a wretched moment, he thought he'd misunderstood and should not have come. But then she smiled so brightly that it felt a little like the warmth of spring sunshine on his face after a long winter. Her cheeks were flushed, and she gazed at him as if she'd just found a long-lost brother she'd desperately searched for. It was entirely possible that she did think that very thing, because he also realized she'd been enjoying the absinthe punch, judging by the near empty glass in her hand.

The two gentlemen looked at him warily.

"Mr. Brendan!" She startled them all by pulling Marek into a one-armed hug. "I am so *happy* you have come! May I introduce you to Mr. Shoreham," she said, planting her hand on the chest of one man and giving him a hard pat. "And Mr. Marks, both of them members of the Philological Society. Mr. Shoreham has just informed me I am not

equipped to be a member!" She said it in a manner that would suggest she was not harmed by this pronouncement, but he knew differently.

So did Mr. Shoreham, who made the unpardonable sin of rolling his eyes. And then he looked at Marek with such superiority and eagerness for Marek to disagree that Marek was tempted to punch him in the nose on principle.

"Mr. Shoreham believes that not everyone is suited for the study of languages," Hollis said.

"More accurately," Mr. Shoreham said, "we are engaged in the study of the structure and relationships of language, and not merely the language itself. Learning a language may be left to a tutor. Have you thought of engaging one, Mrs. Honeycutt?"

Hollis's eyes narrowed dangerously. "Do you know what else may be left to a tutor, Mr. Shoreham?" she asked, and remarkably, she appeared to be squaring off. "I'll tell you what. A—"

Marek moved before she did something like fling herself at the man's throat, and put himself between her and the two men. He said in Weslorian, "Pettiness and misogyny may also be left to a tutor, sir, but I think it better left to a fist in your face, as it is my impression that you are an ass. If you say another condescending word to my friend, I will shove my Weslorian foot so far up your arse I may very well launch you to the bloody moon."

Mr. Shoreham blinked. "I beg your pardon?"

"You should lend yourself to learning the structure of the Weslorian language," Marek said in English, and turned to Hollis. "Mrs. Honeycutt, may I have a word?"

"I would be *delighted*." She put her hand on an arm he had not yet offered, lifted her chin, and gave Mr. Shoreham a look he'd not soon forget as she stepped away with Marek.

He held aside the curtain of garland and handed her through, then joined her. He took her by the elbow and continued with her, escorting her out into the hall, where he had a half chance of hearing her.

In the hall, she threw her arm around him again. "Did you just save me, Mr. Brendan?"

"No, madam—you were doing perfectly well on your own. I merely added my opinion." He carefully set her back.

"What did you say to him?" Her eyes were shining and she looked entirely kissable.

"I said things that ought not to be repeated in the company of the fairer sex."

Hollis Honeycutt laughed with delight, dipping backward a little when she threw back her head. "*Thank* you! That man is insufferable." She suddenly grabbed his arm. "You *came*! What took you so long! I thought you weren't coming, and I don't mind confessing that I was truly devastated! Do you see how quickly we've become friends? I have *so* much to tell you."

She was talking so fast that he had to watch her lips move. But he had trouble concentrating on the words they formed because the idea of kissing her was now firmly entrenched in his thoughts.

"But first tell me, what do you think of the decorations?" She paused and slowly turned a circle, as if taking in the sights for the first time tonight.

"Lovely," he said.

"Have you *ever* seen such a tree?" she asked, leaning into him to view the tree.

He didn't move as he probably should have done. "Never. At least not in a house."

"You see? You're learning all sorts of new things in London."

"Yes, I am," he said softly. Things about himself, mostly. He had learned that he didn't want to live between worlds anymore. He wanted to live firmly in a world where there was a Hollis Honeycutt.

"Guess *what*?" she whispered. "Douglas is here!"

"Pardon?"

"Lord Douglas, with the sheep! I mean the *ship*." She gave a hearty laugh and shook her head.

Marek smiled. "How much of the absinthe have you had?"

"The what?"

He looked at her glass. So did she. "Oh. This is my second. Or third?" She looked up, frowned slightly, and then abruptly reached around him.

Marek turned to see what she was reaching for and watched her take a candied orange from a wreath on the wall. It had been carved into a little bucket. She plucked something from it, held it up, and said, "Sweetmeats!" She tossed the piece into her mouth.

Marek laughed.

"I'm ravenous," she said, and picked another piece. She offered it to him. "I am forever ravenous and I can't wait another moment for the promised Christmas pudding to appear. My own sister said I was bubbling up."

He had to guess at what that meant, but he felt quite adamantly that if she was indeed "bubbling up," she was doing it in all the right places.

She took a third sweetmeat from the little bowl and held it up to him. He shook his head. "You're very disciplined, aren't you?" she asked.

"In some things, I suppose."

"I'm disciplined, too, when I'm of a mind, but lately, I feel as if I'm always in search of something to occupy me.

Widowhood can be rather tedious, you know. One must look for ways to amuse oneself, even if that means losing a bit of discipline." She smiled, and popped the last candied bite into her mouth.

"You are a fascinating woman, Mrs. Honeycutt."

"Mr. Brendan, you flatter me! I think we are in many ways very much alike."

"I don't know… You're gregarious. I'm not. And I don't care for sweetmeats. You seem to enjoy them."

She laughed. "On the other hand, you're alone and so am I. You love Shakespeare and so do I. And you are curious. And…" She smiled and gestured to herself. "So am I."

"You are remarkable," he said quietly.

"And so are you, Mr. Brendan."

"Marek."

"Yes, right you are. Hollis."

Their gazes locked for a long moment, and it seemed as if the watery noise receded from his head, and the candles shimmered a little brighter, and the people—what people?—had all disappeared from view.

Hollis suddenly gasped. "I almost forgot! You must make Douglas's acquaintance!" She grabbed his hand and tugged him along, back into the crowded room. The sounds, the people—everything that had receded from him moments ago—came rushing back in force.

They didn't make it very far into the room when Hollis was accosted by the Duchess of Tannymeade. "Darling, where did you get off to? Caro forced Beck to speak to Lady Northcote, and it was *delicious*. She thanked him for inviting her to the party and he said he didn't, that it was his sister's doing, and *she* said, with a laugh, mind you, that the feeling was mutual as her father had forced her to come, but really, I think— Oh, I beg your pardon," the duchess said, looking at Marek.

"Eliza, this is Mr. Brendan. He's Weslorian!"

"Yes, I see," she said, nodding to the bit of green on his lapel. "How do you do, Mr. Brendan?"

"Very well, thank you." He bowed.

"Lady Tannymeade, you are wanted— Oh."

The duke had come to fetch his wife, and Hollis, still holding the crystal cup, said, "Your grace, this is my friend, Mr. Brendan!"

The duke looked at him, his gaze flicking to the bit of green on his collar. "How do you do," he said curiously. *"Wesloriat?"* he asked in Marek's native tongue.

"Je."

The duke continued in the Weslorian language, as it was very close to Alucian. "You're part of the Weslorian delegation. I remember you—you advise the trade minister."

"Je," Marek said. "Lord Dromio."

Tannymeade's gaze flicked to his wife, then back to Marek. "His lordship seems…" He paused, as if searching for a word.

Idiotic? Ridiculous? Lacking gravitas?

"Well, I don't know what he seems, really," he said, and looked away, as if trying to avoid the conversation he'd started. "Hollis, darling, you've had another glass? Mind you have a care—the absinthe will bedevil you."

Hollis giggled as if he'd meant that to be amusing.

"Oh, look, they are setting up to play Chairs," the duchess said. "You should play, Hollis!"

"Me?" Hollis laughed. "I'd rather—"

"What are you all doing here?" another man said, pushing into their circle.

"Beck, have you met Mr. Brendan? He's Weslorian." To Marek she said, "The Earl of Iddesleigh."

The man, who looked to be a few years older than Marek, had darkly golden hair. He gave Marek a once-over, and said, "How do you do. Come on then, the lot of you. We've another round of Chairs, and unless you want to sorely disappoint two princesses, one of whom had this bothersome idea, you will take your places."

Hollis looked at Marek. He was horrified by the thought—there wasn't enough drink in him for such buffoonery.

"You're Weslorian," the earl said. "Come on, then."

Damn it, but Hollis pushed her glass at the earl and grabbed Marek's hand as if they were children instead of adults. "It will be fun!"

"It won't, you may trust me."

"Are you always so serious?" She tugged Marek along behind her, and much to his horror, he couldn't seem to stop himself from allowing it. She kept looking back at him, always smiling, her eyes sparkling, and he felt a little like a lemming, headed for the edge of the cliff.

"But I've never played this game," he said when they reached the floor.

"How is that possible?" She pointed to the chairs and then said something he didn't quite understand. In fact, he didn't understand anything beyond that point. It was loud, and people were laughing and shouting. But he heard the dull thud of the music in his head and fell in line, walking around the line of chairs with everyone else. The chairs were lined up with every other facing the opposite direction. When the music suddenly stopped, everyone tried to take a seat. On the first go, he was lucky, and happened to be right in front of a chair. Two people were eliminated from the game when they were not able to find a seat before they were all occupied.

A footman came forward and removed a chair. Everyone stood, and when the music began, around they went again. On the second round, Marek beat a gentleman by a nose to a seat. The gentleman was sent out.

Round and round they went, the noise deafening in Marek's good ear and the laughter thrumming in his chest. That was something entirely new adding to the mix—it had been many years since he'd laughed so freely, many years since he'd felt the concussion of it in his chest. It made him feel good. It made him feel like a human.

Marek was bloody well laughing.

CHAPTER TWENTY

The gathering to celebrate the Christmas tree at the
home of Lord Iddesleigh still holds all of Mayfair
in thrall. It has been reported by several, including
this writer, that a future duke and a future queen en-
gaged in a game of Chairs that took such a competi-
tive turn the future duke inadvertently knocked the
future queen from the last empty seat. She vowed
revenge but was spirited away to her palatial abode
shortly before she could exact it, and he was sum-
marily banished to his house nearby.

King Maksim has recently been spotted in the park
of St. James, walking alone with a trail of guards
behind him, looking deep in thought. Is he thinking
he has given too much away? Several in the British
delegation believe he has. Coal is very important for
the development of Weslorian commerce, but he has
allowed it to slip through his fingers, according to
those with firsthand knowledge.

⌐—Honeycutt's Gazette of Fashion and
Domesticity for Ladies

THE GREEN PUNCH had altered Hollis's agility, and she
couldn't seem to take the turn at the end of the line of chairs
very nimbly. She went out in the fourth round, but not before Mr. Harmon, who had claimed the chair she sought,

very loudly and graciously invited her to sit on his lap. She politely declined with a very deep curtsy, and to the applause of everyone, she twirled out of the game. She stood back, short of breath from her laughter, her back against a doorframe, watching Marek as the game progressed.

He was quicker than she was and found a seat each time. He was enjoying himself, and the effect was quite charming. He was so very handsome when he smiled, and the sound of his laugh, a deep rich timbre, seemed to awaken every nerve in her. She was still feeling the euphoria of finding him in this crowd after she had convinced herself he wasn't coming. But here he was, playing Chairs, of all things.

His smile was devastating—it creased his cheeks and sparked in his eyes and her blood rushed so very hot. She found that rather interesting, as he was a different sort of man from any she'd ever known, with the exception of Donovan. He was not terribly refined and urbane, like Beck or the princes. There was something very masculine about Marek, even playing a silly game at a Christmas party.

The peacock went out in the next round, and she sashayed away, clearly miffed that the young Baron Crownhead didn't gallantly give her the seat.

Marek was the next to go out. He pushed through the crowd to where she stood, still grinning.

She straightened and smiled when he reached her. "I'm *shocked*, Mr. Brendan," she said, trying to sound serious.

"Why?" He touched a lock of her hair on her shoulder.

"Because you played the game!" She leaned forward. "*And* you enjoyed it. Don't deny it—you were laughing."

Marek braced one hand above her head against the doorframe. "Of course I enjoyed it. Who wouldn't enjoy such nonsense? I'm not an animal, madam. How shall I explain it?" He paused, squinting a little, as if thinking. "That game—'it is like a barber's chair that fits all buttocks. The pin-buttock, the quatch-buttock—'"

"'Any buttock!'" Hollis fairly shouted. He was quoting Shakespeare to her and her heart was doing leaps in her breast. "I could not have even dreamed of meeting anyone who knows as much of Shakespeare as I do."

He laughed. "Neither could I."

She couldn't have conjured a man like him, either. "Have I told you that you are very handsome, sir?" she asked dreamily.

His smile deepened. "You have not. I am certain I would have remembered such a compliment so freely given."

A cry went up from the crowd, and they turned to look. Beck had been eliminated and was arguing with Mr. Harmon. Hollis turned a smile to Marek—he was watching her. There was something in his expression that made her pulse leap.

She suddenly couldn't seem to look away from his mouth. "Are you enjoying the evening?"

He tilted his head to one side, and his gaze slowly moved down her body, stalling at her bodice before returning to her lips. "*Je.* Very much."

"Are you surprised?"

"More than I can say. Then again, everything that has happened to me since meeting you has surprised me."

She could feel the corners of her mouth curling up. "I will take that as a compliment and be pleased that I surprise new friends rather than bore them."

His eyes shifted down, to her bodice. "How would you ever bore anyone?"

"Another compliment," she murmured. She glanced up, to the mistletoe hanging over their heads. Marek looked up, too. Before he could discern what she was thinking, Hollis caught his lapels and pulled him forward as she rose up on her toes. "Happy Christmas," she said, and she kissed him. She boldly planted her lips on his, and she felt the shock of her impetuous behavior and the fullness of his lips reverberate all the way down to her toes. His lips were so soft, feather-pillow soft, and she could imagine very easily being lost in them.

Just as she'd abruptly kissed him, she abruptly let go. She laughed breathlessly and pointed up. "Mistletoe!" she exclaimed, as if he hadn't seen it. As if he would understand that the sprig would lead to such incautious emotion. Her heart was pounding, and her breath was short and she wanted to slip away with him, to someplace private.

"Je, du mugel," he said. But his words came out like a rumble, and in the next minute, his arm was around her waist, pulling her into his body and pressing against her. He kissed her back. But his kiss... *His* kiss was much more than hers. Whatever Hollis's intention had been, it was swallowed and forgotten and burned in the path of his response. She opened her mouth, felt his tongue slide in between her teeth. He cupped her face, his thumb stroking her cheek as his tongue tangled with hers. He kissed her with an erotic mix of demand and reverence, and while he did, her heart's rhythm turned frantic and she imagined opening her legs and him sliding hard and long into her, his hands on her breasts. She moved against him, arching into him, sliding her pelvis against his body. She felt guilty and exhilarated, excited and buzzy with anticipation. *This* is what she missed. She missed a man's touch, that feeling of being wholly desired. She missed abandoning herself to pleasure. She missed lying against someone, feeling the heat of their skin.

The kiss was wild and unacceptable and dangerous. With everyone's backs to them, it was full of craving and an even strangely potent desire to be caught, to go as far as he would take her.

And then, suddenly, Marek ended his kiss. He let go of her waist and drew back from her. His gaze bore into hers and he slowly wiped the back of his hand across his mouth. His hair was mussed. Had she done that? She couldn't think properly. Everything was muddled because her heart was still pounding, and she was a bit in her cups, and she was on fire.

"What are we to make of this, Mrs. Honeycutt?" he asked, as breathless as she was.

"I don't know, Mr. Brendan," she answered honestly. "But wasn't it diverting?"

His smile matched hers and his eyes glittered in the light of the melting candles, and she felt that glitter in every corner of her soul. It was lust and pleasure and surprise and fascination and everything on which a new esteem feeds. She knew how feelings like this could consume a person, and heaven help her, she wanted to be consumed. She was ready to be consumed.

"We should…" She wavered, and in that moment of wavering, of asking for more, she spotted Lord Douglas. "Wait!" she cried.

"What?" Marek said.

Hollis darted past him. "Lord Douglas!"

Douglas was walking across the hall. He halted and turned around. He looked a little glassy-eyed and didn't even seem to recognize Hollis at first. But when he recognized her, he grinned and walked unevenly toward her.

"Are you standing under the mistletoe and waiting for me, lass?" Douglas asked, and leaned in, as if he meant to kiss her.

Hollis quickly ducked away. "I should like to introduce you to my friend, Mr. Brendan," Hollis said, and deliberately pointed at Marek in case Douglas hadn't noticed the gentleman standing just there.

Douglas looked in the direction of her pointed finger.

"Marek Brendan of Wesloria," Marek said, extending his hand in greeting.

"Marek Brendan of *Wesloria*," Douglas repeated with jovial theatrics, and took his hand, shaking vigorously.

"I know you," Marek said. "It is your ship that carried the lads to London recently."

Douglas gave a snort of laughter. And then he squinted at Marek. "Do I know you, then?"

Marek shook his head. "They are friends of mine, the four soldiers. Weslorian, like me."

Douglas stared at Marek. Then at Hollis. "Who is this man?" he asked, and instead of waiting for her to answer, he looked again at Marek. "Are you one of the king's men?"

"Not me," Marek said, as if that offended him. "I'm a clerk in the trade minister's office. I'm here to tell him he's right." He grinned.

So did Douglas.

"I've heard tell that your ship is the best."

Douglas leaned against the doorframe as another round of Chairs began. "Aye, that she is. Steam-powered. Best on the seas now, if you ask me. You say they were friends of yours?" Douglas asked, then glanced at Hollis. "What's she to do with it?"

"I told him I'd help him find his friends," Hollis said.

"You wouldn't be cooking up something for your ladies' gazette, would you?" Douglas asked.

"Why not?" Hollis said. "Ladies appreciate a man in uniform."

"Ah, lass, ladies appreciate a *man*. Too many of them don't have a proper one. But you'll no' want to write about those four soldiers. They weren't in uniform, for one. And they seemed a bit rough for proper ladies."

Hollis worked very hard to keep her expression neutral, but inside she was shouting—William Douglas had just confirmed the existence of the four soldiers.

"*Je*, that's Wesloria for you," Marek said. "Who was it again who brought them here?" he asked as if he should know the answer but couldn't quite recall. "It wasn't the king, was it?"

Douglas's attention had shifted to the game of Chairs. "That wee princess very nearly pushed the gentleman from the chair. Did you see?"

"Was it the king?" Hollis asked.

Douglas shook his head. "Not that I know. Another Weslorian. Like you, aye?"

"Do you recall his name?" Marek asked. "Might be acquainted with him, as well."

Douglas laughed. "What I recall is his purse, lad. He paid well enough for it. What else is there to remember?"

"What, you sailed all the way to Wesloria and took some man's money to put four men on your ship?" Hollis laughed. "You're teasing poor Mr. Brendan, Douglas. Tell him you are."

"What are you talking about?" Douglas asked. "I've never been to Wesloria. I met the gentleman here. My maiden voyage was to France and back."

"I don't understand," Hollis said.

Lord Douglas, whose attention was firmly on the game of Chairs, sighed with impatience. "Listen carefully, Mrs. Honeycutt. A Weslorian gentleman in London engaged my services a fortnight ago when I planned my first voyage. Asked me kindly if I'd pick up the lads for the journey back and gave me a fat purse. Do you understand now?"

Hollis could tell by the way Marek was looking at Douglas that he couldn't make sense of this tale, either. What gentleman? And why were the four soldiers in France? "Well, no matter," Hollis said lightly, as if she accepted this explanation completely. "Do you know where they've gone?"

"No," Douglas said. "They disembarked and disappeared into the docks. Did you see that, then? She pushed Walters out of the way."

Hollis looked over her shoulder. They were down to four chairs.

"I want to see this," Douglas said. "Pardon." He stepped around Hollis and Marek and walked through the crowd to see the end of the game.

Hollis and Marek looked at each other. "They *do* exist, those soldiers. But I can't say that I'm entirely happy to hear it," Hollis said.

"Agreed," Marek said. "Something is not right with it. I need to find them."

"Yes, I really think we must," Hollis said.

Marek frowned. "Not *we*. I mean to go to the docks. That's no place for a lady."

"I'm not delicate china, sir. I mean to go with you and you'll need Donovan's help. He'll know where to look, and really, Marek, are you not yet convinced that you need me?"

His gaze softened. He sighed and shook his head. "*Je*, I am convinced." He touched her hand with his fingers.

Hollis was thrilled by his admission. She was thrilled to be of use to anyone, but especially to him. Frankly, she was thrilled in so many ways she still couldn't properly catch her breath.

"We're still under the mistletoe," Marek said.

"So we are."

A loud roar of approval—or disapproval—went up from the crowd as someone took the round of Chairs. Marek took Hollis's head between his hands and kissed her softly on the mouth. He lifted his head, laced her fingers in his, and brought her hand to his lips. "Tomorrow?" He kissed her knuckles.

Hollis's fingers curled around his. "Tomorrow." *Tomorrow and today, and all the days beyond.*

He let go of her hand, gave her a meaningful look, then disappeared down the corridor.

Hollis was so enthralled by Marek and his kiss that she completely missed the contretemps between Lord Douglas and Princess Justine, about which guests would speak of for weeks to come.

CHAPTER TWENTY-ONE

The peace summit between Wesloria and Alucia is set to conclude this week. By all accounts, the agreement is a good one for Alucia and has set the Duke of Tannymeade as a popular figure who will one day sit on the Alucian throne. Wesloria has fared less well, and after a brief walk in the park, King Maksim was not seen for a few days. It is reported he is suffering again from an ague from which his recovery is slow.

Rumors of who kissed whom under the Iddesleigh mistletoe are quite shocking, indeed. A venerated solicitor was spotted kissing a peacock beneath the mistletoe. The peacock did not mind, but the gentleman's wife surely did, as the peacock, while sitting precariously on the shelf, is far younger than the unfortunate wife.

Ladies, Mr. Tom Smith's Christmas Novelties include the new Cosaque, *a paper-wrapped treat that when pulled apart reveals sweets or trinkets. This is a delightful game for the Christmas supper table. Mr. Tom Smith's shop may be found at Finsbury Square in the Moorfields.*

⌒—Honeycutt's Gazette of Fashion and Domesticity for Ladies

ELIZA AND SEBASTIAN were forced to depart with the royal princesses, lest there be any more shouting between Princess Justine and Lord Douglas. The contretemps occurred when Douglas slipped into the final seat just as the princess was attempting to take it. Beck had to ask Lord Douglas to take his leave, too, and Douglas did so with élan, bowing before everyone and offering his humble apologies for arguing with a mere girl. He signaled the musicians to play as he marched from the room, pausing only to grab the nearest woman and kiss her beneath the mistletoe before disappearing into the night to do God knew what.

Hollis could not help but smile. She appreciated that Douglas didn't conform to what society wanted him to be. Neither did she.

Beck was less appreciative of Lord Douglas's actions. He glared at Hollis. "It's all your fault," he said. "If the Weslorian king challenges me to a duel, I will demand you be my second. You deserve no less for this tree party," he said, casting his arm wide and knocking one of the candles off the tree.

His house did look as if a riot had broken out. Candles had toppled from the tree, garland portieres had been pulled from the eaves, and crystal cups were scattered across windowsills and mantels. There were even some resting on their sides on the carpet.

"I'll have Garrett arrange a ride home for her," Caroline said sweetly, and put a protective arm around Hollis's shoulders and pulled her away from Beck. "Don't fret," she whispered. "He'll be right as rain when he sleeps off the punch."

Hollis was sent home in the company of Mr. and Mrs. Dawson, whom she only knew as nearby neighbors of hers. But the moment she stepped into their coach, she felt the icy air. The couple was clearly in the middle of a row. "Oh," she said, flustered by it. "I...I'll just step down," she said, but Mr. Dawson grabbed her hand and pulled her all the way in.

"Nonsense. You live not a block from us, Mrs. Honeycutt. We should be delighted to see you home." He looked at his wife, presumably so she could offer her confirmation, but she turned her head and refused to look at either of them.

"Umm...thank you?" Hollis said uncertainly. She eased onto the bench next to Mrs. Dawson. No sooner had the coach pulled away from the curb than the row began in earnest. From what Hollis could gather, it all had to do with whom Mr. Dawson had kissed beneath the mistletoe.

"It was harmless fun," he insisted. "Ask Mrs. Honeycutt. She was kissing one of the foreigners."

"Oh!" Hollis said, startled that anyone had noticed.

"Lady Katherine Maugham is not *harmless*," Mrs. Dawson retorted.

The peacock! She'd kissed this old man? Hollis very nearly squealed with laughter. Granted, Mr. Dawson was a venerated gentleman who handled the private affairs of many well-to-do men, including Beck, and was old enough to be the peacock's father. Or perhaps even grandfather.

"That young woman has not gained an offer and now you've made it impossible," Mrs. Dawson continued.

Hollis bit her lip. She very much wanted to remark that the peacock had made it impossible when she'd tried to gain Prince Sebastian's attention, and then Prince Leopold's, but thought the better of inserting herself into this argument.

"It wasn't *me* who has made it impossible," Mr. Dawson complained. "She's a pretty thing. If there is anyone to blame for her failure to gain an offer, it's her harpy mother. You should pay particular note, madam."

Mrs. Dawson gasped with outrage. And then the shouting *really* started.

Neither of the Dawsons noticed when Hollis slipped out of the coach—well, tumbled out—and ran up the steps to her home. Marek was right—that Christmas punch was the devil.

She let herself in and removed her cloak. "Anyone home?"

"In here!"

She followed the sound of Donovan's voice into the drawing room and found him sitting before the fire. He was waiting up for her. He was much better now, and the bruises had faded from purple to yellow and green. He was working again, too. Just this morning he'd been cleaning windows. He winced only a tiny bit as he came to his feet when she walked into the drawing room.

"How was the party?"

Hollis smiled. She felt weightless, as if she was about to float out of her shoes. She did, in fact, bump into the wall as she stepped into the room. "It was wonderful, Donovan. I wish you could have come."

He grinned at her. "Dear Lord, I can smell your joy from here. What have you been drinking?"

"A terrible thing! It has the taste of licorice, but too much of it. As…something?"

"Absinthe?"

"Yes!" she said triumphantly. She came forward and kissed him on the cheek. "I had more than I ought."

"It would seem," he said as she collapsed onto a chair. He eased himself into the one beside her. "Tell me about it."

"Lord Douglas engaged in a shouting match with Princess Justine over a silly game of Chairs, and then Mr. and Mrs. Dawson had a row because Mr. Dawson kissed *the peacock* under the mistletoe."

"That sounds dreadful for both parties. Anything else?"

"Yes! Marek and I discovered there really *are* four soldiers. We're going to find them. With your help, of course."

"Marek, is it?"

"We're friends, Donovan."

"Mmm," he said, his eyes narrowing slightly. "And you're going to help your friend find these soldiers, is that the plan?"

"Well." She avoided his gaze by fussing with a loose crystal in her gown. "I thought you and I would help him as we would any friend."

"We don't have any friends that we help in that manner. How are we going to help him?"

"Lord Douglas said they are down at the docks somewhere. Marek knows nothing of the docks."

"But I do," he said.

"You know more than him," she said. "Will you please help us?"

Donovan smiled. "You know I'd do anything you ask of me."

"I *do* know. And I'm asking. Hopefully, I'm asking with all due civility and not shouting, but at this point, I really can't say if I am or not. There's a very solid ringing in my ears."

"Oh, I have no doubt of that," he said with a grin. "All right then, it is half-past three in the morning. Off to bed with you."

Hollis yawned loudly and found her feet. Donovan put his hands on her shoulders and pointed her in the direction of the door. "Do you need any help?"

"No, thank you, I can manage. Lord, it's a wonder I haven't popped out of this dress yet." She blew him a kiss and made her way to her room.

Her room was lit softly by a dying fire—Donovan clearly expected her home some time ago. Hollis paused to look around her. Her gaze landed on a painting on the far wall. It was a landscape scene, *Fields at Dawn*, or something like that. She gathered it was meant to evoke gloom, given that a gray mist covered the fields.

She'd never liked the painting. She'd wanted something prettier, something more colorful for this room. But Percy had wanted this one. And Hollis had always done what Percy wanted. She'd done what he'd wanted because she'd loved him so and had been very good about burying her wishes in favor of his. But it was time to add some color to this gray room.

Hollis kicked off her shoes and walked to the painting. It was large and heavy, but she managed to bring it down without breaking a toe or putting a hole in the wall. She turned it around to face the wall and hoped she remembered to tell Ruth to take it out tomorrow.

Hollis walked to her bed and sat on the end, looking at the patch of wall where the painting had hung, where the wallpaper was a little lighter in color than the paper that had surrounded the frame. The lighter patch reminded her of how she felt about Percy. He was a little lighter in the part of her where he'd always existed. And soon, that patch of lightness would fade, too, like Percy had, until she could hardly see it.

Hollis was ready to move on with her life. She'd been ready for a time, she could see that now. She fell backward onto the bed, her arms splayed wide. "Have I mourned enough, Percy?" she whispered. "Say I have and let me go." She closed her eyes and felt herself drifting away.

But she wasn't thinking of Percy in those final moments of consciousness. She was thinking of Marek. She imagined herself on the farm he'd described, tending his animals. Or baking bread. She imagined writing a book or taking long walks with a dog. She imagined sitting next to him instead of Donovan before a fire.

She imagined a lovely, simple life with Marek.

He was so different from any man she'd known. He was taciturn and solemn and surprising in so many ways. She had the feeling there were so many more parts of him she had yet to discover.

Somehow he'd made her feel vibrant and necessary again. He'd made her want again.

Hollis drifted to sleep with want wrapping around her like an old, familiar blanket.

CHAPTER TWENTY-TWO

The heavy rains that have battered Britain for the last fortnight have made some roads to the north impassable. It is expected that some family Christmas celebrations will be dampened as well, as travelers are advised to remain in London rather than attempt the roads.

Mr. Copperstone at Leadenhall Market has said he will have goose in good quantities in time for Christmas, as well as apples suitable for wassail.

Mrs. Compton of Green Street is taking orders for her famous twelfth-night cake. Mrs. Compton said each cake will serve eight persons, or ten if one is frugal, and may be purchased for the luxurious price of one pound, fifty pence.

⌀—Honeycutt's Gazette of Fashion and Domesticity for Ladies

MAREK WANTED NOTHING more than to leave the Green Hotel, but naturally, Dromio caught him before he could to inquire what he was doing. "You look a bit piqued, Brendan," he observed as he studied his face.

"I am perfectly fine, my lord."

"Did you perhaps have a bit too much to drink last night?" Dromio asked. "Or…" He made a very crude gesture to mimic copulation.

Marek said nothing. Then asked, "How did you find the king?"

"Hmm?" Dromio said absently. "Oh, a bit muddled, I'm afraid." He sighed and looked at his hand. "He could not be swayed, unfortunately."

"From?"

"From giving away so much," Dromio said, still looking at his hand. He dropped his hand and looked at Marek. "Where are you off to this morning?"

"To take in the sights."

"What sights?"

"Museums."

"Museums!" Dromio laughed. "Never occurred to me that a man so interested in numbers and goats would appreciate a bit of artwork. Good day to you, Brendan. Try not to look so piqued when you return." He laughed at his joke and slapped Marek's shoulder before turning and walking away.

That man, Marek decided, was perhaps the biggest jackass he'd ever known.

He walked on, to the front doors, but just as he was stepping out, he noticed Lord Osiander sitting alone near a window, his scowl fixed on Dromio. Marek didn't know the man, had hardly exchanged more than a few words with him in the weeks they'd been in London. But it was apparent to him that Osiander didn't trust Dromio any more than Marek did. Which was to say, not at all.

He continued on, out into a dreary, wet day. The air felt heavy around him, and he pulled his cloak tighter to him as he walked.

In spite of the weather, he was feeling buoyant. It was remarkable to him that he was as eager as he was to see Hollis again. At least as remarkable as the kiss he'd given her beneath that mistletoe. Marek had spent so much of his life in the shadows, so fearful of being discovered, that he'd learned to retreat from any male instinct like that. He couldn't recall that he'd ever been so audacious or immodest, but Hollis... Lord that woman had managed to bewitch him. She'd made him feel like the kiss was imperative, like the evening could not end without it. He'd departed that house on Upper Brook Street having laughed as hard and as long as he had ever done. He'd hardly even *smiled* until she had blown her way into his life.

Now that these feelings had been unleashed in him, he didn't know how to tame them, or even if he wanted to. He didn't want to examine them too closely—he didn't want to think too much.

He just wanted to see her again. Consequences be damned, it was as simple as that.

When he arrived at her house, the rain was driving across the street in sheets. He banged on the door, and moments later, Donovan opened it and gestured Marek inside. He shook off the rain from his cloak and removed his hat, eyeing Donovan's face and the fading bruises as he did. There would be a scar on his brow, but it didn't seem as if any other marks would be visible. "You look well enough, all things considered," Marek said.

"Aye, so do you," Donovan said. "New coat?"

Marek looked down. "No."

Donovan smiled wryly. "Come in. She'll be down soon. Never seen a woman so eager to visit the docks."

Marek silently followed him into the drawing room.

"Drink?" Donovan asked. "Whiskey? Tea?"

Marek shook his head. He wished Donovan would quietly disappear so that he could take Hollis into his arms.

But Donovan sat when she came bounding in the door, her face a wreath of smiles.

"Good morning, Marek!"

"Mrs...." He stopped himself, painfully aware that Donovan was watching him. "Hollis," he said. He felt something and glanced down. The yellow cat was twining through his legs.

"Buttercup likes you!" she said with delight. "Buttercup never likes anyone, does she, Donovan? How *are* you this morning, Marek?"

"Very well. And you?"

"I won't lie—my head hurt something fierce this morning. But Mrs. Plum has a concoction that will cure all ills and I am feeling much improved. Shall we go?"

"Are you certain? The weather is dreadful."

"I am very certain! If ever there was a day to find four men, it would be today, don't you think? No doubt they are tucked away in an inn or...someplace. Donovan has some ideas of where to look."

Marek glanced at Donovan.

"What she means is that I know of places where men of questionable character and motive will congregate."

That's rather what Marek thought she meant. "I don't think it's wise for you to accompany us," he said to Hollis.

Donovan suddenly stood up. "Save your breath, Mr. Brendan. Mrs. Honeycutt only grows more determined with every protest or suggestion to the contrary of her wishes. A more stubborn woman you'll not meet."

Marek must be growing accustomed to this strange house and the stranger relationship between Hollis and Donovan, because he was not at all surprised or taken aback, and neither was Hollis. In fact, she laughed as if that amused her. And, he noted, she did not deny it. "Is the carriage ready?" she asked.

"I'll see," Donovan said, and went out of the room.

The moment he passed through the doorway, Marek strode across the room to where Hollis stood, grabbed her hand, and pulled her close to kiss her cheek. And then her mouth. "You look remarkably well."

She beamed up at him. "How could I look anything less after last night? You look very well, too."

"It's come round!" Donovan called down the hall.

Marek was reluctant to take his gaze from her, but with another flash of a smile, Hollis went out of the room. He followed her, and while Donovan helped her into her cloak and bonnet, he put on his own.

"Ready, then?" Hollis asked, and when Marek nodded, the three of them dashed out in the rain and stuffed themselves into the landaulet, and the hired driver ferried them down to the docks.

Their first stop was a public house, The Siren's Song. "What potions have I drunk of siren tears?" Hollis murmured.

"A sonnet," Marek said.

She smiled. "Yes."

"I thought I was the only one to have been made to listen to readings of Shakespeare," Donovan said. "Shall we, Mr. Brendan?"

"*Je.* And Mrs. Honeycutt will remain here," he said, and pinned her with a look before she protested. "Don't even think to argue."

She leaned forward to look out the small window. She groaned but did not argue. Donovan gave Marek the slightest nod of approval. They were from two different parts of the world, but they were united in this—a public house called The Siren's Song on a public dock was no place for Hollis Honeycutt.

Unsurprising, given the wretched weather, men and barmaids were practically stacked to the rafters. The deep rumble of male voices mixed with the high pitch of women's laughter thudded against Marek's good ear. With a grimace, he and Donovan squeezed through the crowd.

Donovan looked very much at home here. He had the walk of a dandy, smiling at men and women alike. They made their way to a scarred wooden bar in back. Donovan braced against it and leaned forward to speak to a man behind the bar. The barkeep responded with a shake of his head. Donovan said something else. Again, the man shook his head.

Donovan turned to Marek and spoke, but Marek shook his head and pointed at his ear. He couldn't hear a blessed thing over the roar. Donovan gestured for him to go out, and they retreated from the public house and jogged back to the waiting carriage.

Hollis threw open the door for them from inside. "Well?" she asked eagerly as they climbed inside and closed the door, shaking the rain from their hats. "What did you find?"

"Nothing," Donovan said. "The bloke said they haven't had soldiers of any sort, but to try the Wilbur Arms. Said he'd heard of them congregating there. The only thing was, he couldn't say where the soldiers were from. They could be British soldiers."

"We carry on, then," Hollis said, and looked at Marek for confirmation.

Marek nodded.

Donovan stuck his head out the window and yelled the direction to the driver.

By the time they'd reached the Wilbur Arms, the torrential rain had lessened to a slow patter, but a cold north wind was settling in. Once again, Donovan and Marek went inside. Once again, no one knew or had seen four Weslorian soldiers.

By the time they returned home later that afternoon, they'd gone to four public houses, a brothel, and a dilapidated inn with an enormous green wooden fish hanging on the outside wall. No one had seen the Weslorian soldiers. Marek hadn't believed the story of the soldiers to begin with, but he found that he was disappointed that it was proving not to be true. He had hoped for something—anything—that might help him uncover the truth.

Donovan left Marek and Hollis in the drawing room to warm before the hearth and returned minutes later with wine and ale. But he'd brought only two glasses.

"Shouldn't there be another—"

"No," Donovan said. "I'm going out. I've someplace to be and you're not to fret."

"I think I've earned the right to fret, given what happened."

Donovan smiled. It was a soothing smile, and Marek could see how the man's charm could work on a person. "You're still not allowed, madam. Mrs. Plum has laid out supper. Invite Mr. Brendan to dine." He nodded to Marek. "Good evening, sir," he said, and strode from the room with Hollis staring after him.

At the sound of the front door closing behind him, Hollis sighed and looked at Marek. "I'm not to fret," she said, resigned. "Will you dine with me?"

"Will it not be remarked, you dining alone with a mysterious male guest?"

Hollis laughed. "No more than the fact that I live here quite on my own with a manservant everyone believes is my lover." She leaned across the space that separated them and pushed a bit of damp hair from his temple. "I don't care what anyone says anymore, Marek. I'm not to fret, and I should very much like you to dine with me. Will you?"

Years of being inordinately careful completely evaporated from him. He decided he didn't care what anyone said about it, either. *"Je,"* he said. *Anything you want. Anything.* "I would like that very much."

HE WAS A bit surprised there was no one to serve them in what looked like a sitting or garden room. It was quite small and there was no hearth. A small, round table with four chairs sat in the center of the room.

A jovial Mrs. Plum greeted him warmly and asked after him, as if they'd all become great friends the night he'd dragged Donovan upstairs. She put platters of food on the table, then removed her apron and bid Hollis a good-night.

"Thank you, Mrs. Plum. My regards to Mr. Plum!"

"As always!" Mrs. Plum said cheerily and went out the door from which she'd appeared.

Hollis went to the sideboard and returned with a decanter of wine. She poured two glasses and invited Marek to sit. She removed the silver dome from the platter and revealed a succulent roast beef and fingerling potatoes. His stomach rumbled at the smell of it.

"Mrs. Plum is an excellent cook," she said, and held out her hand for his plate. She heaped quite a lot of food onto it and then heaped almost as much onto hers.

Marek was famished, and probably dug in to the meal with a little too much enthusiasm. But so did Hollis. There was nothing delicate about her, really—he was beginning to see that in spite of her refined appearance, she was a lusty woman. He liked that. He thought it nice, dining like this.

It was cozy. Intimate. It felt familiar, but new at the same time. It was something Marek could very much get used to.

"This is divine," she said, not for the first time, about the food. "Isn't it amazing how something so ordinary can be the best thing in the world?"

Je, quite amazing.

She asked him about his own home. He had mentioned his farm to her, but she wanted to hear more about it. "A farm sounds so…bucolic," she said. "What's it like?"

He told her about the respectable manor house that had once belonged to a landowner's mother-in-law until her death. He had a small garden, a few farm animals. He told her about the pair of goats he'd acquired that served no purpose other than they kept his lawn trimmed. Sometimes too trimmed—just before he'd departed for England, they'd eaten a sizable hole in a hedgerow and he'd had to engage the lad who looked after his stock to repair it while he was away.

"I've dogs, too." He glanced down at his plate. "I miss them," he said wistfully.

"Cats are not the same, of course, but I would miss my cats if I were gone for a long period of time." Her brow creased slightly. "Is there anyone you miss?"

The question caught him off guard. It was difficult to explain how solitary his life had become, and he wouldn't try. He shook his head.

"Ah." She smiled. "Why have you never married?"

Marek's eyebrows rose as he forked a bite of potato. "That's a rather pointed question."

"Are you surprised by it?" Her eyes glittered with amusement.

He smiled softy. "No."

"Do you mind terribly if I ask? I wondered who was

watching after your dogs while you were away, if you had a Mr. Brimble to mind them, and it made me wonder whether you had a wife to take care of them. You're a handsome man, Marek. I should think ladies would be deliriously happy to entertain an offer from you."

He had to laugh at that. "Thank you… I think. But I should think the answer to your question is obvious."

"Not at all," she insisted.

"No? If it was ever discovered who I am, it could be disastrous for me. I've no doubt Felix Oberon would seek to see me hanged as my mere existence puts another claim to the throne before his. It would be unfair to burden a wife with it."

She frowned. "But you've not been discovered after all this time. Aren't you lonely?"

Was he lonely? Marek didn't know if he would call his state of being lonely. He was alone. Removed. But he hadn't been filled with longing.

At least not until he'd met her.

"I should think if the king knew you were alive, he'd be filled with joy," she said quietly. "Can you imagine, to discover your baby had not met a tragic end, after all?"

"I don't know how he would feel," he said. "Life in Wesloria is not as it is here. People struggle to simply survive in many parts of the country. I believe the king is trying to make things better, but until that happens, everyone is viewed with suspicion. I would be viewed with suspicion. I can't risk it." He put down his fork. He didn't want to think of his solitary life in Wesloria or the isolation he felt from most of the world. "Why haven't you married again, Hollis? You're a beautiful, vibrant woman. I would think gentlemen would be begging for an introduction."

She laughed. "You are too kind, sir. If there are gentlemen wishing to marry a widow, I've scared them all away."

"I doubt that."

"Gentlemen do not always appreciate a woman who is forthright in her actions and words." She looked at him as if she expected him to disagree.

He definitely disagreed. "On the contrary, madam. Gentlemen do appreciate it, but they are not always prepared for it. Society has given us to believe we always have the upper hand."

"*That* is so true!" she exclaimed. She leaned back in her seat, one arm draped over her middle. "Quite honestly, it wasn't until very recently that I felt I could finally let go of my grief over losing my husband."

He understood a little about grief—his was for a life that could have been, and a life that was lost to him. "How did he die, if I may?" Marek asked curiously.

"It was a carriage accident. In weather much like this, his carriage went off a bridge and he drowned."

"Good Lord."

"It was quite shocking. I don't like to think about it. To imagine…" She shook her head, picked up her wineglass, and took a long drink, then put it down. "Therefore, I don't imagine."

"What was he like?"

"Percy?" She smiled fondly. "He was a good man. You would have liked him. He and Donovan were childhood mates, and he brought Donovan into his household when things began to be said about him. But Percy never had an unkind thing to say about Donovan. I think he loved him like a brother, and Donovan the same. Percy was also very curious by nature. He was the one who established the gazette. But his gazette was about very serious things, such as politics and economics." She gave him a very pert little smile. "It was not as popular as my version."

Marek laughed at that. "It's truly remarkable what you've done."

"Not really," she said breezily. "I had help. And what else did I have to do? I meant it as a way to honor his memory, but now—now I…"

She looked away, as if trying to find the right words.

"Now what?" he prodded her.

She turned her gaze back to him. "Now I need more. That's it. I need my life to *mean* something. I can't spend the rest of my years honoring a dead man, no matter how much I loved him. I have…wants," she said, her cheeks flushing. "I want to live. I don't want to live to mourn."

Those words struck a chord in Marek. He didn't want to live to mourn, either, and maybe that's what he'd been doing all this time. He sat up, leaned across the table, and took her hand in his. "I understand."

"Do you?"

"Better than I can convey. I have wants and desires, too. I think I can't live my life without being discovered, and yet, I want meaning, just like you. I don't want to live to mourn—I want to live to live."

Her eyes turned luminous. She turned her hand beneath his, palm to palm, and wrapped her fingers around his. "Would you ever want to be king?"

"No," he said instantly. "I am not prepared for that sort of life and have no wish to be. I have two half sisters who are prepared for it and I have no wish to take that from them. No," he said again, as if she'd challenged him. "That has never been my intent. The only wish I've had at all was to *see* my father. But if he were to see me for who I really am? I think it would do more harm than good."

"You can't be certain of that."

"But think of it, Hollis. Even if he were to believe me, he would naturally face the dilemma of what to *do* about me. What the discovery of me would mean to everything that had gone before and to every decision he'd made and would make. I couldn't do that to him."

Hollis slowly nodded. "I see your point." She pressed his hand between both of hers. "You're a good man, Marek. I would think that most people in your situation would want whatever their true birth could give them. Riches, titles, power."

He smiled. "I suppose I'd rather be a good son than a king." The words sounded sad to him. A man resigned to his circumstances. Of course, there was part of him that imagined the riches, the titles, the power. But it was all too fraught. He liked his little patch of this world and he was not in danger of losing it. His father was in danger of losing something every day of his life. "How is it possible I found you in this storm, Hollis?"

"I found you, remember?"

Something seemed to shift in the air around them. He could feel a charge, a change in temperature, a glow. And as he sat there, his gaze locked on hers, she lifted his hand and tenderly kissed his knuckles. "I'm so happy you are here."

She said it every time she saw him, and Marek believed it was true. He was happy he was here, too. He pushed away from the table, took a few steps to her seat, and pulled her up and into his arms. He roughly smoothed her hair, still damp from the rain. He ran his thumb across her bottom lip. "I don't know what to do with you."

"Come upstairs," she said.

He wanted more than anything to go upstairs, but that wasn't what he meant. He didn't know what to do with his esteem for her. He didn't know how to fit it into his life, but he was desperate to find a way. *"Hollis."* He pressed his forehead to hers.

"We both want to—I'm not blind, Marek, and neither are you."

"Don't say another word or I will lose my mind," he said, and took her head in his hands and kissed her. He kissed her with all the desire that he'd bottled away for years, desire for things he could never have, for things he'd missed. He kissed her and could feel himself sliding into oblivion. All the locks in him were opening and the heat was flooding into him, filling him up. There were so many moments he'd longed for and had not allowed himself to have, and this beautiful woman was offering.

She leaned back, then grabbed his hand and pulled him toward the door. She glanced back only once before darting into the hall. He followed like a puppy. Up the stairs, down a darkened hall, and into a room.

"What of your staff?"

"Donovan won't be home. Ruth won't come unless I call for her, and Mr. Brimble sleeps like the dead."

Still, Marek looked over his shoulder at the open door.

She let go his hand, shut the door, and turned the lock. She leaned against it, her smile sultry now.

They were in the master suite, he thought. There were things around them that he normally would have taken in, assessed, and committed to memory. But at the moment, the only thing that mattered was the need in that room. Raw, monstrous need.

And it was coming from them both.

CHAPTER TWENTY-THREE

The oldest among us will recall a winter when the rain never ceased falling and the Thames froze over. The river has not yet frozen, but scholars predict it will have by the end of January. Mind that you stock coal and peat for the worst months.

In spite of the gloom that has settled on London, the Alucian and Weslorian peace accord is expected to be signed this week and the delegations are likewise expected to depart for home before the New Year.

Ladies, in this season of many Yuletide candles, The Workwoman's Guide *advises that if you find yourself with scorched linens, and the threads are not damaged, you may restore the fabric when boiled in two parts Fuller's earth, one half cake of soap, the juice of two lemons, and a cup of vinegar to restore the fabric.*

      —Honeycutt's Gazette of Fashion and
      Domesticity for Ladies

THE LIGHT IN her room was so low that Marek almost looked like a shadow, but even in that dimness, she could still see the gleam in his eye. "Are you certain this is what you want?" he asked.

His voice rolled through her, turning her sharp edges into soft grassy slopes. She was sliding down a familiar path, but one she hadn't taken in so long she'd forgotten all the twists and turns, and her breath was short with anticipation. She'd invited a man into her room. The words *sounded* immoral, but she didn't feel immoral. She felt fully righteous, actually. She had saved herself for her husband. She'd done what she was supposed to do. But now she saved herself for only her.

Marek was moving toward her, his eyes boring into her. "Are you certain, Hollis Honeycutt? This is not something you can easily return from."

Perhaps he was trying to get her to see reason, but he only stoked the flames in her. She was well aware that this could be a calamity in more ways than one. God knew she and Percy hadn't always been in perfect harmony. And there was always the after, those tender moments when one could only hope that expectations and feelings aligned. But she couldn't think about that—Marek was looking at her as if he wanted to devour her, and it lit her on fire. "I am entirely certain."

Marek groaned. "I thought you'd say that." He reached where she stood with her back against the door. His gaze drank her in, and he lifted his hand and caressed her shoulder, traced a line across her collarbone to her other shoulder, and up her neck, curling around her ear.

Hollis leaned her head back and closed her eyes, feeling her skin turn to kindling in every place his fingers moved.

He bent his head and kissed the curve of her neck into her shoulder, then sank a hand into her hair, dislodging the ringlets and pulling them free. "I am mad for you," he whispered, and followed that with something said breathlessly in Weslorian, before kissing her mouth.

She slid her arms around his neck and he pressed his mouth to her throat. She scraped her fingers through his hair, and he pushed her against the door, his mouth on hers again. The weight of his body was hard against hers. His kiss was impassioned, and hers was frantic with want. She was falling into these feelings and these sensations, and all she could think of was how she needed to feel his skin against hers, to feel his strength envelop her and take her to the heights she had not seen in a very long time.

Marek's lips were agonizingly pleasurable, spreading desire through her so quickly there was nothing she could do to douse it. He turned her around and moved her backward as he worked the fastenings of her gown. The sleeves slid down her shoulders, and when she removed her arms, the gown slid down the chemise and to her waist, where a petticoat held it aloft. *"Deo mea,"* he murmured, and pushed her gown down and over her petticoat. With his eyes locked on hers, he pulled at the ribbon that held the petticoat around her waist. It slid down her legs along with her gown.

Hollis reached for his neckcloth as he shrugged out of his coat and began to unbutton his long waistcoat. When he'd discarded those items, he kicked off his boots, slipped his hand around her waist, and lay her down on the bed. He crawled over her, his lips kissing her from the hollow of her throat, to her collarbone, and down, taking her breast in his mouth.

A vortex of desire was gaining traction in her, spinning her around and around. She was losing herself in her yearning and his touch.

He tossed aside his shirt and kissed her breast again, murmuring something about her galloping heart. White-hot anticipation coursed down her spine and spilled into her groin. Marek pressed his erection against her leg; she pushed a lock of dark hair from his brow and stared into his eyes. His breathing was hard, his golden gaze the sun to her sea of desire. This moment was deeply erotic and profoundly evocative, filling the air around them. Their mutual regard wrapped them in a cocoon.

He hooked a finger under the hem of her chemise and slid it up, then used both hands to pull it over her head so that she lay bare before him. He sat up, removed his trousers, and returned to her. He skimmed his hand over the plane of her belly and down to her thighs. His body was dense and powerful, his hands strong. She relished the feel of a man beside her, on her. She kissed him, slipping her tongue into the seam of his lips at the same moment his fingers slipped into the seam of her.

Hollis was raging with unbridled desire. She had long believed she could never desire a man as she had desired Percy, but she'd been wrong. The desire she had for Marek was potent and hot—because this was her choosing and she had asked for what she wanted. In some ways, that made this more powerful than any intimate moment she'd ever experienced.

Marek was very deliberate in his caressing of her, stroking her body, kissing her, showing her how much he wanted her. She sank into the sensation of his touch, the feel of his body pressed hard against her own. She felt every beat of his heart against her breast. She surrendered to his hands and his mouth and, at last, to his body, when he slid into her with a sigh of bliss.

She was instantly transported. His body in hers was exquisite and unbearable and urgent and inescapable. She moved with him and against him, urging him to abandon. Their eyes were locked with a powerful current of mutual desire, each silently willing the other to crest the wave first.

Hollis was the first to fall, letting herself implode with a gasp and a whimper. With a strangled cry, Marek yanked free of her, spilling onto her thigh.

The heat of his body seeped into hers. It seemed forever before Hollis slowly floated back to earth. She had always feared that she would find love after Percy was solemn and heavy with grief. But this was nothing like that. This was freeing. She felt as if the last shackles of her grief were broken and she was free to love again.

She could still feel Marek's heart beating against her breast. He slowly rolled onto his side and laced his fingers with hers.

Hollis rolled onto her side, cupped his face with her free hand and kissed him. He responded with several kisses to her face before gathering her in his arms and holding her to him.

"I think I am forever changed," she said softly.

Marek said nothing. Hollis realized that she was on his deaf side. He hadn't heard her. She caressed his ear and kissed it, then made him turn his head and kissed him once more. He smiled with such adoration that she couldn't suppress a small shiver. His expression was warm and open, and he wrapped a dark tress of her hair around his finger.

Marek didn't have to speak. He didn't even have to hear her. A bond had been forged between them, and no matter what else came, she would be forever grateful to him for removing the mantle of mourning from her. Hollis felt vibrant, a star shooting across the sky of her life. Her blood still flowed hot in her veins, and she wanted to remain like this forever, the two of them in this bed, in a tangle of sheets, in a space where no one could touch them.

Rain began to fall again, pattering against the window. Hollis pushed herself up and propped the pillows behind her. Marek rolled onto his side to face her, his head resting on his fist.

"This might have been disastrous," Hollis said.

"Why?"

"Two people are not always so compatible."

He smiled and caressed her face. "Did you find us compatible?"

"Exceedingly compatible." She traced her finger down his nose.

They lay like that for a very long time, talking quietly, caressing each other. Marek told her about his childhood. About fishing on the sea with the man he'd always thought was his uncle. He talked about the stark beauty of a remote land, and she imagined a tundra of sorts, rising into rocky mountains, then giving way to the sea. He talked about his farm, about his dogs that would lie at his feet each night, and Hollis imagined one of them putting his head on her lap. She imagined the warmth of the room with the fire he'd built. She imagined this rain pattering on a house far away.

Hollis told him about her favorite pets. She told him about the cats and dogs that had always lived in their house. And the rabbit she'd had as a girl. The rabbit had escaped the garden enclosure and had gone missing. Days later, a neighbor bragged about a most excellent dinner of rabbit.

"Dear God," Marek said, wincing.

She told him about the death of her mother, and her father's blindness.

She told him everything.

Marek listened attentively.

They talked about everything that had gone on in their lives until this moment in this room. There was no question between them of a future, or even a tomorrow. Tonight was about two people brought together by extraordinary circumstances. Two people who had developed a mutual regard against all odds, and who would one day need to recall all the details they shared now so they could make sense of this extraordinary moment.

It was also about falling in love. That's what Hollis was thinking when she climbed onto Marek's body and found him willing and able. They made love again, exploring this new, budding landscape they'd created. Of all the men she'd met and interacted with over the last few years, why was he the man to capture her imagination so completely? Why was it the solemn, partially deaf man who made her feel so exuberant? There was no logic to it. *The course of true love never did run smooth*.

Shakespeare.

Hollis didn't know when she fell asleep in his arms, but she slept heavily, and she dreamed vividly. There were soldiers, and Marek. Beck, too, which should have disturbed her more than it did.

She was awakened in what felt like the middle of the night. The hearth had gone cold, and the room was nearly black. But she was aware of someone moving around in the room. She ran her hand over the bed next to her and found it empty. She sat up, propping herself on her elbows and blinking into the dark. "Marek?"

"I'm here," he said in a low voice. The bed sank to one side with his weight. He touched her face and smiled tenderly. "I should go. Your servants—"

"I have another idea of how to find them," she said, her dreams coming back to her.

"Pardon?"

"The soldiers."

He stroked her hair and tenderly kissed her forehead. "There's no point, Hollis. If they ever existed, they have disappeared into London."

She sat up, drawing up the sheet with her. She pushed a

tangle of hair from her eyes. "I dreamed it. Or thought it, I don't know—but soldiers must be billeted somewhere. They didn't come here to wander the streets, did they? I know someone who might know where foreign soldiers may be billeted. All we need is cake."

He chuckled. "You're still dreaming."

"Donovan and I will pick you up at the hotel at one o'clock. But we must arrive before he has his luncheon."

"You're not making sense, Hollis."

"I know," she said. She came up on her knees, wrapped her arms around his neck, and kissed him. "You'll see. Trust me."

Marek sighed and settled his hands on her waist. "You make it impossible to resist you. You do know that, do you?" he asked, and pressed his lips to the side of her neck.

Actually, Hollis thought it was the other way around.

CHAPTER TWENTY-FOUR

From the hallowed halls of a palace, more than one heard the terrible row between some of the Weslorian ministers and King Maksim. The shouting could be heard all the way to St. James Park. No reason for the argument has been reported, but those who heard the shouting in Weslorian noted that the king sounded quite angry. Could it be that Alucia will have more gains in the new agreement than his own country? Even those of us who are ignorant of the proceedings know there cannot be true peace if one party has more than the other.

The Earl of Kendal and his formidable daughter, Lady Blythe, were recently spotted on Regent Street, and in particular, in the establishment of dressmaker Madame Louisa. A reliable little bird has told us that an astounding twelve gowns were ordered. Perhaps Lady Blythe is building a trousseau.

⌐—Honeycutt's Gazette of Fashion and
Domesticity for Ladies

AT HALF PAST ONE, Mr. Kettle pulled his pail from beneath his chair. It felt heavier than it had in the preceding weeks, and he couldn't help but smile. Mrs. Kettle had at last come home, having apparently discovered that her father was more demanding than she considered her own husband to be. Mr. Kettle felt a bit smug about his wife's epiphany and reminded her that he had told her to expect her father would be less inclined to tolerate her unacceptable behavior, and he sincerely hoped she'd learned a valuable lesson.

If the weight of his pail was any indication, she had.

He removed the linen and spread it on his desk, then balanced the pail in his lap to peer inside.

A hunk of bread rested on top. He removed that and placed it on the linen. This was most assuredly an improvement, and he would freely admit that he had missed his wife's fresh bread.

The next item he lifted from the pail was an uncooked potato. *A potato?* Their argument last night had resulted from his expressed desire for variety in his meals, particularly as he'd been forced to eat the same foods for several days in a row after she'd gone running off to her father's house. But this was not the variety he'd envisioned.

He placed the potato next to the bread. He reached into his pail and removed another potato, this one even bigger than the last. There was nothing else in the pail, and Mr. Kettle once again stared with dismay at his lunch.

"Mercy, your luncheon has not improved, has it?"

Mr. Kettle snapped to attention at the sound of Mrs. Honeycutt's voice. He thought he was done with her. He'd sold his soul to the devil for a piece of cake, but here she was again, smiling at him in that way that caused his skin to tingle. He glared into her blue eyes.

"Good day, Mr. Kettle!" she said, as if they were old friends.

"Mrs. Honeycutt." He noticed she had a basket on her arm, and he could see a cheesecloth peeking from the top of it. His mouth was already watering—he remembered with great fondness the cakes she'd brought last time. To say they were divine was no exaggeration. Perhaps he ought to mention it to Mrs. Kettle. Perhaps she could learn to make cake like that.

"A potato?" Mrs. Honeycutt asked.

Mr. Kettle shook himself back to the present. "To what do I owe this visit?" he asked crisply. "I thought I had your word you'd not bother me again."

"Did I say that?" she asked, her brow furrowing as if she was trying hard to recall. "I don't think I said *that*." She glanced over her shoulder, which is when Mr. Kettle noticed her Adonis standing in his usual spot. "Did I say I would never bother him again?" she asked curiously.

"I can't imagine you'd say that," the man said.

Mr. Kettle noticed someone else. Another man, just as tall as Adonis, but a bit broader in build. He was not as pale as the Englishman, either. He reminded Mr. Kettle of the Spaniards who often sailed into London.

Another thing he noticed was the man's hands. They were enormous. He felt a curious and uncomfortable flush. He imagined those hands could easily wrap around a man's neck and squeeze the breath from him without much effort at all. Had it come to that? Did they mean to murder him for the manifests?

"Mrs. Honeycutt, I've already—"

She didn't allow him to finish his sentence. "I know, and you were so very helpful, too." She reached into her basket and removed whatever was wrapped in cheesecloth and placed it on his desk. With one long finger, she pushed open one flap of the cheesecloth, and then the other. Mr. Kettle couldn't help himself—he leaned forward to see. *Apple tarts.* And not just any apple tarts. These were as thick as his fist and as wide as dinner plates. There were two of them nestled in that bundle.

"As I was saying, you were *so* helpful…but it seems we need one more bit of information to complete our study, and I think you may be able to help with that." She nudged the tarts closer to him then slid onto the chair beside his desk.

She propped her arm on his desktop and leaned forward. He wondered if she knew that her bosom was just there, directly in his line of sight. Sometimes, Mrs. Kettle didn't seem to notice her bosom was just there, either. His gaze moved over the fleshy mounds of her breasts and then up to her eyes again. "Pardon?"

Her eyes were shining. The woman enjoyed tormenting him, clearly. "You're so very knowledgeable. It's a wonder to me you've not risen higher in the ranks. But then again, you very well might do so when your help is revealed to the King of Wesloria."

"What?"

She broke off a bit of one tart and popped it into her mouth, and just like that, his gaze was on the tarts again.

"Would you happen to know where four Weslorian soldiers might billet?"

He snorted. "How would I know something like that?"

"Well…you go to the docks every day, don't you? I should think you might have heard something here or there through the years."

He did hear things, actually. He crept one finger toward the tarts. Mrs. Honeycutt smoothly pulled them out of his reach.

"I just meant to smell it," he said.

Mrs. Honeycutt pulled the tarts even closer to her and took another bite. "Dear Lord, this is *excellent*. Simply melts in your mouth! Where do you think soldiers would billet if they didn't want anyone to know they were here?"

Mr. Kettle's face began to heat with his anxiety. He wasn't sure he really knew the answer to her question, but he was certain that even if he had an idea, he was not to share it. But he wouldn't be telling her, would he? He'd be guessing. A guess for an apple tart.

Mrs. Honeycutt lifted one of the tarts and held it up right

under his nose. He leaned back because the smell of baked apple was torturous, and when he did, his gaze landed on his potatoes.

"I find potatoes are only tolerable when nothing else will do, and then, only cooked."

As if he needed to be told that. He reasoned he was not showing her the manifests, which his lordship had specifically told him not to do. He was not showing her anything at all, really. He was *guessing*. "You might have luck with Mr. Rangold in the Jewish quarter of Hackney," he said. "Well, Hackney Wick, to be more precise."

Her lovely eyes sparked with delight. "Does Mr. Rangold have a first name?"

Mr. Kettle had to think about that. "Ivan, I believe." He'd seen the man a time or two down at the docks, collecting his pay for housing whoever needed housing. And generally, the people he seemed to house looked as if they might not obtain housing in the usual ways.

"You have been most helpful." She pushed both tarts toward him, bumping into his linen cloth and pushing it out of the way, which caused both potatoes to roll from his desk and hit the floor. Mr. Kettle ignored the potatoes, picked up one of the treats, and took a large bite. "No more, Mrs. Honeycutt," he said through a mouthful of tart that was indeed melting in his mouth. "You have caught me at a particular moment that will be rectified this evening," he said, eyeing one of the potatoes. "I will not be bribed."

"*No*, of course not, Mr. Kettle," she said, and rose gracefully from her seat. "Good day." She walked out of his tiny office. The man with the large hands followed her without a word. But Adonis winked at Mr. Kettle before he followed after his mistress.

CHAPTER TWENTY-FIVE

The news that Lord and Lady Chartier, lately of Bibury, have determined to stay on in London through the twelfth day of Christmas has been received with great joy by friends and family alike. Lord Justice Tricklebank will fete the couple and his family at his home on Christmas Day. Lord and Lady Chartier are expected to resume their place in society and attend several soirees intended to celebrate the formal end of the peace negotiations between Alucia and Wesloria. The final accord is expected to be signed this week.

Ladies, with Christmas only days away, Milloy and Drake Company is offering printed invitations on embossed and scented paper. Sir Henry Cole has a selection of Christmas cards for posting to your loved ones during the Christmas season. They are offered for one shilling each.

෨—Honeycutt's Gazette of Fashion and Domesticity for Ladies

MAREK, HOLLIS, and Donovan dined at a restaurant in Belgravia to discuss what Mr. Kettle had revealed. Donovan was flatly against either of them going into Hackney Wick.

"But Hackney is lovely," Hollis said.

"Where your friends reside, aye, it is," Donovan said. "But not all of it. Not Hackney Wick."

"I prefer to go alone," Marek said.

"But you're not familiar with Hackney—"

"I will learn it," Marek said briskly before Hollis could argue her way into this. "If they are there, I'll have better luck alone, Weslorian to Weslorian." He wanted to be free to talk to these soldiers on his own terms, in his own way, and to take as long as the task required. He didn't think he could accomplish that with a woman in tow—no offense to Hollis, certainly—but he knew how men were. He didn't want Donovan, either. A reasonable man on foreign soil might suspect Donovan of being with an authority they didn't want to encounter.

Quite a lot of discussion ensued, particularly as Hollis was dismayed that neither of them thought it safe for her. At last, she conceded when Marek promised her he'd come straightaway to Mayfair to tell her everything that he had learned.

He meant to keep that promise when he walked away from the restaurant. But events had a way of unfurling when a person least expected it.

It was easy enough to find Mr. Rangold's town house. The area was home to people who worked hard for their living, judging by the women who trudged down the street with small shopping baskets, and the men in worn suits striding purposefully across the bowling green.

The Rangold house, he discovered, was a nondescript, redbrick town house identical to the other town houses on that block.

A woman selling apples thought nothing of it when he offered her two shillings to point him in the right direction. He took his apple, and made his way to the street she'd indicated. Once there, Marek intercepted a gentleman, who pointed to a faded door near the end of the block. No one paid him any heed as he walked up to the door and used the tarnished knocker to rap.

A woman eventually came to the door. She looked as harried as the rest of the people on the street. Her gown was brown, her hair gray, and she wore a dirty apron and a lace cap. She wiped her palms on her apron as she peered at him, as if she thought she might know him. When she spoke, it was a language he didn't know. Polish, perhaps? "Do you speak English?"

She blinked. "Who are you?" she asked in heavily accented English.

"A friend."

She did not look convinced.

"Is Mr. Rangold in?"

"No." She moved to close the door, but Marek quickly put up a hand to stay her. "I am Weslorian," he said. "I'm looking for my friends. I understand they are housing here, with Mr. Rangold."

She eyed him suspiciously.

"I have important news for them."

"No one home now," she said. "Come again later."

"Can you tell me where they've gone?"

"Where," she scoffed. "I clean, I clean. Come back later." She physically pushed him back and shut the door.

He supposed that meant he'd have to wait. It was terribly cold and damp, but Marek took up a position in the bowling green, determined to wait until one of the soldiers appeared. He sat beneath a tree, his back to it, and felt the cold and damp seeping in through his clothes. He pulled his wool cloak tightly around him and his hat down as far as he could for warmth. He folded his arms across his body, then fixed his gaze on the house.

No one came or went in the time that he sat there. Marek

inadvertently dozed off, and was startled awake by a sound or movement—he never knew what—and woke just as a man reached the steps leading up to the door of the town house.

Marek leaped to his feet. He couldn't cover the distance to reach the man before he entered the house, so he instinctively yelled *"Odaat!"* *Wait*.

The man whipped around at the sound of his native tongue. He was scarcely more than a boy, Marek realized as he jogged across the street to him. He forced a smile as he reached the bottom step. *"Wesloriat?"* he asked in his native tongue.

The young man glanced around, as if expecting someone to appear.

"So am I. Obviously," Marek said in Weslorian, and laughed nervously. "I am here with the Weslorian delegation. I have news."

The young man softened. "Oh." He came down off the landing. "What, for me?"

"All of you," Marek said.

"But I'm the only one here. They've gone to meet the gent."

The gent. "Ah," Marek said. "I think it best we don't talk here. Is there a public house nearby?"

"Je." But the young man hesitated and looked back at the door. "I'm to dine here."

"I won't keep you from supper. What do you say to a pint? A toast to the home country."

The young man gave him an appraising look. Then he shrugged. "Aye, then. Let's hear your news. What's your name?"

"Vilcot Tarian," he said, borrowing the name of his neighbor.

They walked to the corner public house. It was the end

of a workday and the common room was crowded. Marek feared he'd not be able to hear what the young man said. He caught that his name was Lorenz, and Marek squeezed in next to him on the bench, insisting Lorenz sit first so that he would be on Marek's right. He had to lean in quite close to hear the lad above the din, but he laughed and claimed to be an old man.

Lorenz didn't seem to mind it. As it turned out, he was young enough that he was desperately homesick. He might have been fifteen years old, Marek guessed. Lorenz missed his mother, he missed his sister, and the voyage had made him ill. He clearly needed the opportunity to talk, and talk he did, until Marek didn't think he could absorb another word.

He told Marek he and the others were here to protect Queen Agnes and the princesses. He felt honored to be selected from the ranks for this important mission.

"And the other lads?" Marek asked. "Were they selected, as well?"

Lorenz nodded. "We're friends, all of us. Dominick's the one who knew the gent. None of us have ever been away from Wesloria. And we heard Princess Justine is beautiful." He looked at Marek. "Is she beautiful?"

Marek considered this. "All women are beautiful," he said. "And what are you to protect the queen and the princesses from?"

Lorenz shrugged. "I don't rightly know. I thought you might know. They said the king is weak and can't protect them himself. The gent said he might not even live to see Wesloria again!" he said, his voice full of wonder. "Is that true?"

"No," Marek said. "He is not as ill as that." He wondered if it had occurred to this young man that the king would travel with a small army to protect him and his family. He wondered if it had occurred to him to inquire why the advisors to the king would allow him to take such a journey if he was weak and might not survive.

Marek drained what was left in his pint and ordered Lorenz another one. "Did the gent say any more than that?"

Lorenz looked at him curiously. "You said you had news."

"I do. But if you've already heard it, what is the point of repeating it?" He smiled.

Lorenz thought about that a moment and seemed to accept it. "He said we'd see London and the princesses, that's all. And to keep it a secret. It's a special mission, aye? He said there might be a spot of trouble here and there."

Marek nodded. "There could very well be. Did he say what sort of trouble?"

Lorenz shook his head as he accepted the pint from the serving girl.

Marek rubbed his face with his hands. This...child was here to protect the queen, so he thought, and had no more clue of what he was doing than a simpleton. He lowered his hands and turned to face Lorenz. "I want to understand you completely, Lorenz."

The lad nodded.

"A man—a gent you don't know, by your own admission, and apparently don't know even his name—comes to you and your friends and offers you a voyage to London and a chance to see a princess if you will protect the queen."

"Aye," Lorenz said, and drank thirstily from his second pint.

"He tells you that your king—the sovereign you serve and have vowed to defend—is weak. And that there may be trouble. You've no idea what trouble, or what you are doing, or why, and you don't think to question any of it. Does that not sound odd to you?"

Lorenz swallowed. He looked at Marek. "Pardon?"

"You're pathetic," Marek said.

Lorenz hesitated. And then he laughed nervously. His skin was turning splotchy.

"You come here as you have, and cry for your mother and your sister, drink the ale a perfect stranger offers you, and you can't give me one word about who this man was."

"What...? Who are you?" Lorenz asked. "I don't know who he was. How was I to know him?" The lad seemed frightened now. A lot of good this one would be if there was indeed any trouble. "He was a minister or something, that's all. Dominick said he was high up and I didn't... I don't know what..."

"What did he look like?" Marek demanded.

"I don't know. Tall. Thin," Lorenz said desperately. "Light brown hair."

"Jovial in his demeanor? Laughs easily?"

Lorenz nodded.

Marek was not surprised, really. It felt almost as if he'd been waiting for someone to point a finger at Dromio all along. Naturally, he couldn't be entirely certain it was Dromio, but in his gut, he knew that it was. What Dromio was about was the question.

Marek reached into his pocket and withdrew a five-pound note and handed it to Lorenz.

Lorenz looked astonished. "What's this?"

Marek didn't answer him. He picked up his hat.

"Wait!" Lorenz said, sounding desperate. "You said you had news!"

What a stupid lad he was. "I do," Marek said. "But it's

not for you." Without another look at the ridiculous man-child, Marek walked out of the public house.

His pulse was pounding at his temples. He wasn't certain what he had to do to prevent what was happening—whatever it was—but he wanted to kill Dromio with his bare hands.

A LIGHT SNOW had begun to fall by the time Marek returned to the Green Hotel. He had expected to find the common room empty, assuming that preparations were underway for the signing ceremony tomorrow. But there were Dromio and Van, two glasses of whiskey before them, laughing together.

"Brendan!" Dromio said when he spotted Marek walking toward them. "Join us. You've made yourself scarce of late. Your paramour must be quite good at what she does." He waggled his eyebrows.

"Have a seat, Mr. Brendan," Van said, and with his foot, moved a chair out from underneath the table for him. "Join us in toasting the successful conclusion of a peace agreement. You may rest comfortable in your Weslorian bed now." He lifted his glass so abruptly that whiskey sloshed over the rim.

They were drunk, congratulating themselves on a job well done. The question was, what was the job they had done?

"I am surprised to find you celebrating," Marek said, shaking his head at the footman who came forward to offer a whiskey. "The accord is not particularly favorable to Wesloria."

"It went better than we thought, all things considered," Dromio said. "You shouldn't be so glum all the time, Brendan." He looked at Van and laughed.

"When do we sail?" Marek asked. How much time did he have to prevent whatever was about to happen?

Van shrugged. "The king is not well, as you know, so the exact plans have not yet been made." He slid a look at Dromio.

Dromio smirked. "But perhaps sooner rather than later?"

They were forgetting themselves, these two. Their emotions about the king were plain for anyone to see. Well. Except Lorenz, of course.

Marek looked down at his hands. He had very little time to stop whatever they were about, and he was at a strong disadvantage not knowing what it was. All he knew was that they had sabotaged the peace agreement. And that he was just one man. And he had very little time to do anything. He suddenly stood from the table.

"Whoa, man," Dromio said. "What are you doing? You've not yet had a drink."

"Thank you, but I am unwell," Marek said.

Dromio snorted. "Mark me, Brendan—your aloof manner will be your downfall one day."

Van chuckled.

Marek didn't spare the two traitors as much as a glance as he strode away from the table. His thoughts were racing—he needed help, and he knew only one person who might even consider helping him, and really that was a winged prayer. But he had seen the way Osiander had looked at Dromio and Van.

He knew that it was entirely possible that Osiander was just as treacherous as the other two. Marek didn't know whom he could trust—besides Hollis, that was.

He had to try. He couldn't reach the king on his own. Osiander was his only hope.

Marek strode to the room he knew Osiander to occupy

and knocked on the door. No one answered. He strained to hear some movement behind the door, but it was pointless—his hearing was too weak.

Marek put his hands on his waist and stared at the carpet at his feet. This was it, then. Short of storming the palace and demanding to speak to the king, there was nothing more he could do. He could go to the Alucians, but why would they help him? They had everything they wanted from this summit.

The door suddenly swung open. Osiander stood in the door, his hair wet, a towel wrapped around his waist. He looked Marek up and down. *"Je?"*

Marek stared at him. The words he needed to say would not form as quickly as he would have liked. How exactly did one say he suspected two ministers were plotting against the king?

"Out with it, man," Osiander said in Weslorian.

Marek drew a breath. He leaned forward and said softly, "I have reason to believe that Lord Dromio and Lord Van are plotting against the king."

Osiander's gaze turned hard, and he glowered at Marek. For a moment, Marek fully expected guards to be summoned to detain him. What would they do to him—hang him? Drive him out of London and drop him in a marsh? Toss him overboard on the voyage home? Incarcerate him and make him stand trial before his father?

"Come in," Osiander said, and then looked up and down the hall to see if anyone was about. "Don't stand there, come in," he urged him, and opened the door wider.

CHAPTER TWENTY-SIX

King Maksim, the Duke of Tannymeade, and Prime Minister Russell gathered at the House of Lords to sign the accord between the kingdoms of Alucia and Wesloria. Peace has been achieved, although some say at a great cost to Wesloria. King Maksim had to be helped to the dais, as his health has been weak of late. While the accord was being signed, reports from the continent arrived citing unrest in the Astasian coal-mining region between the two countries.

It would appear that the desire to address social ills is only for warmer days, as the Coalition for Morality and Decency has not been seen near Piccadilly Circus, nor any other public place since the colder weather set in.

◇—Honeycutt's Gazette of Fashion and Domesticity for Ladies

HOLLIS PACED IN front of the hearth until Donovan made her go to bed. "He's not coming tonight," Donovan said firmly, and put his hands on her shoulders and turned her toward the door.

"But he said he would."

"Aye, he said he would come as soon as he was able, but it would appear he is not able tonight. And you'll be no use to him if you are dead on your feet. But he will come, Hollis."

"What if something has happened to him?" Just voicing the thought aloud made her feel queasy. She'd felt this way once before—the day Percy hadn't come home when he was expected. "I shouldn't have let him go," she said with a moan.

"He's a grown man, love. You couldn't have prevented him. Go on, then, go to bed. I'll send Ruth to you when he comes."

Hollis did as Donovan requested—she went upstairs and began to pace there. But eventually she tired herself out and lay down on her bed, fully clothed. She couldn't sleep. Her mind kept racing around thoughts of Marek. She imagined that the four soldiers had beat him just like Donovan had been beaten. He could be dead by now. Donovan said Hackney Wick could be dangerous.

She thought of the way he always looked at her, with that half smile that made him look somewhat amused, somewhat confused, but mostly intrigued. She thought of the way he watched her lips when she spoke. Of his quiet strength. Of the heat of his body, and how easily he held her.

Lord. She'd gone and fallen in love with him like a fool.

She eventually did sleep, and her reward was to be rudely awakened by Donovan. She heard him whisper her name, and when she opened her eyes, he was looming over her. *"Aiiee!"* she shouted and rolled away from him. "What the devil are you doing?" She pressed a hand to her wildly beating heart.

"Pardon, but Ruth has gone out to the market. Get dressed and come downstairs."

"Has something happened?"

"Aye, something has happened." He suddenly smiled. "Mr. Brendan has come."

With a gasp, Hollis clambered out of bed and ran to her vanity. She could hear Donovan chuckling as he went out of the room.

Hollis assembled herself as quickly as she could, knotting her hair loosely at her nape, and buttoned the last buttons of her blouse as she flew down the stairs.

Marek was pacing before the hearth in the very place she'd paced just hours ago. He looked grim and his eyes were shadowed with exhaustion. He didn't hear Hollis come in, didn't notice her until she'd moved into the room. But when he did notice her, his whole countenance changed. His face filled with light, his eyes sparked gold.

She raced across the room, leaping into his embrace. He buried his face in her hair and let out a long sigh. "What happened?" she begged him.

"So much that I hardly know where to start." He set her on her feet.

"Did you find the soldiers?"

He nodded. "Only one, but only one foolish lad is necessary. He was homesick and stupid, and hardly old enough to be out from behind his mother's skirts." He shook his head.

Hollis pulled Marek down beside her onto the settee. He dropped his head back and closed his eyes a moment. "It's Lord Dromio," he said. He opened his eyes and sat up. "He's the one behind it."

"How?" she asked.

Marek began by telling her what the young soldier had said, and that the "gent" he referred to could be none other than Dromio. "It makes sense. He came a fortnight before the rest of us. He was here when Lord Douglas was paid to bring them. He meets the description the lad gave me." He stood up and began to pace again. "I could have done more. I've long had a bad feeling about him, but it was nothing I could prove or put into words." He shook his head and looked away for a long moment.

"You couldn't have known, Marek. Did you confront him?"

Marek shook his head. "I am no one. He doesn't care what I say—he can easily counter it, or claim I'm disgruntled. No one would take my word over his." He glanced at her. "I sought the help of Lord Osiander."

"Who?"

"Our minister of labor. He's rather new to his post. He's young and ambitious, and by everything he says, I believe him to be interested in seeing Wesloria evolve into a modern country. When I told him what I knew, he confessed that he shared my suspicions. He's heard rumors, and said every time he tried to engage Dromio or Lord Van, he was pushed back or dismissed or left out altogether."

"Oh, my," Hollis said. "Then it's all true, isn't it? Someone does mean to overthrow the king?"

"I believe so," Marek said. "But Osiander and I agree—there is not enough proof. We spoke at length and...we decided we must take our suspicions directly to the king. Before he sails. Hopefully before he signs the accord."

"But that's today!" She looked at the clock on the mantel. It was half past twelve. The signing was to happen this afternoon. "There's no time, Marek."

"It is out of my hands," he said. "Osiander is attempting to get an audience but thus far has been denied. They say the king is unwell and there is much to do. Dromio has managed to remove him from any meetings with the king, and he doesn't know what he's been told."

"He can't sign the agreement!" Hollis exclaimed. But

the moment she spoke the words, she realized that she was wishing to undermine her own brother-in-law.

"He likely will, Hollis. It seems too late to stop the wheels in motion. And even if there were a way to stop it, Alucia would never agree to any delays. They've got what they came for, *more* than what they came for. Both delegations are preparing to sail. The British prime minister is hosting a final reception this evening for all parties. To try and undo it now would be…a disaster. But it may not be too late to stop what else might be planned."

Hollis thought of Eliza and Sebastian. Eliza was so proud of her husband—this was a victory for them. This would endear Sebastian to his people. She thought of Marek, who not only had to watch his father be swindled, possibly overthrown, but also had to watch it as he carried such a burdensome secret. She thought of the people of Wesloria and Alucia, who were relying on this peace agreement to bring prosperity.

And she thought of herself. She could feel a quake rumbling in her, a true crack in her foundation. So many things felt as if they were on the verge of exploding in her. She looked at Marek. "Do you have to go now?"

He shook his head. "Not yet. I left word with a footman where I might be reached if Osiander sends for me."

Hollis couldn't even bring herself to look at Marek when she asked her next question. "What now?"

He didn't answer her with words. He sat on the settee beside her again and drew her into his arms, kissed both cheeks, and then her mouth.

Hollis put her hands on his cheeks and forced him to stop. "You're leaving."

He looked surprised. "*Je*. Did you—did you expect different?"

Hollis bit back a sob and shook her head. "I didn't dare to expect anything. I didn't dare to dream of anything. But I…" There seemed to be no words to describe what was racing through her heart just then. Despair and resignation. "Everything has happened so fast, and I didn't expect, but—"

"Hollis, *milas*," he murmured, and lowered his head to hers, lingering there a long moment. "This may be the last opportunity we have to be alone together."

"Oh." She winced. "That is the saddest thing you've said yet."

"Hollis." He suddenly dropped down to one knee before her and gathered her hands in his. "This time with you has meant everything to me. You've given me more happiness than I have had in many years. *Je?* I can't begin to express the depth of…what is the word," he said, and pressed his forehead to her knees. *"Ledan,"* he said. "It means…it means perhaps hope. Yes, that's it. Now I have hope that life is not closed to me. Now I have hope that I can feel things I thought were barred to me."

"Oh, Marek," she said sadly, and leaned over his head. "You gave me *ledan*, too."

He rose up, and this time, caught her hand and pulled her up with him. "We have this moment, if you want it."

"I want it." Her gaze fell to his mouth. *"I want it."*

And so it was that she found herself in Marek's arms again, her hands on his bare chest, her fingers skimming over the hard wall of his abdomen, his chest and nipples. And so it was that she crawled on top of him and slid onto his body. She braced herself against him while he cupped her hips. She allowed herself to leave her thoughts behind and only feel, to remember what it was like to be cherished and adored and maybe even loved.

She remembered what it was like to love someone in return.

He moved her onto her back, and with his gaze locked with hers, he drove her to a climax they could share. Hollis's cry of pleasure was too loud, but so was Marek's. She had a fleeting thought of raised eyebrows through the house, but she didn't care. Let them think what they wanted. Let them all think ill of her and wonder what had happened to her morals. She didn't care, she didn't care, she didn't care.

All she cared about was this moment with this man, of the freedom she'd gained from her grief, of the love she felt burgeoning in her heart. Her body seized around his with her last cry; he grabbed her hips and thrust into her one last time before pulling free with his own strangled cry.

They lay there, tangled around each other, spent, exhausted, and wordless. Marek stroked her hair and her shoulder. He looked at her with so much tenderness that it made her heart ache. After a moment, it seemed as if he couldn't bear to look at her at all. He rolled over on his back and slung an arm over his eyes.

With the pad of her thumb, she traced the line of his jaw, felt the stubble of his new beard. "I want to tell you that I… I've fallen in love with you."

Marek sighed. He hadn't heard a word. She was aware she was on his left side. But she'd needed to say it. But she didn't need to complicate the bitter end of them with those words.

They spent the afternoon in her bed, talking as their fingers traced paths to memorize each other's contours. They avoided the difficult subjects in favor of laughter and secrets.

Until the very end. Until the light began to fade from

the window. Until it would be time for Marek to go. "What will you do when I'm gone?"

Hollis traced a circle around his navel. "I don't know. It feels like so much is changing. Everyone is leaving and I... My whole world is changing. It's an upheaval." She looked at him. "What will you do?"

"Mourn," he said simply. "'I would not wish any companion in the world but you.'"

"Shakespeare," she whispered sadly. "Marek, I—"

She meant to try again to tell him what she felt, to leave nothing unsaid that should be said. But an ill-timed rap on the door prevented it.

Hollis donned a dressing gown and went to the door, peeking around the edge of it.

Donovan gave her a bit of a smirk. "I never knew this side of you, Mrs. Honeycutt. Will you please tell your... friend that a footman has come with a message. He is wanted at the Green Hotel in half an hour."

Hollis closed her eyes. "Thank you." She shut the door and turned to look at Marek.

"Has he sent for me?" Marek asked.

She nodded.

He threw off the covers and grabbed his trousers, dressing quickly. As he buttoned his shirt, Hollis brushed his hair. When he was dressed, he turned around to her.

There was no time to say all the things that needed to be said. Hollis grabbed his hand. "Will you write to me?" she asked desperately.

"Every day," he said without hesitation. "Will you?"

"Every day. Come to Christmas," she said. "You'll still be here, won't you? Come to Christmas at my father's house. I'll send the direction around to your hotel."

He looked impatiently at the door. "We may have sailed by then."

"Yes, but if you haven't, please come."

He caught her chin and tilted it up, then kissed her. When he pulled back, he opened his mouth as if he wanted to say something. He didn't speak. He kissed her once more, and then slipped out of her room.

And perhaps out of her life?

Hollis suddenly felt sick. She pushed her hands into her belly and sank onto her bed.

CHAPTER TWENTY-SEVEN

The King and Queen of Wesloria and their daughters have been invited to share Christmas supper with Queen Victoria, Prince Albert, and the royal family. They may expect to enjoy a roast beef raised on the queen's estate, as well as boar's head, game pie, and one of the queen's favorites, plum pudding. The Weslorian contingent is scheduled to set sail the day after Christmas. The Alucian delegation, led by the Duke and Duchess of Tannymeade, will depart a week later.

The Coalition for Decency and Morality has turned their attention to caroling this Christmas season with their rendition of "O Come, All Ye Faithful."

Ladies, use brandy liberally in your mince pies to enhance the flavor and keep any complaints about the meal to a minimum.

〜—Honeycutt's Gazette of Fashion and Domesticity for Ladies

MAREK FELT ALMOST as if he was outside of his own body as he stood in the king's suite of rooms at St. James Palace. He'd been in a room with the king before, but only twice, and both times there had been a crowd of people. He'd stood back. Out of sight.

Today, however, it was only him and Osiander.

A butler had shown them into a small antechamber, with

a table and two chairs at the center, an upholstered bench against one wall, and the requisite portraits to add some interest. The butler had disappeared into the adjoining room. Neither Marek nor Osiander spoke.

Haral Osiander was a man of average height and a paunch in the belly. From appearances, he did not look like what one might expect to take down a conspiracy. He walked nervously back and forth across the little room, his brow furrowed in thought. He looked as exhausted as Marek felt. But he also looked grimly determined. As he'd said to Marek, this plot could weaken Wesloria for generations.

The door to the adjoining room swung open and the butler walked through. He stood to one side. "His Majesty, the king," he intoned.

Marek's breath caught as King Maksim walked through the door. He looked even more diminutive than he had in crowded rooms, and he was clearly a full head shorter than Marek. But he was also clearly his father—he had the same golden-brown eyes and the streak of white at his forelock. His pallor was gray, and when he spoke to Osiander, his voice was soft and hoarse. Marek worried he wouldn't be able to hear him.

Osiander looked at Marek. "Mr. Marek Brendan," he said.

Marek bowed. "Your Majesty."

"Brendan," the king said, looking into Marek's face. Did he see what Marek saw? Did he notice any similarities? "There was a small fishing village near the northern border called Brendan. Named after a warrior, if my memory serves me. When I was a boy we took our fish from there." He sat heavily in a chair at the table. The butler came forward and laid a cloth before him.

The king propped himself on one arm of the chair and

said, "My lord Osiander. You have arranged this private meeting. Speak."

Osiander cleared his throat and began. "I beg your forgiveness, Your Majesty, but as the son of a coal baron, I cannot sit by. I am compelled to speak."

The king nodded.

"I was terribly dismayed to see our country bargain away rights to the coal mines in the Astasian region."

The king frowned. "They were not bargained away. We've come to an agreement to share the resources."

Marek stiffened. That sounded like what the king had said before they'd left St. Edys. An equitable sharing of resources. Had he not read the agreement?

"Unfortunately, that is not entirely true," Osiander said. "There is very little sharing to be done." He explained that Wesloria had given the coal mines to Alucia, and in return had claimed the right to find coal in a smaller, rockier part of the range. The king's face remained impassive as Osiander explained the harm that would cause the region as a whole. "The people there, they earn their living in the mines. Now it will be Alucians taking food from their tables."

The king frowned slightly. "This is not what I've understood from Dromio."

"No, I'm certain not," Osiander said. He said that he'd argued with Lord Dromio about this very thing. "But his lordship claimed to be acting on your wishes at your behest, Your Majesty."

The king's face darkened slightly as the butler laid a plate before him.

"If you had concerns about the agreement, why am I just hearing about them? The agreement has been signed, my lord."

"*Je*, Your Majesty," Osiander agreed. "Up until yesterday, I believed we were doing what you wished. As ill-advised as I thought it to be—and not only me, but one of your best advisors of economics," he said, with a nod toward Marek. "It was too late to stop the agreement from going forward. But I think there is still opportunity to improve on some of the tenets."

The king shifted his gaze to Marek. "Is this true?"

"*Je*, Your Majesty," he said.

"And yesterday you had an epiphany, as well?" the king asked curtly.

"No, Your Majesty. I have been advising against the terms of the agreement all along."

The king snorted and looked at the table. "Are you implying that my minister of trade and my foreign minister have intentionally misguided me?"

A footman, as young as the soldier Marek had visited, entered the room. He was carrying a bowl of soup on a silver platter. He stood silently to one side, holding the tray and the bowl.

"I believe they have," Osiander said. "Just a few days ago, we learned of the existence of four Weslorian soldiers here in London, brought by way of a Scottish merchant vessel, at the behest of a gentleman who believes the king is so ill he may not survive the journey home."

The lad holding the soup jostled the tray slightly; the silver clinked together. By some miracle, Marek heard it and glanced at the footman.

So did the king. He said, "Put it down, Heiner." He turned back to Osiander. "I *have* been quite ill, that is true. The doctor advises it is an ague, a result from this bloody damp air. That's why I must get out of it as soon as possible."

The young footman inched closer to the table.

"Your illness, as sudden as it was, has kept you from the negotiating table, Your Majesty. And Dromio and Van have managed to keep me from attending you with news of the negotiations."

"Is that their fault? They have said you have a penchant for too much drink and can't be roused in the morning," the king said calmly. "Who should I believe?"

Osiander blanched. "That...that is not true," he said, clearly appalled.

The footman still hadn't put the soup before the king, and from where he stood, Marek noticed a thin line of perspiration at his hairline.

"What proof have you of anything you allege, Osiander?"

The footman managed to put the soup before the king.

"The soldiers," Osiander said. "The peace accord. I assure you it is not what you have been told. The truth is buried in the pages."

"That may be, but Van said the Alucians wouldn't support any of our demands."

"That is not true. The Alucians want peace and to prosper, like you. They were willing to make concessions on the grain exports as well as the coal mines, but we conceded."

The king considered him. And then Marek. "It all seems rather far-fetched. It's a pity my prime minister isn't here to enjoy this tale."

Marek was stunned. The king didn't believe them. Osiander looked completely flummoxed by the realization. "There is more," Marek blurted.

The king gestured for him to speak. Osiander nodded. Marek told the king about the shipment of grain to Finland that had rotted in port, and how Finland was persuaded to turn to Alucia for grain.

"One shipment is not a conspiracy, Mr. Brendan."

"There were the engines for the textile factories, as well. While en route, someone had them routed to Helenamar."

"It's been a bad season for sea-faring trade," the king said. "More than one shipment has been held up or diverted because of storms." He picked up his spoon. "Who stands to benefit if any of what you say is true?"

"With all due respect, Your Majesty," Osiander said. "Felix Oberon would have everything to gain."

The king put down the spoon. The footman glanced at his feet. "How dare you mention him to me."

"Dromio's father has a large interest in the coal mines," Osiander said.

"But you said Dromio just gave them away. What sense does that make?"

"If I may speak frankly...it makes you look weak at home. They say you are ill. They say you gave away the mines to the Alucians when many in that region depend on the work. They say you undercut our grain exports and then insisted on a tariff, and now the landowners must increase costs."

"We must raise revenue," the king snapped. He picked up his spoon. The young footman watched the king dip the spoon into the soup bowl, then looked directly, and nervously, at Marek.

Marek would never know what he saw in that young man's face. Fright, maybe? A desire to be free? But he looked at Marek, and Marek heard himself say, "Don't eat it."

The king looked at him. "I beg your pardon?"

"It's poison. That's why you've been so ill, Your Majesty."

The king looked at the bowl, then at the footman.

The color drained from the footman's face.

"My guess is that they mean to poison you to death.

That's why the rumor goes round that you may never leave England alive."

Osiander loudly cleared his throat, but Marek ignored him. He had to voice his suspicions. "Those soldiers are here to take the queen and the princesses into so-called protective custody. But they won't return to St. Edys if you die, Your Majesty. Felix will step in, use everything that happened here to make his case, and the queen and the princesses will be in danger."

Marek didn't know what he expected, but he didn't expect the young man to suddenly fall to his knees and beg for mercy.

"Your Majesty, it wasn't me," he cried.

"Pardon?" The king stared down at the footman. A quick-thinking Osiander lifted a hand to signal one of the guards. "It's all right, Heiner," the king said. "Take a breath."

Heiner took a breath. But he was shaking so badly that Marek feared he might be having a seizure. "I did what they said—they threatened my family and I've a newborn son."

King Maksim put his hand on Heiner's head. He looked up as the guard reached Heiner. "Take him. Then go to the queen and princesses and don't let them from your sight," he said calmly. Two more guards entered the room, and the king removed his hand from Heiner's head. "God save you, Heiner," he said to the young man as the guards took the footman in hand.

There was more commotion, more guards, and Marek had to cup his good ear to hear what the king said amid all the voices. He was asking questions. He was demanding that Dromio and Van be brought to him. He wanted the four soldiers rounded up, and to know who'd brought them to London and why. He asked if anyone in St. Edys was involved.

When Marek was finally dismissed, leaving Osiander with the king and his guards and personal secretary, the king looked even frailer than before. But it was not a frailty born of sickness—it was the frailty that comes with bearing the weight of the world on one's shoulders.

As Marek bowed to the king to take his leave, the king asked Osiander, "Who is he again?"

I am your son. For a single moment, Marek felt compelled to admit the truth. To say it out loud.

"A civil servant of the crown, Your Majesty," Osiander answered for him. "An expert of economics. A patriot."

The king looked at Marek expectantly, as if he thought he might add to that brief description. Marek stood there mutely, his thoughts far outpacing his tongue. He noticed how weary the king looked. He thought of his farm and his animals, his quiet, peaceful existence. He thought of Hollis and how light he felt in her presence. He thought of how sick he was of living partially in two worlds, but not fully in either.

So he said nothing.

"Thank you, that will be all," the king said to him.

Marek turned to go. It had been a tedious, anxious experience—all of it—from the day his aunt died until this moment. But Marek felt relieved. He'd made his choice. He knew where he was supposed to be.

CHAPTER TWENTY-EIGHT

Prince Albert has very graciously sent decorated Christmas trees to schools and barracks around Windsor to celebrate the spirit of the season. The trees are reportedly decorated with gingerbread figures that are suitable for eating.

Two Weslorian ministers were brought before King Maksim to review the newly signed trade agreement, as the king has found it lacking.

Might wedding bells sound in the New Year? Observers say that a widower of great means will offer for a peacock who has searched far and wide for her perfect match.

∽—Honeycutt's Gazette of Fashion and Domesticity for Ladies

THIS WAS SUPPOSED to be a joyous time of year, a time to celebrate family and friends and the birth of new beginnings.

Hollis was anything but joyous. She hadn't heard a word from Marek since he'd walked out of her house two days past. She'd heard nothing about what had happened at St. James with the king. The only thing she'd heard had come from Beck, who said the foreign contingents were busy preparing for their voyages home.

Marek wouldn't leave London without saying farewell to her. At the very least, a letter. *Something.*

When she heard Donovan answer the door with a hearty "Happy Christmas!" on Christmas Eve, her heart leaped. He'd come! She raced down the hall, nearly colliding with Donovan in her haste to greet him. But when Donovan stepped back to admit entry, she stopped. Her face fell. It was Eliza and Caroline. "Oh," she said.

"I beg your pardon!" Caroline responded. She and Eliza were holding a giant box between them.

"Happy Christmas, darling!" Eliza said as Donovan took the box from them.

"It's heavy," Donovan observed.

"Yes, well, her Christmas dress required extra fabric because your mistress will not make use of a proper corset," Caroline said.

"Can't say that I blame her." Donovan hoisted the box onto his shoulder and walked down the hall to the drawing room.

"Hollis? You've not said a word of greeting," Eliza said. She wrapped her sister in a hug.

"I wasn't expecting you. How *did* you…? Ah." She spotted the guards posted outside her house.

Eliza glanced over her shoulder at them, too. "Oh, that's Bas's doing, of course. What with all the turmoil in Wesloria." She shut the door behind her.

"Where is Cecelia?"

"With her father. I hope you don't mind. You'll see her tomorrow, but we've hardly had any time together, just the three of us, and I am desperate for it. And I want to see your dress! Caro speaks of it like it is spun gold."

"Not spun gold. Silk and satin," Caroline corrected her. "Very expensive silk and satin"

"Have we visitors?" Mr. Brimble appeared, carrying Marcus, the black-and-white cat.

"Mr. Brimble!" Eliza said, and hugged him, too.

"Well, well," Mr. Brimble said, smiling. "Who have we here? Are they carolers?"

"I am *not* a caroler," Caroline said, sounding a bit miffed that anyone would think she was.

"It's our family, Mr. Brimble," Hollis said. "Shouldn't you see about feeding Marcus?"

"Oh, I should, shouldn't I?" he said, as if he'd just remembered he was holding the cat. He toddled off.

"His memory is decidedly worse," Eliza said, watching him go.

"What have you been doing with yourself?" Caroline asked, linking her arm through Hollis's and making her walk down the hall to her drawing room.

"Me? Waiting, I suppose."

"For Christmas? I called on the judge today. He's got a goose and he's very proud."

"Does he?" Hollis asked.

Caroline nodded. "It's in the garden. And those two little beasts won't stop barking at it. Poppy said Mrs. Spratt has come by twice to complain."

"Forget the goose, Caro. Tell her who is coming to Christmas with us," Eliza said as they entered the drawing room. Caroline let go of Hollis's arm and sailed deeper into the room, to the box Donovan had put on a table.

"Who?" Hollis asked.

"Can you not *guess*?" Caroline asked excitedly.

"Who?" Hollis insisted.

Caroline's face was about to crack open with her smile. "Lady Blythe Northcote and her father."

"No," Hollis said dramatically. "Does Beck know?"

"Not yet," Eliza said with a girlish giggle.

"Caro! You can't surprise him Christmas Day! He'll be furious!"

"I'll tell him tonight. And he'll be ridiculous about it, of course. But I think he really rather likes her. He's mentioned her more than once."

"Really? What has he said?"

"Let me think. That her laugh reminds him of the bray of a donkey. And he's always been suspicious of gingers."

Eliza laughed. "That's what makes her perfect. She's not the usual sort." She fell in a cloud of blue onto the settee.

"I almost forgot! You will never guess what I heard," Caroline said excitedly.

"Have you been going around to the Mayfair salons?" Hollis asked.

"Yes. Why do you look so surprised? Because of my scandal last year?" She waved her hand at her. "No one is a pariah forever. And besides, Leopold and I are married, so that eases the crime for some. So much is forgiven if you marry, you know."

"Especially if you marry a prince," Eliza said. She and Caroline looked at each other and burst out laughing.

"What did you hear?" Hollis asked.

Caroline beamed at her. "Katherine Maugham has received an offer, after all!"

"Impossible!" Hollis cried. "From *whom*?"

"Lord Middleditch."

Hollis gaped at her. Lord Middleditch was a widower nearing his fiftieth year. He had two grown sons, both of them nearer to the peacock's age than she was to his lordship's.

"And everyone says she will accept. He has fifty thousand a year, he didn't beat his first wife, and she really has no other prospects."

The three of them fell silent a moment, thinking about their nemesis and her long quest for an offer.

"Well," Eliza said. "I hope she's happy."

"I do, too, really," Hollis said. "Maybe she won't be so wretched in her demeanor if she marries?"

"That's the happiest part of this news," Caroline said. "Middleditch makes his home in Leeds." She walked to the box and removed the lid, then pulled the gown out with a flourish. The skirt fluttered open in soft gold waves.

"Oh, Caro," Hollis said softly.

The gown was beautiful. The first thing Hollis noticed was that it reminded her of the color of Marek's eyes. It was so beautiful, and she would be beautiful, and Marek would never see her wear it. He'd never see her at all.

"Hollis? What's the matter?"

Eliza's arm was suddenly around her.

"I don't know," Hollis said tearfully. "I'm…lost," she said, and turned into her sister, holding on to her. "Everything is changing too fast! I hardly catch my breath and then it all changes again!"

"What are you talking about?" Caroline asked. She placed her hand on Hollis's back.

"Donovan!" Eliza called, sounding a little frantic.

Donovan appeared at the door.

"We need something," Eliza said. "Hollis is weeping."

"I know just the thing." He disappeared again as Hollis tried to wipe her sudden tears, appalled by them, but Eliza held her so tightly she couldn't lift her hand high enough.

Caroline and Eliza eventually steered Hollis to the settee and made her sit, then flanked her, both of them looking at her with concern.

Donovan returned with three tots and decanted whiskey.

"That's not what I think Eliza meant," Caroline said.

"No, but it will do," Eliza said, and took one of the tots from the tray.

"Pay me no heed," Hollis said, wiping her tears and trying to smile. "It's the time of year, that's all."

"That time of year?" Donovan sighed. "You're always so unflappably honest, madam. Don't dissemble now."

"What? What does that mean, Donovan? Hollis? What does that mean?" Eliza demanded.

"Tell them," Donovan said, and then strolled from the room, pausing first to admire the dress.

"I hate him," Hollis murmured.

"No, you don't. You love him!" Eliza insisted. "We all know that."

"Of course, I *love* him," Hollis said. "But sometimes I hate him. He knows me too well."

"I *knew* it," Caroline said triumphantly.

"Not like that, Caro, for God's sake. I love Donovan as my dearest friend."

"That can't be true, because *I* am your dearest friend," Caroline said.

"All right, then. He is my very good friend."

"Then what is it?" Eliza asked, nudging her.

"You won't believe me. You'll be shocked. But I love someone else. At least, I think I do. Oh, I don't know! What does it feel like to be in love?"

Caroline and Eliza looked at each other. "Well, darling," Eliza said carefully, as if dealing with a madwoman, "you loved Percy once. Remember?"

"But it was so long ago and I was so young, and I really can't recall."

"It feels like your insides are being clawed by a cat," Caroline said, and tossed back her tot of whiskey.

"Caro," Eliza said disapprovingly.

"What? My point is, being in love can be very painful. Who is he, Hollis? And how dare he not return your affection. And why is this the first we are hearing of it?"

"When might I have told you? You're both at so many events and soirees. He's—he's Weslorian."

Eliza frowned with confusion, but Caroline gasped. "The peculiar one?"

"Yes, him…but he's not peculiar. He's the most wonderful, interesting man. I think I love him, and he's leaving, and *you're* leaving, and Caroline will return to the country, and Pappa wants to leave and even Beck has found someone. Beck! Beckett Hawke!"

"I agree, Beck is very shocking," Eliza said.

"Oh, darling," Caroline said, and threw her arms around Hollis.

Eliza did, too. "You must invite him to Christmas. We must meet him. How can we not meet him?"

"I did. But he won't come, and even if he did, everyone would talk."

Eliza laughed. "You're worried about talk? Everyone talks about you, anyway, living here with Donovan, and publishing your gazette—"

"And your many, *many* visits to the library and the foreign secretary's office, and your stubborn refusal to wear a corset," Caroline added.

Hollis couldn't help herself. She laughed. "I sound delightful."

"You are," Eliza said. "You are the most delightful person I've ever known and he is a damn fool if he doesn't come."

"I don't know," Hollis said with a weary sigh. She was exhausted from trying to understand what existed between her and Marek now. "Maybe it isn't the same for him. It's entirely possible that I dreamed it all."

"Tell us more," Eliza asked.

So Hollis did. About how strange she'd thought him. Aloof. But then discovered he was deaf in one ear. She told them he'd studied Shakespeare, like her. And that they had a great deal in common—they were two people standing in the world alone. She even told them about his farm, and how she'd imagined herself there.

She didn't tell them about the things she and Marek had discovered. She didn't mention Wesloria or Alucia at all. That was very much beside the point. The point was, he was perfect for her.

Caroline and Eliza listened intently. They were silent for a moment when she finished.

"Well, you best be prepared if he does come, darling," Caroline finally said. "There is nothing more satisfying than being dressed like a queen when the object of your desire looks in your direction. Shall we try on the dress?"

Hollis sniffled. The dress really was beautiful. So beautiful that she felt a little cheered by it. "Yes."

Eliza downed her whiskey and clapped with delight.

CHAPTER TWENTY-NINE

Christmas is upon us! We wish you good cheer and peace be with you.

Ladies, remember that Madeira wine is a good substitute for sherry in your eggnog.

—Honeycutt's Gazette of Fashion and
Domesticity for Ladies

CHRISTMAS DAY DAWNED with a dusting of snow beneath gray skies. Hollis and her household walked a well-worn path to her father's house. As they passed rows of houses, the air filled with the scent of roasted chestnuts and wood. It smelled as if all of London was gathered around a bonfire.

At Bedford Square, Hollis was pleased to see that Poppy had done a fine job of decorating. A very large wreath graced the front door—Donovan had come earlier in the day to help Ben hang it. The wreath was bursting with apples and berries and red ribbons, and really, it was the first thing to catch one's eye when they entered the street.

"That's lovely, isn't it," Mr. Brimble said. "Makes one long for Christmas."

"Aye, it does," Ruth said, and looped her arm through Mr. Brimble's.

They walked up the steps to the door but hadn't even knocked when they were greeted with the frenzied barking on the other side. "It's me, you mutts!" Hollis shouted gaily at the door. Moments later, Ben opened it, stepping over the dogs. "Merry Christmas," he said joyously. And to the dogs he commanded, "Walk on, you beasts, walk on!" with his arm pointing away from the door as Hollis, Ruth, Donovan, and Mr. Brimble crowded in to remove their cloaks and hats. Mrs. Plum had not joined them, as she has a rather large family of her own.

"They're all in the drawing room, madam," Ben said. "I'm to help Margaret in the kitchen with the goose. It's the size of a pig, it is."

The house smelled like roasted goose and holly, and Hollis and her household entered a transformed drawing room. She gasped with wonder—it looked nothing like it had before. Poppy had outdone herself. She'd draped boughs of holly around the broken clocks Eliza had left on the mantel and hung what looked like silver bells in them. She'd used some of the many books that were stacked around the room as a base for the Christmas tree, which she'd proudly placed in the bay window. She'd even hung an enormous cluster of mistletoe from a chandelier near the hearth.

Everyone shouted a Christmas greeting at them, and Hollis went around the room, greeting all of her family.

"This is lovely!" Hollis exclaimed. "Where is Poppy?" she asked when she reached her father. His knitting had been put away for the day, she noticed. Pris was in his lap. So was a goose feather.

"She said there is much to be done for the meal," her father said.

"I'll lend a hand, shall I?" Ruth asked, but she was already headed out of the drawing room.

Hollis scooped up Pris from her father's lap and handed the cat to Mr. Brimble. "Ah, here is Marcus," he said, stroking the cat's head.

Beck was on the settee, sitting so languidly that he took up half of it until Caroline made him move over. Then she took up the rest of the settee.

Leopold and Sebastian had moved to the hearth. They were talking in low tones, probably discussing the growing reports of unrest in the Astasian region. Eliza had confided yesterday that her husband had been obsessed with the news from home and was eager to return.

Eliza and Cecelia were on the floor. Eliza had dressed Cecelia in a white gown trimmed in Belgian lace. She reported that as soon as they arrived, her daughter had spit up her cereal, and the stain of it trailed down her front.

Hollis realized, as she looked around her, that it was the last time they would all gather like this in her childhood home. The realization prompted a swell of sadness in her.

Eliza, Sebastian, and Cecelia would all be gone soon, sailing back to Alucia, and really, Hollis couldn't say when she might see her beloved sister again. Caroline and Leopold would return to Bibury and her saplings and her trousers, and occasionally, she would come to London to check on Beck. But only occasionally.

Beck, well…he would always be in London, Hollis suspected, complaining about this or that.

Her father, who was smiling at the sounds around him, his sightless gaze on the wall, was moving to Sussex with his entire household, including Jack and John and Pris.

And where would she be? Eating her meals alone? Stuffing her body full of loneliness and restlessness? Where would Marek be? On his farm with his dogs and chickens? She thought where she would want to be next year at Christmas, with everyone scattered. In Sussex, with her father? No—she would rather be on a little farm in Wesloria. With Marek.

She winced a little when she shifted in the chair she'd taken. In spite of having made the gown a little looser, it was still tight. But it was truly stunning—Ruth had said she looked as pretty as she'd ever seen her when she'd helped her dress her hair this morning. Hollis wished Marek was here to see her. This is the way she wanted him to remember her.

"Is Molly coming?" Mr. Brimble asked as he passed by Hollis, stroking Pris. "She'll be late, I think." He walked on.

Hollis stood and went to the Christmas tree. There were little gifts inserted in the boughs, the paper tags tied to them sporting Eliza's handwriting. There were new knitting needles for Pappa. A tiny notebook for Hollis. A trouser belt for Caroline.

The dogs startled them all when they suddenly leaped to their feet and began barking as they raced from the room. Hollis could hear Ben's deep voice, and her heart caught, hoping the next voice was Marek's. But, no, the next voice was that of a woman, and moments later, Lady Blythe Northcote and her father entered the room.

Beck immediately clambered to his feet. "My lord," he said to her father. "Lady Blythe."

"Happy Christmas, Lord Iddesleigh!" Lady Blythe said cheerfully. "Happy Christmas to you all." She was wearing pale blue that showcased her large bosom, and her ginger red hair had been dressed with leaves of holly. Hollis liked this cheerful woman.

"Wonderful!" Caroline said. "Now that you've arrived, let the festivities begin."

The introductions were made, and Ben and Margaret, Poppy and Ruth joined them, crowding in beside the tree. Caroline had always been a consummate hostess, no matter whose house it was, and today was no exception—she made sure everyone had wassail or eggnog. She even convinced Donovan to lend his voice to some carols. Donovan said he would only if Ruth joined him.

Lady Blythe proclaimed them both true talents and handed her glass to Beck to be refilled. "I can accompany you on the pianoforte," she suggested, looking at the one that had been pushed in the corner of the room.

"Oh, dear, Lady Blythe—it has sat unused for many years," Eliza said.

"Oh, let's try it. It's Christmas!" Lady Blythe said. She pulled it away from the wall herself, then sat and began to play. Hollis supposed Lady Blythe's playing was adequate, but the pianoforte was so out of tune that it sounded wretched.

"With all due respect, madam, you are butchering what would otherwise be a lovely carol!" Beck complained.

"What's that?" Lady Blythe said.

Oh, but Hollis *really* liked her.

"I *said* you are ruining the music!" Beck shouted.

"My lord, you really must look on the bright side of things!" she insisted.

"I fail to see the bright side of an instrument so out of tune."

She stopped playing. "The bright side is that you have Christmas carols and your loved ones and everyone is having a grand time." She laughed and continued playing with heavy hands, while Donovan and Ruth gamely carried on.

Hollis stole a glance at Eliza and Caroline. The three of them smiled pertly at each other, silently agreeing that yes, Lady Blythe was the one.

When they'd finished their attempt at caroling, Leopold and Sebastian were pressed to perform an Alucian carol, which, Sebastian sheepishly pointed out, was a drinking song. Cecelia clapped with delight as her father and uncle sang. Upon the conclusion of that rousing song, Ben announced, quite formally, "Dinner is served, Your Honor."

"What are you putting on airs for?" Poppy asked as she breezed past him. "This way, everyone, if you please!"

They all made their way across the hall to the dining room, then squeezed around the table. Margaret had gone to a lot of trouble. The goose was cooked to a golden-brown. She'd prepared oysters and Yorkshire pudding and, she said proudly, "A sweet mince pie."

As they found their places and began to hand the food around, Jack and John went from chair to chair, looking for bites and bits.

Lord Kendal, Lady Blythe's father, asked Beck about his plans for Iddesleigh. Beck, who had taken a large bite of goose, didn't answer straightaway.

"What can possibly be done with Iddesleigh?" Lady Blythe asked. "It's no bigger than a deer's dropping."

Beck's head snapped around to Lady Blythe. And in that moment, Hollis would later say, she saw his gaze change. "That's what *I've* said."

"It really makes one wonder why an earlship was named for it, doesn't it?" she said. "Do you suppose it was punishment?"

Beck put down his fork. "It certainly is for me."

Lady Blythe laughed. And Beck did not take his eyes from her after that.

Hollis's father asked if all his children were present.

Eliza laughed. "You've only two children, Pappa, and we are both here."

"I have more than two. I've at least four of you from long ago, and now with the princes, I have two more. Not to mention my grandchildren."

"Grandchild," Hollis said.

"For now. I should like your attention, be you a relative by blood or by heart. I have an announcement to make."

Everyone turned toward the head of the table.

"I have accepted a bench in Sussex. Ben has found us a lovely manor home and we will be making the move early in the year."

"What? So soon?" Hollis asked.

"But…what of this house, Pappa?" Eliza asked.

"I'll leave it to my daughters to decide," he said. "And, yes, Hollis, darling, so soon."

"I'll look after the house for you if you like, Your Honor," Donovan said. "Ruth will help me, won't you, Ruth?"

"Of course," Ruth agreed.

"Thank you," the judge said.

"Cheers, Your Honor," Donovan said, lifting his wineglass. "I'll make it a point to visit you often in the country."

"See that you do, Donovan. And bring my daughter."

As everyone congratulated the judge, Hollis could see that everyone but her had come to terms with it. Her father deserved the peace of the countryside. But she felt so alone.

Lord Kendal brought up the peace accord. "Quite a new beginning for your country."

Sebastian sighed. "It may be more symbolic than practical in due course. We learned this morning that Weslorian forces have seized the coal mines in the Astasian region."

"What's that? After the peace accord has been signed?" the judge asked.

"Unfortunately, peace was not as close as we'd hoped," Sebastian said.

Everyone was solemn for a moment. Cecelia broke the tension by looking at her grandfather and babbling at him.

It was nearly seven o'clock in the evening. Most of them

had finished their meals and had pushed aside their plates. Margaret had brought in a bowl of plum pudding that was so large Leopold said he might swim in it. They'd all had a fair amount of wine and nog, and the talk had turned to their childhoods, with Beck relating some unbelievable tale about Eliza and Caroline crawling up to the roof at Bibury with sheets tied as capes, prepared to fly.

"We didn't mean to *fly*, Beck," Caroline said.

"We were cold!" Eliza said, laughing.

"How lovely. It's obvious your brother cares very much for you," Lady Blythe said.

"See?" Beck said to his sister. "Even Lady Blythe can see what I do for all of you."

Caroline rolled her eyes. "Then allow me to—"

They all heard the knock at the door at the same time. Jack and John launched into the hall and scrambled for the door. Caroline pinned Hollis with a look, and with her head, indicated she should go.

Hollis could only hope it was Marek. If it wasn't, she might expire with disappointment then and there. "Excuse me," she said, pushing away from the table so quickly that she very nearly tipped her chair over.

"Sit, Hollis. Let Ben—"

"She's closer, Pappa," Eliza said, and gestured for Hollis to hurry.

Hollis stepped into the hall. Her heart was beating so hard she could scarcely get a breath. Jack and John were barking furiously at the door. *Calm yourself. It's not him.* He would have come by now, he would have sent word. Still, Hollis steeled herself when she reached the door, prepared to let the disappointment settle into her marrow.

She yanked open the door.

"Merry Christmas," Marek said.

Hollis was breathless. *Speechless.* She had to stare at him for several minutes, she had to reel her thoughts and hopes back to where they'd been days ago.

He looked down at the two dogs jumping up on his legs.

"Jack! John! Down!" she commanded.

He tilted his head and smiled curiously at her. "May I come in?"

CHAPTER THIRTY

The New Year is the time for new beginnings, and Lord Iddesleigh might have found one under his Christmas tree. His sister reports that he will offer for a ginger beauty from the north, and no one could be happier than this author.

Word has reached London that Wesloria has invaded the Astasian region in spite of having signed a peace accord. Travelers from the continent have reported unrest in the capital city of St. Edys.

Ladies, the perfect gift for making calls on New Year's Day is a bit of clover tied with ribbon. Clover is considered good luck if one possesses it at the start of the year.

⌒—Honeycutt's Gazette of Fashion and Domesticity for Ladies

MAREK DIDN'T REALLY know what to expect. He'd thought he wouldn't be able to come at all, not after everything that had happened. But with the king and his family swept away to Windsor, where they would remain until they sailed the next day, and Lord Van disappearing, and with Dromio caught in a tangled web of deceit, Marek had found the time and space to be away. Osiander was leading the charge to have the two ministers, and whoever else was involved, brought to justice. He'd managed to slip away in all the confusion among the Weslorian delegation.

He was prepared to be rebuffed at this door. After all, he'd not been able to send word for nearly three days now. But he needn't have worried—Hollis grabbed his hand and pulled him inside.

"Who has come?" her father called from the dining room.

Hollis threw her arms around his neck. "*You* have," she said, her voice rough. "You have come, Marek. I thought you wouldn't, I thought you'd gone."

Marek cupped her face with his hands. He didn't glance down the hall, didn't remove his hat, didn't care what he'd feared. He kissed her with desperate longing, and he knew by the way she kissed him back that her longing has been just as desperate.

He lifted his head. "My God, you are beautiful. I came, Hollis. I should have—"

"Mr. Brendan."

Donovan had appeared in the hall. He glanced back into the dining room. "We have a place for you at the table." He stepped back inside the room.

Hollis smiled and took his hat from his head. "It's Christmas supper," she said. "At least take a meal with us before you…speak."

How could he deny her? He shoved out of his cloak and let it drop onto a stool behind him. A cat hopped up and curled on top of it. Maybe he ought to hang it, but Hollis was pulling him down the hall and nothing else mattered.

At the door to the dining room, she looped her arm through his. She smiled up at him. "You came, and I am *so happy* to see you." And with that, she pulled him into a room full of people. "We have a guest!" she announced with great enthusiasm. She proceeded to introduce Marek to her family. And servants. And two dogs. Everyone in her world was here, and by the look of it, everyone in her family preferred to think of their servants as family.

He heard some of what she said as she introduced him, and something about how they'd met, but she kept turning her head, and he missed half of the introduction. When she'd finished, she beamed up at him.

"Ah. Thank you. Merry Christmas to you all." He bowed.

At first, no one moved. Everyone at the table had their gazes fixed on him, undoubtedly trying to work out his relationship to Hollis. He didn't care what they thought—all he cared was that he was here, with her, for either the last time, or hopefully, if he was to have his Christmas wish, the first time.

"Well…perhaps you ought to sit," Donovan suggested.

"Yes!" the duchess cried. "Yes, sit, sit." She hopped up and hurried to get a plate.

Someone had put a chair and place setting next to Hollis, and as she filled his plate to nearly overflowing, he politely answered as many questions as he could, even those Hollis had to repeat to him. Yes, he'd come from the Green Hotel, where the Weslorian contingent was packing belongings to be sent to the docks and loaded onto a ship. Yes, it was true the king and his family had moved to Windsor for safety reasons. He believed most Weslorians would sail tomorrow night. He wasn't certain quite yet when he would voyage home—it depended on a number of things that he was not at liberty to discuss.

No, he couldn't say what had happened, as he had not been privy to all discussions, but agreed that Wesloria had given more than she ought to have done. Yes, he liked London very much. And then he looked at Hollis and said, "I have found much to admire here."

"Oh," Beck said. He looked around at them all, then at Hollis. "It's like that, is it?"

Lady Blythe propped her chin on her hand. "I think it's lovely. Is it not lovely, Lord Iddesleigh?"

"He is a Weslorian, Hollis," Leopold pointed out. "I thought you were on the side of the Alucians."

Hollis laughed and looked at Marek. "I think I've changed my mind."

The conversation eventually turned from Hollis and Marek. They were talking about family traditions during the holiday season, but Marek didn't hear much of it. His attention was on Hollis, and hers was on him.

After he finished his meal—or half of it, as Hollis had put enough for two men on his plate—they all retired to the drawing room. He liked the look of it in here. It looked well used, the sort of room where a family would often gather. He wanted to know what that was like, to be with a family every day of one's life.

There was mistletoe, and the married couples among them made a show of sharing a kiss beneath it. The judge talked about a new house he would move into soon and said he understood it had a view of the lake, and when he thought of it, he thought of the lake at Bibury.

The duchess, who had returned from putting the princess to sleep, announced they all had gifts in the tree. There were a few of them, and Marek watched as Hollis received a tiny notebook, and a necklace from her father that he said had belonged to her mother.

It was a lovely evening, but Marek grew more anxious as it progressed. He was aware of a ticking clock, aware of how much needed to be said, of how quickly time was passing.

It was Lady Chartier's idea that they go around and announce their Christmas wishes.

"Must we?" Iddesleigh groused.

"Yes," she said, and poked him in the ribs.

"Very well. My Christmas wish is that you would not make us state our Christmas wish," he said.

"My wish is Lord Iddesleigh be made to go again," Lady Blythe said, and everyone laughed.

"Very well." He stood up and cleared his throat. "My sincerest Christmas wish is that we all find peace and prosperity in the New Year."

"Hear! Hear!" the judge said, lifting his wineglass.

"Me, me, me!" the duchess cried, hopping to her feet. "My Christmas wish is for Cecelia to have a sibling."

"Or, as we in the palace call it, a spare," Leopold drawled. More laughter.

"Caroline?" the duchess said.

"My Christmas wish is that my saplings grow and that our new home for the foreign-born women displaced from domestic service will be full this time next year."

Marek didn't know what she meant, but Iddesleigh smiled fondly at her. "Whoever would have thought that you would become the charitable one?"

His sister slapped him playfully on the shoulder. "I did! It's your turn, Your Honor," she said.

"My wish is for clean country air," he said. "Poppy?"

The young woman he'd met in front of the Green Hotel blushed. "My Christmas wish is the same as it is every year, Your Honor. I wish for a beau." That earned her whistles and applause.

"Do you mean Donovan?" the duchess asked slyly.

The poor maid turned crimson, but Donovan laughed. "Poppy, if you will do me the honor—"

"No!" Poppy cried. "I've always said you're too handsome for me, Donovan. Your grace?"

The duke sighed. "My Christmas wish is for peace. We all deserve it." He lifted his glass in toast to Marek. "Leo, to you."

"My Christmas wish is to be reunited with my parents. It's been too long," he said, and glanced wistfully at Caroline. She caressed his face. "Ah... Donovan," Prince Leopold said.

"What, mine?" Donovan shrugged. "That we might all put aside our differences." He glanced at the floor, lost for a tiny moment, then lifted a smile to the rest of them. "Your turn, Ruth."

"Oh, my Christmas wish is very simple. I should like to learn how to make Margaret's plum pudding."

"How lovely!" Margaret said. "Then my Christmas wish is to teach you. Come round this week. Ben?"

"My Christmas wish is a hunting dog. I mean to do some game hunting in Sussex, and not with the likes of them," he said, pointing at Jack and John. He glanced around the room. "Mr. Brimble."

"Mr. Brimble, do you have a Christmas wish?" Hollis asked.

Mr. Brimble's old eyes watered. He looked down at Jack, who had managed to put himself on the man's lap. "My Christmas wish is to see Molly," he said, and tears began to slide down his cheeks.

"Mr. Brimble!" Ruth said, and moved to sit beside him, patting his arm and drawing his attention to the dog. Poor dear—they would probably never know who Molly was.

"And you, Hollis?" Eliza asked. "Let me guess—your Christmas wish is for the gazette to become the premier purveyor of news by the end of the year."

Hollis smiled. "Last year, I might have said so. But my Christmas wish is that everything stop changing so fast. But if everything must change, that I be allowed to change with it."

"I don't know what that means," her father said. "What does that mean?"

"Just that everyone is leaving, Pappa, and lives are changing, and I am…not changing. I am standing right where I've been for a very long time."

"Oh, Hollis," Caroline said sadly. "It won't be as bad as you think."

"Well," she said with a lighthearted shrug. "It seems that way to me. Mr. Brendan, it is to you."

All eyes turned to Marek. He'd been thinking since this game started. Of how little time he had left. Of the things he'd learned about himself since he'd arrived in London. Of regrets and lost opportunities. "Someone asked me recently who I am," he said. "And I realized that for many years, I've been between two worlds, neither firmly in one nor the other. It is difficult to explain, but I've been in a land of no one." He'd kept himself apart from the living. It was a wonder he hadn't turned into a ghost.

Everyone was looking around, clearly confused. "It's impossible to explain, but my Christmas wish is to plant myself fully in one world."

"What world?" the duchess asked.

"A world where there is laughter and love and companionship." He looked at Hollis. "A world, *any* world, where Hollis is, frankly."

Someone gasped. Lady Chartier grabbed the duchess by the wrist, her eyes wide. "Did he…? Did I hear…?"

"Sssh," the duchess said, and leaned forward, her gaze on Marek.

But Hollis didn't move. Her gaze was on the floor. She was entirely immobile, and he wondered if he'd said the wrong thing.

"This is not how I meant to say it, Hollis," he said apologetically. "But as they say, 'Make use of time, let not advantage slip.'"

"Ah," Donovan said, nodding appreciatively. "A little Shakespeare for you, Mrs. Honeycutt."

She slowly lifted her head and met Marek's gaze with two pools of blue. He couldn't guess what she was thinking. He felt a little as if he was swinging at the end of his rope. In an effort to make it right, he stepped closer. "This is not how or when or really even what I meant to say it… but I am painfully conscious of the time and will not let the advantage slip. I am asking you to come with me, Hollis. Come to St. Edys, to Wesloria. I am twice the man I am when you are near."

"Oh," the duchess murmured. "Oh *my*."

"What is happening?" the judge asked.

"I don't know, exactly, Pappa," the duchess whispered loudly.

"To *Wesloria*?" Hollis asked, her voice a whisper. She searched the faces around her, as if she thought it might be a joke.

Marek took her hand and forced her to look at him. "Do you love me?" he asked. "God knows that I love you."

Her mouth dropped open. He had stunned her. Hell, he'd stunned them all. Now everyone was gaping. *He* was stunned. He was nothing like the man he'd always been in this moment. All these years, quiet as a mouse, kept to himself, and this was the way he would step into the world he'd chosen?

"Hollis," Donovan said beneath his breath.

She blinked. "Yes," she said to Marek. "I—I do. I *do* love you."

There were more gasps, but Marek ignored everyone but her. "Then come to Wesloria. You don't have to answer me straightaway. But…unfortunately, you must answer me soon. Do you understand, Hollis? You know I must return. You know why. But my hand to God I don't want to return without you."

"I can't," Hollis said. "This is not… I don't know what…" She looked at Donovan.

"Aye, she needs a bit of time to think it through," Donovan said crisply.

"She doesn't!" the duchess exclaimed and gained her feet, moving to her sister's side. "Hollis?" She took her sister's face in her hands and forced her to look at her. "You love him. The cat is clawing you apart, remember? You've lamented that we're all moving on. You grieved Percy well, darling. You were the best widow a man could ever hope for. But you are young, and you love him—what holds you?"

"Is this true?" her father asked. "My daughter loves this man?"

"I think she does, Your Honor," Lady Chartier said, her voice shaking with emotion.

"Why have *I* not heard of it?" Iddesleigh demanded, his voice shaking a little, too.

"Sometimes life is happening right below our noses, isn't it?" Lady Blythe asked cheerily.

Hollis had her gaze fixed on her sister. "But there is so much to consider. Donovan, and Mr. Brimble and Ruth, and Mrs. Plum."

"This is divine!" Lady Blythe said. "This is true Christmas magic. It's as if you trained a horse and he's won the race."

Iddesleigh jerked his gaze to Lady Blythe. "That's what *I* was thinking."

"Hollis," Marek said, pulling her back to him. "I will vow to you now, before God, before your family, before the bloody Alucians, even, that I will honor you all your days and do whatever I must to make you happy." And then, to prove it, he put his arms around her and kissed her on the mouth beneath the mistletoe.

The cheers that went up sounded deep and ominous to his dead ear. But when he lifted his head, Hollis's blue eyes were swimming with love and the faces around him were smiling.

"More wine! Someone bring more wine!" Iddesleigh bellowed.

But Marek was aware that Hollis still had not answered him.

CHAPTER THIRTY-ONE

When the New Year bells ring, we may expect new matchmaking, as bachelor gentlemen make their rounds of open houses and leave their calling cards. We join all the happy families who hope that perhaps this year will bring the sound of wedding bells into their lives.

It is now apparent that in spite of Britain's best efforts, and the earnest negotiations between Weslorian and Alucian delegations, peace has not come to the two countries as hoped. In response to news that Weslorian troops had invaded the Astasian region, Alucia has advanced troops to counter. "In war, events of importance are the results of trivial causes," wrote the great playwright, William Shakespeare.

Revelers walking to the home of Lord Pennypiece were witness to the arrest of Lord Dromio of Wesloria, who has been taken into custody for crimes against the king and was quickly put on a ship bound for St. Edys.

Ladies, if your New Year's wish is to conceive a child, it is recommended that you put your corset aside, as it is known to suppress the natural process of conception by squeezing all your necessary parts together.

๑—Honeycutt's Gazette of Fashion and Domesticity for Ladies

DONOVAN HAD A gift for Hollis when they returned home from her father's house. He grinned as she unwrapped it. It was a silver fountain pen. "Oh, Donovan. It is beautiful," she said, admiring it in her hand.

"You seem to always be writing," he said proudly.

They'd been home for half an hour, just the two of them in the drawing room. Christmas Day had ended with hugs and kisses around. The farewells were the worst for Hollis, and she'd cried through most of it. Her family thought she was weeping with happiness after Marek's declaration.

The truth was that she was weeping with sorrow. She already missed her family.

Marek had returned to the Green Hotel to prepare, he said, for his departure. "May I call in the morning?" he'd asked. His eyes had searched hers, as if looking for a hint of what her answer would be.

"Yes, of course," she'd said, trying to hold her tears at bay. She'd been so stunned and so moved by his declaration. And so...*confused.* How could she make a decision like that so quickly? How could she even think of leaving her home? It didn't matter that Eliza and Caroline had pulled her aside and begged her to consider her own happiness if she truly loved him. It didn't matter that her father had hugged her tight and said he knew she would do what was best for her. It didn't matter that she'd actually imagined being in Wesloria with him. She had never thought it could actually happen. There was so much to think about!

Thank God for Donovan—he knew she needed time to think. To talk. It simply wasn't that easy. Was it?

"I have a gift for you, too," she said, and went to the window and reached behind the brocade drapes for the package she'd hidden there. She brought it to him.

"Well," he said. "That's a very large package." He tested

JULIA LONDON 337

the heft of it, then smiled up at her as he began to open it. "A new saddle?"

"You don't have a horse."

He moved aside the paper and pulled out a shirt. Not just any shirt, but one made of the finest linen money could buy. "Because your good shirt was ruined that night."

"Ah. Indeed it was." He held it up to examine it. "It is perfect. Thank you, Hollis." He put one arm around her and kissed her cheek. "Now may we talk about what happened tonight?"

Hollis pressed her hands to her abdomen. "What *did* happen?"

Donovan laughed. "The stuff of dreams, love. A man declared his love for you and asked you to run away with him. You cannot imagine how many times in my life I've dreamed of that very thing. And there you were, standing like a simpleton—"

"A simpleton! I was in shock!"

"And letting the poor chap lubber on."

She couldn't help but laugh. "I was speechless!"

"Aye, of course you were. Didn't think Brendan had that sort of surprise in him." He grinned, thinking about it. "You're going to go, aren't you?"

Hollis instantly sobered. "No. How can I? My family is here."

"Here? No. Half your family is in Alucia, which, I dare say, will be easier to reach from Wesloria than from England. The other half is dispersing to the country. And if you want to know what I think, your hesitation is not about your family at all. I know what keeps you from making this your Christmas wish." He sat on the settee, his arm stretched along the top of it.

"What?" she asked, sinking onto the settee beside him.

"Me. Ruth and Mr. Brimble, of course, and Mrs. Plum. But mostly me, I believe."

She couldn't deny it. She loved Donovan. And if she wasn't here, who would protect him? Who would love him? Where would he live? "You're right," she said morosely. "I can't leave you, not after what you did for me after Percy died."

Donovan picked up her hand and kissed it, then held it tight. "I think we might start there. I love you, Hollis, I do. The reason I stayed when he died is that I couldn't bear to see you with all that grief. And then—then our friendship blossomed and I didn't want to leave you because I cared about you and didn't want to see you alone."

"But now?"

"But now, you've found someone who loves you better than I ever could. I want you to have that."

"But what about you? I care about you, too, Donovan. I don't want to leave you alone."

"Well that's the beauty of this, then. I won't be alone. What have I always said?"

He'd said so many things. "Don't fret?"

"Aye, don't fret for me." He shifted forward. "Where do you think I go in the evenings? There *is* someone, Hollis. There has been someone for a long time."

Someone. What did that mean? Why had he never said so? "What are you…? Do you mean you have a…?"

"Lover," he said for her. "Someone I care for very much and have for a year or so now. In Maida Vale."

Hollis gaped at him. How could she not have known? She suddenly pulled her hand free and backhanded his shoulder. "Why did you never tell me?"

"And have you fret?" He reached for her hand again.

"Trust me, love, it is better for you if you know very little. I would never have you involved in anything I've done."

"But I—"

"Listen to me, Hollis. This is not about me—I will not be alone and I'll be perfectly fine. This is about you. You don't want to be alone, but you might be if you hesitate. You love him, don't you?"

She gulped down a sob and nodded. "Very much, I think."

He smiled as if that genuinely pleased him. "I will miss you as I've missed Percy, but go, love. Find your happiness again. You were the best wife to a good man. But you could be a better wife to this man. And he could be a better husband to you."

"Don't say it—"

"I will. Brendan understands you. Percy loved you, but I don't know if he understood you. You're a different person now. A confident, vivacious woman. You deserve a man who appreciates you as you are, and I think Brendan does."

Her heart was swelling. She thought of that little farm. Of waking up beside him. "Do you really think so?"

"I know so."

"What about the gazette?"

He shrugged. "Take it with you. Do you think you will lack for intrigue or news in Wesloria? You can sell your house or leave it. I will look after this along with your father's house. I will look after Ruth, and Mr. Brimble. And even Mrs. Plum, although she doesn't need me. And it would make me the happiest of men to know that you were loved and cared for and understood, and I helped make that possible for you by tending things here."

Tears of gratitude were already clouding her vision. Hollis hadn't realized how much she needed to be released from Donovan.

He stood up. "It will break my heart to see you go. But it will also be one of the happiest days of our lives." He leaned down and kissed her cheek. He took his linen shirt and went out of the drawing room, leaving her to ponder her future.

HOLLIS COULDN'T SLEEP. She tossed and turned, her mind churning over all the possibilities. What if she went? What if she didn't?

When the day dawned, she climbed out of bed. She needed this over and done. Whatever the next big change would be, she wanted to go on with it.

Ruth came to help her dress, and she put on the best gown of those that fit. "I shouldn't have had a second helping of the plum pudding," she complained as Ruth helped stuff her into a gown.

"But it was so *good*," Ruth said. "I can hardly bear to ask, but what do you mean to tell the Weslorian gentleman?"

Hollis sighed. "I don't know."

"Ah, Mrs. Honeycutt. That was the most romantic thing I've ever seen in me life."

"Me too," Hollis said softly.

She went downstairs to eat breakfast, but she couldn't make herself. Her stomach was in twists and knots. She alternately paced and stared out the window, watching the clock tick down to eleven o'clock.

Marek was punctual. When he arrived, Donovan solemnly showed him into the former dining room, where Hollis had gone to occupy her hands with needlepoint as she waited. Marek looked past the cluttered table, and the proof sheets of her next edition hanging from the linen sheets on the wall, to where Hollis was sitting in her favorite chair.

This was it, then. She put aside the needlework and stood up and rubbed her damp palms on her skirt. She was immediately struck by how wan he looked as he approached her, as if he hadn't slept, either. He didn't come all the way to her—he paused halfway into the room. His gaze softened. "Hollis."

"I am *so* happy to see you," she said. She took a step forward, but he held up a hand.

"Allow me to just…look at you, please. If this is the last time I am to see you, I want to remember it all."

Hollis slowly lifted her arms, then slowly twirled in a circle. She dropped her arms and said, "Did you mean what you said?"

"Every word," he said instantly. "I didn't know how much I needed you—needed love—until you gave it to me, Hollis. And now I can't imagine being without you." He took a step closer. "I know I ask too much. I know Wesloria is not the life you are accustomed to. But I will make it a good life, I swear it." He took another tentative step. "So, then? What is your answer? Will you come, Hollis?"

She sighed. She pressed her fingertips to her brow and squeezed her eyes shut for a long moment. "I don't know what to say," she said, and dropped her hands. "I thought about it all night, and I still don't know what to say."

Marek stiffened. His jaw clenched.

"I'm scared. I'm uncertain," she admitted. "I don't know what to expect and I fear I will miss my family terribly, and there are people who rely on me."

"I understand," he said, and looked down at his hands. "I knew it was—"

"But I could no more let you leave without me than I could leave off the plum pudding last night. Promise me, Marek. Promise me you'll always love me and care for me, and you won't be alarmed if I write things, and you won't try and tell me what to do, and if I start a philological society, you won't object."

His face lit with a happy smile of surprise. His amber eyes seemed to cast the room in gold. "Are you mad? I will be your first charter member. We'll start with the study of Weslorian."

"I mean to write a lot of things. And sometimes the things I write anger people."

"I will bring you pen and paper."

"I may annoy you from time to time. Donovan says I can be very annoying when I'm of a mind."

"I like to be annoyed."

"But I will be a good wife to you. I will love you and honor you and I will keep all your secrets."

"I know."

She grinned. "Then, yes, Marek Brendan. I will go with you to your farm and your dogs and cows and sheep in Wesloria and pretend I don't know who you really are and write bits and pieces about things that should be brought to light and—"

Marek caught her up before she could finish the list of all the things she would do and kissed her—her cheeks, her mouth, her forehead.

She threw her arms around him and hugged him tight. "I love you," she whispered.

He didn't say it back. He hadn't heard her.

Hollis smiled. She'd have to get used to that.

EPILOGUE

A trial has commenced in the case of His Royal Majesty the King vs. Mr. Felix Oberon in the plot to usurp the throne. This follows the trial of former ministers of trade and foreign, respectively, for attempting to poison the king. Mr. Oberon is accused of orchestrating a coup through the peace process. It is said the plan was a complicated one—to cause unrest in the regions where Weslorians are considered the poorest by bartering away their livelihood, then enlisting those poor souls in an uprising against the king. Furthermore, the plot was to make the king appear to be weak and sick and incapable of making good decisions for the country.

Mr. Oberon had planned to claim the throne through a distant relation. In the wake of this terrible scandal, the Weslorian parliament has secured the succession of the throne to the firstborn child of the king, with no male relatives able to supercede. Princess Justine will one day be queen.

The kingdom of Alucia has agreed to negotiate once more around the lucrative coal mines in the Astasian region. Lord Osiander, the minister of labor, will lead the negotiations for Wesloria. It should be acknowledged by all that peace is a precarious thing and must be negotiated at regular intervals.

In happier news, it has been widely reported that the Alucian Duchess of Tannymeade is expecting her second child in the autumn. In England, the future looks just as bright for the Duke of Tannymeade's brother, Prince Leopold, who, with his wife, recently visited his family in Helenamar and reported the healthy growth of new saplings at his English estate. The prince and his wife were accompanied by Lord and Lady Iddesleigh of England. Lady Iddesleigh delighted in taking Alucian dance lessons during her stay. Lord and Lady Iddesleigh continued on a tour of the region and visited Wesloria, bringing with them news and letters from home to the author of this gazette.

King Maksim has recovered from the attempted poisoning of his person. Talk has turned to finding a match for Princess Justine, and as would be expected, princes and sons of dukes from the world over have sent gifts so that she might take notice of them.

Ladies, when welcoming a newborn in the summer months, take care to eat fruit and sit in the sun for at least an hour a day, as that will aid in the baby's digestion of mother's milk. This writer has discovered that a good helping of cake will also aid in the little prince's digestion, as well as his mother's digestion.

○—The Brendan Gazette of News, Advice, and Musings

A LETTER FROM DONOVAN had come yesterday, but Hollis had saved it until today. She'd taken her baby, Maksim, named for a grandfather he would never know, out into the grassy field behind the modest manor home she lived in now. The house sat at the base of the mountains, and the loveliest copse of elm trees provided shade from the noonday sun.

Brutus, the biggest dog with the shaggy black-and-white coat, had come along, and stretched across the blanket she'd put on the ground for his midday nap. His snoring had chased the sheep across the field.

Hollis put her baby to her breast and opened Donovan's letter. His handwriting was atrocious, and she had to squint to make out some of the words.

He wrote that he'd let her house to an American family with four daughters, all of them on the hunt for wealthy Englishmen, which he clearly found amusing. He and Ruth and Mr. Brimble had taken up residence in her father's home, and Mrs. Plum came round every other day to cook for them. Marcus, the cat, had slipped away one night and had never come back, and while Mr. Brimble still had Buttercup, he was so distraught about Marcus that Donovan had found another black-and-white cat to soothe him.

He said the peacock's wedding was held at Westminster, because her father knew someone who knew the queen.

He reported that he was in excellent health and quite happy. As usual, he offered no more than that. He said that the news of Maksim's birth had filled him with joy and he longed to see the baby. He wrote that he missed Hollis terribly, but that he could tell from the brevity of her letters she was well occupied and happy, too. He did hope one day she would return to London to visit.

The rest of his letter was filled with gossip, which kept her enthralled until the very end. She had changed a lot, but the desire to peek into other lives was still very much a part of her.

Hollis folded the letter and stuffed it in her pocket, then lay down on the blanket with Maksim. Every once in a while she caught the smell of the bread she'd baked this morning, wafting over them, teasing her belly. Oh, but she'd grown a bit round since coming to Wesloria. Mrs. Tarian, the neighbor, had taught her how to cook. And Mrs. Tarian had a baby slightly older than Maksim. He was her fourth, and thank goodness for it—Hollis and Marek had been helpless when Maksim had been born. Mrs. Tarian always knew what to do.

Hollis dozed a little. This was her favorite thing to do on summer afternoons, to have a lie-down in a field with a dog and a baby beside her. Her next favorite thing to do was to lie next to her husband in their bed. She blushed a little, remembering last night.

When Maksim began to fuss, she got up, nudged Brutus off the blanket, gathered it up, and walked back to her house. The cat, Mr. Whiskers—they had allowed the Tarian children to name him—was sitting in the window, watching them. Brutus barked at the cat, as he did every day, and the cat stared down at him with superior intelligence, as he did every day. With Maksim on her hip, Hollis opened the garden gate and stepped through. From here, she could see the road, and just as she knew he would be, Marek was riding up the lane, on his way home.

The sight of him filled her with so much love and joy. He had kept his word to her—he'd made her so very happy. In everything he did, in every way. She couldn't dream of what prayer she'd uttered through the years to have brought him to London.

Marek easily dismounted and walked forward, kissing her first, then Maksim's head. Then, of course, he bent down to greet Brutus. "What do I smell?" he asked, looking toward the house.

"Bread."

He grinned, his eyes flashing gold at her. He put his arm

around her waist. "That makes me indescribably happy." He kissed her cheek.

They walked into the house. But just as they reached the door, the sun caught some crystals she'd hung from a fruit tree. It fractured the light and it looked as if someone had sprayed them with sunshine. Maksim gurgled. Marek took him from Hollis's arms and carried him inside, Brutus on his heels.

Hollis paused on the doorstep and looked around at her little world. It was perfect. There was not a thing she would change about it. Change was over for her—she had found where she belonged in this world, and she could not have been more content.

She turned and walked into her house to join her family.

* * * * *

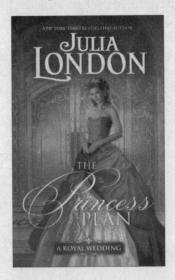

Don't miss the second book in A Royal Wedding series by *New York Times* bestselling author

JULIA LONDON

Every prince has his secrets.
And she's determined to unravel his...

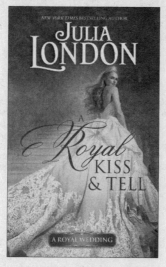

Order your copy today!

HQNBooks.com

PHJLBPA0720Max

Get 4 FREE REWARDS!

We'll send you 2 FREE Books plus 2 FREE Mystery Gifts.

FREE
Value Over
$20

Both the **Romance** and **Suspense** collections feature compelling novels written by many of today's bestselling authors.